Praise for
STARFIST I: FIRST TO FIGHT

"CAUTION! Any book written by Dan Cragg and David Sherman is bound to be addictive, and this is the first in what promises to be a great adventure series. *First to Fight* is rousing, rugged, and just plain fun. The authors have a deep firsthand knowledge of warfare, an enthralling vision of the future, and the skill of veteran writers. Fans of military fiction, science fiction, and suspense will all get their money's worth, and the novel is so well done it will appeal to general readers as well. It's fast, realistic, moral, and a general hoot. *First to Fight* is also vivid, convincing—and hard to put down. Sherman and Cragg are a great team! I can't wait for the next one!"

—RALPH PETERS
New York Times bestselling author of
Red Army

By David Sherman and Dan Cragg

Starfist
FIRST TO FIGHT
SCHOOL OF FIRE
STEEL GAUNTLET
BLOOD CONTACT
TECHNOKILL
HANGFIRE

By David Sherman

The Night Fighters
KNIVES IN THE NIGHT
MAIN FORCE ASSAULT
OUT OF THE FIRE
A ROCK AND A HARD PLACE
A NGHU NIGHT FALLS
CHARLIE DON'T LIVE HERE ANYMORE

THERE I WAS: THE WAR OF CORPORAL HENRY J.
MORRIS, USMC
THE SQUAD

By Dan Cragg

Fiction
THE SOLDIER'S PRIZE

Nonfiction
A DICTIONARY OF SOLDIER TALK
GENERALS IN MUDDY BOOTS
INSIDE THE VC AND THE NVA (with Michael Lee Lanning)
TOP SERGEANT (with William G. Bainbridge)

HANGFIRE

Starfist
Book Six

David Sherman
and
Dan Cragg

A Del Rey® Book
BALLANTINE BOOKS • NEW YORK

A Del Rey® Book
Published by The Ballantine Publishing Group
Copyright © 2001 by David Sherman and Dan Cragg

All rights reserved under International and Pan-American Copyright Conventions. Published in the United States by The Ballantine Publishing Group, a division of Random House, Inc., New York, and simultaneously in Canada by Random House of Canada Limited, Toronto.

Del Rey is a registered trademark and the Del Rey colophon is a trademark of Random House, Inc.

www.randomhouse.com/delrey/

Library of Congress Catalog Card Number: 00-109920

ISBN 0-345-43592-3

Manufactured in the United States of America

First Edition: April 2001

10 9 8 7 6 5 4 3 2 1

Dedicated to
"Shaman" Gary B. Clark,
"The Healing Hand"

PROLOGUE

Looming black against the bright sunlight from the arena, two gladiators clomped under the arch and down the corridor to the dressing rooms. Filmed with sweat, breathing hard, they congratulated each other on their performance. The crowd had loved them despite the emperor's disappointing decision to spare the loser. Outside, the spectators screamed and stomped their feet, demanding another performance. They'd get it.

The two paused briefly in front of where Gilboa Woods sat wearily, one arm chained to the wall, his face showing signs of recent beatings. He was dressed as a lightly armored secutor, as befit the Caligulan theme of the park. The gladiators said nothing, just nodded sympathetically and passed on down the corridor. Woods's turn was coming up soon.

Noto Draya shifted his huge bulk comfortably and put an arm around his nearest consort, a beautiful Turko-Asian girl he'd bought from the Old Woman. He held up his goblet and a servant—a real boy, not one of those idiotic servomechs—poured more wine. Other members of the Draya Family lolling about in the emperor's box above the stadium saluted him with their goblets.

"Long life, boss!" Noto's counselor said across the rim of his goblet.

The crowd had grown silent, attention riveted on the two men circling one another in the dusty arena below. They bore the arms and armor of first-century gladiators. The Pompeiian was the odds-on favorite, but his opponent, trained in Capua, was a good contender. They were attired in the Thracian heavy-armored style. Of course, the gladiators who fought in the Havanagas Roman theme park actually trained in modern facilities. But one attraction of the park was that it re-created precisely the atmosphere of Imperial Rome circa AD 37–41, the reign of the emperor Caligula. Exact reproductions of the amphitheater, the gladiatorial schools—the whole city of Rome, in fact—existed for the pleasure of the park's twenty-fifth-century patrons. The other attraction was blood.

The two circled each other warily, their feet kicking up tiny puffs of dust. Then the sharp sound of the Pompeiian's sword against the Capuan's shield brought the crowd to its feet. Beside him Noto's consort suppressed a scream of delight as she clutched her tiny fists in anticipation. Noto grinned. He was sponsoring the Pompeiian so he stood to win a substantial bet if his man won, and if the man lost, it would be up to him to decide if he lived or died. Either way, he would enjoy himself.

The Capuan darted inside his opponent's guard and his sword stabbed at the Pompeiian's left leg, striking the greave but slicing upward and drawing blood from the other man's thigh. Not an incapacitating wound, but the first of the battle. The crowd went wild. "One for me," a tiny voice said in Noto's left ear. He glanced downward toward a spectator box and grimaced at Johnny Sticks. Sticks, counselor to the Ferris Family, grinned as he gave Noto the finger.

"Hey, up yours, Johnny," Noto whispered into his throat mike. "Tell Homs I got your man by the balls." Homs, head of the Ferris Family, looked up and waved cordially at Noto. Homs had been emperor last month, and Noto had lost heavily to him then.

The Pompeiian suddenly rained blows against the Capuan's shield, driving him back. The crowd jumped to its feet again. The Capuan staggered under the onslaught, tripped, and fell backward. The spectators surged to their feet, and Noto screamed for his man to finish the Capuan while Homs and his party shouted at the Capuan to get up and return to the attack. The Capuan rolled, jumped to his feet, and slashed his attacker across the right forearm. The tightly wrapped leather bands there protected the Pompeiian, but the crowd saw the blow as a skillful counterattack and roared approval.

Hidden back in the shadows under the gladiators' arch, a trainer spoke into a throat mike, frowned when he got no response, then realized he'd picked up the utility radio rather than the crypto. "Slow it down, boys, slow it down," he cautioned the fighters. "Drag the fight out. They expect it. See if you can go a full ten minutes this bout." Obediently, the two slowed to circling one another warily, each looking for openings in the other's guard. They feinted and maneuvered for a full minute.

Noto turned to his counselor. "When's our boy up?"

"Next, boss. Everything's ready."

"You're sure they can't jump up into the stands?"

"Sure, boss. The vet operated on their leg tendons. But they're still plenty dangerous. He won't last long."

The families particularly enjoyed shoving agents into the arena because what happened to *them* was real.

Another scream of delighted rage erupted from the spectators as the two gladiators leaped at each other, furiously hacking and smashing. Their shields slammed together and the sound of swords banging off them resounded throughout the amphitheater. When the blades crossed, sparks flew from the metal, to the immense delight of the crowd. Then they were on the ground, rolling in the dust. Their weapons flung aside on impact, they were using heads, elbows, feet, and fists.

Using a wrestling maneuver, the Capuan managed to throw the Pompeiian off and jump to his feet. He retrieved his sword and, before the other man could recover, placed its blade under the Pompeiian's chin. The fight was over. The Capuan looked up at the emperor's box. Noto leaned over the railing, his ample body quivering with rage. His first reaction was to get rid of his defeated fighter. If he did that, though, he couldn't put the man back into the arena for the rest of the month, and despite his loss, the Pompeiian was still Noto's best chance to win big another time.

Noto gave the thumbs-up. The crowd booed and cursed as one. People threw things into the arena. A wave of angry sound washed over the emperor's box. "Fuck you!" Noto shouted back. "Who runs this place, me or you?" he asked in a lower voice. He turned to his counselor. "They want blood? All right. Give 'em Woods."

For six years Noto Draya had been head of the Draya Family, since removing his brother. When the Drayas had joined with the Ferris Family to run their enterprise on Havanagas some twenty years ago, his brother had moved to Havanagas so he could maintain better control over business matters while keeping an eye on the Ferris Family. The bitter wars between the two crime families that had characterized their relations before the Havanagas deal were not so far in the past that they'd been forgotten.

Now Noto, the ruthless and ambitious second son of the infamous capo James Ferguson Draya, was head of the family. As soon as he could manage it, the Ferrises would be history. Then he would deal with the local rebels. But for the moment he would show the Ministry of Justice it couldn't send its agents to spy on him.

Two burly guards came for Woods. After days of brutal interrogation, a bridesmaid could have handled the agent, but Noto was taking no chances.

"Wa'uh, wa'uh," Woods mumbled. The guards ignored his request for water. Noto had had his tongue cut out. No matter what he screamed in the arena, nobody would understand him.

The guards hauled him to his feet and half carried, half pushed him toward the sunlit archway leading into the arena. Outside it was so bright that, after the gloomy interior, Woods was blinded at first. One of the guards thrust a short-bladed sword into his hand and shoved him out into the amphitheater, where he tripped and fell to his knees. Behind him a solid door slammed shut. He staggered to his feet. As his vision cleared he saw the detritus of combat strewn all over the arena, broken shields, discarded swords, and fragments of armor.

The arena was about two hundred meters in circumference, surrounded by stone walls four meters high. Above the walls were boxes and stands for spectators. Woods knew very well what went on here. The contests were all fixed, and gladiators seldom died in the arena. Men suffered terrible wounds sometimes, but most of the gore was artificial. Woods knew his wouldn't be.

The arena was empty.

Woods stared at the wall opposite where he stood panting, waiting for his opponent to emerge from the staging area. Would he be a retarius, a net-fighter armed with a dagger, trident, and net? Woods hefted his short sword. In his current physical condition, even another secutor would make short work of him.

The crowd began to chant, "Bring on the fight! Bring on the fight!" The roar swept over Woods. Suddenly the opponent's door clanged open. The crowd went instantly silent. For a full thirty seconds nothing emerged from the black square. Then two agile, bipedal, reptilian creatures bounded out into the amphitheater, and the crowd gasped in surprise. Behind them two more scaly animals colored in irregular stripes of yellow, green, and brown appeared in the doorway. Their heads, half the length of a man's forearm, had gaping jaws lined with fearsome serrated teeth. They bounded into the amphitheater on massive hind legs that had three dagger-like claws on each foot. Stubby forearms held shorter but no less lethal-looking claws. The creatures stood a meter tall. An agile, heavily armored man could easily deal with one; two were always a little more difficult. But, the year before, the best of the Gauls had fought four of the beasts at one time and emerged with only a few wounds. The spectators rose as one and shouted approval.

Disoriented by the roar of the crowd, the beasts tried to leap the walls into the crowd at first, but the severed tendons in their legs prevented them from jumping that high, normally not a difficult thing for this species.

And then they saw Woods.

The raptors bounded at him quickly.

Woods placed the tip of his blade just under his sternum and threw himself to the ground as hard as he could. The crowd screamed in anger and disappointment as the blade pierced his chest but settled down immediately as the beasts set about reducing Woods's body to red chunks.

CHAPTER
ONE

Getting from highway to the side of the headquarters building was no problem; the Marines' chameleon uniforms easily hid them from the crowds of HQ workers milling about outside during the lunch break. Those same crowds confused the motion detectors and other passive surveillance devices around the building's perimeter so the sensors didn't notice the intruders either. Just where the intelligence report had said it was, they found an open window to an untenanted office.

"Rock," Corporal Kerr said into his helmet radio. His infra screen showed Lance Corporal Rachman Claypoole slithering through the open window. Kerr followed immediately and had to move immediately to keep PFC MacIlargie from landing on him inside the office.

By the time Kerr got to his feet, Claypoole was next to the hallway door. Kerr checked his HUD and shook his head. He was amazed that it didn't show guards in the hallway. But *nobody* seemed to be there. He thought that was amazing for so large a building. Of course, most of the people who worked at the headquarters were civilians, and civilians didn't act like military personnel.

"Go," he said softly into his radio. Claypoole's next move was the first true test of the infiltration—intelligence didn't know if there were passive surveillance devices in the headquarters' corridors.

Claypoole pushed the door open and darted through. No

alarms sounded, but that didn't mean none were blinking somewhere else, alerting guards to the intruders. Kerr tapped Claypoole's invisible shoulder and gave him a push. The three Marines sprinted to the nearest radial corridor and down it to a vending alcove. Kerr rechecked their route on the floor plan in his HUD, made sure his men knew where they were going next, and then they were off once more, soft-footing their way. Their objective was the command center deep in the center of the large building. So far there were no signs of pursuit.

They next stopped outside a door on an inner ring-corridor, and Kerr once more examined the building's floor plan on his HUD. Three green dots indicated the positions of he and his men; the door icon showed its lock was engaged. Five ill-defined red dots inside the room showed where its occupants were. Maybe. The dots were indistinct because his sensors weren't sure the hot spots were people; they could be over-heated equipment. The floor plan showed another door leading from the room deeper into the building. It didn't show another route to where they had to go—unless they blasted through a wall. Blasting through a wall was out of the question; for their mission to succeed, they had to infiltrate the interior of the building undetected. They weren't even carrying anything that *could* blast through a wall.

This was a good test, Kerr thought, of how three Marines could quietly subdue five people. It wasn't a good idea to rush in and try to physically overpower them. Even if the five were trained navy guards instead of ordinary sailors or civilians, the Marines had a distinct advantage since they were effectively invisible in their chameleon uniforms. Three highly trained, invisible Marines bursting in unexpectedly should have little problem subduing five people, even trained security men. But could they do it before one of the five managed to sound the alarm? In any event, they had to get through a locked door before they could deal with whoever was in the room. But breaking the lock would alert the people inside, and if the lock was tied into a security system . . .

The corporal quickly inventoried the equipment available to him. Like the stunguns that were their main weapons, all their grenades, were nonlethal. The flashbang wouldn't do, its bang was too loud, the gas in the coldcock grenade would take seconds to fill the room and knock out the occupants, and one of them might set off an alarm in the interval. The neurophaser grenade worked fast enough to take all five down before they knew what was happening, but it would also affect the three Marines if they didn't give it enough time to stop radiating before they entered—and they didn't have much time. The best items they had were the put-outs— gas-impregnated cloths capable of rendering a normal-size person unconscious in just a couple of seconds if held over the mouth and nose. But they'd work only if the Marines weren't outnumbered, as they were. Of course, they could simply rush in, stunguns blazing, and knock out everyone that way—but if the people were civilians, it wouldn't be right to treat them so roughly.

One of the red dots on the HUD moved toward the door. The door opened and a man in civilian clothes stepped into the corridor. Before he shut the door a female voice asked him to remember the extra sugar in her coffee. He laughed, said, "You're sweet enough without the extra." He let the door swing shut on its own as he turned down the corridor and almost stepped on Kerr's foot.

Kerr moved fast. He threw an arm around the man's chest to lift him off the floor and clamped a hand over his mouth and nose. The man flailed his arms and kicked wildly, but his soft-shod feet only connected with Kerr's shins and made little noise and less damage.

Almost immediately, Claypoole was on the man, his fingers pinching his carotid artery to knock him out. Simultaneously, MacIlargie grabbed the door to keep it from shutting all the way and relocking. The door remained ajar by the width of his gloved fingers.

"Good thinking," Kerr said, "both of you." The comm unit in his helmet transmitted his words to his men and not beyond. They were committed now; the security system might set off an alarm if the door remained held open. They had to go in. He shifted the unconscious man so he held him up with one arm, leaving the other free to give instructions. He made quick marks on his HUD and transmitted them.

MacIlargie flung the door open then dashed through and to the left. Claypoole was right on his heels, darting to the right. Kerr came last and headed straight ahead, holding the unconscious civilian like a shield.

"Back so fast?" the female voice asked. The woman looked up and her eyes bugged when she saw her coworker's inert body advancing on her. It slammed into her and knocked her off her chair before she could scream. To her right, MacIlargie had already stunned one civilian and was shifting his stungun's muzzle to another. On the other side, Claypoole had disarmed a navy guard and was engaged in a silent struggle. Fortunately, the sailor, distracted by having to wrestle with an unexpected, invisible opponent, was too panicked to yell out a warning.

Kerr dropped the man and slapped a put-out on the woman's face. She tried to draw a deep breath as she kicked and flailed her arms. The breath was a mistake and she went totally limp.

"Sorry about that," Kerr murmured. He was afraid he might have injured her when he slammed her coworker's body into her.

A rapid-fire *thump-thud* to his right spun him in that direction. Claypoole's sailor dropped like a rock.

In his infra Kerr saw Claypoole look toward him. "I had to bounce his head off the wall," Claypoole said. "He might have a concussion."

Kerr grunted. Suffering serious injury or getting killed was a chance sailors, soldiers, and Marines took.

"Secure them," he ordered.

In a moment all five people had their wrists cuffed behind their backs and their ankles held together with the self-adhering security bands the Marines carried for that purpose. The Marines used wide tape to close the mouths of the five. Last, they used strong cords to link the people's ankles to their wrists.

One of them, the corridor man, regained consciousness before they were finished.

Kerr knelt next to him and flipped up his shields so the man could see him. "Just lay there and relax," he said. "You're not going anywhere without help, and nobody's seriously injured." He flipped his infra and chameleon shields back into place and stood. His HUD indicated that the next room was vacant. "Let's go. Mac, me, Rock."

MacIlargie opened the inner door and zipped through. Kerr and Claypoole followed just as fast—they wanted to get away from the door in a hurry in case their sensors were wrong about nobody being in the adjoining room.

The three Marines trotted along the narrow passage between a rank of desks and a bank of data stores to a doorway on the far side of the room. The HUD floor plan showed a broad corridor beyond the room. The sensors also showed a number of people, mostly singles but some in pairs or trios, walking in both directions along it.

Kerr checked the door. The locking mechanism was disengaged, that much was good. The rest of it wasn't.

Impatiently, he watched red dots moving along the corridor on his HUD. It quickly became obvious the Marines would have a long wait for the corridor to become vacant; there might not even be a moment when nobody was walking in the direction of this door. They had to take the chance that nobody would notice when the door opened and no one came out. Keeping an eye on the moving dots on the HUD, he gave instructions.

The door opened to the left. At a moment when nobody was coming toward it from the right, he opened it and MacIlargie rushed past him into the corridor.

"What's that?" Kerr asked in a voice that could be clearly heard by nearby people.

"You've got to finish this before you go," Claypoole replied just as loudly. He ducked past Kerr into the corridor.

"But—oh, all right," Kerr grumbled, then stepped away from the door and let it close. He glanced left along the corridor. Nobody seemed to notice anything. They headed deeper into the building, closer to their objective.

A man effectively invisible can move without, in most places, being noticed, as long as he moves quietly. But in a corridor with even moderate traffic, being quiet isn't enough. People automatically avoid obstructions they see; they don't avoid obstructions they don't see. An invisible man is an unseen obstruction. The three Marines had to duck, weave, and occasionally backstep to avoid people who were about to bump into them. They weren't successful one hundred percent of the time.

"Excuse me," a man in a flight suit said absentmindedly when MacIlargie found himself stuck between two people moving in opposite directions. The young Marine was able to avoid one but not both. MacIlargie grunted something and spun away. The flight-suited man, with his hands swooping through the air, continued his conversation with his equally intent and swoop-handed companion. A few paces later the man in the flight suit realized he hadn't seen anybody where he'd bumped into someone and stopped to look back.

"What's the matter?" his companion asked.

"I bumped into somebody, but nobody's there."

"Sure there is." The companion pointed his chin at the person MacIlargie had managed to avoid when the flight suit bumped him.

"No, I saw her. It was a man's voice that said 'No problem.' "

The companion looked at the doors lining the corridor. "Whoever it was must have gone into one of those offices."

"You think so?" Flight Suit wasn't sure there had been enough time for the man he bumped to make it to one of the doorways and through it before he looked back.

"Of course I'm sure. What else could it be?"

Flight Suit shrugged. "I guess you're right. There's no such thing as an invisible man—and there aren't any Marines here." They resumed walking and returned to their conversation. Their hands began making flight patterns once more.

At last the Marines reached their next way point, a janitor's closet off a short side corridor, and ducked inside among the cleaning robots. Kerr shrunk the scale of his HUD floor plan, then rezoomed on the section that showed the route from there to the command center that was their objective.

"It should be tougher from here on," he said softly. "We're likely to start running into guards."

"The one in that first office was easy enough," Claypoole snorted, forgetting how much trouble he'd had subduing the sailor.

"From here in, they'll probably be more alert."

Claypoole stifled a remark about three Marines' swabbing up a headquarters full of squids, instead listening for his fire team leader's next orders.

Despite Kerr's concern, the only guards they encountered between the janitor's closet and their next way point were two petty officers flanking the ornate entrance of what was probably an admiral's office. The guards, standing at parade rest, appeared to be more ceremonial than functional.

The next way station was their last. Kerr's HUD sensors showed no red dots nearby so they appeared to have a clear passage along the next two, short, corridors. He knew there was a guard station right beyond the range of his sensors.

According to the intelligence reports, nobody could pass the guard station without being identified and cleared.

Kerr touched helmets with his men and said, "Here's what we're going to do . . ."

A minute later, halfway down the second corridor, a warning tone in their earpieces froze the Marines in their tracks. A sensor had picked up the emanations of a motion detector.

Kerr checked his HUD. The warning device was on the opposite side of the mouth of the next corridor on the right, the last corridor they had to follow. The motion detector was probably tied into a control panel at the guard station. They withdrew a few steps while they considered what to do about the motion detector. By that time they were close enough to the guard station for the HUD to show two dots representing the guards. The two dots were motionless, so either the motion detector hadn't picked up the Marines or the Marines weren't acting suspicious enough to draw the guards' attention—yet.

The Marines weren't carrying anything that could unobtrusively disable a motion detector. There was only one thing they could do.

"Plasma shields up," Kerr ordered. He hefted his stungun. "We go fast and take the guards down." And hope they didn't have projectile weapons, he thought. The plasma shields would protect the Marines if the guards had blasters, but they weren't wearing body armor. "Our objective is right beyond them."

Claypoole and MacIlargie acknowledged him then turned on their plasma shields and readied their stunguns.

"On three. One. Two. Three."

The three Marines sprinted the ten meters to the adjoining corridor and skidded around its corner. The guards had noted movement on their monitor and were drawing their hand-blasters.

"Where are they?" shrieked one when he looked up from

the monitor that told him three targets had just run into their corridor.

The other guard, eyes wide and mouth open in surprise, raised his hand-blaster to fire blindly, but he convulsed as shots from two stunguns hit him before he could press the firing stud. His weapon fell from limp fingers and he collapsed over the railing of the guard station. The other guard was twitching and falling before the first dropped his weapon.

"Go!" Kerr shouted in the clear.

The three Marines bounded through the guard station, burst through the double doors beyond them, and scattered into the command center.

"Everybody, you're dead!" Kerr shouted as he raised his helmet shields.

Most of the two dozen people in the room looked toward him with disgust.

Three other grinning, chameleoned Marines were already there, helmets off. They shouted friendly greetings. A cluster of high-ranking officers, including three Confederation Marines in dress reds, stood at the far end of the command center.

Rear Admiral Blankenvoort, commander of the Confederation Navy supply depot on Thorsfinni's World, and the highest ranking member of the Confederation military in the sector, looked glumly at the second trio of Marines to burst into his command center, then hung his head and shook it ruefully. "I really need to tune up my security chief. Probably replace him. This is downright embarrassing."

The lieutenant commander who, as provost marshal, was responsible for security, blanched.

Blankenvoort looked sideways at the Marine lounging next to him. "I hope your Marines didn't injure any of my personnel."

Brigadier Theodosius Sturgeon, commander of the Confederation Marine Corps' 34th FIST, and Thorsfinni's World's second-highest ranking military officer, replied, "I don't think they did, Admiral. I impressed on them that civilians and sailors, even navy security personnel, are fragile creatures compared to Marines and that they needed to be gentle with anyone they couldn't avoid." He couldn't keep a touch of smugness out of his voice. "And, Admiral? Don't be too severe with your provost marshal."

"Why not?"

"A couple of reasons. First, no matter who the nominal security chief is, you're ultimately responsible."

When Sturgeon didn't immediately give the second reason, Blankenvoort asked through a clenched jaw.

"Commander Van Winkle's infantrymen are very, *very* good." Sturgeon and one of the other Marines exchanged grins.

"How many other fire teams do you have in the building?" the admiral asked. Anger and despair fought for control of his voice.

"Four."

The top navy people in the room groaned.

The three Marine officers courteously refrained from grinning.

Ten minutes later the sixth and final Marine fire team burst into the command center and announced that everybody was dead. The command center had six entrances; each fire team had entered through a different one. Brigadier Sturgeon and Colonel Ramadan, his chief of staff, went with Admiral Blankenvoort and his staff to debrief the results of the security exercise, while Commander Van Winkle took the infiltrating Marines, two fire teams from each of the three blaster companies in his battalion, into a room where his S-2, intelligence officer, waited to debrief them.

"Did you kill anybody?" Van Winkle asked as soon as the door was closed.

"Nossir," the fire team leaders barked.

"Any serious injuries? Other than the guards you had to overcome at the entrances to the command center?"

"Sir, we might have given a guard a concussion," Corporal Kerr said. He gave the number of the room where they'd subdued the five people.

"Sir, a guard put up a pretty good fight," said a fire team leader from Kilo Company. "I think we broke his nose and an arm." He gave the number of the room where they had stashed the man.

Nobody else had anything more severe than bruised egos to report. They were all pretty smug.

"Don't feel too good about yourselves," Van Winkle told them. "Imagine if it had been actual hostiles who burst in here? There'd be quite a few dead people here, and we'd be getting ready to move out on a live operation. With the navy command center in hostile hands, we'd have no way of knowing what we were up against or how much intelligence they had about our strength and intentions." He looked at his Marines sternly. He was pretty sure, though, that no one else could have made it all the way to the command center without being discovered the way his six fire teams had. If for no other reasons than nobody else was likely to have the floor plans.

"Well done, Marines," he finally said. "Now Lieutenant Troud will debrief you. Lieutenant."

"Sir!" Troud came to attention.

Van Winkle left the room and the debriefing got under way. The navy was going to want to know every detail of how six Marine fire teams got from outside the building all the way into the command center in its heart without anybody sounding an alarm.

CHAPTER TWO

It was a quiet Sixth Day night in Big Barb's. Only a half-dozen or so fights had broken out. No more than three patrons of the combination bar, restaurant, ships' chandler, and bordello had to be carried out insensate from the vigor of the fisticuffs. The usual raucous singing seemed muted, fewer voices than normal shouting imperfectly remembered lyrics. Raised voices didn't stay raised for long—the more boisterous speakers seemed cowed by the hollow booming of their voices in the relative quiet.

There wasn't anything in particular wrong. It was simply that the Marines of Lima Company's third platoon, the main military habitués of Big Barb's, were tired from the training exercise late the night before. And the fish the inhabitants of the Niflheim area of Thorsfinni's World called "herring" were running, so most of the fishermen and other seamen who were the bulk of Big Barb's clientele were at sea.

Tired Marines and absent sailors made Big Barb less than her normal jolly self—she wasn't making as much money as on a normal Sixth Day night. Her great bulk threatening a stool's integrity, she sat alone at one end of the scarred bar and glowered out at the half-empty room. She sniffed; not even wonderful Charlie Bass was there. She remembered the deal she'd made with him for the promotion party nearly a year earlier, and a smile threatened to break up the storm cloud of her face, but she battened the smile down.

Several Marines from third platoon sat at a table in the

corner nearest the kitchen exit. A few of Big Barb's girls kept them company—partly because they enjoyed the company of the Marines, partly because they hoped to entice some of them to the private rooms upstairs, where the girls made most of their money.

Carlala, a new girl, sat on Claypoole's lap. With the fingers of the arm draped around his shoulders, she idly played with the short hair on his scalp. She leaned against him so that a breast settled lightly on his chest. From time to time, in seeming casual movement, her cheek gently brushed his. Carlala might have been new at the business, but she already had distinct ideas of how to arouse a man without being overt. She *wanted* to jiggle her bottom on him because her subtlety didn't seem to be getting any reaction, but jiggling would be too overt.

Instead of being aroused, Claypoole absently lay an arm around her waist and let his hand curl slightly where it rested on her thigh. His other hand moved languidly between the stein of Reindeer Ale he sipped from and the Fidel on which he puffed just enough to keep it from going out. Truth was, he was barely aware of the young woman on his lap; his thoughts were elsewhere.

Carlala was certainly pretty enough, and Claypoole had cheered and whistled as much as anybody else a few weeks earlier when she made her first appearance at Big Barb's. She was a bit shorter than average, but her smile and sizable bust made her appear taller in men's eyes. Claypoole had been upstairs with her more than a couple of times. If he'd been in a normal mood that evening, he'd be reacting strongly to her. Probably he'd even be thinking that of all Big Barb's girls she was his favorite. He might even think he'd like to take her away from Big Barb.

That did happen sometimes; Bronnoysund, the liberty town outside the main gate of Camp Major Pete Ellis, was home to a fair number of fat, happy housefraus with a brood of children—in a couple of instances, grandchildren—who had once been Big Barb's girls.

These Marines were behaving in a most uncharacteristic manner. Not one attempted to steal a kiss or tried to feel the softness of a breast. None even patted a nicely rounded bottom. Neither did they seem to have any great interest in getting drunk. They'd had a robust dinner when they arrived a couple of hours earlier, but they hadn't eaten with any of the high gusto with which they normally tore into their reindeer steaks. Since then they'd drunk slowly and talked quietly about inconsequential things, paying the girls no more attention than they might have given kittens hunting wild yarn about their feet.

All the Marines present that night had been stationed with 34th FIST for more than the two years, the normal duty assignment for FIST Marines. Not that Marines were always transferred after two years; sometimes, simply by happenstance, a Marine might stay in one place with one unit for two and a half or even three years. But Thorsfinni's World was classified as a hardship post, and the Confederation Marine Corps was conscientious about transferring men from hardship posts on time.

"CARLALA!" The booming voice rang out over the bang of the door its owner flung open.

Carlala—and all the other girls—looked toward the main entrance to Big Barb's. A dozen big men rolled in. Big Barb herself looked up and momentarily forgot to glower. One of the fishing boats had come to port, and its crew was primed for a night out.

Carlala looked at Claypoole and very deliberately said, "Someone wants me. Do you mind if I go to him?"

Claypoole gave her an absent smile and said, "Have a good time."

With her mouth little more than an inch away from his, Carlala reconsidered the kiss she was about to give him. She gave one wiggle on his lap, just to remind him of what he was missing, then rose and danced off toward the fishermen who'd just arrived. The other young women were already on their way. In moments each fisherman, one or more of Big Barb's girls clinging like lampreys to him, was headed to satisfy his heart's most immediate desire—to a table for his first good meal in more than a week, to the bar for his first drink since sailing, or for the stairs, to the private rooms on the second floor.

The Marines continued to drink slowly and talk quietly about nothing in particular. Until . . .

"Think they forgot about us?" Lance Corporal Van Impe asked. He'd been with 34th FIST for more than two and a half years.

"Not a chance," replied Corporal Dornhofer. Of the nine Marines around the table, he'd been on Thorsfinni's World the longest, and he'd been a Marine longer than the others. "There are a lot of things Mother Corps forgets to give her Misguided Children. Mother Corps forgets to promote people." He nodded at Lance Corporal Chan, who had been filling a corporal's billet for longer than normal. "She sometimes forgets to give people medals. She even forgets to issue us gear that works right." Schultz, Claypoole, and Dean smiled; they knew *that* drill by heart. "But one thing Mother Corps is real good about remembering is rotating people off hardship posts."

"Mother Corps thinks *everybody* deserves to get the shit duty." Corporal Goudanis chuckled without mirth.

Claypoole, Dean, and Chan looked at each other. They'd arrived on Thorsfinni's World together. The other six had been with 34th FIST longer than they had. Even though they were past due for rotation, they didn't quite feel they had the right to complain in such company.

"We aren't the only ones, you know," Lance Corporal Watson commented.

Corporal Linsman nodded. "Gunny Bass, Staff Sergeant Hyakowa, Corporal Kerr—"

"Kerr doesn't count, he was away for almost two years," Van Impe said.

"Recuperating from wounds suffered on a deployment with us," Dornhofer reminded him. "That counts."

"—Lance Corporal Dupont," Linsman continued, ignoring the interjection, "all three squad leaders, half the gun squad."

"Captain Conorado, Top Myer, Gunny Thatcher," Dornhofer said, picking up the roll call. "Hell, everybody in the company headquarters unit."

"And that doesn't count the men from the other platoons," Goudanis added.

"Anybody know about the rest of the battalion?" Dornhofer asked.

Nobody had enough friends in the other blaster companies—or any of the FIST's other units—to have any idea whether it was just Lima Company that wasn't getting transfers or if the stagnation had spread further.

"We've got a lot of new men in the platoon," Goudanis said. "But every one of them was a replacement for a Marine who was killed or injured too badly to return to duty." He shook his head. "I don't remember the last time we got a new man as a replacement for someone who rotated out. Except Corporal Doyle."

"Special situation," Linsman said.

"Doyle's a pogue," Van Impe said. "Pogues don't count."

"That's a good point," Dornhofer said to Goudanis, ignoring the remarks about Corporal Doyle. "And it really bothers me. A few FISTs, most particularly the 34th, have an unusually high number of deployments. That means we suffer a high number of casualties. Normal procedure is to transfer a Marine out of one of these high-deployment FISTs into a unit that doesn't deploy so he gets a break from being the tip of the pointy end." He glanced around the table. "I think every one of us has a wound stripe. Several of us have more than one. The longer a Marine is in a high-deployment FIST, the worse the odds against him surviving."

He looked at Schultz. "What do you think, Hammer?"

Schultz grunted. "Mother Corps sends, I go." It really didn't matter to Schultz where he was stationed or for how long. All he asked was to remain a lance corporal until he retired after forty years' service and to be in a unit that had a lot of combat deployments. Thirty-fourth FIST was the best assignment he'd had so far—perhaps no other unit in the Confederation Marine Corps had as many deployments as it did. If he spent the rest of his career with 34th FIST, that was fine with him.

They were silent for a long moment, each man thinking his private thoughts, then Dornhofer leaned his elbows on the table and said, "Something's going on. I've been thinking about requesting mast to find out what it is."

"Request mast?" Chan asked. "You don't have to be so formal about it, the Skipper will see any man in the company who knocks on his door."

Dornhofer shook his head. "I don't mean Captain Conorado. I mean Brigadier Sturgeon."

Every Marine had the right to "request mast," to go to the commander at the appropriate level to get a problem resolved. He didn't have to explain the problem to anyone under that commander—no one could shunt the problem aside or bury it. Request mast was a very serious matter, and never undertaken lightly or for frivolous reasons.

"Brigadier Sturgeon!" several of them exclaimed.

"You don't fool around," Linsman said.

"Why not go to Commander Van Winkle first?" Goudanis asked.

"Because the battalion commander doesn't know anything that the FIST commander doesn't, and the brigadier probably knows things Van Winkle doesn't."

"Don't you think if the brigadier knew he'd have told us by now?" Dean asked.

Dornhofer didn't answer. He knew what Dean was thinking. Confederation Marine Corps officers were all commissioned from the ranks. Every one of them knew what it was like to be on the bottom of the chain of command and have to carry out the orders or live under the dictates that came down that chain. Every one of them knew from firsthand experience what the junior enlisted and junior noncommissioned officers were capable of. Even if the institution the enlisted men sometimes called "Mother Corps" was occasionally negligent, the officers could be counted on to do their best for their Marines.

"If something's going on that affects us like this, either he doesn't know or he's under orders to not tell us," Linsman said.

"If he doesn't know, somebody needs to tell him. If he's got orders not to tell us, those orders are wrong." The others, even Schultz, who was content being with 34th FIST for an extended period, made movements or noises of agreement.

There was nothing they could do about the situation that night other than complain. But Marines on liberty, with money in their pockets, beer at hand, and willing women nearby, don't stay disgruntled for long. After a while they set about getting happily drunk and started looking for proper female companionship.

As it turned out, by the time Dornhofer filed for his request mast, he couldn't see the FIST commander.

CHAPTER
THREE

It was snowing heavily in Fargo on the day Assistant Attorney General Thom Nast had his second interview with Madame Chang-Sturdevant, President of the Confederation Council.

That first time he'd been only a special agent of the Ministry of Justice, laughed at by superiors who thought him a fool. Madame President, however, knew better and she had given him the job of cleaning up the poaching operation on Avionia, which had resulted in the arrest of numerous government officials, chief among them the Attorney General herself. Nast had subsequently been promoted to Assistant Attorney General and put in charge of the Organized Crime Directorate.

"Why the hell didn't you take the Metro, Thom?" Hugyens Long groused. He nodded at the swirling snowstorm just outside the landcar's window. "Or we could have taken a hopper," he added grimly. It was nearly forty kilometers from the Ministry of Justice's headquarters in Davenport to the Confederation Council Complex at Dilworth, east of the river. It would take them a good hour to travel that distance on the surface. Despite the fact that they would never have to go out into the storm, Chief Long had insisted on bringing along a warm overcoat. "You never know," he had said when Nast asked him if he thought the coat would be required.

"I thought we might want to talk, Chief. Privately."

"Don't count on it, Thom," Long grunted. "Sweet Persephone's tits, you don't know where the bugs might be! This is a company car, goddamnit." Spying had become endemic at the ministry during his predecessor's reign. When she had been arrested for her role in the Avionian operation, Long was called back from retirement to replace her. Unlike his predecessor, Long was a cop, not a lawyer, so to him the law was to be obeyed and enforced, not used for personal gain or advantage.

As Attorney General, Long had managed to find out more than he was authorized to know about the ultrasecret Avionian Project, and some prominent politicians and businessmen had gone to the penal colony called Darkside for their role in the poaching there. Since his appointment he had discovered, to his utter dismay, that the Ministry of Justice was riddled with officials on the take, every one of them left over from his predecessor's administration. He was rooting them out, but slowly. Many of Nast's investigations into racketeering, for instance, were thwarted because someone in the Organized Crime Directorate had been leaking information to the syndicate bosses. The other directorates were equally riddled with highly paid informants.

Nast refused to talk about his plan in any office at the ministry. Long respected Nast's precaution and he respected him as a professional law enforcement officer. Nast had proved his worth on Avionia. So Long readily acceded to the younger man's request for a private meeting with the Confederation President. If Nast didn't want to talk about his plan until he was sure it would not be compromised, and if he felt its success required the special intervention of the president, Attorney General Long would support him.

"I did have this vehicle swept," Nast said.

Long grunted. "Just keep what you know to yourself, until we're in with the President. Besides, you only wanted to take surface transportation because you like the goddamn snow, Nast!"

They both laughed. "It is beautiful, isn't it?" Nast said.

Long snorted. "Hate the stuff myself. Here we are in the capital city of the Confederation of Human Worlds and the goddamned government can't even put a climate dome over the place, so we have to endure this—crap." He shook his head. "Smoke?" He fumbled in his loose-fitting jacket and produced a handful of cigars. "I have Clintons and Fidels."

"Thank you, sir," Nast replied. "A Fidel, please. The Clintons are too tasteless for me."

They lit the cigars and smoked in silence for a long moment, savoring the Fidels' richness.

"Ah, Thom, me boy, a cigar is a cigar, but a Fidel is a smoke." Long stretched luxuriously and blew the smoke out slowly through his nose.

Nast marveled at how calm his boss was. Another man would have demanded to know what his plan was, possibly refused his request for an interview with the president as going out of bounds over a matter that belonged within the ministry. But not Long. The Attorney General was actually content just to wait to hear the details of his plan. Known affectionately as "Chief," because he'd run a planetary police force for many years, Hugyens Long believed that reliable subordinates should be allowed to exercise their own initiative. Even to the point of calling for a meeting with the confederation president if need be. Even to the point of enduring an hour's ride in a landcar in a snowstorm.

Nast had come up with a plan to gather the evidence he needed to break up the mob's activities on Havanagas, the "leisure world" owned and operated by some of the biggest crime families in the Confederation. Almost every agent so far sent to Havanagas had died. Nast had managed to keep two alive—code names Bistro and Copper—because he was the only person in the ministry, Chief Long included, who knew their identities. Bistro's cover was so deep and his position so low-level, he had not yet been able to develop useful access; Copper figured prominently in Nast's plan to destroy the mob's hold on Havanagas. But to carry off his plan, Nast required presidential authority. That was good enough for an old cop like Long.

"I've known Chang-Sturdevant for some years, Thom," the Attorney General said, "But you actually worked for her on that Avionian thing. What's your impression?"

Nast shrugged. "I like her, Chief. She's not afraid to make decisions, and she trusts you to do your job. She knows how to run a government. Not a bad looker for a gal in her seventies either. I'd say she was a knockout when she was in her forties."

"Would you share a Fidel with her?" Long joked. The expression "to share a Fidel" was a distinct sexual innuendo.

"Yeah, I'd share a Fidel with her, and a number of other things." He laughed.

The landcar wound its way through the towering canyons of Fargo's government buildings, mostly the minor ministerial departments of West Fargo. About half a kilometer behind them another intrepid traveler's car plowed bravely through the drifts, its lights intermittently visible through the swirling snow. They crossed the frozen Red River of the North while the two passengers smoked contentedly, the landcar's guidance system carefully negotiating the patches of ice and snowdrifts along the highway. In the blizzard, it was impossible to make out the soaring edifices of the Council Complex that dominated the city's eastern skyline. Five kilometers beyond the river they entered a tunnel at Dilworth that led into the vast underground city that lay beneath the complex. More than a hundred thousand people from every world in the Confederation lived and worked there.

The car glided to a smooth stop beside a busy unloading platform. Its doors swung open and the pair dismounted. A vast underground plaza, crowded with shoppers, stretched off into the far distance before them. Despite the storm roaring on the surface, the underground city basked in warm artificial sunlight, its citizens going about their business in shirtsleeves. "Gentlemen, we have arrived," the landcar's feminine voice announced. "Take the Red Walkway to Tower B7. The President's suite is on the 101st floor. Enjoy your business, gentlemen." The car sped off.

They mounted a high-speed walkway marked RED and were carried across the plaza toward a huge bank of elevators. Chief Long carried his overcoat over one arm. He had begun to perspire slightly. "Thom, one thing I can tell you for sure," he said, running a handkerchief over his brow.

"What's that, Chief?"

"We're flying back to Davenport."

In the unloading zone, the car that had been following them pulled to a stop and a tall man wearing an overcoat hopped out. He stood for a moment, rearranging the garment about himself. He ordered the car to wait for him in a nearby parking zone.

He stood looking about, getting his bearings. When he caught sight of the two officials some distance ahead of him on the moving walkway, he smiled grimly and followed them.

No one was allowed access to the elevator bank without first passing through a full-body security scan and retinal ID. There were no exceptions, not even Madame Chang-Sturdevant or her cabinet ministers, although one station was exclusively reserved for officials of cabinet rank. A long row of scanners manned by security police blocked the way. The pair picked one with a short line. First their identities were established and then they were asked to surrender their sidearms until they were ready to leave the complex. Chief Long stepped into the scanner first.

"Where have you been eating your meals, sir?" one of the guards asked.

The question came as a surprise. Long shrugged. "Mostly in the ministry cafeteria. I spend most of my time at the office."

"Step around here and look at this, sir." The guard indicated Chief Long should come around to his instrument console. "See that?" He pointed to a tiny dot on the screen. It was located in the sigmoid flexure of his colon.

Chief Long nodded. "Thom, a goddamn bug! There was a bug in my goddamn food! I knew we were smart not to talk in the car."

"This one has almost worked its way through. Someone in the cafeteria is feeding you these things on a continuous basis, sir, since if you're regular, uh, you know . . ." He shrugged his embarrassment. "I'm afraid, sir, we'll have to, er, move it all the way on before you can pass through. No pun intended." He handed Long a large vial. "The rest rooms are over there, sir. In just a few minutes it'll be out of your system. The laxative is very powerful. You're early for your appointment, I see, so you should still make it on time. Oh." He handed Long a waxed carton. "Please, um, use the scoop provided to put it all in here. We'll have to retrieve the device and pass it on to Technical Services for evaluation."

Long turned to Nast. "Thom, I knew the cafeteria food was bad, but this is ridiculous. Good damn thing they weren't trying to poison me, eh?" He addressed his stomach: "Get an earful, you dirty bastard! I'm gonna get you!" Then he marched grimly off to the lavatory.

Three more bugs were discovered in Nast's clothing.

"Are you feeling ill, AG?" Madame Chang-Sturdevant asked Chief Long as he took his seat in her office.

"Nothing serious, ma'am. It was, er, something I ate," he replied with a sickly smile.

"I apologize for not talking to you more often, AG. You're doing a wonderful job over there. Thank you. Thom . . ." She turned her attention to Nast. "Good to see you again! Congratulations on your promotion, by the way." She turned back to Chief Long. "Mr. Nast did a bang-up job, cleaning up that poaching operation. Some of my administration's worst enemies went to Darkside over that." She smiled. Of course, the arrests had been made based on criminal acts, not party membership.

"Refreshments, gentlemen? Larry," she said, addressing the servo that rolled soundlessly out of its niche at the sound of her voice. "See what my guests would like to have."

"Good afternoon, Mr. Long," it said in a basso profundo. "May I offer you refreshment? May I hang your coat, sir?" Long's overcoat lay draped across his knees.

"No, no," he answered, a bit too quickly. Putting anything in his stomach was the furthest thought from his mind just then. "Thank you anyway," he responded.

"Good afternoon to you too, Mr. Nast," Larry greeted Thom. "Good to see you again, sir. Would you have a Schwepps, sir?" Larry actually laughed pleasantly as he served Nast.

Madame Chang-Sturdevant and Nast sipped their drinks. The floor beneath them quivered slightly. "It's the wind," Chang-Sturdevant announced. "This building sways up to two meters in high winds. Did you know that? Well," she went on, "you asked for thirty minutes and time's a-wasting. Mr. Nast?"

Nast cleared his throat. "Ma'am, as we all know, Havanagas is owned and ruled by several crime families. We've been trying to get inside the organization there to obtain the evidence we need to put them out of business. First, we know they never pay taxes when they can avoid it. We've been working with the Ministry of Finance on that, but so far nothing's come of that effort since Finance has the same problem we do—agents sent to Havanagas never live long enough to make a report."

"We've lost six agents over the last few months, ma'am," Long interjected, "murdered in the most horrible fashion." He described briefly what had happened to Gilboa Woods.

"That's not to say we don't have anybody out there," Nast said. He turned to Long. "Sorry, Chief, but I set up two agents on my own and didn't tell anyone about it." Long nodded. Nast turned back to the president. "One is under very deep cover and not highly placed, so hasn't developed much of anything yet. But the other's a different matter, and I'll get to him.

"Tax evasion, murder, and obstruction of justice are not the only crimes the mob's committed," Nast continued. "There's the slave trade. They sell young women throughout Human Space to be used as prostitutes. The mob there also makes millions off the illegal traffic in drugs like thule—and avoidance of customs duties in the process. And then there's the sexual exploitation of children held prisoner in the brothels of Havanagas. And worst of all, ma'am—I hesitate to say it— 'snuff parties' where women and boys are slowly tortured to death for the pleasure of well-heeled perverts."

"You can literally get almost anything you want on Havanagas," Chief Long said.

"Yes, gentlemen," Madame Chang-Sturdevant said, "I know some of the details. But Havanagas operates legitimate business enterprises too, all legally chartered, taxpaying ventures that cater to the perfectly natural desire of people to enjoy themselves in a pleasant atmosphere. Havanagas is a resort world, and millions enjoy vacations there every year. When was the last time either of you watched *Barkspiel*, gentlemen?"

Nast grimaced. The syndicated quiz show was watched avidly by billions of people throughout Human Space. It offered its contestants, ordinary working men and women, the chance for instant riches. All they had to do was answer correctly a set of very simple questions while revealing the most intimate details about their personal lives. The prizes were so huge nobody could blame a miner from Diamunde, or a waitress on Wanderjahr, for instance, for divulging the details of their sex lives to hundreds of millions of other people. The show ran on dozens of worlds, each with its own host. The contestants, men and women perfectly groomed, were ageless personalities virtually worshiped by their audiences. And the Grand Prize on each show was an all-expense-paid, top-of-the-line month-long vacation on Havanagas.

"Gentlemen," Chang-Sturdevant continued, "in this regard, our policy toward Havanagas is ruled by show biz. Shut it down and," she shrugged, "I take heat I don't need. Running the Confederation Council is work enough by itself, I don't need legitimate investors and a trillion fans screaming for my head because I've ruined their fantasy. Shut Havanagas down, no; clean it up, yes. And I don't want anyone to know about it. And if things go bad, I've got to be able to deny my administration had anything to do with it. You take the heat if the operation blows up. I hate to say that, gentlemen, but to survive in politics sometimes you have to lie or sacrifice your loyal supporters."

Nast and Long exchanged glances. They nodded; losing their jobs would be worth it if they could clean up Havanagas.

"Also, gentlemen," the president continued, "don't forget there is a highly fragmented, indigenous resistance movement on Havanagas, people who want the mob out of their lives. They're not in the majority and they are largely ineffective, but the movement is alive. They could complicate things. They will want to fill the void when the mob bosses are gone. Have you thought about that, Mr. Nast?"

"My plan will be executed with utter discretion, ma'am," he replied. "I call it 'Operation Hangfire' and—"

Chang-Sturdevant raised an eyebrow. " 'Hangfire,' did you say? Translation, please!"

"Oh, sorry, ma'am. The expression goes back to the days of gunpowder firearms and literally means a cartridge that does not fire immediately. But in another sense it means a slow and deadly reaction, and that's what Operation Hangfire will be to the mob."

"Thank you, Thom." Chang-Sturdevant smiled. "Please continue."

"Well, you mentioned the resistance movement, ma'am,

the Havanagas Liberation Front, it's called. I am going to use it to rid Havanagas of the mobsters. And to answer your other question, no, ma'am, I hadn't thought about who'll run the place afterward. But shouldn't that be left up to the citizens of Havanagas and the legitimate stockholders in the enterprises that support the world's economy? I assure you, we can pull this off without destroying Havanagas or embarrassing your administration in the process."

"How?" Chang-Sturdevant and Long asked at the same time. They looked at each other and laughed. "How, Mr. Nast?" the president asked.

"By snatching the leadership. I don't need convincing evidence of all their crimes, only one, and when I've got it I can take them all into custody. Many great criminal leaders over the centuries have been destroyed because they were convicted of relatively minor felonies. Tax evasion is one. As soon as I have the hard evidence I need, I'll take them." Briefly he explained how he would do it. "You see," he concluded, "the plan is flexible."

Chang-Sturdevant and Long were silent for a moment, thinking. "It might work," Long said at last. He sighed and shifted his bulk in his chair. But it might not work, he reminded himself. "Larry, I think I'll have that drink now."

"Very good, sir. I recall you enjoy bourbon with a dash of distilled water?"

"Today, I want a cold Reindeer. Don't leave a head on it, Larry."

"Tell me this, Mr. Nast," Chang-Sturdevant said. "I appreciate your coming here and briefing me on this plan, and I support everything you wish to do. But otherwise, why do you need special help from my office? This whole operation is something you can handle within the Ministry of Justice."

"I was getting to that, ma'am," Nast replied. "I need your help because I need you to order the Commandant of the Confederation Marine Corps to detail three men to me—no explanation offered—to be my special undercover agents on

Havanagas. They will make contact with my one agent who has the goods on the mob and the resistance. Discharged Marines, spending their savings on liberty on Havanagas, it's perfect cover. Here," he continued as he loaded a crystal into a reader, "I've got the files on the three men I want for this operation."

Madame Chang-Sturdevant gasped. "I know these men, two of them anyway!"

Chief Long gave Nast a long and thoughtful look before announcing that he too knew lance corporals Joe Dean and Rachman Claypoole. "They worked with me on Wanderjahr, Thom," he said. "Damned good men, but . . ." He was now having doubts about the success of Nast's plan.

"Mr. Nast, these men saved the life of an ambassador on Diamunde," Madame Chang-Sturdevant said. "I will not have them sacrificed to bring down the syndicate on Havanagas. I will not!"

Nast had not anticipated Chang-Sturdevant's reaction. He'd picked Dean and Claypoole because they were brave and resourceful young men, and both Chief Long and the president knew them. He thought this would increase their confidence in his choice of the Marines for the mission.

"Madame President, I fully understand how you feel," he said. "I picked these men because they have the qualities needed to pull this operation off and survive. They will be under the guidance of Corporal Pasquin, who is a brave and resourceful NCO, but the two lance corporals, Dean and Claypoole, can think on their feet too. They have all been under fire. Ma'am, you know how desperate the fighting was on Diamunde. Dean and Claypoole were in the thick of it. That's what Marines do, they go into tough situations and survive. The Corps will send them into battle again and again as long as they wear the uniform. Like beat cops, they swear an oath to put themselves in harm's way to protect those who can't protect themselves. They are trained to take care of each other. That technique has worked to help Marines survive over the centuries. It'll work with these three men on Havanagas too. I need them for this operation, ma'am. It won't work without them."

Chang-Sturdevant was silent for a long time. "Can you guarantee me their safety?" she asked at last.

Before he could reply, Chief Long answered the question: "No, we can't. But as Thom just pointed out, Madame President, they are aces at survival." Long had concluded that if Nast thought these men were good enough to make his plan work, then he would support it.

"I will personally monitor the entire operation, ma'am," Nast added. "I'll be with the reaction teams. We'll go in at the first sign the Marines have been compromised."

Again Madame Chang-Sturdevant was silent. At last she said, "Guarantee me one thing, gentlemen. You will not sugarcoat this mission. You will tell them just how dangerous it can be. Give them the option of refusing to go."

Nast sighed mentally with relief. "Yes, Madame President, I promise you I will do that," he pronounced gravely.

"Well, your time is up, gentlemen." She stood up and her visitors did the same. "I have to prepare for a reception for the new ambassador from Ivanosk. Keep me briefed on this operation, Chief. I'll tell my secretary you get in to see me whenever you have news."

They were halfway to the door when the President stopped them. "One more question: Why did you pick three Marines, Thom? Why not two or four?"

Nast had not expected the question, but he was ready, "Well, three is the normal composition of a fire team, ma'am, and these three men were in the same fire team. They know how to work together."

"And," Chief Long added, "Havanagas is only one world. If we'd wanted to clean up two worlds, we'd have picked four Marines instead of only three."

*　　*　　*

Madame Chang-Sturdevant was still chuckling as she prepared for the reception. She pondered what it was Thom Nast had wanted to "share" with her besides that Fidel. She had not survived in Confederation politics without knowing just what it was her enemies—and her allies—were saying about her.

"Thom," Long said as they entered the elevator, "let's stop in one of those cafés on the plaza. I'm feeling better now and I want to eat something that doesn't have a damned bug in it."

They retrieved their weapons at the security station and started across the plaza toward a row of shops and cafés three hundred meters from the elevator bank.

"Mr. Nast? Mr. Nast?" someone called from behind them. Nast turned. A tall man was approaching them, an off-worlder by his clothing. "I have important news for you, sir," he said as he drew back his coat and leveled a black tubular object at Nast. Nast dived for the ground as Chief Long flung his overcoat at the assassin. There was a stunning *flash-bang*. Razor-sharp titanium slivers from a flechette round struck sparks off the flagstones of the plaza before ricocheting into the crowd. Firing upward from where they lay on the ground, Nast and Long simultaneously sent plasma bolts through the man's chest. The bolts burned through and dissipated harmlessly into the air as he crumpled into a lifeless, smoldering heap.

The plaza turned into a madhouse as hundreds of people ran for cover, some with slight wounds from the flechettes. Others were injured in the mad rush for safety. Security police, weapons at the ready, rushed to where the trio lay sprawled on the ground.

Nast tossed his pistol to the ground and stood up, his hands raised over his head. "We are police officers!" he shouted.

"Turn around! On your knees! Hands behind the back of your head!" one of the officers shouted, his weapon leveled directly at Nast. Nast assumed the position. "Cross your feet at the ankles!" the officer shouted. Nast complied. "Don't move!" Another officer covered Nast while the first holstered his pistol, kneeled on his legs and snapped on the cuffs. He assisted him to stand up. "Do you have any other weapons on you?"

"No, sir, and if you reach into the inside left pocket of my coat, officer, you'll find my credentials. That fat man on the ground is the Confederation Attorney General. The dead man is a hired assassin. Now would you mind uncuffing me?"

"I'm hit," Long said from where he still lay, a pool of blood seeping out from under his legs. "Some of those goddamned flechettes got me in the legs. '*Fat* man?' " he groaned. "I'll show you 'fat,' you young whippersnapper," he mumbled. Emergency medical personnel were already attending to his wounds. "Hell, I'm all right!" Long shouted. "See to those civilians!"

"No, you aren't," a medic replied. "Lay still. Don't worry about the civilians."

As the first policeman uncuffed Nast, another came up to where they stood. He had retrieved the assassin's gun. "It's a Brady Shot Rifle," he announced. "Modified with a three-round tube magazine and the barrel cut down to thirty-five centimeters. Very deadly and very professional."

"Yeah," a third officer said, "but not professional enough." He nodded toward the still smoldering corpse.

"He probably had to be sure of his target," Nast said. "Otherwise he'd have shot us in the back from three meters and that would've been it. We were damned lucky."

"I'm very sorry, Mr. Nast," the first policeman said as he returned the handcuffs to his carrier. "We didn't know who you were." He handed him his credentials and his weapon.

"No problem," Nast said. What the police officers had put him through was only normal procedure to ensure their safety in a potentially deadly situation. He'd have done the same thing himself. "Who's your station commander? I want a full check on this guy, find out all you can about him." It would probably be useless; they'd find nothing on him, but the checks had to be run anyway. Maybe they'd get lucky again. He turned his attention to Chief Long. "Chief, how you doing?"

"So I'm a 'fat man,' huh?" Long groused. "I heard you! Bugged, given the shits, shot, and now *insulted*, all in one day! You haven't got many points left with me, Nast."

Nast smiled. "I apologize, Chief. You are not fat, Chief, only *lipoid*."

"That's more like it. Doc, how am I doing?"

"You have some nasty lacerations in your lower legs, sir, but we'll have you back out on the street in a few hours. Gotta transport you to the hospital, though." He signaled for a litter from the waiting ambulance.

Long reached up and tugged Nast's sleeve anxiously. "Thom," he whispered, "they're on to you, lad. They know you're up to something. Be careful. Be careful!" he shouted as he was carried off to the ambulance.

After giving instructions to the officer in charge, Nast asked one of the security officers for a ride to the hospital.

It had been a long time since he had felt real fear. He didn't have time to be afraid during the shooting, but Long was right, the mob knew he was on to them, and that knowledge struck fear into him.

"That was some good shooting back there," the officer remarked as they drove through the tunnel complex to the infirmary. Nast fingered the butt of the hand-blaster under his left armpit and smiled. The hand-blaster he could trust—always. He could trust Chief Long too—and those three Marines, he could trust them. But that was it.

Of course, whatever agents had been following them, including the dead man, must have talked, but none of them knew anything about his plan. So the syndicate on Havanagas had to know he was looking at them. He thought of the murdered agent and the fear melted away, to be replaced with anger. Thom Nast was too professional to give in to emotion easily, but he was mad, and that was a bad sign for the mob.

CHAPTER FOUR

Brigadier Theodosius Sturgeon, commander of 34th FIST, pondered the data on his desk display for a time, then swiveled his chair to face the window overlooking the parade ground, where two company-size units were going through close-order drill. Normally Sturgeon watched them closely and made mental notes, but he didn't focus on them this time; his mind was on the data he'd just studied, twisting its way through it, trying to make sense of the numbers and find meaning in their implications.

Knuckles rapped sharply on the frame of his office door.

"Come," he said without looking to see who was there. Footsteps crossed his office floor and came to a stop on the other side of his desk.

"Speak." He still didn't look to see who his visitor was.

"I take it you looked at that data," said Colonel Ramadan, 34th FIST's Chief of Staff.

Sturgeon turned to face his visitor and lifted a hand to indicate he should sit. Ramadan settled himself in the nearest chair and looked expectantly at his commander.

"What do you make of it?" Sturgeon asked.

Ramadan shrugged. "Somebody at HQMC G-1 slipped up." He thought that an unlikely possibility. The G-1, personnel department, at Headquarters Marine Corps on Earth was more efficient about some things than field commanders would wish, and they weren't known for slipping up on routine matters, especially priority routine matters. "Or something's going on that nobody's seen fit to tell us." That, he thought, was more likely.

"How long ago did you notice this anomaly?"

"Lieutenant Wakenstrudl brought it to my attention a month ago." Wakenstrudl was Sturgeon's F-1, the FIST personnel officer. "I wanted to see what I could find out before I brought it to your attention."

Sturgeon cocked an eyebrow. "You found out something already?" Communication between worlds was slow, messages could only go via faster-than-light starcraft and their delivery had to take into account transportation schedules. One month wasn't anywhere near enough time for a query to reach Earth from Thorsfinni's World, the home of 34th FIST, much less for a reply to make its way back.

Ramadan shook his head. "I waited for the next courier. One came yesterday." He chuckled. "That lieutenant is probably still quaking from the grilling he got from a colonel."

Sturgeon waited, no need to ask the obvious—Ramadan clearly hadn't gotten any information from the courier that wasn't in the dispatches and orders he carried, information and orders that didn't address the anomaly he'd discovered.

Ramadan had nothing more to say, and outwaited the FIST commander.

"Somebody's messing with my people," Sturgeon finally said. "It's incumbent on me to find out who and why."

"Not only your people," Ramadan said. "You're past due for rotation too. So am I, for that matter."

Sturgeon nodded. "It began with third platoon, Company L of the infantry battalion. Then the rest of Company L, the infantry battalion's command element, and a platoon in Dragon Company. It includes you, me, and Sergeant Major Shiro. There have been no routine changes of duty station in that group in up to a year and a half." He paused and recalled the data. "That clerk, Corporal Doyle, the one we shipped out a couple of months ago, he's the only man from Company L who has rotated in quite a long time."

"You'll remember, sir, we shipped Corporal Doyle out pending orders."

"Right." Sturgeon nodded. "That was a tough one. His first sergeant wanted to court-martial him for insubordination, and an army general wanted to give him a medal for the same action." He shook his head. Some problems defied rational solution. Well, that problem had been solved: no court-martial, no medal. The brigadier returned to the immediate problem. "Furthermore, there have been no routine rotations in any element of the FIST during the past four months. Four months. Have you ever seen a FIST go four months without anybody being transferred out?"

"Nossir. Except for a few times on major deployments." Colonel Ramadan snorted. "I've even seen men yanked out of units on combat deployment for routine changes of duty station."

"Very strange," Sturgeon mused. He looked sharply at his second in command. "We get replacements for every combat loss. G-1 at HQMC hasn't misplaced us. They are deliberately avoiding transfers. Why?"

Ramadan knew the question was rhetorical and kept quiet.

"Colonel, 34th FIST and Thorsfinni's World are officially classed as hardship duty. Thirty-fourth FIST has more deployments than perhaps any other unit in the Confederation Marine Corps. And Thorsfinni's World . . ." He shook his head. "Have you ever made the 'Grand Tour'?"

Ramadan chuckled. "Indeed, I have, sir." Niflheim, where Camp Major Pete Ellis, the home base of 34th FIST, was located, was a large island about the size of the Scandinavian peninsula on Earth, and closer to Thorsfinni's World's north pole than to its equator. The island was craggy, rocky, windswept, and harbored little vegetation higher than mid-thigh on the average man. Niflheim nestled in a gray, crashing ocean, reminiscent of Earth's North Atlantic. The only city of noticeable size on the entire planet, the capital city of New Oslo, was located near the southern end of Niflheim. On the "Grand Tour," Colonel Ramadan had visited many other islands—Thorsfinni's World had no continental landmasses—from pole to pole and around the planet's equatorial belt. "The whole damn place looks like this." He gestured at the landscape visible through the window. "Temperatures change, but the islands all look alike."

"Right. All the Marines stationed here have for off-base recreation is Bronnoysund," the liberty town just outside the main gate of Camp Ellis, "and an occasional leave to New Oslo." He shook his head. He'd been to New Oslo. On almost any other civilized planet in the Confederation of Human Worlds, New Oslo wouldn't rank better than a third-rate provincial town.

"That and neo-Viking steddings." Ramadan nodded.

"Frequent deployments and lack of decent amenities. That's why this is a hardship post. Nobody's supposed to be stationed here for more than two and a half years. Most Marines are transferred out after two years. I've got people who have been here nearly three and a half years. Someone's messing with my people. I'm going to find out who and why and put an end to it," Sturgeon said. "I don't care who has what reasons for this, there isn't a man in this FIST who deserves that kind of punishment." He stood abruptly. Ramadan also stood. "I haven't taken leave in five years. I'm taking leave—to Earth. Colonel, you're going to be in command here for a few months."

Ramadan started. He'd had no idea what Sturgeon would do about the data he'd brought to his attention, but taking leave, even to Earth, hadn't even made his list of possibilities.

"Sir?"

"I'm going to find out what's going on, and nobody had best get in my way."

"But—"

"Don't you think you're competent to command a FIST?"

"Yessir, but—"

"Then command, Colonel. I'm going to Earth."

*   *   *

It wasn't that easy, of course. Nothing is ever that easy on a remote outpost. Most member planets of the Confederation of Human Worlds have a busy starport with several starships arriving and departing daily, one heading for Earth every day or two. The station crews of most worlds' starports lived in orbit, at the starport. Life for the crew of Thorsfinni Interstellar was much more languid—most of them lived planetside and only went up to orbit when there was work to do. For the "control tower," that could be as infrequent as twice a week, even with the Confederation Navy using the civilian starport instead of going to the expense of building one of its own. Brigadier Sturgeon had to wait eight days to catch passage on a freighter to New Serengeti, where he expected to quickly find a starship headed for Earth. Because of his abrupt decision and the difficulty of interstellar communications, he had no chance to book passage from New Serengeti before he reached it.

A week into the first leg of his month-and-a-half journey, Sturgeon started wishing medical science had perfected cold storage for passengers on interstellar flights. He'd never been bored during the many-weeks-long passages on deployments, had always been busy drawing up plans and seeing to the training and preparation of his Marines. But this time he was traveling alone, with nothing to do but plan his actions once he reached Earth, and to use the freighter's limited recreation and entertainment facilities. He didn't even have the workings of the ship as a distraction. The captain, a lifelong merchant mariner, had no use for the military and told Sturgeon on the second day of the voyage that he'd be pleased if the Marine stayed out of the way. Well, he thought, it'd be just another week and a half to New Serengeti, where he should have no trouble booking passage to Earth on a better equipped ship. At least, he hoped it would be better equipped.

The fast frigate CNSS *Admiral Stoloff* was better equipped.

A McKnight class fast frigate, it was one of the most modern starships in the Confederation Navy, and its captain was delighted to let a Marine brigadier hitch a ride to Earth.

"I've got a cousin and a nephew who betrayed family tradition and joined the Marines," Commander Ishmala Yazid said jovially. "The Yazids have been navy since sailors first sailed wooden dhows on water seas, and they had no use for landlubbers until my generation, when Roger Yazid joined the Marines." He gestured expansively. "And then so did his son Anhel. So that makes you brother to my cousin Roger and my nephew Anhel, which makes you family to me. Family is always welcome on board my ship."

Considering it had been more years than Sturgeon wanted to contemplate since he'd last been at Earth's navy starport, he was surprised at how little it had changed. He watched the approach on a viewscreen in his cabin. The navy starport first appeared as a sprinkling of lights above the dawn terminator that blinked out as the spaceport moved around Earth's edge and into full sunlight. The lights, by then much larger and seemingly more numerous, reappeared nearly an hour later as the spaceport reappeared on the other side of Earth. Slowly, as the *Admiral Stoloff* continued braking to orbital speed, the lights enlarged and resolved into the familiar oblates, spheres, and polyhedra of Confederation Navy Base Gagarin, moving slowly in their ponderous, stately waltz.

Soon, the viewscreen allowed Sturgeon to distinguish ships resting within repair and maintenance bays or nestled alongside loading docks. Here and there, tugs pushed and prodded starships away from bays and pierage and far enough out from the structures that they could safely turn on their engines.

Other ships stood apart from the starport structures, waiting their turns in the bays or at the docks. As spaces opened, tugs pushed and prodded them into place. A first glance might show the aimless, almost manic movement of ships guided by tugs, but more careful study showed the movement to be carefully choreographed as the moving starships danced a more spritely minuet through the structures of Gagarin Navy Starport.

At length the *Admiral Stoloff* matched speed with the starport. Tugs nudged it into position in the queue awaiting docking space. Sturgeon could make out the tiny dots of space-suited sailors as they flitted around the ships, inspecting, making repairs, repainting, and doing the myriad other things sailors did to ships in port. On mysterious missions, shuttles drifted hither and yon among the structures. Every five or ten minutes a shuttle arrived from planetside or dropped for Earth's surface; most of them were navy Essays, though some looked to be commercial craft.

The shuttles making the Earth-orbit transit all took the long way planetside, three degenerating loops to the surface. Obviously, none of them carried Marines; shuttles bearing Marines always took the express route, nearly straight down. Sturgeon idly wondered if he'd find a platoon of Marines waiting their turn to head planetside when the *Admiral Stoloff* docked, and whether he'd go with them at "high speed on a rocky road," or if there were only sailors and civilians awaiting transit planetside.

Despite the apparent crowding, the starport was very efficiently run. The *Admiral Stoloff* waited little more than an hour before it turned the gravity off to let tugs push and prod it into the minuet and snuggle it against a dock. The starship filled with whistles, bells, and intercom commands as its crew bustled about doing the necessary work.

In his thirty-five years as a Marine, Sturgeon had cumulatively spent more than four years on board navy vessels, yet he understood almost nothing more of the running of a starship than he did the first time he rode one on his way to Boot Camp on Arsenault. That was all right; he doubted there was a sailor alive, officer or enlisted, capable of commanding a Marine blaster platoon. With the very notable exception of the medical corpsmen attached to FISTs, almost any sailor would be a liability with a ground combat unit. It wasn't a question of superiority or intelligence; the navy and the Marines had different functions, their training different.

Sturgeon waited patiently in his cabin, out of the way of the crew. His packing hadn't taken long, he was ready to leave the ship when permission was given. The whistles, bells, and piped commands gradually diminished in frequency. A knock sounded on his cabin hatch.

"Come."

The hatch opened to reveal a bosun's mate first class.

"Sir," the bosun's mate said crisply, "with the captain's compliments. He would welcome the Brigadier on the bridge."

"My thanks to the captain, bosun," Sturgeon said, rising. "If you will be so good as to lead the way?"

"Aye aye, sir. Follow me." The bosun's mate turned and began following a towline toward the bridge.

Sturgeon didn't need the guide. He knew the way from his cabin to the important places on the ship; the officers' wardroom, the library, the gym, and the bridge. Observing naval courtesy, however, he followed on the bosun's mate's heels. The passageways were beginning to fill with sailors in liberty uniforms.

"Sir!" Commander Yazid said when Sturgeon propelled himself onto the bridge. "It has been a pleasure to have a brother of my cousin Roger and my nephew Anhel as a passenger on my ship."

All the stations on the bridge were occupied, as they had been every time Sturgeon had been on it. But the usual air of alertness was absent. Many of the bridge personnel seemed to be shutting down systems or running maintenance checks. Most of the others were relaxed, their final duties on arriving at port finished.

Yazid extended a hand and Sturgeon gripped it. "Captain, the pleasure has been mine. Let me assure you, this has been the most pleasant voyage I have ever undertaken on a navy vessel."

Yazid beamed. It was wonderful to have a flag officer on board who wasn't looking over his shoulder and second guessing his every move. "Sir, with your permission? We have reached port. My crew is anxious to begin their long-awaited liberty call. Flag officers must debark before the enlisted men can make their break for revelry."

"By all means, Captain, let us not keep your crew waiting. My bags are ready. I can debark at your pleasure."

"Sir, I will have someone take your bags pierside." Commander Yazid signed to a bosun to see to it. "If you wish, I can have someone escort you to the transient terminal. I'd do it myself," his face fell, "but my flotilla commander demands my presence in his office at the earliest."

"I understand fully, Captain. You have already overextended yourself in hospitality. And it won't be necessary to supply a guide; I've been at Gagarin before, and it doesn't look like it's changed much."

"Yes, while very much is new, at the same time very little has changed."

The dock wasn't in null-g, but its "gravity" was slight enough that no one would plummet to the deck on leaving the starship. Sturgeon slipped his feet into a comfortable pair of shufflers to avoid a too-vigorous step which would send him into uncontrolled flight, then took his two bags from the bosun's mate, who stood over them. The sailor saluted.

"Thank you, bosun," Sturgeon, unable to return the salute with a bag in each hand, said with a nod. He looked around to get his bearings and headed, in the proper short-step shuffle that kept the shoelets attached to the deck, toward a sign that read TRANSIENT TERMINAL SHUTTLE. He stepped out of the shufflers before boarding the local shuttle. The transient terminal was maintained at 0.5-g, so he wouldn't need magnetic assistance to stay on the deck there.

Several Marines were waiting for transportation planetside, mostly couriers, junior officers, and mid-level noncommissioned officers. Sturgeon exchanged proper greetings with them. He was on leave, so he had to buy a ticket on a United Atmosphere shuttle. He and the couriers ignored each other, though the juniors were all acutely aware of the brigadier and behaved themselves better than they would have had a flag officer not been present. The army and navy personnel—an army major the highest rank among them—did their best to ignore the presence of a Marine brigadier.

The wait for the shuttle wasn't long. A steward, following proper military protocol, held Brigadier Sturgeon aside until everyone else boarded, then sat him closest to the exit so he, as the highest ranking person on board, could be the first off when the shuttle landed at Lynn J. Frazier International Airport outside Fargo, home of the Confederation Council— in effect, the capital city of the Confederation of Human Worlds.

Sturgeon might be on leave, but he wasn't going to waste any time being a tourist. He would go directly to the heart of the Confederation military establishment—both the Combined Chiefs of Staff and Headquarters Marine Corps were in Fargo. His first order of business would be to find a place to stay.

CHAPTER
FIVE

Housing was provided for military personnel assigned to duty at the Combined Chiefs or the headquarters, but visitors were on their own. Brigadier Sturgeon managed to find a room in a modest bed-and-breakfast a short tube ride from the Hexagon. It was a somewhat longer tube ride to HQMC, on the top of what passed for a hill in southeastern North Dakota—the Marines had always liked to keep themselves separate from mere soldiers and sailors.

Brigadier Sturgeon didn't bother to completely unpack before he put on his dress reds and his overcoat. It was May, mid-spring, but the temperature hovered not far above freezing. Properly dressed, he headed for the Hexagon to pay a visit to the C-1, the Combined Chiefs personnel department. Regardless of what he'd said to Colonel Ramadan, he suspected the foul-up lay with the Combined Chiefs rather than HQMC.

Brigadier General (Select) Wolford M'Bwabor-Onorosovic, IV, Second Deputy Director, Assignments Division, Confederation Armed Forces C-1, welcomed Brigadier Sturgeon into his office most fulsomely.

"Brigadier! Welcome to the Hexagon!" M'Bwabor-Onorosovic grasped Sturgeon's hand in both of his and pulled him to a visitor's chair. "It's quite rare that we receive a current commander of any combat arms unit, much less the commander of one of those Marine FISTs." He rolled his eyes toward the ceiling as though seeking guidance. "As a matter of fact, I believe you are the first FIST commander, current or former, I've ever had the pleasure of meeting." He gave an impression of skipping as he walked to the far side of his desk and sat in his commanding chair. His chair was on a low platform, not visible from the desk front, so that he sat higher than his visitors and they had to look up at him. Seated, he clasped his hands and leaned over his forearms, which lay on the desktop. His smile was broad, intended to be infectious. Sturgeon didn't return it.

"How do you like Fargo so far? Is this your first visit?"

"Haven't seen anything but a couple of tubes and a B-and-B so far, but I've been here before, so I know what I'm not missing."

M'Bwabor-Onorosovic laughed loudly, but short of a guffaw. "I know what you mean, Brigadier, I do indeed." His head shake failed to budge his grin. "I cannot for the life of me comprehend why anybody would put a city, much less a capital city, in such a barren location. I grew up on Argent, you know. Have you ever been? The most beautiful planet in all of Human Space. Marvelous, towering forests, waterfalls to dwarf Angel Falls, seas so clear you can still see everything around you at a depth of a hundred feet, fruits and flowers that could have served as the model for the Garden of Eden myth." He chuckled, then started and looked pop-eyed at Sturgeon. "No offense intended; I mean if you are Judeo-Christian. I don't intend to slight anybody's religious beliefs."

"None taken, General," Sturgeon said with a patience he didn't feel. He wanted to conduct his business, but he had to humor the man, who seemed to him more and more a buffoon. "I'm a Marine. We swear by the most shocking things."

"Yes, well." Right. The general realized that the man before him was not an administrator or bureaucrat. He quickly eyed the panoply of ribbons on Sturgeon's scarlet tunic. Some of them he recognized, such as the Gold Nova—the military's second highest decoration for heroism—and the Bronze Star with gold starburst, another decoration for heroism in action against an enemy. Most of the others he didn't recognize, though he suspected they were campaign medals. One made him blink: the Marine Enlisted Good Conduct Medal. Then he remembered that all Marine officers are commissioned from the ranks. He shuddered internally. Sturgeon was a real combat Marine, almost the only one he had ever faced, definitely the only one he'd ever been alone with. The broad smile disappeared while he cleared his throat, then slapped itself back into place.

"Well, Brigadier, you didn't make the trip all the way from Thorsfinni's World"—*Where in Human Space is that?*—"to hear me prate about my home world." He changed his voice from jolly to sincere and lowered the beam of his smile. "What can my office help you with?"

"General, as you know, I command a FIST. Thorsfinni's World, as you may know, is classed as a hardship post. The normal tour of duty is two years, two and a half at the outside. Some of my people have been there three and a half years. No one has been transferred out in . . . well, when I left there hadn't been any changes of duty station in four months. If there weren't any transfers while I was in transit, it's now nearly six months. I fear the Assignments Division has somehow—inadvertently, I'm sure—misplaced 34th FIST."

The sincere smile stayed on the Second Deputy Director's mouth, but his eyes went blank. *Misplaced a FIST?* "That's impossible, Brigadier. The Assignments Division doesn't make the change-of-duty-station transfers. That is done by the chiefs of the services. We receive the change-of-duty-station requests, verify them, and issue transfer orders under the titles of the services. We are a conduit, not an originator."

"Headquarters Marine Corps doesn't make such mistakes," Sturgeon said firmly. "The Marine Corps is a small organization. Everyone in the Corps knows where each unit is. It's easy for us to keep track of our people. As you said, all transfers are funneled through your division. That's a lot to keep track of. It doesn't at all surprise me that a small unit in an out-of-the-way place could get overlooked."

"But my dear Brigadier . . ." The general brushed his hand over a contact spot on his desktop and a display and keyboard morphed out of its surface. He tapped several keys and watched the display come to life. His smile morphed into a moue and his eyes from blank to confused. Slowly, he looked at the Marine. "There is no record of orders for change of duty for anyone in 34th FIST entering the system in the past eight months." He pulled himself fully erect and said with the sincerest gravity he could muster, "Brigadier, I'm afraid your 'small organization' did indeed manage to lose track of some of its people."

Moments later, a very dissatisfied Brigadier Theodosius Sturgeon was following a guide through the warren of hallways and pedestrian streets in the Hexagon, on his way back to the tube. He was very annoyed by his meeting with the Second Deputy Director of the Assignments Division of C-1. They had to have somehow lost the requests that came to them from HQMC. The Marines *never* made such mistakes. Never.

He'd go to G-1 at HQMC and get hardcopy of the orders. Then take them back to the Hexagon and wave them under the nose of that supercilious Brigadier General (Select) Wolford M'Bwabor-Onorosovic IV—though he'd rather not have to deal with that ass again. He snorted. For all of his bonhomie, M'Bwabor-Onorosovic had kept the formality of them calling each other by rank, instead of using first names as flag officers more commonly did in private.

I guess he likes being called General, Sturgeon thought. As a brigadier general (select), his actual rank was colonel, but he was in a flag position. Sturgeon knew he outranked him, but M'Bwabor-Onorosovic was not in his chain of command. He snorted.

*   *   *

Brigadier Sturgeon had no trouble finding a seat; the tube car he rode in was almost empty. At the first stop along the way he looked out the window on the opposite side of the car and saw crowds of people waiting on the platforms leading into Fargo. He glanced at the time: It was after 1600 hours, quitting time for government workers. Too late to find anyone in G-1. Then he finally noticed the rumbling in his stomach. He'd been in Fargo for six hours. How long was it since he last ate? He remembered breakfast on the *Admiral Stoloff*, nothing since. No wonder he was hungry; he hadn't had lunch and it was near the dinner hour. What to do: Get off at the next stop and head back into the city? Come back in the morning, maybe make an appointment instead of just dropping in as he did at the Hexagon?

His stomach rumbled again. No, that would take too long. He'd only been a commander on the one other occasion he visited HQMC, but he remembered there was some sort of flag officers' mess. Surely his uniform and ID would get him into it for an early dinner, even though he wasn't headquarters personnel.

The Fargo tube system had gaily decorated stations, each unique, often with colors and designs representative of their location. Stops in residential areas usually had murals of the neighborhoods, images of children playing in parks and the like. A mural at the main campus stop for the Confederation University of the Worlds displayed ivy-covered walls and cap-and-gowned people striding along flagstone pathways, even though no ivy grew on the university buildings and nobody wore caps and gowns any longer, even at graduation ceremonies. The HQMC stop was no exception. Sturgeon was almost the only person who got off the tube car, and he paused to take in the mosaics.

The walls had scarlet and gold tiles in the form of the Confederation Marine Corps emblem, a rampant eagle standing on a globe floating on a starstream. Off to the sides the various campaign medals Marine units had been awarded were picked out in brightly colored tiles. A frieze along the base of the walls displayed the colors of the many enemy units the Confederation Marines had defeated in battle. At both ends of the platform were the emblems of the two Marine Corps directly ancestral to the Confederation Marines: the United States Marine Corps and the British Royal Marines. There were more campaign medals and enemy colors depicted than the last time he visited. He recognized most of the medals—he wore several of them—and there were a few colors he had helped take. His chest swelled and a lump formed in his throat at the sight.

Alone, Sturgeon faced the Royal Marines emblem and saluted it. He about-faced and saluted the emblem of the United States Marine Corps. He knew that without them the Confederation Marine Corps would not exist as the premier fighting organization in human history, and he would not have the Corps as the family he loved so deeply. Moisture formed in the corners of his eyes, and he wiped it away as he turned to head for the lift into the HQMC building complex.

At the surface was a small plaza that split into several walkways headed in different directions. He took the one that went straight ahead to a gate watched over by a small guardpost. A few people trickled out through automated side gates that checked their identification.

A lance corporal with a military police band wrapped around the upper left sleeve of his dress reds overcoat stepped out of the gatehouse and stood at parade rest. He carried a hand-blaster in a shiny white holster hanging from a white Sam Browne belt, a sparkling brass whistle was suspended from the lapel of his overcoat, and a scarlet and gold aiguillette was wrapped around his shoulder. When Brigadier Sturgeon approached within a few paces, the lance corporal snapped to attention and saluted with a white-gloved hand.

Sturgeon came to a halt in front of the MP and returned his salute.

"Sir, how can I help the Brigadier?"

"I'm visiting Earth on leave, Lance Corporal, and have been eating civilian and navy food for the past couple of months. I'm here hoping I can come aboard to get some good Marine Corps chow," he said with a twinkle in his eye.

The lance corporal repressed a laugh. "Good Marine Corps chow" sounded like an oxymoron to him. He said out loud, "I believe that can be arranged, sir." He gestured to the gatehouse.

Sturgeon stepped inside, removing his hat as he passed under the lintel. Almost immediately he saw the ID verifier. He stepped close to it and stripped off his black leather gloves while the MP, who hadn't removed his hat, went to the comm unit and called the sergeant of the guard to report the visitor.

"Been stationed here long?" Sturgeon asked when the lance corporal completed his call.

"Six months, sir." The lance corporal faced him, again standing at attention, with a small table between them.

"At ease. This is your post. You don't know me."

"Thank you, sir." He slipped easily into parade rest but didn't lock his hands behind his back. Though unlikely, there was always the possibility that the brigadier was a spy or saboteur and that the guard would have to go for his weapon. Strange brigadiers simply didn't show up at 1630 hours very often.

"Good duty?"

"You know it, sir."

Sturgeon chuckled. "Actually I don't. I've spent my entire career in FISTs or on Fleet staffs. This is only my second visit to Fargo."

"Yessir, I can see the Brigadier's been around." He nodded toward the ribbons on Sturgeon's chest.

The small talk was necessary. Sturgeon knew it would take a few minutes for the sergeant of the guard to get the officer of the guard, and for the OG to reach the gatehouse to check his ID. Talking passed the time and prevented the buildup of tension. Military protocol required that an officer, not a junior enlisted man, verify the identity of a high-ranking officer whenever practical.

In minutes the officer of the guard, a lieutenant, arrived. Like the MP, he did not remove his hat as he stepped inside. He came to attention and saluted. Sturgeon nodded and the lieutenant cut his salute.

"Sir, I'm Lieutenant Ehrhardt. Welcome to HQMC." He stepped to the ID verifier. "If you please, sir."

Sturgeon put his wrist inside the sleeve on top of the apparatus. "Brigadier Theodosius Sturgeon, Commander, 34th FIST." He pulled up his left sleeve to expose his ID bracelet then slid his forearm into the verifier sleeve. The OG studied the data that appeared on the verifier's small display.

"How can I help you, sir?" Ehrhardt asked, satisfied that the visitor was indeed who he said.

"As I told your very efficient lance corporal"—he hadn't missed how the MP positioned himself with a table between them and maintained alertness—"I'm on leave and have been eating civilian and navy food for a couple of months. I'm hungry for some good Marine Corps chow."

Lieutenant Ehrhardt wasn't as good at controlling his face as the lance corporal. His mouth twitched; he also considered the phrase an oxymoron. But then, he'd heard that the Henderson Flag Club had excellent chefs for its dining room. Maybe the chow there was better than what he ate in the junior officers' mess, or what he used to eat in enlisted mess halls.

"Certainly, sir." He glanced at the clock on the wall. "I don't believe the dining room at the Flag Club will be open for dinner for a short while yet, but the bar that adjoins it should be open by now. If that's acceptable, sir."

Sturgeon nodded. "That's quite acceptable."

"If you will come with me, Brigadier, I'll escort you."

Sturgeon looked at the lance corporal. "Stay sharp, Lance Corporal. You're doing a good job."

"Thank you, sir." This time the lance corporal couldn't

prevent the flicker of a smile; it had been his experience with officers above the rank of captain that they generally ignored junior enlisted men. He wasn't accustomed to such politeness.

Ehrhardt opened a door in the back of the gatehouse and Sturgeon stepped through and waited for the OG to take position to his left.

"This way, sir." Ehrhardt pointed. Sturgeon stepped off and the lieutenant adjusted his pace to walk in step with him. They passed a few structures built in generally uniform military architecture. Ehrhardt stopped in front of one that was different; it was constructed of rough-cut stone and had window frames and doors that looked like real wood. A red-on-gold sign set in the spacious lawn in front of it said:

LIEUTENANT COLONEL ARCHIBALD HENDERSON

FLAG CLUB

FLAG MESS

HEADQUARTERS MARINE CORPS

(members and guests only)

"Here we are, sir."

Sturgeon looked at the sign. "I don't have a membership," he said softly, annoyed at himself for not anticipating a membership requirement.

"Yes you do, sir. The nova on your collar gives you admittance. I believe there is a nominal membership fee, but they'll have to tell you about that inside."

"Well, thank you, Lieutenant Ehrhardt. I guess I can find my own way from here."

Ehrhardt came to attention and saluted, then about-faced and headed back toward the officer of the guard office when Sturgeon returned the salute.

Sturgeon looked at the sign again and wondered why a Flag Club was named after a lieutenant colonel. It suddenly came to him. Archibald Henderson had been the fifth Commandant of the U.S. Marine Corps, a legend.

As Sturgeon approached, the door to the clubhouse opened, not on automatic, which he might have expected, but by a live human being who held the door open and gave a shallow bow as he stepped in, all to Sturgeon's startlement. Since he'd been close to flag rank, he'd never been assigned anywhere that had a flag officers' club; he wasn't prepared for the high degree of personal service given to generals and admirals.

"Are you a guest, sir?" the man asked when he straightened from his bow.

"I'm afraid not, I'm merely visiting—and looking for some dinner."

"Certainly, sir. This way please." The functionary, dressed in an archaic black suit with starched white shirt front and white gloves, led him to a small but ornately carved desk and indicated he should sit at it. A data screen and keyboard morphed from the surface of the desktop. "I'm afraid I must ask you to fill out a membership form, sir. Simple visitors are not allowed, but the form and a nominal fee will allow you full Flag Club member's benefits for the duration of your visit."

"Thank you," Sturgeon said, and read the membership form and club rules.

The functionary, in response to a signal Sturgeon neither heard nor saw, went to the door to open it for new arrivals.

Sturgeon was vaguely aware of the voices of the new arrivals as he began filling out the form—and yes, the fee was nominal, less than he'd expected.

"Ted!" a voice interrupted him. "Ted Sturgeon, is that really you?"

Sturgeon looked up, surprised. He was even more surprised when he saw that the man addressing him wore a single gold nova on the collars of his tunic.

"General Aguinaldo!" he said, jumping up to stand at attention.

Aguinaldo strode to him, clapped him on the shoulder and warmly grasped his hand. "It's not 'General' in here, Ted.

Here we're on first-name terms, from the assistant commandant on down to the newest brigadier." He chuckled. "The Commandant, of course, is the Commandant. What brings you to Fargo? Wait, I forget myself." He turned to the men who'd entered the room with him. "Ted, I'd like you to meet Sam Saoli and Hank Tui." Sam Saoli wore the three silver novas of a Marine lieutenant general, Hank Tui the two novas of a major general. "Gentlemen, I want you to meet Ted Sturgeon. His FIST was the first wave to cross the beach on Diamunde, and he was one of my Corps commanders there."

Admiration was evident on the faces of the two generals.

General Saoli stuck out his hand to shake. "I've heard about you, Ted. Pleased to make your acquaintance. That was a hell of a job you did." He shook his head and added with a touch of envy, "I've never had the opportunity to command a Corps myself, you'll have to tell me what it's like."

It was exceedingly rare for a Marine to command a Corps-sized unit, and unheard of before Diamunde for a Marine to command one in which his subordinate commanders were army generals who outranked him. Brigadier Sturgeon had commanded a Corps with army major generals commanding the divisions that made up the Corps.

Major General Tui grabbed Sturgeon's hand as soon as Saoli released it. "Ted, your fame precedes you. It's an honor to meet you."

"So what are you doing with that?" Aguinaldo waved at the desk.

"Joining the club, sir, so I can get some chow."

Aguinaldo looked at him quizzically. "You haven't been restationed here; I'd know if you were. And it's Andy here, not 'sir.' "

"I'm on leave—Andy."

"Well, why didn't you come directly to me? Don't throw your money away on a membership. You're my guest for the duration of your stay. Where are you staying, by the way?" Before Sturgeon could answer, Aguinaldo turned to the functionary. "Franz, anything Ted gets while he's here is on my tab. Understand?"

"Brigadier Sturgeon's bills are on your tab. Absolutely, sir."

"Fine." He turned back to Sturgeon. "Ted, we're on our way to cocktails and then dinner. Will you do us the honor of joining us?"

"The honor is mine, Gen—Andy." Calling the Assistant Commandant, the second highest ranking member of the Confederation Marine Corps, by his first name would take some getting used to.

Tui laughed, draped a companionable arm over Sturgeon's shoulders and walked with him behind Aguinaldo and Saoli into the bar. "You'll get used to it, Ted. I was in a FIST when I made colonel, and stayed in FISTs until I got my second star. Then I spent a year as Inspector General for Seventh Fleet until I got assigned to HQMC. This is the first place I've been that has a Flag Club—or anyplace where I ever saw more than one or two other flag officers at a time. Even then, most were navy, and they usually didn't want a Marine underfoot. I know how strange it is the first time you address a full general by his first name, and how much stranger it is with the ACMC himself. But comfort will come soon."

The four of them seated themselves in club chairs grouped around a table. Discreet sound baffles rose around them to provide a modicum of privacy. While they chatted and sipped drinks, a liveried waiter came around with menus. They ticked off what they wanted and the waiter picked up the menus on his return trip. Shortly after, a bell chimed and a sonorous voice intoned, "Gentlemen, dinner is served."

They stood and everyone in the bar looked to Aguinaldo, the highest-ranking general present, to lead the way.

"Gentlemen," Aguinaldo said in a voice loud enough to carry clearly throughout the room, but looking at Sturgeon, "a good commander always makes sure his people are fed before he gets his own chow. So I will enter last." Then he looked around at the assembled generals and added, "Except for Brigadier da Cruz, who is responsible for making sure there's enough to feed us all."

There was light laughter at the mention of the Deputy Director G-4, Class IV supplies, and the generals, most of whom had their wives along as guests, began filing from the bar to the dining room. True to his word, Aguinaldo was the last one in. Even Brigadier da Cruz preceded him—the Deputy Director G-4 was unobtrusively overseeing kitchen and dining room operations.

Following the most exquisite dinner Sturgeon had ever been served on a Marine Corps installation, the four retired to the bar to continue drinking and talking. Saoli and Tui were most anxious to hear Sturgeon's account of the war on Diamunde. They couldn't quite get over the thrill of a Marine brigadier commanding a Corps.

The hour was getting late when Aguinaldo announced, "Gentlemen, it's getting late and *some* of us have to report for duty in the morning. I suggest we adjourn."

"Indeed," the others agreed, standing.

"Ted," Aguinaldo said as they headed for the exit, "I've arranged for a car and driver so you don't have to brave the hazards of the tube." He raised a hand to forestall any objections. "It's late and a long ride back into the city. And I want you to come by my office in the morning. Is ten hours all right with you?"

"Ten hours is splendid with me, Andy." More than enough time for him to get there. And a meeting with the Assistant Commandant! That will solve the problem, he told himself. *Then I'll be able to cut my leave short and head back to Thorsfinni's World where I belong.*

CHAPTER
SIX

A captain was waiting for Brigadier Sturgeon when he arrived at the tube gate of HQMC, and escorted him directly to the Assistant Commandant's office, where he had to wait only a minute or two before an aide showed him in to Aguinaldo. He expected to find that the Assistant Commandant of the Marine Corps had a larger office than any other general's office he'd ever been in, and it was. What did surprise him was its decoration. The usual Confederation and Marine Corps flags flanked the massive desk along the rear wall, but that was the only thing he'd seen in every other general's office. To the visitor's left of the Confederation flag was a display of quarter-sized flags he didn't recognize. On the right of the Marine Corps flag was a similar display, but of flags Sturgeon did recognize—various Marine Corps units from battalion on up, probably the colors of units Aguinaldo had commanded. It seemed reasonable to assume that the display of unrecognized flags were the colors of enemies that the units he'd commanded had defeated. Rather than the usual array of trids of the general posing with dignitaries he had trids of places, and of Aguinaldo with people Sturgeon mostly didn't recognize. Then he spotted a couple of images he did know and knew what the rest were. There was a trid made on Diamunde, and another with Aguinaldo standing with Sturgeon and his other major commanders on that campaign. Those weren't images showing the Assistant Commandant with people of dubious importance, they were images of places where he'd gone to war and the men he'd gone to war with.

"Brigadier Sturgeon!" Aguinaldo said, striding from behind his desk, hand extended, the first name informality of the previous evening out of place on duty in his office. "Thank you so much for coming."

"General, it's my pleasure to visit the Assistant Commandant in his lair."

They shook hands.

"Please, Brigadier, have a seat." Aguinaldo guided Sturgeon to a conversational grouping of chairs around a small table. His hand grazed a touch-plate when he sat. Almost immediately a side door to his office opened and a corporal entered, bearing a silver tray with a silver coffee setting with porcelain cups and saucers. Each shimmering silver piece had the Marine Corps emblem embossed on it, and the porcelain cups and saucers had the emblem enameled in scarlet and limned in gold.

"I trust you do drink coffee?" Aguinaldo asked. "This is the best, Jamaican Blue Mountain."

Sturgeon salivated. "Thank you, sir. I've heard of Blue Mountain. Its reputation is superb."

"Thank you, Corporal," Aguinaldo said when the junior NCO set the tray on the table. "I'll take it from here." The corporal left without a word.

Aguinaldo made a small ceremony of pouring the coffee, and the men held the delicate cups to their faces, inhaling the aroma, then sipped slowly, savoring the taste.

They made small talk for a couple of minutes, then Aguinaldo cut to the chase.

"So tell me, Brigadier, what are you doing on Earth?" He had never seen, or even heard of, a FIST commander leaving his unit for the length of time it took to visit Earth from such a distance as Sturgeon had traveled. He knew Sturgeon and his reputation well enough to know he had to have an exceptional reason.

Sturgeon wasn't surprised by the abrupt change of subject; he was surprised the casual conversation that preceded it had taken place at all. He cleared his throat before beginning.

"Sir, 34th FIST seems to have been forgotten by somebody. I've been in command for four years. My Chief of Staff and sergeant major have been with me that entire time. My infantry and air commanders have been with me nearly as long."

Aguinaldo raised an eyebrow. He knew 34th FIST and Thorsfinni's World were hardship assignments. FIST commanders, the major subordinate unit commanders, and their top people were assigned there for three-year tours, everyone else two years.

"Interesting," he said. But he didn't believe Sturgeon took three or four months away from his command to complain about not being reassigned to a staff position somewhere. Most Marine officers from the rank of brigadier on down craved assignment as a FIST commander—and most higher-ranking generals wished they still were commanding the Corps' prized combat units.

"But that's only the tip of the iceberg. None of my people have received normal rotation orders in four months. Excuse me, I forgot transit time. Unless orders have come through since I left, none of my people have rotated in six months. I have enlisted people and junior officers who have been with 34th FIST for nearly as long as I have."

Aguinaldo's expression closed in concentration. That was most peculiar. He'd heard nothing about it. Surely he would have been officially informed if a FIST was removed from the normal rotation of personnel. He stood suddenly, but waved Sturgeon to remain seated.

"Excuse me a moment," he said, "I want to check something." He walked briskly to his desk and leaned over it. He morphed a data screen and keyboard out of its surface and tapped in a few commands. He frowned at what he saw, then tapped in another command. Again, he frowned at the display. Slowly, he sat down and tapped more commands. Again and again he was displeased with what he saw. Brusquely, he dismissed the computer, stood, and returned to sit with Sturgeon. His expression was quizzical but not particularly concerned.

"I have to make a few inquiries. Somebody seems to have slipped up somewhere. I think I can guarantee that by lunchtime tomorrow the situation will be cleared up and the order-cutting process will have begun." He stood; the meeting was over. He grasped Sturgeon's hand and guided him toward the door. "How about if you come by at 1200 hours tomorrow, we'll have lunch at the club, and we can have a laugh at the expense of whatever chucklehead goofed. Do you need a guide to show you the sights in our fair capital?"

"Thank you, sir. No, I won't need a guide. I'll be back tomorrow."

In the outer office Sturgeon asked the captain who had brought him, "Could you show me to the museum, please? Once in a while it's good to review our history."

"Yessir," the captain replied. "The museum is this way."

As his guide led him deeper into the HQMC complex, Sturgeon thought something was odd about the way Aguinaldo had checked the records then quickly dismissed him.

When the door closed behind Sturgeon, Aguinaldo stood for a moment, staring at his desk. Moments ago he'd found that routine rotation orders had been issued all along for the Marines of 34th FIST. Progressively, starting with one infantry company and gradually spreading out to the entire FIST, those orders had been quietly rescinded. There was no annotation in the records he had access to—and so far as he knew there were no Marine Corps records he *didn't* have access to—that indicated who rescinded those orders. Something was wrong. By all the gods, he was going to know who was messing with the careers and lives of his Marines—and why. And when he found out, he would correct the problem and someone's head would likely roll.

Promptly at noon the next day Sturgeon arrived at the Assistant Commandant's office and was escorted in without having to wait.

Aguinaldo didn't get up from his desk or indicate that Sturgeon should sit.

"Ted, I'm sorry, but I have to renege on our luncheon. Something's come up that I have to deal with right now." He glanced at the clock. "I have just enough time to get to a meeting at the Hexagon." He stood up and headed for the outer office. "Walk with me, please." To his secretary he said, "You know where I'll be." Back to Sturgeon as they headed out of the building to where a car waited for him, "This is going to take the rest of the afternoon. It should be cleared up before 1600 hours, but it won't last beyond that. I want to make it up to you for having to leave you on your own like this. Listen, first go to lunch. Flag Club, my tab. Today is Friday, Fifth Day, as you call it on Thorsfinni's World." He barked a laugh. "We keep regular office hours here. From 16 hours until 8 hours on Monday I'm officially off duty. I've got a cabin on the Snake River and I'm going fishing for the weekend. Do you fish? I'd like you to join me."

Fishing? Sturgeon had gone fishing three times in his life and never caught anything. But an invitation from the Assistant Commandant was the same as an order.

"I'd be delighted to go fishing with you, sir."

"Fine." Aguinaldo's driver stood at the side of the car, holding the passenger door open. "Don't worry about fishing gear, I've got extras of everything that I can lend you." He grinned. "You're in for the time of your life. The Snake River valley is one of the most picturesque wilderness areas in all of Human Space. Tell my secretary where you're staying. I'll pick you up there at 17 hours." He got into the car. The driver trotted around to the driver's door, got in, and drove off.

More and more peculiar, Sturgeon thought. He wondered if the something that had come up or this meeting had anything to do with his problem. He also noticed that during the few minutes they were together, Aguinaldo had oddly enough returned to first-name informality. Was that his way of saying, *Trust me,* or *Bear with me, I'm on your side*? He had clearly said nothing about the problem that brought them together here.

Sturgeon went back to leave the address of his B-and-B with the secretary, and quietly fought off the anxiety that suddenly threatened to overwhelm him. At the Flag Club, Sturgeon wondered how the brigadiers and generals managed to stay fit if they ate so well every day. Or maybe they didn't. Only three or four others were present for lunch hour, and they seemed to eat lightly, unlike the crowd at the previous evening's dinner.

CHAPTER
SEVEN

Colonel Ramadan, acting commander, 34th FIST, shot up-right in his chair. He stared unbelieving at the vidscreen before his eyes. In more than thirty years as a Marine he'd never before seen a similar message. And it was no hoax.

As temporary commander of 34th FIST, Ramadan followed Brigadier Sturgeon's routine and personally reviewed all incoming messages from 4th Fleet. He read the operational orders first, because they would have an immediate effect on the unit mission. Then he read traffic dealing with logistical matters—ammunition, fuel, supplies, maintenance, rations, the "sinews" of war—because while he could count on his Marines never to give out, his supplies were only finite.

As Sturgeon's deputy, Ramadan usually assigned action to all incoming communications, distributing them to the FIST and subordinate unit staffs after Sturgeon had read them first and noted their content. Often Sturgeon annotated a particular message with a personal comment—sometimes very pithy—or suggestions on how to proceed to fulfill whatever requirement Fleet or Headquarters, Marine Corps, might be placing on his unit. Ramadan sat at his console, tapping in a note here, an exclamation there, indicating on a pull-down screen who on the staff should get a particular message for action and who for information. He was a meticulous man, so he preferred to key in his comments personally instead of using a voice-activated writer. That way he could review his annotations at leisure and get them just right. He saved everything to the brigadier's personal file, so Sturgeon could see what had come in while he was away.

The intelligence reports went to the F-2, but Ramadan read them all first. It was important to know what was going on, especially in 4th Fleet's sector, because a hot spot anywhere within Fleet's area of responsibility could mean another combat deployment for 34th FIST. Those reports were all classified, so Ramadan had to enter his personal password to read them. He reached for his wallet and withdrew a crumpled fragment of paper. It was strictly against security regulations to write down passwords, but if he didn't he could never remember what his was. They changed every thirty days anyway. When he did this in someone else's presence, he always said he was reaching for his mother's photograph, to give him inspiration "in these trying times."

He saved the personnel traffic for last, not because it was the least important; personnel transactions were in fact most important: morale and manpower matters are the heart and soul of any military unit. They are also the most interesting. All personnel actions were routinely passed to the FIST F-1, the personnel officer. Matters dealing with individual Marines would pass from there to battalion or squadron S-1, and then to the individuals' company commanders. He looked for orders on incoming Marines first, and then reviewed the officer promotion lists and the enlisted promotion allocations. All were very short. He noted a new ensign, a chaplain, was on the way, Scientific Pantheist. Ramadan snorted. He was nominally a Muslim. In his view, if there was a God, he was a Marine, not some ill-defined unifying "life force."

When he got to the end of the file, an icon blinked on his screen. There was a classified message still to be read. Now, that was strange. Normally, personnel messages were encrypted for transmission only. He entered his password.

CONFEDERATION MARINE CORPS
HEADQUARTERS BATTALION
FOURTH FLEET MARINE FORCE

In Reply Refer to:
1320/2
CONAD
220949

FIRST ENDORSEMENT ON CCMC 201830Z APR 49

From: Commanding Officer, Headquarters Battalion, 4th
Fleet Marine Force

To: Corporal Raoul Pasquin, 2000842R/01, CMC, L/34
Lance Corporal Joseph F. Dean, 2033768B/01,
CMC, L/34
Lance Corporal Rachman Claypoole, 2013242L/01,
CMC, L/34

Subject: TEMPORARY ADDITIONAL DUTY ASSIGN
MENT ORDERS

1. Effective delivery above named enlisted Marines stand detached from present station and duties and are directed to proceed most expeditious route and report to CNSS *Wanganui*, Soma Chundaman, Novo Khongor, for duty. Period of TAD: Indefinite.

2. Authorized 0 days leave. Addressees will bring only items of personal hygiene and 1 (one) dress scarlet uniform. Prescribed travel uniform: garrison utility.

N. CORMAN
COMMANDING OFFICER

What? Ramadan thought. He clicked the link to the Commandant's message that Fleet was endorsing. Headquarters Marine Corps sending three of his men to—to—where the hell *was* this Novo Khongor anyway? He scrolled down to the authority line. What he saw there caused him to snap straight up in his chair:

AUTH: VOCCMC

Colonel Ramadan tapped a button on his console. "Sergeant Major Shiro, get Commander Van Winkle and Sergeant Major Parant up here fast, and all of you come in to see me."

Carefully, Bass looked at the cards Staff Sergeant Hyakowa had just dealt him. Two Odins, a Frigga of clubs, a six of hearts, and a ten of spades. Hmm. It was Thors or better to open, progressive all the way, trips to win, so he could open and he had a nice pair to draw to. He had forgotten just how many times the cards had been dealt in this game of five-card-draw poker since nobody had yet gotten three of a kind or better to win. But, judging by its size, the ante heaped in the middle of the table had grown to at least a hundred kroner, a pot worth winning. He hoped nobody else had openers.

"Openers?" Hyakowa asked.

Top Myer, just to Hyakowa's left, tossed in two silver kroner. Damn! Bass thought. Lucky old bastard! The large coins clinked authoritatively into the ante. Myer turned to Bass and grinned, fiercely, a thick black 'Finni cigar clamped tightly between his teeth.

"I call," Bass said sourly, reluctantly matching Top's opener.

"I call and raise six kroner," Sergeant Major Parant announced just to Bass's immediate left. Shit! Bass thought. He was betting the limit! Bass could swear the table shook as the sergeant major tossed the coins onto the pile, where they landed with a metallic thud.

"Oh, there's the power!" Hyakowa observed. Sergeant Major Parant smiled cryptically and settled farther back in his chair. One of the silver kroner rolled across the table and came to rest directly in front of Hyakowa. "Ah, a sign! A sign!" he shouted as he reluctantly shoved the errant coin back into the center of the table.

"You're pretty damn free with *my* money, young man," Myer said in reproach to the battalion sergeant major. "Damned if your lucky ass'll ever get invited back to one of our games. Goddamned staff pogue."

"I call, dammit," Hospitalman First Class Larry Horner, Company L's chief corpsman, said, counting out eight kroner. "I better win this," he muttered. "It's my stake for a vacation on Havanagas, after all." He grinned widely as he shoved the money into the pot.

"You'll get to Havanagas when kwangduks whistle," Staff Sergeant Ord Boyle, the battalion mess sergeant, replied, counting out eight silver kroner. "It's bad enough I gotta feed your bottomless stomachs, now you want every goddamn kroner I earn—and I gotta send money home to my sick mother," he whined in mock sorrow. "You bastards are taking the very medicine out of her mouth, I just want you to know that." He raised his eyes heavenward as he shoved the money into the pot. "She may have already passed on, since I missed my last payment. May her poor soul find solace in heaven. She won't get any in this cruel world." Boyle did not have a mother but he was an excellent cook.

"I been doctoring scratches in this damned FIST for *three* long years," Horner said, "and I have concluded our stomachs have no bottoms 'cause Ord's chow's eaten holes straight through them. I am due for rotation any day now, gentlemen, and when I get back to civilization, first thing I do will be to get me a stomach transplant. They're doing wonderful things with synthetic organs these days. Boyle, the Corps should dock your pay for impersonating a food service representative."

"Dock my pay, Doc?" Boyle shot back. "What's the charge for practicing medicine without a license? And speaking of short-timers, I'm so short I could sit on one of them kroners and my legs wouldn't reach the floor. Hey, Sar'n't Major," he said, turning to Parant, "what's the story on orders, anyway? How come Personnel's not been burning up space with messages back to Fleet? I'm way overdue for rotation."

"You ain't the only one overdue for rotation, Boyle. But in your case the Corps is keeping you here because the battalion's grown immune to that poison you serve them in the mess. Send you anywhere else and we'd have a riot on our hands—after a lot of Marines passed on to their gods. Now are you guys gonna play cards or sit here all evening weeping in your beer over 'personal' problems?"

"Well, I call, gentlemen," Hyakowa announced, adding his pile of coins to the ante. "Cards to the gamblers?" He turned to Myer.

The noncommissioned officers of Company L held poker games once a month. They played cards the old-fashioned way, with pasteboards. Very large sums of money were never bet or lost, though, because they played for the enjoyment of the game and the comradeship, not for the money. Of course, a casual observer would've thought differently, because once seated around the table they pretended to be vicious competitors out to cut each other's throats. That was part of the charade. Regard for rank was temporarily set aside for the evening, so the games were unruly, noisy affairs, with plenty of good-natured grousing and cursing. Brags, insults, and gossip flew about the smoke-filled room. Even business of one sort or another might be conducted over a slow hand of cards. And sometimes, as on that evening, they were joined by senior NCOs from battalion headquarters.

They played in a back room at Big Barb's, where buxom serving girls kept the beer flowing and it was not unusual for an evening's big winner to treat the bar afterward—and the girl of his choice, upstairs. They could have played back at Camp Ellis in the NCO quarters, but at Big Barb's they could put aside the strict military discipline that ruled their lives. The raunchy exchanges that were such an important part of these monthly get-togethers stayed inside the little room. It just would never do for a lance corporal casually passing by to overhear a staff sergeant and his first sergeant nonchalantly calling each other names and then laughing it off. But such name-calling was confined strictly to that little back room at Big Barb's.

The cards they used were the type the 'Finnis liked to play with, decorated with designs of gods from the ancient Norse mythology. Aces were represented by Ymir, the primeval giant, the equivalent of Chaos to the Greeks. Kings bore the image of Odin, and queens were Frigga, Odin's consort. Jacks were Thor, the second principal god after Odin. Tens through deuces were identified by their value, and otherwise the 'Finni decks consisted of the traditional fifty-two cards in four suits—clubs, spades, hearts, and diamonds. The games they played were also traditional dealer's choice, draw and stud poker mostly, with some ingenious variations. Wild cards were not permitted.

"Gimme *one*," Top Myer announced, holding up a huge forefinger.

Aha, Bass thought, two pair! He could outdraw Myer. "Three, please," he announced.

"An honest man," Hyakowa said as he dealt Bass his three cards.

When Bass got the cards, he did not look at them, just shuffled them together with the Odins. He would not look either, until he'd seen what the other players were taking.

"I'll play these, thank you very much," Sergeant Major Parant announced. He smiled smugly and folded his hands across his stomach.

A bluff? Bass asked himself. Not likely. The most Bass

could expect to hit was three of a kind, maybe a full house, if he was lucky. Parant had to have a straight or a flush or a boat if he really was standing pat. But Bass knew that if he folded, he was out until the game was over, that was the rule. So he *had* to stay in—and probably lose.

"Pat hand, you lying bastard?" Top Myer almost shouted.

"Looks like it," Horner said glumly. "I give you blood when you're wounded, you suck my blood in these games. It's only fair. Give me three cards, please, Wang."

Hmm, Bass thought, another pair. How high?

"One card for me," Boyle announced.

Easy hand to read, Bass thought: drawing to a straight or a flush.

"Dealer," Hyakowa announced smugly, "takes—*none!*" He smiled victoriously at Sergeant Major Parant, who smiled back and just shook his head slowly.

"Great Buddha's cock on a platter! *Two* freaking pat hands at one time! You unbelievable lucky turds!" Horner shouted, banging the table with a fist so hard the coins jumped.

"Careful, there, clap-checker," Sergeant Major Parant cautioned, "that's my retirement fund you're disturbing." He grinned again, showing his teeth to Hyakowa.

"Fragile vessels for liquid excretional matter, that's what you are, all of you," Boyle muttered as he looked at his cards and grimaced.

"Pisspots? Don't you use them to cook our stew?" Hyakowa asked innocently.

"Naw, he drinks outta 'em," Horner said. "Whose bet is it?"

Hyakowa nodded toward Sergeant Major Parant. "Our fearless enlisted leader raised; it's his bet. Bet a lot, Top, I need your money."

"You guys been to college, or near one at some time or other. You should have guessed I'm betting the limit, gents. Please contribute generously." He shoved six more kroner into the heaping pile of coins.

"I see that obvious bluff and raise back six kroner," Horner announced calmly.

Shit! Bass thought. He hit! With two pat hands in the game Horner couldn't be raising on three of a kind, the most likely combination, since he took three cards. Bass made up his mind to fold when it came his turn. He couldn't compete with those guys. At least one of them had to have a winner.

"And I raise—you—all—back," Boyle said, carefully pronouncing each word as he shoved eighteen kroner into the pot.

Now Bass considered himself more an observer of the game, not a player. Well, Boyle had hit his flush, and probably a high one at that.

"Ahem, my *dear* friends and comrades," Hyakowa said gravely, counting out a stack of coins, "I reluctantly—I emphasize 'reluctantly,' because I hate to take money from the mentally retarded—raise you all *back* six kroner. This is the last raise, gentlemen, only three to a hand. House rules."

"We all know the goddamn rules," Boyle muttered.

"Twenty-four kroner to you Top, you too, Charlie," Hyakowa said as he shoved a pile of coins into the ante, a dangerously smug expression on his face.

"Fuck you!" Top Myer snarled, "Next goddamn deployment, I'm gonna brief your ass the whole flight! I'm out." He showed two Ymers openers and some other cards that Bass did not see before the old first sergeant tossed them into the center of the table atop the coins and the other discards.

"Charleee, it's on you." Hyakowa grinned. "You might—I only suggest it—look at your cards now, before you reluctantly, but with your usual gracious and consummate good taste and superb sportsmanship, fold and let me at last scrape into my hugely depleted coffers the winnings I have so richly earned."

Bass shook his head. Wouldn't hurt to look. Bass looked. He pursed his lips. He scratched his head. "Uh, I need some change," he said, drawing a fifty-kroner note out of a pocket.

He tossed it into the ante and counted out twenty-six one-kroner coins in change. "I call," he announced.

"Well, girls, read 'em and weep," Sergeant Major Parant said as he laid down a full house, three tens over a pair of fours.

"Beats my small straight," Horner admitted, throwing in his cards. "I'll go to Havanagas next year, maybe."

Boyle showed a spade flush, Ymer and Frigga high. "The fate of my sainted mother is now on your head, Sergeant Major," he announced sadly.

Hyakowa grinned and spread out four nines. The other players groaned. Sergeant Major Parant disgustedly gathered up his full house and pitched it into the center of the table. "Wang, you eat shit and whistle at the sailors."

"He never whistled at *me*," Horner announced sadly, and pouted.

"Yes, yes, indeed, my most respected sergeant major—you have too many teeth, Larry," Hyakowa said as an aside to the corpsman. "And now, Charles, the finest platoon commander in the Corps, what, pray tell, are you holding onto so tightly over there? It is only you, Dear Gunnery Sergeant Charles Bass, who stands between me and the delightful spread of fiduciary opulence on the table. Reveal thyself!"

"Well," Bass said slowly, grimacing, "I have two pair."

"Charlie!" Top Myer shouted. "What are you doing still in this game with only two pair?" The other players looked at Bass as if he'd lost his senses. Hyakowa laughed and reached for the money in the pot.

"Not so fast, respected and dearly admired platoon sergeant," Bass said. "That's two pair of Odins. With a five kicker." He laid his cards down and spread them out. "One, two, three, and four. Four Odins. You can keep the five-spot kicker, Wang. I got two Odins on the draw." Bass grinned victoriously at Hyakowa.

Hyakowa, entirely deflated, slumped back in his chair. "Four nines and I get beat," he whispered incredulously.

"God?" he shouted toward the ceiling. "Why are you screwing with me like this?"

"Fine hand, Charlie," Sergeant Major Parant said. "You played it like you knew what you were doing." He leaned over and whispered, "When the game's over, I need to see you and Top Myer in private for a little while, okay?"

Parant would not say what it was he wanted to talk to them about until they were back in his quarters at Camp Ellis. He handed each a cold beer produced from a tiny kitchenette and indicated they should take seats in the small alcove that served as a living room just off his sleeping compartment. Bachelor NCO quarters at Camp Ellis were comfortable but cramped.

"I had a little talk with Sergeant Major Shiro this afternoon," he began, nodding in the direction of the FIST sergeant major's room, just down the hall from where they were sitting. "Did you know Brigadier Sturgeon's gone back to HQ at Fargo?"

Top Myer's eyebrows shot up in surprise. He glanced over at Bass, who shook his head slowly. "The word we got was he took home leave. Fargo? Was he called back?" A worried expression crossed the first sergeant's face, and Bass leaned forward anxiously. The character of a FIST was determined by its commander. Thirty-fourth FIST was the best strike team in the Corps because Brigadier Sturgeon could bring out the best in a Marine. If he was being reassigned, that certainly was news, and it would affect every man in the unit.

"He took home leave to go back to HQMC and talk to the Commandant," Parant announced slowly. The others just stared at him. Take home leave to go on official business? That was unprecedented. "Something's not right in this universe, and he took it upon himself to go back to Earth and find out about it. I don't need to tell you, we've got Marines in this FIST who are way beyond their scheduled rotation dates. Way beyond. That's unprecedented. We are being deliberately isolated on Thorsfinni's World, and the brigadier wants to know why." Parant paused and took a sip of beer. "Gentlemen, I think it's got something to do with Lima Company and its deployments to Society 437 and Avionia.

"Now I don't know what you did on those deployments and I don't want to know," Parant continued, "but no Marine commander would *ever*, I mean *ever*, quarantine a whole combat unit just because some of its Marines had gone on a hush-hush mission somewhere. Negative. So if this does have something to do with your company, it means someone very—*very*—high up is fucking with us."

"And the brigadier's gone all the way back to Earth to find out about it." Top Myer shook his head. "That's only what I'd expect him to do."

Sergeant Major Parant took a long drink of his beer. "That's not all," he announced. "Colonel Ramadan got a message from Fleet this afternoon. Charlie, the Commandant *himself* has issued verbal orders assigning three men from your platoon TAD to some—some," he shrugged, "nowhere-place for an unspecified period of time. No explanation, just do it."

"Who are they?" Bass set his beer carefully on the table. A cold knot of fear was beginning to form in the pit of his stomach.

"That new corporal of yours, Pasquin, and lance corporals Dean and Claypoole. A whole fire team."

Oh God, Bass thought, they talked! They're going to Darkside and this "temporary additional duty" crap is just the Corps' way of handling it quietly!

"Captain Conorado will have battalion orders on his desk first thing in the morning," Parant continued. "I just thought you should know."

"Well, I've been in the Corps all day," Top Myer said, "and this is not the first time I've been told to jump through my ass. So we'll get those lads ready to go, won't we, Charlie? And they're keepin' us all here on Thorsfinni's World till we croak?" He shrugged. "That ain't so bad, long's I got Charlie Bass commanding my third platoon." He laid his hand on Bass's shoulder.

Bass smiled weakly. Hell, he thought, before long they'll have the whole damned FIST in that penal colony! Then he did smile. A pissed-off Marine FIST on Darkside? Worst mistake those Ministry of Justice farts could ever make!

Captain Conorado sat at his console, reviewing Company L's training schedule for the next month. A block of three days had been set aside for low-gravity training on a navy vessel in orbit around Thorsfinni's World. Marine Corps regulations required that every Marine undergo the training annually unless excused by his commander. He was about to ask for a personnel status projection for the coming month, to see who wouldn't be available for one reason or another—men were always being detached for schools and special duties—when his console blinked a warning that a high-priority message was coming through.

Damn! he thought at first. Another deployment? He was both angry and excited: angry because he felt his company had had its fair share of deployments recently, the affair on Society 437 involving his third platoon, and then the Avionian affair that had almost gotten him court-martialed. But he was also, paradoxically, thrilled, because deployments are what Marines live for. Then he thought, No, it's about those orders from Fleet. Top Myer had briefed him first thing that morning on the news Sergeant Major Parant had given him and Bass after the poker game last night. Sure enough, it was Commander Van Winkle, his battalion commander. "Captain, I'll be in your orderly room in five minutes. Be sure your first sergeant and Gunny Bass are there." The screen went back to the personnel projections, but Conorado was no longer interested in them.

Gunnery Sergeant Bass reported to his commanding officer

three minutes and twelve seconds after the battalion commander's image blinked off Conorado's computer screen; Commander Van Winkle and Sergeant Major Parant arrived one minute, fifteen seconds later. Conorado, Top Myer, and Bass were waiting when they came through the door.

"You're early," Conorado joked as they came in.

"Into your office, Captain." Van Winkle nodded toward Conorado's open office door, not taking the humor of the moment. The four Marines trooped in and the door closed behind them, leaving the three enlisted Marines sitting in the outer office looking at each other in astonishment.

"I don't like it when things I don't understand begin to affect the men assigned to my command," Van Winkle began without preamble. "This," he handed Conorado a set of battalion orders, "I do not understand." Conorado glanced at the orders, looked up questioningly at his battalion commander and then handed them to Myer and Bass, who pretended to look surprised when they read them. Sergeant Major Parant, standing behind his commanding officer, nodded at Myer and winked.

It was just like Top Myer had said. The authority line on the orders read VOCCMC, "verbal orders, Commandant of the Confederation Marine Corps." The Commandant himself had given the order to detach the three Marines and send them off to—to someplace so remote nobody had ever heard of it before.

"Any idea what's behind this, Captain?" Van Winkle asked.

"No, sir. I was going to ask you that same question."

Commander Van Winkle shook his head and sighed. "I guess we're not supposed to know what's up with L Company, Captain. God knows, it's got to be harder on you than anybody else. Well, better get them up here and break the news."

"Where are they now, Charlie?" Conorado asked.

"Down in the VR chamber, practicing aerial gunnery spotting, Skipper," Bass replied. "I'm on my way." He left without further protocol.

"Now I want to know if you have been talking," Bass demanded. Pasquin, Dean, and Claypoole stood at rigid attention before their platoon commander's desk in his tiny office.

"About what, Gunnery Sergeant?" Pasquin asked.

"About Waygone or the Avionia deployment, goddamn it! Have you three been talking down in Bronnys or *anywhere* to *any*body? Out with it!"

"No!" all three answered as one.

Bass stared at the trio silently for what to them seemed a full minute. "Okay," he said at last. "All right. You know the penalty for talking about those operations. Well, digest these, then," he said, handing each a copy of the battalion order.

Each read them once, then twice. "Holy Hanna," Pasquin exclaimed. "Where's No-Novo Khongor, Gunny? What's the *Wanganui*?"

"One set of dress reds?" Claypoole asked, reading the orders. "What kind of deployment is this, Gunny?"

"Khongor is way the hell and gone from here, and we're nowhere," Bass replied. "The CNSS *Wanganui* (AGS 742) is a goddamned *surveying* ship," he added disgustedly.

"Oh, no," Dean whispered. "Surveying" reminded him of Society 437. "Gunny, are we being sent out as Marine guards on some surveying mission?" The question was so preposterous Bass had to laugh. Dean's face turned red. Pasquin and Claypoole joined in the laughter, but they weren't so sure the question was such a dumb one.

"Okay, here's what this means," Bass said at last. "The Commandant of the Marine Corps *himself* has issued verbal orders detaching you for some kind of duty on the *Wanganui*. I thought at first you'd blabbed and this was just the Corps' way of covering up an embarrassment, three of its men being sent off to Darkside—"

"Shit!" Pasquin exclaimed. Dean and Claypoole started violently.

"Belay that!" Bass commanded. "Belay that. I don't think that's what this is all about. I did at first, but not now. You said you didn't blab, so you didn't. Besides," a wry smile crossed the platoon commander's face, "who ever heard of going off to jail in your dress reds?

"All right. We're going up to see the Skipper, and then Top Myer wants to talk to you three."

Within twenty-four hours every man in L Company was convinced Pasquin, Dean, and Claypoole were in fact on their way to Darkside, and each began uneasily reviewing every word he'd said, drunk or sober, since the company had returned from Avionia. One thing they all knew for sure: Pasquin, Dean, and Claypoole were definitely in some very deep shit.

Top Myer accompanied the trio into orbit. There he swung every bit of weight a first sergeant can swing to be allowed onto the fast combat support ship, the CNSS *Yi Sun Pok*, which would carry them to Novo Khongor and eventual rendezvous with the *Wanganui*. He needed a private meeting with his Marines before the starship launched.

He closed and dogged the hatch to the small compartment the three men would live in during this journey to . . . wherever the hell Novo Khongor was. Then he stood, feet spread, fists jammed on his hips, and glared at them long enough to make them very nervous. He kept glaring until they began to sweat.

"I don't know where you're really going or what you did," he began softly, "but it can't be anywhere or anything good. What did you do?"

The three cast quick glances at each other. Pasquin, as senior man, spoke. "We didn't do anything wrong, Top. Honest."

Myer snorted. "A corporal and two lance corporals? Infantry? You expect me to believe you didn't do anything wrong? What, do you think I've spent my career as a chaplain's assistant?" They later swore that smoke and flames shot from his nostrils when he snorted.

"All right, then, answer one question for me—and tell me the absolute truth." He waited until each of them agreed. "Did any of you say *anything*, I mean word one, to anyone outside of Company L about what really happened on Avionia?"

"No, Top!" they said simultaneously.

"Absolutely not, First Sergeant," Corporal Pasquin said. "We all know what would happen to anyone who let it slip. I think before anybody in the company would let anything slip you'd have to get him so drunk he *couldn't* talk."

Myer peered intently at them. They didn't flinch, and he decided they were probably telling the truth.

"Well, then," he said in a more conversational voice, "the three of you, for reasons unknown, are departing on a deployment to a place nobody I know has ever heard of on an unspecified mission. As you well know, every time Company L or an element of it deploys, I give an unofficial briefing to the men before we arrive on-station. Sometimes I have information to impart that is unavailable to our commanders. Sometimes I put a different slant on the mission." As he spoke he removed his fists from his hips and clasped his hands behind his back. He began pacing from side to side; the compartment only allowed two steps in each direction. "This is the only chance I have to brief you on this mission, and it's very difficult because I have no idea where you're going or what your mission is." He shook his head and a corner of his eye twitched. Three of his Marines were going somewhere and he had no idea what harm they would face. What could he possibly say to help them accomplish their mission and stay alive and unharmed?

"You are Marines. Moreover, you are members of the most

decorated combat unit in the Confederation Marine Corps, 34th FIST. Even more than that, you are members of Company L, the best infantry company in the entire Marine Corps. You know that." He wheeled on them and glared. "Don't let it go to your heads! It doesn't matter how good a Marine you are or how good your unit is. All it takes is one lucky shot and you're dead! That's what combat is, it's a toss of a coin." He stopped glaring and resumed pacing.

"Wherever this place is you're going, whatever your mission is, once you get there, remember four things. You are among the best of the best. You represent not only yourselves, but Company L, 34th FIST, and the entire Marine Corps. You will accomplish your mission, whatever it is, and you will return to Camp Ellis alive and in one piece." He glared again. "Just remember, if you don't come back to me alive and in one piece, your asses are mine." He came to attention. "Corporal Pasquin, Lance Corporal Claypoole, Lance Corporal Dean, good hunting." He grasped each of their hands to shake, then spun about and left, almost forgetting to undog the hatch before opening it.

"Don't you ever scrub the air in this scow?" he snarled at the first sailor he passed. Particles in the air had to be the explanation for his watering eyes.

CHAPTER
EIGHT

This happened a dozen years earlier:

"Mud. That's all this damn place has," First Geologist Donny Yort snorted.

Only one of the people seated at the conference table in the senior staff meeting room reacted to the geologist's blunt statement, Dr. Horter Hottenbaum, the administrative chief of the exploratory mission to the planet Society 362.

"But—" Hottenbaum began.

Yort looked levelly at his boss and cut him off. "Mud to a depth of up to a mile in places." Yort enjoyed making people think by using archaic units of measurement. He pushed a button on the control panel set into the tabletop in front of him. A series of 2-D images marched past on vidscreens placed so everyone at the table could see them without turning around. The display wasn't necessary, but Yort also enjoyed showing graphically what he was talking about—he believed it made people think what he was saying had great importance and they would pay it closer attention. Some of the images were of low, shallow-sided hills, others of plains; several showed forests that appeared more to drip than to grow. Inset in the corner of each image was a close-up of the ground, which was uniformly brown and wet. "Nowhere less than a hundred meters. My opinion is that just getting through the mud to begin drilling for minerals could make drilling cost-prohibitive."

"But Engineering's got . . ." Hottenbaum twirled a hand in

front of his chest; he was a botanist and couldn't think of the term. ". . . got stuff to harden mud so it can be drilled through." He looked at Chief Engineer Baahl for confirmation.

"Polyfrazillium-3," Baahl said. "Inexpensive, easy to use. Can cake a hundred-meter-diameter column of firm dirt through a mud lake half a kilometer deep."

"So—" Hottenbaum looked triumphantly back at Yort, but Baahl interrupted him.

"On a dry day." The chief engineer shook her head.

Hottenbaum was so dismayed by her comment he didn't notice the way her hair billowed out when she shook her head, a sight he normally loved. "Beg pardon?" he said.

"Polyfrazillium-3 won't set on a day with humidity over seventy-five percent. I don't think anyplace on this planet ever dries out that much." Baahl glanced at the chief meteorologist for confirmation.

"To put it in layman's terms," Chief Meteorologist Slyvin said with a shrug as he pushed a button on his console, "the sun never shines here." He stifled a smile when that pompous Yort's images were replaced by his. The images of the planetary surface were replaced with a picture taken of the planet during the exploration ship's approach several months earlier. It showed solid, globe-girdling cloud cover. "The average humidity planet-wide is ninety-two percent. Average number of days per annum without rain in all reporting areas, 0.7. Average annual rainfall in all reporting areas . . ." He shook his head. "I don't understand why Society 362 isn't covered with a worldwide ocean."

Society 362 had an unofficial name, Quagmire, but nobody ever used it in staff meetings or anyplace else it would be recorded.

"But—" Society 362 was the first exploration mission on which Hottenbaum was chief administrator. He dearly wanted it found habitable so it could be colonized. Few scientists ever served as chief administrator on more than one expedition. He needed a finding of habitability to ensure his place in history.

Dr. Achille Marcks, the expedition's chief psychologist, knew that and wasn't about to let Hottenbaum raise another objection. He cleared his throat loudly and said, "Dr. Hottenbaum, let me remind you that nearly three-quarters of the members of this expedition are veterans of at least one other BHHEI mission, and several hundred have multiple explorations behind them. We have been here for eight standard months. The weather, with its constant overcast, is such that 943 out of the 1,006 people on this expedition have had to be treated for the form of depression known as 'seasonal affective disorder.' At this time . . ." He consulted his personal vid even though he could have used the tabletop console to put the data up for all to see as the geologist and meteorologist had. ". . . 261 are unable to perform more than the most rudimentary functions of their roles due to SAD. Perhaps a few score of them will require extended talk and/or chemical therapy after they leave here. Psychology has no choice but to recommend, in the strongest terms, against colonization."

"But the centauroid life-forms are so interesting, they have to be studied." Hottenbaum turned pleading eyes toward the faunal life-form group head.

"Come on, Horter!" said Chief Biologist Winny Rendall. "We've seen heptapods on enough other worlds; they've lost their novelty."

"But they don't have heads—"

Rendall cut him off with a sharp laugh. "So what? When you look at the location of the sense and ingestion organs, everything is within the normal range of location and relationship." He shrugged. "Casing the brain inside the thorax makes more sense than our exposed housing. The head and neck are pretty vulnerable to injury, you know."

"Colonists aren't necessarily the best people to do an in-depth study of a new world's biota." Dr. Angela Streeth, the chief botanist, jumped in before Hottenbaum could raise another objection. "They're too busy trying to make the planet habitable to expend resources on studying flora and fauna. A specially designated and designed scientific study group can do the job better." She grimaced. "My team hasn't found anything interesting yet, and more than half of my people are working at less than full capability." She nodded at Marcks.

Dr. Horter Hottenbaum looked from face to face and sighed. Every department head was opposed to opening Society 362 for colonization. "Then there's no need . . ." He couldn't bring himself to finish asking the question.

"I recommend we go home *now*," said First Deputy Administrator Egon. "We can write our reports on the journey."

They left a month later on the next supply ship. The ship didn't take them directly back to the Bureau of Human Habitability Exploration headquarters on Earth, it first stopped at Kingdom, a colonized world just three light-years from Quagmire, to drop off a consignment of intestinal flora culture. Kingdom's theocracy wanted the world to be totally independent, but not all of the nutrients necessary for healthy human life were readily available yet. A recent plague had attacked the intestinal flora of the colonists, and they were facing famine from their reduced ability to digest food. Only crew who were needed to transfer the floral consignment and receive the minerals Kingdom used as trade goods were allowed off the ship during the two days it was in orbit. This wasn't by command of the ship's captain, it was by order of the theocracy. The monks of the Holy Regiment of the Shepherd's Crook, who served as customs agents inside the ship, permitted no unauthorized persons to debark. The monks looked like they were fully prepared to use the Confederation military blasters they carried. An armed shuttle hovering outside the transport's docking bay backed them up. No one on the ship to Kingdom objected: the planet was subject to frequent rebellions by those colonists who believed Kingdom should allow more individual freedom.

As the mission's shuttles took off from Quagmire, from the edge of the nearby rain forest a small group of centauroids unlike any the BHHEI mission had encountered in nine months of study watched quietly. When the last of the shuttles vanished into the upper atmosphere, they regrouped into a circle.

"The monsters have gone," one said with relief.

"Have they truly gone or will they return?" another asked, watching the sky through his dorsal eyes.

The biggest centauroid lashed out to thump the worrier between his retracted primary eyestalks. "Look at us when you talk," he snarled. "You are being rude."

The worrier instantly retracted his dorsal eyestalks and extended his primaries. He lowered his torso and pointed his primaries at the leader's mid-feet. "Those monsters frighten me. Four limbs are unnatural." His voice was muffled by the mud inches below his mouth.

Another shuddered. "And those huge lumps where their primary eyestalks should be! They are uglier than any demon the shaman warns us about."

Others began babbling of their disgust at the appearance of the monsters. The leader ignored them. He extended his torso to its fullest height and aimed his primary eyestalks at the just-abandoned BHHEI base. He came to a decision.

"They had many tools and other objects," he said. "Maybe they left something in those . . ." His vocabulary failed him. The centauroids didn't construct buildings or live in caves, their nests were roofed with living branches teased into place for that purpose and had open sides. "We must search." He slapped one of the others on a forelimb. "Go. Bring back our females and young. Also more hunters."

The designated messenger dipped his torso and bounded up into a nearby tree. He used all six limbs to scramble along the branches from tree to tree—arboreal travel was far faster than slogging through the undergrowth.

A hunter who had been silent swiveled his primary eyestalks toward the base. "What if they set traps?"

"Our females and young will find them," the leader said

firmly. Secretly he wasn't so sure his kind could find all the traps the monsters might have left. What sort of traps might monsters such as the ones who just left be capable of conceiving?

The humans hadn't set any traps; the vid, trid, and audio recorders left running didn't count. In any case, the record the vids, trids, and audios made would never be seen by a human unless another mission was sent to Quagmire. Even then, the next mission would have to visit Central Station and retrieve the recordings before the dank atmosphere degraded the storage media beyond recovery.

Neither had the mission left behind anything usable—usable to humans, that is. The centauroids, on the other hand, were fascinated by the decomposing foodstuffs in the composters. Even more interesting to them were the items they were able to dig out of the nonorganic trash pit: rapidly corroding broken screws, a cracked bubble matrix, the partly carbonized innards of a comm unit that had overloaded and burned out. One searcher thought she was caught by a trap when she squeezed a mostly used tube of adhesive and it stuck the phalanges of a forelimb together. She thought she was crippled for life, but a few days later the normal scaling of her dermis sloughed off enough surface cells to remove the adhesive. Most fascinating of all were the few wrappers from consumable items that hadn't yet degraded. The wrappers were impervious to just about everything and could be torn only at their tear strips, which, of course, had already been torn. Because people found such wrappers useful for more than merely preserving consumables between manufacture and use, they were designed to not degrade until they had been buried in a landfill for several days. The leader gathered the wrappers to be tied together for use as ceremonial capes. He thought they would be far more impressive than the leaves normally used for that purpose. The centauroids moved on and eventually migrated away. Nothing else untoward happened for a dozen standard years. Then monsters came again.

*　　*　　*

The hunter hunched behind the foliage of a tree at the edge of a sluggish river. He watched the monsters on the island for a long time. Soft rain gently pelted his shoulders and back, and ran down his body to drip onto the ground below. Finally he decided to move closer to the monsters. He was too young to have seen the monsters that had visited earlier, but he'd heard all of the stories and thought these might be different. According to the tales, the earlier monsters were more uniform in size, about the same size as people. Some of the new monsters looked to be at least twice the size of people, and the smaller ones were the size of young people, not adults. He was pretty sure the smaller ones weren't immature monsters; it was always the small ones who seemed to be leaders and the big ones were workers. Were they different kinds of monsters? That was as peculiar a thought to the hunter as the monsters coming in different sizes: his kind had not domesticated animals. He had never heard of the earlier monsters striking each other. During the time he watched from the tree he had seen several monsters strike each other, sometimes smaller ones striking larger ones. The large ones never hit back.

He couldn't be sure, but the skin color of the monsters seemed different from what he had been told about those who had left half a lifetime earlier. Their outer coverings were all the same color and pattern. He'd not heard that the earlier monsters all had the same coverings; the older hunters, who had seen them frequently, described them as wearing many different coverings, most in colors nobody had ever seen before. One thing he was sure of from his own experience: the nests the new monsters constructed were different from the nests the others had made; he had been one of the young who searched the monster camp after the others left.

He wasn't going to go closer in the open; two other hunters had come into this area in recent days. They hadn't returned. The hunter suspected the monsters had killed them. He would get closer to the monsters, but they wouldn't see him. Then he would return to his clan and report what he learned.

Keeping foliage between himself and the island, he swiftly clambered to the ground. He lay his spear where he could find it easily on his return and lowered himself to his belly. He dropped his thorax as well, with his shoulders hunched high enough only to keep his mouth out of the mud, and slithered into the water. The patter of the rain on the river's surface masked the small wake he made entering the water. Completely submerged, he paddled to the middle of the river to take advantage of the slight current. There, next to a leafy branch drifting with the current, he buoyed upward enough to break the surface with his dorsal eyestalks and snorkeled his nostrils. If monsters on the island saw his eyestalks and snorkel, they would think the organs were leaves on the branch. Maybe when he got closer he would find a way to bend his body so he could raise a tympanum above the water and listen to the monsters. The sounds of the monsters might have meaning to the shaman and the elders.

The river ran very slowly and it took considerable time for the hunter to get appreciably closer to the island. He swiveled his dorsal eyestalks to take in as much detail as possible, but almost none of what he saw made sense to him. All of the monsters were doing something, none were simply relaxing on that fine, drizzly day. Most of them rushed from one nest to another, many hunched as though they disliked the rain. Why would monsters dislike rain? As one smaller monster went from one nest to another; a larger monster accompanied it, holding a large leaf over it so the drizzle didn't fall on it. Very peculiar. Sometimes monsters moved objects from a nest into a smaller nest then climbed into the smaller nest. Then the small nest moved! The first time he saw that, the hunter was so frightened he almost swam away. But the small nest didn't move toward him, so he stayed. None of the small nests moved toward him. Instead, one by one, they all went to the largest nest and entered it, so he stopped being afraid. After he witnessed that phenomenon several times, he recognized a pattern to the movement: the small nests loaded objects from one particular small nest, went into the largest nest, then returned to the first nest and repeated the process. They must have been moving things into storage. But why move them if they were already in a nest? That didn't make any sense to him.

Then the nest from which things were being taken roared so loudly the hunter could clearly hear it even under the water. It was the loudest thunder the hunter had ever heard, and it terrified him even more than the small nests did when they first moved. His astonishment when he saw the nest lift into the sky was so great that he opened his mouth and forgot to breath through his snorkel. He choked on the water he swallowed and had to raise up to clear his breathing passage. As soon as he could breathe again, he ducked back down to expose only his dorsal eyestalks and snorkel. He quickly swept his gaze over the island, but none of the monsters seemed to have noticed him. He looked upward and saw the nest that roared shrink into the sky. Then he remembered hearing that the monsters from before had used flying nests to leave. He should have known immediately what was happening—but no one had told him about the roar. Briefly he asked himself, did this mean the monsters were leaving? But only briefly; the monsters had been removing things from the flying nest and putting them in a nest that was surely too big to move. More likely the flying nest was on its way back to where the monsters came from to get more things to move into the large nest. He wondered again what the objects were and why they were being moved into one location.

The current drew him around the end of the island, and he saw that several of the smaller monsters were at the bottom tip of the island. They were naked and held spears. The worrisome thing was, they were wading in the water. Well, they wouldn't see him if he simply submerged completely and retracted his snorkel. He could easily hold his breath for the length of time it took to reach the bank along which he'd left his spear. He took a deep breath, retracted his dorsal eyestalks and snorkel, then headed toward the shore, with his pectoral eyestalks extended for guidance. His midlimbs and aft limbs stroked powerfully, but with an upward thrust; he moved his forelimbs in an opposite direction to keep from surfacing.

The hunter only got a short distance before he saw something that startled him. One of the small monsters was swimming along the bottom of the river.

The small monster held a short spear extended before him. The spear had a barbed point that glittered more than the sharpest stone. The hunter didn't know how the monsters perceived their surroundings without eyestalks, but he could make out nothing on the monster's dorsal surface that looked like a sense organ. He thought if he stayed well above it and didn't swim so powerfully, the monster might not notice him and he could pass by safely.

The monster suddenly did something with his spear and it shot forward to impale a fish. A cord so thin the hunter could barely make it out trailed from the spear to the monster's hand. The monster thrust forward with its aft limbs and reeled the cord in with its forelimbs. The hunter took advantage of the monster's distraction and kicked vigorously forward to pass it. The strength of his thrust carried him back to the surface and he extended his snorkel to take a deep breath. When he was nearly directly above the monster, it suddenly twitched around and the hunter saw glimmering spots on the front of the growth on the monster's shoulders. Had they stalks he would have *known* they were eyes; without them he could only guess they were. An opening on the front of the monster's shoulder-growth opened and closed rhythmically; it had to be the monster's mouth.

The monster had almost brought the spear back to its hand when it sensed the hunter. It twisted around to reach the spear. With the sharp point extended at the hunter, it pushed against the riverbed and shot upward.

Panic flashed through the hunter; he was unarmed except for his skinning knife. But the panic was only a flash. The spear was encumbered by the fish that still dangled from it, he should be able to avoid the point. He was bigger than the monster and had just taken a breath at the surface. He didn't know how long the monster had been submerged, but surely it couldn't hold its breath much longer. If he dodged inside the jab of the spear and grappled with the monster, he could use his midlimbs and hindlimbs to pinion its limbs, hold its spear away with a forelimb, and use his knife with his other fore-limb. He plunged down to meet the monster and managed to swat the spear away before it could cut him.

The monster was strong, much stronger than a young cen-tauroid of the same size. The hunter had to wrap his aft limbs about the monster's body to keep from being pushed away to where the spear could be brought into play. Fortunately, the monster's aft limbs couldn't grasp and their range of move-ment was far less than the hunter's. He gripped the monster's forelimbs with his midlimbs, but it was a struggle to keep a grip, much less pinion the monster's limbs. Frantically, he groped for his skinning knife, a chert sliver with animal hide wrapped around one end. The monster wrenched one forelimb free and clawed at the hunter's pectoral eyestalks. The hunter gave up his plan to stab the monster. Instead he wrapped all six limbs around it and squeezed. He had breath left; squeezing would force out any breath the monster still had. A current of water pulsed against the hunter's mid-limbs. The monster's mouth changed its shape. The hunter couldn't know what that meant, but the monster was smiling. It stopped struggling and wrapped its forelimbs around him. It squeezed and a bubble of air was expelled from the hunter's mouth.

All of the hunter's eyestalks extended. He needed to break free and swim to the surface, he desperately needed to breathe, to get to the air. He let go with all of his limbs and tried to break away, to swim upward, but the monster maintained its forelimb grip and wrapped its aft limbs around the hunter's hindquarters.

Too late, the hunter realized the flow of water he had felt on his midlimbs came from the monster's sides; too late, he recognized the way the monster's mouth opened and closed was the same as some fish did. Too late, he realized the monster was breathing water.

The monster held the hunter down as the hunter's world turned red, then gray, then black. The hunter's struggles slowed, then ceased. He went limp. The monster rolled him onto his dorsal side and prodded his abdomen. A string of tiny bubbles dribbled out of the hunter's mouth and his body sank, to rest rocking on the riverbed.

CHAPTER
NINE

"Hit me," Claypoole muttered as he studied his down card carefully. Pasquin dealt him the Thor of hearts faceup. "Damn!" Claypoole shouted. "Busted!" He flipped over a ten to go along with a seven and the Thor showing.

"I'da stayed on seventeen," Pasquin said. He took Claypoole's bet and then looked expectantly at Dean.

"I'm good," Dean said.

Pasquin flipped over the Odin of diamonds to go with the eight of spades showing. "Dealer pays nineteen," he announced.

"Pay me," Dean said, flipping a Frigga of spades to match the ten of hearts on the table. Pasquin paid Dean from a thick stack of bills sitting to one side. The game had been in progress since early morning and it was suppertime. The room was littered with empty beer bottles, mute evidence of a long day indeed.

"Lessee, Rock, you owe me, um, six hundred?" Pasquin said, shuffling the deck. "Payday stakes, I guess, since you don't have any cash left?" Pasquin laughed and drew mightily on his Fidel. He exhaled a huge blue-white cloud of tobacco smoke, adding to the haze already hanging over the small table in their tiny hotel room. The one thing they had been sure to bring with them on the mission was a good supply of cigars. They'd have brought more cash but neither Dean nor Claypoole had counted on Pasquin's luck—or skill, they weren't sure which—at cards.

"Loan me fifty until my luck comes back, won't you Deano? Hey, ain't it against regulations for an NCO to gamble with enlisted men?" Claypoole asked Dean, nudging Corporal Pasquin as he spoke.

"It is, it certainly is," Dean answered, "we being only lowly lance corporals and him a corporal and enlisted leader. And if I lose, I'm complaining to the captain of the *Wanganui*, assuming there is such a vessel and assuming it ever makes port again."

For more than a month the trio had been sitting in a flophouse in Soma Chundaman, Novo Khongor's only city of note, waiting for the *Wanganui* to make port. Considering that it had taken the *Yi Sun Pok* two months to get them there, they'd been on the mission three months and still didn't know what it was all about.

Novo Khongor was one of the most inhospitable worlds in Human Space. Its seas were brackish, almost lifeless, uncharted reaches continually agitated by violent storms, and its continents were mountain fastnesses, swept by dry, freezing winds. Soma Chundaman was situated on a high plateau above the sea, and on a calm day the wind howled down its streets with enough force to make walking into it a chore. Windblown salt spray from the ocean coated everything left outdoors for more than a few minutes, so most of the town's facilities were underground. To resist the winds, the few buildings on the surface were built like reinforced bunkers, no more than one story high. And there was always dust in the air.

The chief industry on Novo Khongor was mining. The men who worked the mines were mostly descendants of Mongolians who'd immigrated generations before, when the planet's rich mineral resources were first discovered. A hardy, hospitable people, they were the only feature of the place that made the Marines' stay there endurable, but even their hearty drinking habits and natural affability were beginning to wear on the trio after a month in the place with virtually nothing to do.

The Confederation Navy had selected Novo Khongor as the *Wanganui*'s home port because it was on the far reaches of Human Space, a convenient jumping-off place for a survey vessel. It had been the *Wanganui*, seconded to the Bureau of Human Habitability Exploration and Investigation, that had first surveyed Society 437, that ill-fated world where the skinks had first revealed themselves to humanity. In fact, most of the voyages undertaken by the *Wanganui* were in support of the Bureau, so its crew was more used to working under civilian control than military.

"I don't see why the Navy didn't send the *Wanganui* to Thorsfinni's World to pick us up instead of making us cool our heels in this place for months on end," Claypoole groused as he looked at the new cards Pasquin had just dealt.

"What? To pick up three Marine *enlisted* men?" Pasquin snorted. "They're off exploring and charting somewhere, and when they're done, we'll join 'em and find out why in the living hell the Corps has sent us out here." Pasquin shivered. "Damned place reminds me of Adak Tanaga, when I was with the 25th FIST there." His two companions said nothing; Adak Tanaga was where Pasquin, in charge of a force recon team, had gotten men killed because of negligence. In the eyes of the men of Lima Company, 34th FIST, the corporal had more than redeemed himself on Society 437 and Avionia, where he had demonstrated he was a good combat leader with guts.

"Well, we've only been here thirty-seven days," Dean said.

"Yeah, and six hours, thirty-two minutes, and fifteen seconds," Claypoole answered. "I've been keeping count."

"Maybe the skinks got them," Dean said, and immediately clapped his hand to his mouth.

The other two started violently. "Goddamnit, Marine, keep your mouth shut!" Pasquin shouted.

"Jesus, Deano," Claypoole gasped.

"Sorry! Sorry! I wasn't thinking . . ."

"Talk like that can get us all into trouble, Joe," Pasquin said. "Ah, what the hell," he relented, "is the Ministry of Justice or whoever gonna bug a shithole like this, just to see what three Marine grunts are talking about? Just watch it from now on, okay?"

Pasquin glanced at his watch. "Hey, it's suppertime. Suppose we mosey down to the Gobi and eat, maybe lift a few?" The Gobi was a one-star—Claypoole's rating—restaurant that catered mostly to single miners. A one-star rating was as high as Claypoole would rate anywhere on Novo Khongor, and from what the three had seen the past month, that was generous. Pasquin stretched. "Maybe Miss Shandra will be accommodating tonight."

At the mention of Shandra, Claypoole felt a sharp pang. The way the waitress and Pasquin had hit it off reminded him poignantly of the bar girl on Wanderjahr who died in his arms. Jezu, Claypoole thought, I went through a war on Diamunde, fought aliens on 437 and Avionia, and I still can't get over Maggie.

"Something wrong?" Pasquin asked, seeing the sorrowful expression that had come over Claypoole's face.

"No, no," Claypoole answered quickly, shaking off his thoughts.

Dean, who had been with Claypoole when Maggie was shot, said, "He's just sorry he lost so much money."

"Don't blame him; a real Marine likes to win at *everything*!" Pasquin answered, hefting his winnings. He divided the bills into three even stacks, shoved one at Claypoole and the other at Dean. He did that with his winnings at the end of every card game.

Lieutenant Aldo Perizzites, captain of the *Wanganui*, gave the Marines' orders only a perfunctory glance. "I knew you were coming but I don't know why and I don't care," he said. Perizzites was the most unmilitary officer any of the Marines had ever met. His uniform was dirty and wrinkled and his hair was long even for a navy man. He could not have shaved in several days.

Survey ships had a bad reputation in the navy, anyway, and the *Wanganui* was living up to it. The first sailor Pasquin had observed when they came aboard had a ring in his ear. The Marines were scandalized when a seaman addressed the chief of the boat by his first name and the petty officer never batted an eyelash. Rumor had it that once a man was assigned duty on a survey ship he stayed there for as long as he was in the navy, because he'd never fit in anywhere else after a cruise on such a vessel.

The civilian scientists and technicians who'd endured the *Wanganui* for an entire year took their leave of the crew with hugs and high fives.

"Another science team's coming aboard in a few days," Perizzites told the three Marines, "and we're headed for Society 461. It's all the way *beyond* the other side of Human Space, so it'll take us three months to get there. You'll be on this mission for a total of eighteen months. Stay out of our way and you'll be all right. Your duties, I'm guessing, will be defined by the chief scientist when he gets aboard." He turned to the chief of the boat. "Ron, get these guys squared away in the crew's quarters, will you?" He turned his attention to a rating who had presented him with a loading manifest. The rating was actually wearing a bandanna on his head.

The chief of the boat, an unkempt, burly man named Riggs, gestured for the Marines to follow him. "I don't much like jarheads," he told them as he turned and headed for the companionway. The three glanced at one another but said nothing.

"Oh . . ." Perizzites turned back to the three Marines. "Where are your weapons?"

"We didn't bring any, sir," Pasquin answered. Perizzites stared at Pasquin as if he hadn't understood the answer, then shook his head and went back to his manifest.

*　　*　　*

Sailors always live better on shipboard than troops. But when on shipboard, Marines do not like to be berthed with sailors. That is not because Marines do not appreciate the relative comfort of navy billets. It is because, to coin a metaphor, hunters don't have much in common with farmers. But on the trip out to Novo Khongor, the three Marines had been consigned to crew's quarters for two months, so they were not too disappointed to be berthed with the crew of the *Wanganui*. The racks were soft and the chow was said to be good.

And the crewmen, despite Chief Riggs's prejudices, did not seem to mind three Marine infantrymen in their quarters. Despite their disregard for military dress and protocol, the crew knew the ship and their duties. The first night, a second class had come over to where the Marines were bunked and asked them to join a poker game just starting up. That time Pasquin did not give any of the money back.

"Marine contingent, report to the bridge! On the double!" the watch officer blared over the ship's PA system. Calling the three Marines his "contingent" was Lieutenant Perizzites's idea of a joke, and his crew played along gleefully. The three Marines just took the ribbing and simmered quietly.

Pasquin put his cards away. "Let's spruce up a bit," he told the others as he put on his dress reds tunic and slid into his shoes. "Can't let the captain think we've turned into sailors."

"Or worse, members of his crew." Dean laughed.

"Well, maybe we'll get the word at last," Claypoole ventured hopefully. It had been two full days Standard since the new survey team had arrived and loaded its equipment onboard the *Wanganui*. Despite the fact that the vessel was almost at its jump point into Beamspace, the Marines had not yet met the chief scientist or any of his party. The trio had watched them coming aboard from a remote corner of the ship's loading bay—they'd been ordered not to get in the way of ship's operations. The scientists hadn't brought much baggage with them, and there was something vaguely unsettling about the men. They didn't talk to anyone and they just didn't look the way the Marines thought scientists should.

Lieutenant Perizzites, together with the dour, uncommunicative junior-grade lieutenant who was the ship's executive officer, and the chief of the boat, were waiting impatiently on the bridge.

"We got here as quickly as we could," Pasquin apologized, thinking the lieutenant was miffed because the Marines had taken so long to respond.

"The *Wanganui*'s a big ship, Corporal," Chief Riggs commented sarcastically, "so we figured it'd take you jarheads a while to find your way around her." Riggs was a huge slob of a man who never missed an opportunity to poke fun at the Marines, but the trio did not resent his sallies very much because he poked fun at everyone. His leadership style, if it could be called that, was to motivate by ridicule rather than by shouting.

Perizzites made a dismissive gesture with a hand. "Actually, we're waiting for the chief of the scientific party to get here. He's got some news. Where the hell is he?"

"Maybe he got lost?" the exec ventured, grinning at Chief Riggs.

"I don't know why he wants the Marines up here too," Perizzites groused, pacing back and forth, his hands clasped tightly behind his back. "We're only thirty minutes to jump point. I don't know why he couldn't have called the meeting after the jump. Goddamn, we'll be three months getting to Society 461. Goddamn scientists anyway, bunch of—"

"Actually, Captain, we're not going to Society 461 after all," a mild voice said from the companionway. "Sorry I'm late, gentlemen," Thom Nast said, stepping onto the bridge. "Ah, Lance Corporal Dean! How's Owen?"

The three Marines stood dumbfounded, their mouths hanging open.

"Mr. Nast!" Dean exclaimed. "Um, well, er, O-Owen's a— a—" He struggled to find the right words. "—a man of leisure," he said, blurting out the first thing that came into his mind. "Top Myer's taking care of him while we're . . ." His voice trailed off and he shrugged, a stupid grin on his face.

Nast shook hands with the three Marines and turned to Lieutenant Perizzites. "Thom Nast, Captain, Confederation Ministry of Justice."

It was Perizzites's turn to look astonished. "Ministry of Justice?" he stammered, not understanding. "You—You're not a scientist? This is a s-scientific survey vessel, Mister— Mister—"

"Nast, Thom Nast, Captain. Assistant Attorney General, Confederation Ministry of Justice. I have the protocol rank of a four-nova admiral." Nast smiled engagingly. "This is not a scientific mission, gentlemen," he continued, turning to the others. "This is a law enforcement operation. We are not headed for Society 461 either. We're going first to Renner's World, where we'll drop off our Marines, and then I'll tell you our ultimate destination." Nast handed Perizzites a crystal. "Change of orders," he said. "They come from the highest authority through the Chief of Naval Operations."

"Well—Well—" Perizzites checked the time to jump. Too late to make a course change. He turned to his exec. "Have Navigation plot a new course for when we reach our next jump point." He knew enough not to ask any questions of Nast. "Uh, gentlemen, you'd better return to your quarters for the jump in, uh, two-zero minutes."

"Oh, Captain Perizzites, two more things," Nast said as he turned to leave the bridge. "No liberty for anyone, repeat, anyone, on Renner's World—and move these Marines in with my party. They will have no more contact with your crew while they are on board this vessel."

"Just as well," Chief Riggs muttered, "they got nearly all the lower ratings' pay."

*   *   *

Lieutenant Perizzites stared at the orders on his screen. They had been properly authenticated, and sure enough, they came from "on high," straight from the Ministry of War in fact. The orders were full of the usual gibberish until he got to the part where they announced, "Ch sci party will ann final dest upon dep RW." Now that was unusual. Oops, this guy is no scientist, Perizzites reminded himself. But what was this "law enforcement" mission and why did they pick his scow anyway?

Perizzites was impressed despite himself. He ran a hand nervously over his jaw and briefly considered changing into a clean uniform. *Maybe I should shave too, spruce up for this guy, Nast?* Nah, he told himself on second thought, who gives a damn?

There was almost no room for the four men in Nast's tiny stateroom, but Pasquin, Dean, and Claypoole made themselves as comfortable as they could. "You guys sure do get around," Nast said, then laughed. "Your big buddy, Madame Chang-Sturdevant, told me I had to take damned good care of you two on this mission."

"Wh-What mission is that, sir?" Claypoole asked.

Nast noticed a strange expression on Pasquin's face. "Corporal?" he nodded at Pasquin to speak.

"Sir, the president of the Confederation of Worlds? Does she really know these guys?"

"Only by reputation," Nast smiled. "She was quite grateful for the way these two saved the life of her plenipotentiary, Madame Wellington-Humphreys, during the Diamundian operation. You didn't hear about that?"

Pasquin gave an embarrassed smile. "Endlessly, sir, endlessly. Well, I guess I've got to apologize, guys. I always thought you exaggerated that story a bit."

"No," Claypoole blurted out. "Actually, we played it down." They all laughed.

"Oh, I almost forgot." Nast snapped his fingers. "Chief

Long—remember him?—is now the Confederation Attorney General. He sends his regards too."

"The Attorney General? Come on, sir," Pasquin begged, "this is like one of those old jokes, my fire teammates know the Attorney General?" He looked disbelievingly at Nast and shook his head.

"Since when has the chief been Attorney General?" Dean asked.

Nast laughed, then continued to Pasquin, "I admit, Corporal, it's one hell of a coincidence. They worked for Long when he was advising the Wanderjahrian Stadtpolizei. The Commonwealth called him back from retirement for that one, and then, after the clean-up following the Avionian business, the president appointed him AG."

"Well, I'll be constipated for life!" Pasquin exclaimed.

"All right, men," Nast continued, "back to business. What I am going to tell you now is known only to the president, the attorney general, and me. Neither the minister of war nor the chief of naval operations or anyone on their respective staffs knows our mission; my own men do not yet know where we're headed. They were recruited from all over the Confederation for a 'special mission' and that's all they know about it for now. But I'm going to tell you three."

The three leaned forward expectantly. "Any of you ever watch *Barkspiel*?" Nast asked suddenly.

The question caught them by surprise. "Yessir," Claypoole responded. "That's the stupid game show where they give away big prizes for answering dumb questions. Sure, everyone watches it sometimes."

"Yeah, Claypoole was on it once but he missed all the questions," Dean said.

"Boy, you wouldn't even be alive now if I hadn't killed the shit-eating dogs on Elneal," Claypoole said.

"Boot, those dogs wouldn't even give a coprolite like you a sniff," Dean responded.

"Dude, you wouldn't—"

"Belay that. Listen to the man," Pasquin interjected.

"So we all have watched the program," Nast continued. "And what's the biggest prize of all?"

"An all-expense-paid trip to Havanagas!" Claypoole replied.

"You got it. Ever want to go there yourself?" Nast looked expectantly at the Marines. They in turn looked at one another and shrugged their shoulders.

"I guess so, sir. But hell, none of us'll ever get on *Barkspiel* to begin with, much less have enough money to afford to get to Havanagas on our own."

"Yeah, but I sure would like a chance at one of the fancy bordellos they have out there. I have always wanted to experience that scenario where they lower a girl in a wicker basket over you and she—"

"Cut it out, Claypoole!"

"It's called the 'Chinese basket'—"

"Well, you three are going to Havanagas," Nast announced. That stopped Claypoole in mid-sentence, which was good because both Pasquin and Dean were preparing to thump him. "You three are going there to do something for the Ministry of Justice. I handpicked you for the mission. It'll be very dangerous, but there is no backing out; we're committed. I am sincerely sorry you weren't given a chance to volunteer, but I need you three and you are going, just as you've done on plenty of wartime missions since you've been in the Corps. Only this time you're working for me."

"Dangerous?" Dean asked. "Uh, how dangerous, sir?"

"Very. I'll explain everything later."

The three were silent as they considered what Nast had just told them.

"How bad can things be on a place like Havanagas?" Claypoole exclaimed at last. "Besides, if I can get into one of those fancy cathouses, that's a hell of a lot better than fighting—" He almost said "skinks!"

CHAPTER
TEN

Pasquin rubbed his left wrist gently where the ID bracelet had been for ten years, since he was inducted into the Confederation Marine Corps. It wasn't that his wrist felt any different. But now that the bracelet was gone he just felt different. His entire military personnel, finance, and medical files had been encoded into that bracelet, and it had been updated every time he went on deployment, had a personnel action, got paid, went on sick call, and so on. After ten years the bracelet had become a part of him.

"Dean, you're next," Nast said. Dean stepped up to the table where Nast had set up the ID fitting device.

"Gee, Mr. Nast, I thought only the induction centers were authorized to use these things," Dean said as he stuck his left wrist into the ring on the top of the machine.

Nast pressed a green button on the console and instantly the bracelet snapped off Dean's wrist. Nast dropped the bracelet into a pouch. "Right, he said, gesturing for Claypoole to step up to the device. "Major military hospitals have them too. Your Commandant himself arranged the loan of this device for my exclusive onetime use. Claypoole?" Claypoole stepped up and stuck his wrist into the fitter. "Gentlemen, for the duration of this mission you are now officially discharged from the Confederation Marine Corps. Your bracelets will be refitted when this job is over. Your record will show an uneventful tour of duty on the *Wanganui* as 'Marine Security.' New policy, you know? Security against pirates and *whatever*?" Nast paused. "There will be no record of what you are going to do for me, understand?"

The three Marines nodded. But, since the orders to join Nast had come from the highest level, they waited silently for the other shoe to drop.

Nast handed each man a crystal. "Pop these into your readers when you get back to your corner. They contain a slightly revised version of your service records. Dean, Claypoole, we had to give you somewhat altered dates of service and so on to get the three of you discharged honorably at about the same time. Read these records, memorize everything that is new. You probably will not be questioned too closely, but if you are, you must be consistent." He handed them each a small packet. "Inside are your discharge certificates, travel orders, tickets, everything you'll need for a week on Havanagas."

Claypoole glanced inside his packet and gave a low whistle. He took out a wad of bills and held them up for the others to see. Each packet contained a similar amount of cash and travelers checks. Nast laughed. "Look in your finance records, fellas. You all put the maximum into Soldiers' and Sailors' Deposits. You were able to save more than enough to pay for a trip to Havanagas with something left over. Oh, and when this mission is over and you are back in the Corps, you will have that money in those accounts. Least I could do for you."

"Thank you, sir," Pasquin said. "I'm already beginning to like this assignment." He grinned at the others as he riffled the wad of money.

Nast held up a cautioning hand. "Don't be too sure, Raoul. All right, for now go back to your areas, put up your screens, and study your new service records. I'll be asking you questions about them the rest of this voyage until you get to the point where you really believe what's in there. We'll get together again after chow and I'll start your briefing on the mission. And Corporal Pasquin?"

"Yessir?"

"Corporal, don't use any of that Havanagas money if you gamble with my men on this voyage."

Back in their corner of the compartment, set aside for them by Nast, the trio viewed their altered service records on the readers they'd been provided. "Jezu," Claypoole exclaimed, "I've been with 34th FIST eighteen months longer than I thought."

Dean laughed. "No, you just went on an unusually long drunk and don't remember those eighteen months. You're lucky, Rock, I've got four freaking years of stuff to remember." Nast had to invent four years of service for Dean in order to bring him up to the end of a normal enlistment.

"Who'd ever notice anyway? Looks like we're all assigned to 34th FIST for life," Claypoole answered, a sour expression on his face.

"I got it from Sergeant Souavi in Supply that the brigadier went back to Earth just to check up on that," Pasquin said. "But you guys should be able to figure out why they're keeping us together." He made an expression like a skink and pretended to be spraying them with an acid gun. They grimaced and nodded. Cautiously, Dean activated a one-way window in the privacy screen that shielded them in their corner and looked out at Nast's men, sixty or so husky, mean-looking individuals in plain gray jumpsuits, lolling about in the open bay, smoking, reading, cleaning weapons and equipment. A group of four was playing a quiet game of poker in one corner.

"Okay, okay, guys, come on now. We gotta get this crap memorized. Dean, what's your base pay entry date and when did you get to Boot Camp?"

Nast had added four years to Dean's life to bring him up to the end of a normal enlistment. He had him born in 2423 instead of 2427. The details of the first half of his cover story were not hard to memorize, nondescript assignments in various backwaters. Wisely, Nast had arranged for the other two to share some parts of those assignments, which dovetailed nicely with Pasquin's actual experience, so he could help fill in some of the details for Dean and Claypoole. In reality Dean was halfway through his eight-year enlistment. That came as somewhat of a surprise because until then Dean had hardly given a thought to what he would do when this enlistment was finally up. Other Marines he knew kept short-timer's calendars, marking off the passage of every day until their discharge. But for Dean it made no sense to volunteer for the Corps and then anxiously count the days until his enlistment was up. That would have been an embarrassment; Joseph Finucane Dean had found himself a home in the Marine Corps.

After an hour Pasquin sighed theatrically and said, "If anyone questions us, you guys let me do the talking. Buddha's blue balls, you dildos couldn't remember your numbers if you had them tattooed on your foreheads." He deactivated the curtain. As soon as it went down, a large man with prematurely gray hair approached them.

"My name is Welbourne Brock," he said, sticking out his hand and shaking with the three Marines. To that point the trio had only nodded occasionally at Nast's men, not sure how much contact they were allowed with them. "Want to join us at poker? My partner," he nodded toward where the game had stalled, "is gonna get some shut-eye. Six hands should be interesting."

Pasquin remembered that Nast had told him not to use the Havanagas money if he played cards, so that must mean if he used his own money it'd be okay. "Why not?" he asked the others, and they nodded eagerly. Introductions were made all around as they took their seats. "Are you guys from the Bureau of Investigation, or whatever it's called?" Pasquin asked.

"Nah," Brock answered. "Mr. Nast recruited us from all over the Confederation. Nast personally interceded with our departments to spring each of us for this mission. Most of us have seen service in the army or the Marines. Now we're just beat cops with training in special weapons and tactics. I'm from the Fairfax County, Virginia, PD, for instance."

"Hey!" Dean exclaimed. "We were on a troop ship named *Fairfax County*! Remember, guys? Whatever happened that they named a starship after the place where you live, I wonder?"

Brock shrugged. "Not much ever happened there. Oh, back during the First American Civil War there was some activity. That's where Mosby, the Confederate Ranger, pulled off one of his most famous and daring raids. Captured a Union general right in town and got clean away." The Marines looked at him blankly. "Never heard of that, huh?" Brock shrugged. "I'm a First American Civil War buff, you know? I have one of those detector machines that gives you a three-dimensional image of what's buried in the ground? In my off-duty time I go out and dig up relics. You ought to see my collection of bullets and buckles and buttons, hundreds of years old . . ." He shrugged again, seeing that his guests apparently were not interested in his hobby. "Well, we don't even know yet what we're supposed to do or where," he continued, bringing himself back to the present. "All we know is that it's absolutely top secret and after we leave Renner's World, Nast is going to brief us. How 'bout you Marines? You're going under deep cover, aren't you?" Brock said, more a statement than a question. They did not answer. "Been there, done that." Brock sighed. "This whole operation, all the secrecy, breathes of a really important undercover job."

"That's what it is," Nast said, laying a hand on Brock's shoulder. He had come up on them without being noticed. "Don't take these lads for too much, Welbourne," he went on. "Pasquin, don't forget, first thing after chow." He laughed at that. Their compartment was so small a man could throw a spitball from one bulkhead to the other.

"How'd he sneak up on us like that?" one of the officers asked after Nast had returned to his corner.

"Well, I guess that's one reason he's still alive," Pasquin said. Brock, realizing the corporal knew more about Nast than he was letting on, looked up at him sharply. "Deal 'em!" Pasquin shouted, rubbing his hands together eagerly.

He lost.

"All these guys here"—Nast indicated the other men in the crowded compartment outside his privacy screen—"I recruited because I can't trust anyone in the Ministry of Justice. It's been penetrated by the Havanagas mob." He told them briefly about the attempted assassination of him and Long. "They know something is up." He told them about the agents he'd lost on Havanagas. "I have two still there. One is your contact. The other," he smiled, "is my ace in the hole, and nobody knows the person's identity but me. If things go according to plan, you never will either.

"All right, in brief, here's the situation on Havanagas. Some years ago two of the biggest crime families in the Confederation pooled their resources and literally took over the planet they now call Havanagas. Those were the Draya and Ferris families. They did it by degrees, moving in slowly, buying up and developing real estate, buying local officials. Before the original inhabitants were aware of it, the families owned everything. Many of the people who live there now are employees of these two families, as are the descendants of the original settlers, and for the most part their businesses are legitimate. But Havanagas is merely a secure base these families use to run their enterprises throughout Human Space. They are into everything and they are everywhere. Oh, there's been resistance to the takeover, but the mob rules by crushing opposition ruthlessly. Still, there's a tiny resistance movement on Havanagas, but I'm not into politics and the resistance won't count in any of this.

"Anyway, the mob's made Havanagas a keyword in tourism and entertainment. That's legit. I don't want to interfere with that. But I do want to shut these families down by taking their leaders. I can get the evidence I need to stick them away forever, but I've got to get it off Havanagas. That's where you guys come in."

"Why not just snatch them and send them off to Darkside, like you did with those—ah hell, you know what I mean." Claypoole was referring to the pirates they captured on Avionia.

"I will," Nast answered. "But I've got to have the evidence to back me up on it."

"Why do you need us to get it?" Pasquin asked.

"My remaining agents have survived so far because they've never made any direct attempt to contact me or get anything off the planet."

"Then how do you know they've got anything you need?" Pasquin asked.

Nast smiled and nodded at the corporal. "I knew you were a sharp one, Pasquin. Well, one has managed to contact me using a very roundabout method, so I know what I need is in their hands. But I'm telling you, the families believe in security, and their security works on Havanagas. Nobody gets off the planet without a full-body scan. The same for their luggage. Be surprised how many towels and ashtrays the tourists try to steal in a year. But you three should be beyond suspicion."

"I trust you, sir, but what if we're compromised? What if something goes wrong? Something unforeseen?" Dean asked.

Nast shrugged. "I won't dukshit around: they'll kill you." He told them about Special Agent Woods. "But that won't happen to you."

"Jezu!" Dean shuddered. "We went up against those raptors on Wanderjahr!"

"Yeah," Claypoole said, "but they weren't hamstrung. Put me in the ring with one of them, and swish!" He made as if brandishing a blade. Dean looked at him unbelievingly.

"They get me in there," Pasquin said, "and I'm pullin' a Woods myself."

"They won't get you," Nast emphasized. "And if things do go bad, I won't be far away."

"Uh, how far away would that be, sir?" Pasquin asked.

"A matter of minutes. I've selected a landing site not too far from Placetas, where I can set up a secure base. We've got a stealth suite that should defeat any electronic detection system they have on Havanagas."

"How far is that?" Pasquin asked.

"You don't need to know." Nast smiled tightly. "The less you know about what I'm up to the better. If things go bad and you are taken, they will torture you. If they apply the full suite of horrors, you'll tell them everything. But I emphasize again, they aren't going to get you."

"How will we contact you, sir?" Claypoole asked.

Nast handed each man an electronic bookreader.

"Bookreaders?" Dean exclaimed. He looked at Nast and shook his head. "I don't understand, Mr. Nast."

"Look in the index. What books do you have on them?"

"Well, there's—ah! *The Soldier's Prize,* and wow! *Knives in the Night!* Two military classics! I've read both of them several times, Mr. Nast!" Claypoole exclaimed happily.

"Okay. Open *Knives* and find the words *chieu hoi*." They did. "Now, highlight that word and open the thesaurus." Immediately a high-pitched pinging noise sounded in the tiny space. Nast took a tiny device out of his pocket and shut the pinging off. "This is a radio receiver. Those," he pointed to the readers, "are transmitters. If for some reason the transmissions are monitored, it won't make any difference because we'll be coming in too fast for them to react, even if they figure out what the signal means, and they won't, I assure you. We will be monitoring this one around the clock. Clever, eh?"

"So it'll be just some minutes before you arrive?" Dean looked dubious.

"Ten or fifteen at the most." Seeing the anxious looks on

the Marines' faces, Nast went on quickly, "Hey! You guys can do that standing on your heads! The message comes in you've got the evidence, my guys swoop down on your location and I pick you up. I home in on the readers, you see?"

"Yeah, yeah," Pasquin said quickly. "It'll work just fine."

"Oh, boy, are we in the shit!" Claypoole sighed as soon as they were back in their corner with the privacy screens up.

"It could be worse," Dean offered. "Hey, we're going to Havanagas, we got plenty of money, and we got three full days on the ground there before we contact this guy, Lovat Culloden, Chief of Security for the city of—"

"Placetas," Claypoole said. Placetas was the main port of entry for Havanagas. Tourists went through customs there before moving on to one of the ten fantasy worlds of their choice in other cities situated throughout the planet. Placetas served as the seat of what government there was on Havanagas. While not a theme world itself, in Placetas every kind of vice and pleasure known to man was available. Many tourists never had to leave it.

"And don't forget, we got a neat trip on the *Ben Gay* from Renner's World to Havanagas! One of the finest luxury starships in all of Human Space, and we're ridin' free of charge," Dean reminded them. Their tickets showed them booked from Thorsfinni's World to New Serengeti and from there to Renner's World, the last stop before Havanagas. The trip from Renner's World would take about a week.

"So on the third day in Placetas we meet this guy, Culloden, at the Free Library. Who in the name of the Seven Hells ever heard of a whorehouse with a goddamn library—a real library—in it? Marines in a whorehouse, I can see that, but a freaking library?" Pasquin laughed.

"We go in drunk, Raoul," Dean reminded him. "We sort of wander in at sixteen hours on the third day and raise some hell. We send the message and fifteen minutes later Nast picks us up and we go back to 34th FIST having gotten laid seventeen times and our bank accounts overflowing!"

"Oh, it's brilliant, freaking brilliant," Claypoole exclaimed. "It's so complicated and screwed up it can't help but work perfectly. No, I'm not kidding. Who'd ever believe it was a setup and we're the drop-off for the data Nast needs to hang everybody? I bet if you told one of them Draya or Whatsit Family screws the whole plan, he'd just laugh in your face."

"I know, I know, I know," Pasquin said. "Culloden's been showing up there on a regular basis, sampling the 'books,' looking for a prearranged contact with the right code word."

" 'Whores, fours, and one-eyed jacks!' " Claypoole shouted. "Whoever thought that one up? Ideal for a place where gambling is a prime activity. I wanna be the one to say it!"

"He shakes us down," Pasquin continued, "gives us the crystals, and we call in the cops. I think you're right, Rock. This plan is so far out it'll actually work!" He laughed and slapped Claypoole on the shoulder. "But for right now, I'm gonna find Welbourne and try to get some of my money back."

He did.

CHAPTER
ELEVEN

Brigadier Sturgeon stood in his rented room looking ruefully at the small collection of garments he'd brought to
Earth. Two sets of dress reds, one of dress whites, in the event
he had to attend some formal function, and a set of garrison
utilities. No civilian clothes, certainly nothing suitable for a
fishing expedition. He shrugged off his threatening anxiety
and concentrated on his wardrobe. Maybe he could get away
with wearing his utilities. He'd have to come up with a heavy
coat of some sort; his dress reds topcoat wasn't designed for
wear in the wild. Hell, he thought, if he had to go out and buy
a coat, he might as well buy a complete boonies outfit. He
started to reach for his topcoat when his comm unit beeped.
Who could that be? he wondered. Hardly anybody knew
where he was.

It was the B-and-B's matron. A deliveryman was at the
door with a package for him. The brigadier's signature was
required.

A moment later he was downstairs, signing for a package
the size of a valise. The address label said it was from Frederico's of Minneapolis.

"What's Frederico's?" he asked the matron when the deliveryman was gone.

She looked at the label. "Oh, it's a very fine clothing store,
sir. I believe they have the contract to clothe Marine officers."
She looked at him blandly. "You weren't expecting it?"

"I wasn't expecting anything," he said, and returned to his room with the parcel.

A note was inside the package:

I know you're equipped for evenings at the Flag Club, but you probably don't have anything to wear on the Snake River. Please accept these with the compliments of the Marine Corps.

Aguinaldo

Under the note were three shirts, two pair of trousers, three pair of cushion-soled socks, a pair of heavy, watertight boots, and a thigh-length coat. The shirts and trousers were cold-weather/all-weather, rated to zero degrees Celsius. The garments were all lightweight; they automatically compensated for the ambient air temperature, and could be comfortably worn inside a heated structure or keep their wearer warm without a coat in temperatures just cold enough to freeze water. The coat would keep him warm in arctic conditions.

Sturgeon smiled and shook his head, then reread the note. ". . . compliments of the Marine Corps," it said. General Aguinaldo must have a slush fund he could tap. Just as well he hadn't had to buy them himself, Sturgeon thought, since he wouldn't be able to take them back to Thorsfinni's World with him, and anything he bought would be money into the void. He looked at the garments again. Good quality, all of them. Hmm. Maybe he could find a way to ship them back that wouldn't cost more than the price of the garments.

A car came at 1700 hours. General Aguinaldo wasn't in it.

"Sir," said the driver, a sergeant, "the Assistant Commandant said he'd meet you at the airport."

It was a twenty minute drive to Coen Airfield, a smaller airport than Frazier International, which handled flights to North American destinations. The driver showed Sturgeon to the check-in counter, where a ticket was waiting for him, then left. Sturgeon wondered why they were flying civilian; surely there was a military installation somewhere near the Snake River, and the ACMC swung enough weight to get them a hop on a military aircraft making the flight between Trainor Military Air Station at Fargo and whatever was in Idaho. Anxiety, pretty much forgotten the past couple of hours, stabbed at him again.

Aguinaldo didn't arrive until boarding was called. When he did, he was already dressed for the wilderness. A corner of his mouth twitched upward when he saw Sturgeon in his reds. "I can't speak for you, Brigadier, but *I'm* off duty."

Sturgeon fought embarrassment. "Sorry, sir. I figured Marine general officers traveling—"

"In a civilian suborb, off on a weekend jaunt." Aguinaldo grinned and clapped him on the shoulder. "No problem, Ted. You can change in Boise. My cabin may be rustic, but it's civilized enough to have a closet where you can hang your monkey suit."

Miraculously, or so it seemed to Sturgeon, they had reserved seats together. Aguinaldo let him have the window seat—he'd made the trip often enough to have seen the landscape below many times, but it was a first for the FIST commander, and a commander always wants to observe the terrain. Not that he'd be able to see much of it; the suborb flew high, and nightfall would overtake them before Helena.

They didn't talk about anything that remotely approached the reason Sturgeon made his unprecedented visit to Earth, or anything else of a military nature on the flight. Instead, Aguinaldo kept the conversation on the pleasures of the Snake and the joys of angling. He even avoided Fargo politics and the follies of high-ranking bureaucrats. His jovial rectitude served merely to increase the unease that had been nibbling at Sturgeon since their brief meeting at noon. Sturgeon didn't even try to observe the landscape they flew over.

Aguinaldo kept up the light conversation during the two-hour drive in a rented car from the Boise airport to his cabin.

He didn't have to try hard—Sturgeon was too involved in struggling with his anxiety to try to get the Assistant Commandant of the Marine Corps to talk about something else.

They drove the last three kilometers to the cabin in silence. The last bit of road was roughly paved with gravel, and twisted and turned down a steep incline to the river. Half a kilometer beyond the bottom, with the rush of the river penetrating the soundproofing of the car, a shallow valley jutted a short distance into the mountainside. The "cabin," a one-and-a-half-story stone and log edifice, nestled against the side of the valley.

"Home away from home," Aguinaldo said when he pulled the car up in front of the cabin. "With enough of the conveniences of home that you don't think you're on a combat operation."

Inside the cabin Aguinaldo nodded, satisfied. At least one of the two calls he'd made from his car on the way to the Hexagon turned out the way he wanted. His wife hadn't been as understanding as he'd thought she'd be. She'd alternately screamed and cried about him missing the opera, and declared there was no point in her going to the opera without him. It wasn't that she wanted to see the Chang-Thorsdale work again; she'd seen it at least once too often herself. But many higher-highers, from both government and the military, were attending the opera that night, and she wanted him to be there to take the opportunity to further his career. Further his career! He had to snort at the idea. She wouldn't be mollified during the short time he'd had to talk to her. When he got home he'd have to do something nice to get back in her good graces.

But the other call, yes, to the domestic maintenance company, that went well. The cabin was clean and already warmed, and a quick inspection showed it to be in good repair and properly stocked. He made the inspection under the guise of showing Sturgeon around. The ground floor rooms were large. The living room could easily accommodate fifteen or more people with seating, more than twice that if they stood about. Adjoining in the front of the cabin was a dining room that wasn't crowded by a table large enough to seat a dozen. Behind it was a kitchen.

"Fully equipped and partly automated," Aguinaldo said. "We can punch up breakfast and a lunch to go, then do our own cooking with the fish we catch for dinner," he said proudly.

The master bedroom, complete with its own bathroom, occupied the final corner of the floor. Another bathroom was under the staircase to the upper level, where there were two bedrooms, each with its own bath, and a half bath off the short corridor, "In case we're hosting a party and the one on the first floor is busy."

They put their luggage, just one bag apiece, in their rooms, and had the kitchen make a quick dinner for them. Then Aguinaldo said, "Ted, I know it's still early, but it's been a long day and it gets late early up here. Besides, I want us to get an early start fishing tomorrow. So it's rack time for me." Aguinaldo held out his hand to shake, then went into the master bedroom and closed the door without another word.

Sturgeon stood in the middle of the kitchen where they'd eaten at a small table and hung his head. He seemed no closer to knowing why his men weren't getting rotated than he had when he left Thorsfinni's World. The way Aguinaldo had been acting, they were on no more than a weekend fishing expedition. Was he to get *no* answers? He fought and knocked down his anxiety, then slowly made his way to the second floor. Once in the bedroom, he felt that it really did get late early up here and undressed and got into bed. He tossed and turned for what seemed like half the night, but the muted rumbling of the river eventually soothed him, and then he fell asleep.

Sturgeon was jolted awake by the age-old barracks call, "Reveille, reveille, reveille! Drop your cocks and grab your socks!" bellowing up the stairway. He groaned as he brushed the covers off and rolled into a sitting position on the side of his bed. He felt the cold of the wood floor through the small rug under his feet. He turned bleary eyes toward the window, saw it was still dark outside, and groaned again.

"You awake up there?" Aguinaldo shouted.

"I'm awake," Sturgeon called back, his voice already strong.

"Hit the head, I'll have breakfast ready in fifteen minutes."

Sturgeon couldn't hold back a grin. Fifteen minutes, the amount of time he had for head calls in Boot Camp all those years ago. He wondered if he could still make a head call in fifteen minutes. A body in its late fifties took a lot longer to cleanse itself than a body in its early twenties did. And then he'd still have to get dressed.

It took him nineteen minutes.

Breakfast was on the table in the kitchen. A plate with Canadian bacon and over-easy eggs, still steaming from the food servo, waited for him. A mug of hot coffee stood next to the plate, along with a glass of what could only be real orange juice.

Aguinaldo was already digging in. He swallowed a mouthful with a gulp of coffee and said, "I can order up sourdough flapjacks with real maple syrup if you prefer."

Sturgeon cocked a disbelieving eyebrow at him. He'd encountered sourdough flapjacks and maple syrup in his American history studies, but had no idea anybody still made them. "Really?"

"Really." Aguinaldo shoveled another forkful of breakfast into his mouth and masticated while looking a challenge at Sturgeon.

The sight and smell of the food and coffee suddenly got to Sturgeon. His stomach rumbled and saliva flowed. Lunch and dinner the day before had been light. Abruptly, he was ravenous. "How about both?"

Aguinaldo swallowed. "You got it." He turned to the servo and gave instructions.

Both men wolfed, but the servo still served up two plates of flapjacks before they finished the first course. They ate in silence, relishing that the taste of the food was somehow much better than the same meal would have been in the city—or even in a flag mess on base.

No sooner did they finish eating than the servo *pinged* and offered up a package and a large jug.

"Lunch and enough coffee to last us until mid-afternoon," Aguinaldo said, standing. He handed the jug to Sturgeon and took the lunch parcel himself. "I've already got the fishing gear stowed in the car. It's warm enough that we won't need our coats until this evening. Let's march."

A couple of kilometers upstream the river widened out and made a quiet pool amid a jumble of boulders. They got into their waders, took the rods Aguinaldo had ready, and their other gear, and waded into the water.

Even as inexperienced as he was with fishing, Sturgeon thought Aguinaldo led them into a piece of river running too fast for fishing.

"Lousy place to catch fish," Aguinaldo said over the roar of nearby white water, confirming what Sturgeon had thought, "but a great place to talk without our voices being picked up by listening devices." He cast his line and began fishing.

That startled Sturgeon. Listening devices? Why would anybody want to eavesdrop on them?

"I came up with some interesting information. It seems to be classified so far beyond ultrasecret, it must be rated 'kill your source before he tells you this.' Ted, at least pretend like you're fishing."

"Why would anybody want to watch us?" Sturgeon asked as he made an awkward cast.

"Maybe nobody is, but I'd rather not take any chances." Aguinaldo snorted. "*Chances.* Just meeting privately with you is taking a chance." He slowly reeled his line in, giving it an occasional jerk. He cast again. "You stumbled onto something even the Commandant himself isn't authorized to know."

Sturgeon pretended to concentrate on his fishing rod, but his mind was roiling.

"You know an army general by the name of Cazombi." It was a statement, not a question. Sturgeon flinched but didn't reply. "He's one of a very small handful of people in the military authorized to know a certain secret." He reeled in and cast into the shadow of a boulder. "It's a secret not you, not me, not even the Commandant is cleared for. Only the Chairman and one other member of the Combined Chiefs are cleared for it. Cazombi told you part of the secret."

Sturgeon remembered. The information Major General Cazombi told him following Company L's recent deployment to Avionia had to do with alien sentiences—Cazombi had been in overall command of that mission. Twice, elements of 34th FIST had encountered intelligent aliens. Company L on Avionia and, before that, Company L's third platoon on the research planet Society 437. Sturgeon wasn't supposed to know about those encounters, but Cazombi had risked his career to tell him in the belief that a commander has the absolute right to know what his people do. The army general had told him and his top people—and sworn them to absolute secrecy. Illegitimate possession of that knowledge could get them condemned to life on the penal colony Darkside.

"There's more?" he asked.

Aguinaldo barked a bitter laugh. "A lot more, Ted." He cast again. "You know, if someone is observing us, they'll notice you're just standing there while the current drags your line downstream. Do what I'm doing." He gave his fishing rod a jerk and reeled in a bit of line.

Sturgeon did his best to mimic him, saw his line had trailed far downstream, reeled it in and recast.

"Don't worry too much about watchers, I'm probably just being paranoid. But I've encountered so many startling

things over the past two days, not to mention a level of secrecy I've never even heard of, I'm seeing shadows.

"Damn!" He jerked on his line, but it was snagged. Mut-
tering to himself, he started wading toward where the fly was
stuck, reeling in the line as he went. When he reached the fly,
he probed underwater for it. In a moment it was free, and he
waded back with the object it caught on in his hand.

"People used to be awful careless," he said as he showed
the shapeless, faintly milky object to Sturgeon.

Sturgeon looked at it, concerned. Was it some sort of disguised listening device?

"If it wasn't in such lousy shape, this would be a museum
piece. If it wasn't isolated in the river, an archeologist would
wet himself over it."

Startled, Sturgeon looked at him. "What is it?"

"A plastic beverage container." He looked upstream. "Centuries ago, someone on a hiking or fishing trip finished his
drink and discarded the container. Over the centuries, it got
washed into the river and eventually lodged under the edge of
that boulder." He looked at it again. "It probably got lodged
more than once. Otherwise it would have reached the Pacific
Ocean a long time ago. Come on. I'm not paying enough attention to what I'm doing if I let my fly get hooked on a piece
of flotsam caught under a boulder." He waded toward the
river bank. "And let's dispose of this properly."

Aguinaldo stowed the ancient soda bottle in the car's rub-
bish compartment and got out the coffee jug and two mugs.
He picked a flat rock for them to sit on and poured. While
Sturgeon took a first sip, Aguinaldo withdrew what looked
like a miniature emergency radio transceiver from his shirt
pocket. Sturgeon asked.

"It *is* an emergency transceiver." Aguinaldo set it to the
weather band. "It's also a white noise generator." He pressed a
button on the transceiver's side. "This should keep any snoop-
ing devices from picking up our voices. It's more obvious if
we're under observation, but we can always claim we're dis-

cussing classified subjects and wanted to block any casual eavesdroppers." He laughed. "And that's the absolute truth."

"So what else is there? And how'd you find out?"

Aguinaldo studied him for a long moment, then said slowly, "I'm the Assistant Commandant. To answer your second question, one doesn't reach this high without making powerful friends and doing favors along the way. There're a remarkable number of people who owe me. I called in some favors." He laughed at Sturgeon's pained expression. "Don't worry, I didn't call in favors from anyone who only owed me one. There are as many people in my debt today as there were before you arrived in Fargo." He sat erect, as though coming to a decision.

"The 'skinks,' as some of your Marines called them, and the Avionians aren't the only alien sentiences out there. There are at least a half-dozen others within or near Human Space. None of them seem to be technologically superior to us. Most of them are relatively primitive, like the Avionians. It's pure happenstance that it was an element of 34th FIST that was the first military unit to encounter hostile aliens. Or at least the first to live to tell the tale." He solemnly shook his head. "It's not positive, but fairly certain, that a few small military units or other groups of humans have encountered hostile aliens and been wiped out."

"That's startling," Sturgeon said in what he knew was a gross understatement, "sentient aliens. But what does it have to do with my Marines not getting routine rotation orders?"

"Your Marines were the first military unit to survive what was once called a 'close encounter of the third kind,' one where actual face-to-whatever contact is made between humans and aliens. Because of that, 34th FIST has been designated as the official alien-encounter force."

Sturgeon's eyes widened. "Why haven't I been told?"

Aguinaldo shrugged. "Because the existence of sentient aliens is a state secret. Nobody's supposed to know about the existence of sentient aliens—including you and everyone else in your command who hasn't personally encountered them. In order to hold the secret as close as possible, no one from 34th FIST is to be transferred to another unit. Everyone has been involuntarily extended for 'the duration.' Nobody in 34th FIST will be transferred, released from active duty, or placed on the retired roster until further notice." He grimaced. "Or until the politicians stop being so scared of little green men and change their policy."

He sighed. "On the bright side for you, you're going to remain in the most coveted position in the Marine Corps—in command of a FIST. And, bluntly, you weren't going to be promoted anyway." He gave the brigadier a gentle smile. "You've made more enemies than friends along the way, my friend. And I'm sorry to say I made some of them for you on Diamunde." He shook his head ruefully. "All my talk of making friends.

"I made some powerful enemies for myself on Diamunde when Admiral Wimbush relieved General Han and replaced him with me. Then I made even more enemies when I replaced his Corps commanders with Marines." He looked Sturgeon in the eye. "Do you know that the army high command mounted a campaign to block my appointment as ACMC? They did. But they took too long to get organized and I was already in the billet by the time they fired their first salvo." He shrugged. "In my case, it doesn't matter. This is a terminal assignment; ACMC never gets promoted to Commandant, so the only place up for me is Chairman of the Combined Chiefs, and you know the army and navy will never accept a Marine as chairman." He snorted and shook his head again, remembering his wife's concern about his "career advancement" the day before.

Then he sighed. "Even though they were too late to block my appointment, the army high command made it quite clear that they would take it very badly if any of the Marines placed in command of higher ranking army generals on Diamunde were subsequently promoted. I'm truly sorry, Ted."

Sturgeon shook it off; just now he was dealing with bigger problems than when or whether he'd next be promoted.

"Anyway, that's the big secret," Aguinaldo continued. "Thirty-fourth FIST is the designated alien encounter force. Everyone in it is there for the duration. Death or permanently crippling injury is the only way out." His expression turned angry. "There's even talk of quarantining Thorsfinni's World just in case any of your Marines leaks the word out to the civilians."

"Quarantine Thorsfinni's World? That's unconscionable!"

"People have used many terms to describe the Confederation in the generations since it was founded. 'Benevolent' has rarely been one of them."

"But to hold secret the knowledge of sentient aliens, and quarantine an entire civilized world to keep the knowledge secret . . ."

" 'Humane' is also a term seldom used to describe government policymakers."

"To think we serve them," Sturgeon said, momentarily disgusted with himself and what he'd spent his life doing.

"We don't only serve the government, we help people too. Sometimes we even protect them from the government."

Sturgeon looked away.

"Look at what your FIST has done in the past few years. You defeated a murderous power structure on Elneal and helped destroy a rapacious government on Diamunde. And how you changed the government on Wanderjahr was nothing short of splendid. One of your companies even prevented the disruption of the development of an alien sentience, which disruption would have had unimaginable consequences. Yes, we do the Confederation's bidding—and we do good wherever the opportunity arises along the way."

"But—"

"No buts. We are Marines. It's our job to fight and to kill. It's in our nature to protect and to help. We do both."

For long moments they sat in silence broken only by the

river running past. Then Sturgeon said, "I have to tell my Marines what's being done to them."

"Not yet." Aguinaldo shook his head.

"Some of my Marines are a year overdue for rotation. I have to tell them."

"I'm still owed favors and still have influence—despite my enemies," Aguinaldo said. "I agree with you that the policy is wrong. Tell your Marines that you've got the Assistant Commandant of the Marine Corps working on the problem and that he'll get it fixed."

Sturgeon looked intently at him. "You can fix it?"

"I'll do my absolute best." There was another moment of silence, then Aguinaldo said, "One more thing. There's a corporal, a clerk, name of Doyle. You shipped him out when he returned from Avionia."

"Doyle. Oh, yes. It was part of a settlement. General Cazombi wanted to give him a medal for coming up with the way to make the Tweed Hull Breecher work. His company first sergeant wanted to court-martial him for insubordination. No medal, no court-martial, and a transfer. His tour was almost up anyway."

"He's been interdicted; he falls under the no-transfer policy. He's being held in solitary confinement at HQMC. You have to take him back with you."

After that there wasn't anything else to say on the subject. They went back into the river and caught enough fish for dinner and the next morning's breakfast, after which they returned to Fargo. Corporal Doyle was handed over to Brigadier Sturgeon and they caught a ride on a navy starship headed in the general direction of Thorsfinni's World.

But one thing kept nagging at 34th FIST's commander: General Aguinaldo had said he'd do his best to change the policy. The Marines lived by an ancient adage: *Don't try it. Don't do your best. Do it.*

CHAPTER
TWELVE

It was raining in Placetas when the three Marines smoothly departed the *Ben Gay*. All arrivals in the capital city were required to process through Havanagas Intourist, an official travel agency and customs service. Over six hundred passengers got off the *Ben Gay*, and while they were waiting to have their reservations and baggage checked, two more ships landed, with another thousand tourists each.

"This is not a busy day for us," a customs inspector remarked casually as he conducted a perfunctory scan of their luggage. The Intourist operation was very efficient. Each arrival's ticket was checked and he was booked onto a suborbital flight to whatever theme city was reserved for him. Since the Marines were scheduled to spend their stay in Placetas, hotel reservations had been made for them in advance.

The Intourist reception area was enormous, almost the size of a small city. The departure areas were also crowded with hundreds of happy tourists lugging bags of mementos and souvenirs, waiting patiently for flights home. The air was charged with the exciting sound of announcements for flights, people being paged, the muted roar of several thousand persons all talking at once.

Claypoole glanced at the dome a hundred meters over their heads. "Look at the rain," he muttered. "Does it rain like this often?"

"You bet," the customs agent responded. "In this hemisphere in this season it rains all the time. Most of the people

who come here this time of the year get reservations for an
onward flight to one of the theme cities where the weather is
better."

"We didn't know," Pasquin said.

"Well, according to your tickets, you have that option if
you would like to go somewhere else before your week is up.
Just contact the reservations desk over there if you'd like to
visit another city on Havanagas. Shame to spend all that
money and then just stick around here for a week."

"Ugh. I hate rain." Claypoole made a face.

The customs agent looked up from his scanner as Dean's
luggage went through. "I would think you boys'd be used to
rain, after your time in the Corps."

For some reason Claypoole saw this remark as a criticism.
"Hey, buddy," he almost shouted, "I got more time in the rain
than you got—"

"Okay, okay, Rachman, let's get moving," Pasquin interrupted. "We gotta a lot of beer to drink and ladies to visit."

"—on the shitter," Claypoole muttered as Pasquin guided
him toward the reservations desk.

The ticket agent was very young and very pretty. Claypoole's attitude improved instantly. "You gentlemen don't want
to visit one of our theme cities?" she asked as she checked
their tickets and made entries on her computer.

"No, ma'am, we're planning on spending our time right
here, rain or not."

"As you wish. But you can change your venue anytime you
like. You have a special option that gives you free choice of
any of our theme cities. You can fly out anytime until your
stay is up. Here, take these crystals and see if any of our other
facilities interest you." She looked at them speculatively.
"That's a very expensive option. You must've saved for a long
time to make this trip." She smiled.

"We sure did," Dean answered. "I saved my whole enlistment. Of course, if you knew some of the places the Corps

has sent us, you'd know we didn't have much opportunity to spend our pay." They all laughed.

"Miss, we'd like to change into civvies," Pasquin said. "How do we get to our hotel?"

"Go down the red ramp to Concourse A for ground transportation. You're booked into a double room at the Royal Frogmore, a five-star hotel, gentlemen. Just wait at the Frogmore platform, it's clearly marked, and a landcar will take you there. Enjoy your stay." She returned their tickets.

The Royal Frogmore was indeed a posh hotel. "I could live like this all the time," Claypoole exclaimed as he tested the bed.

"We got one week, Rachman, so better enjoy all this while you can," Dean said.

"Let's take a look at these crystals the lady gave us, get an idea of what's available. Hey, who knows? Maybe we'll up and visit one of them theme cities," Pasquin suggested.

"Not me, Raoul," Dean said from his bed, where he was stretched out comfortably. "All I want to do is get some first-class booze, play some cards, and hire me a fine lady for a night or two."

There were a dozen theme cities on Havanagas. The ones that interested the Marines the most were the Polynesian and Ancient Roman venues, but there was also the theme city of the ancient Greeks, where the battle of Marathon was reenacted once a week; and Europe in the Middle Ages, with sword fights in the streets and monumental royal feasts. "I wonder if they have the Black Plague too," Dean mused sourly.

"I sorta like this Raratonga, with them little brown women dancing hulas and everyone down to his drawers and eating roast pig on the seashore," Pasquin said.

"Rome's the place for me," Claypoole said. "Gladiators, Roman legionnaires and senators, pizza, Chianti, and all that stuff."

"Yeah," Dean said sourly, "and that's where—" He almost said Agent Woods was murdered, but caught himself at the last instant. "—they feed Christians to the lions every Sunday." Pasquin looked at him sharply and shook his head briefly. Dean resolved to be more careful in the future.

They reviewed the crystals on their readers. Placetas had a permanent population of about thirty thousand. During the tourist season this increased to over 100,000, but it was an off season, as the customs man had told them. Few people lived permanently in the downtown area. Small suburban enclaves dotted around the outskirts of the city contained housing areas where the residents conducted their private lives in relative comfort. Nast had told them that the majority of permanent residents on Havanagas was quite happy there; the mob took care of its own. The only dissatisfied elements in the population were the descendants of the original settlers, but even they were forced to make their living off the tourists, and if it weren't for the mob, there'd be no tourism on Havanagas.

Placetas abounded with good restaurants, casinos, bordellos, theaters, every other form of amusement known to man, but it had no exotic theme parks. Its places of entertainment were just straightforward business enterprises that catered to every human desire in its infinite variety.

"There's this casino right down the street from the Frogmore," Dean said. "I'm heading on down there, see if I can find an honest game of blackjack, Raoul." He winked at Claypoole.

"Well, shouldn't we stick together? At least have dinner together before we split up? Hell, I thought we was buddies," Claypoole said.

"We've been stuck together for years in the Corps and on the trip out here," Dean answered. "I want one freakin' night to myself, if you don't mind."

"Okay," Pasquin said, "whatever. Let's meet back here tomorrow morning for breakfast and then we can plan the rest of our time." He nodded knowingly at the other two, tacitly reminding them that they had three days on their own before they were to make contact with Culloden.

The name of the casino was The Suicide King, and its logo was a huge king of hearts, the king with the sword thrust behind his head, thus the sobriquet "suicide." The restaurant there was excellent, even Reindeer Ale was available on tap. Wanderjahrian thule was also available, and Dean smoked several cigarettes with his after dinner steak—steak from real cows, the first he'd had since leaving Earth to join the Corps. The steak was huge and juicy, fully as savory as the reindeer steaks served on Thorsfinni's World. Puffing on a huge Fidel, he wandered over to the blackjack table.

The dealer, a young woman with long, delicate fingers, was playing solitaire when Dean came up to her table.

"Hi," she said, "my name is Tara. Would you like to play?" She held out her hand and Dean took it and squeezed lightly.

"Sure. My name is Joe. What's the bet?"

"Whatever you can afford. The house will cover any bet you wish to make."

"Slow night?" Dean asked as he took a seat opposite Tara.

Her face colored slightly and she smiled. "This is the off season. You're my first customer of the day." It was already way past eight P.M. Tara broke out a new deck and they played for an hour.

"When do you get off duty?"

"Midnight. The casino closes at midnight this time of the year. Why?"

Dean shrugged. "I came here with two friends, we just got out of the Marines. They're off on their own tonight. I wanted to ask you to dinner with me . . ."

Tara looked up at Dean speculatively. He noticed her eyes were dark green. "Sure. Why not? Oh, they call me Fingers around here, 'cause I'm such a good dealer." She held up her long, delicate fingers and smiled.

"Thanks, Tara, er, Fingers. But look, I'm going over to the poker table for a while; you're too good for me." He laughed and gathered up his chips. "See you at midnight."

Pasquin looked into Giselda's warm brown eyes. They'd been smoking thule, laughing, talking, telling each other their life's stories. Giselda was one of the most beautiful whores Pasquin had ever imagined. Her long auburn hair perfectly complemented the delicate bones of her face. Her breasts bulged invitingly, and when she crossed and uncrossed her sinuously long legs the movement jolted his heart. Her hand was cool, soft and delicate, nails perfectly manicured. All in all, Giselda was a very classy escort.

"They call me Jizzy," she'd announced when Pasquin asked if he could sit in her booth. Pasquin smiled.

They kissed passionately. Pasquin slid a hand inside her blouse. My God! he thought. Wonderful endowments! She leaned back in the booth. He reached inside her skirt and gently massaged her thigh.

"Uh, um . . ." Pasquin sat up quickly and slid to the end of the booth.

Giselda straightened her clothes and sighed. "You know," she said mournfully, "I can still show you a good time if you'd only—"

"Ah, no, no. No thanks, Jizzy. I guess I made a mistake." Pasquin's face had turned a deep red. Nervously he glanced around the bar to see if anyone had noticed. No one had. The few other patrons were too deeply engaged in their own conversations to take note.

"Well, thanks, Jizzy. Thanks all the same." Pasquin shuffled some banknotes onto the table. "Sorry to take up your time like this. See you around." He got up to leave.

"You know where to find me, honey, if you should change your mind," Giselda said, stuffing the notes into her bra.

Fat fucking chance! Pasquin thought as he stomped out of the bar. He walked in a driving rain all the way back to the

Royal Frogmore and straight into the lounge, where he ordered a triple whiskey on the rocks. Goddamn! he thought as he swished the raw whiskey around in his mouth. First night on the town, pockets full of dough, a dozen whorehouses within a block, and I gotta pick—He cursed long and terribly.

In the dark, in his bed waiting for the others to come back, Pasquin laughed at long last. Buddha's blue busted balls, he thought. From the waist up she was perfect!

It was not yet light when Tara rolled over and kissed Dean. "Joe?" She shook him gently. "Joe?"

"Um, ah?"

"Joe, wake up and get dressed. There's a shuttle flight to Rome in one hour. We can be there by lunchtime and back here tomorrow before noon."

"What are you talking about? I gotta meet my buddies for breakfast—"

"Joe, I'm off today. You've got an open ticket. You've paid for the trip even if you don't take it. I can fly free as a casino employee. You can be back here by noon tomorrow. Call the Frogmore and tell your friends you're taking me to Rome."

Dean hesitated a moment before placing the call.

Dean was both frightened and excited to be sitting in the Coliseum. He was very much aware that it was where Special Agent Woods had met a terrible death. But the gladiator contests he was watching were just very well-staged dramas, though unbelievably realistic.

Tara pointed to the emperor's box at the opposite side of the arena. It was full. "That fat man sitting in the middle is Noto, head of the Draya Family," she said. Dean wished he had a blaster; he could have ended the careers of the Havanagas families very quickly.

The crowd thundered approval as the gladiators slashed and cast at each other. The action in the arena was furious. The clash of alloy and steel reverberated throughout the arena.

From where he was sitting, Dean heard the heavy breathing of the contestants as they flung themselves at one another. He impulsively inserted his credit card into the slot provided. "Fifty on the guy with the red hair," he said. The machine confirmed the bet and returned his card and a receipt. The odds were printed on the back of the receipt. Dean raised an eyebrow. Six-to-one against the guy with the red hair. He'd have a pile if his man won. He looked at the clock. The betting was over. The odds would stay the same until the fight was decided.

Tara quivered with excitement beside him. A thin rivulet of perspiration coursed down the side of her face. Her fists were clutched so tightly her whole body was shaking. Her full attention was riveted on the fight below where they sat. Dean leaned back in his seat. These people take this crap seriously, he told himself. And here I am, betting on it! he chided himself.

The red-haired gladiator's opponent was down. "Mohammed H. Christ, I've won!" Dean was exultant, but the crowd was on its feet, roaring for blood. Dean stood so he could see what was going to happen. He looked around the crowd. Everyone was screaming and gesturing thumbs-down. Suddenly, Lance Corporal Joseph F. Dean, Confederation Marine Corps, was pissed off. None of those foolish people had ever killed a man, much less seen men really die, and there they were, screaming for blood. "Fuck you! Fuck you!" he shouted and thrust both thumbs upward. Nobody seemed to notice. The red-haired gladiator looked up at the emperor's box, nodded once and plunged his sword into his opponent's stomach.

The crowd quieted down immediately as the "corpse" was unceremoniously dragged out of the arena.

"Whew!" Tara exclaimed from beside him, fanning herself with a program. "Boy, that was some fight, huh? And Joe, you won! You won!" She leaned over and kissed him. "What's wrong, honey, you don't look very happy?"

"Nothing. It's just I've never seen people act like this before." He told her what he'd done on places like Elneal and Diamunde. "I mean, this is so damned real." In fact, it was real, for some people, like Agent Woods.

"Well, we all know it's not for real, honey. It's like watching a trid, you know? Where you can be part of the action? People have been enjoying spectacles like this for years."

"It's not that, Tara. This is not like that. It's the way the spectators acted. In the trids and vids it's always the good guys who win, so you got something to root for, but here, these people don't really care who wins, so long as someone loses."

"Settle down, Joe! After this is over we'll all go back to being normal again. With what you've won we can really enjoy ourselves tonight. And look at the program: next up is Christians and lions!"

Claypoole went into the first bar he could find and ordered a beer. He had just begun sipping the golden brew—these people know their beers, he reflected, because Reindeer Ale is available on tap!—when a shapely, dark-skinned woman sat down beside him. She held out her hand. "Hi, my name is Katie Wells and I'm a whore! Katie's not my real name; that's Keren Begemdir, but I heard an old song once about a girl who died young, Katie Wells, and I liked that name."

Claypoole almost choked on his beer but he took her hand and managed to get his own name out. "Claypoole is my name, miss. Rachman Claypoole. Call me Rock."

"Need someone for tonight?" she asked, smiling and tossing her head back. She regarded Claypoole frankly. Her approach was so sudden and straightforward, Claypoole struggled to reply, so she went on, "Cost you 150 to get me out of here early, 150 for my services and whatever entertainment we decide on afterward. I'll stay with you through breakfast tomorrow, and it'll cost you all told maybe five hundred. If you like it, I'll stick around, give you a reduced rate. Whadaya say?"

Claypoole regarded her cleavage. Nice legs too. He felt a real twinge of emotion as he realized she reminded him very much of someone he'd known a long time ago. He shrugged, but inwardly he knew she was the girl for him. How could I be so lucky? he wondered. "Okay. Sure. Who do I pay to get you out of here?"

"The bartender. Say, I could use some steak and eggs!" Katie patted her stomach as she spoke. "I know a nice place just down the street. We can eat and just make the first performance at the Biograph. You like Shakespeare?"

"Er, as in William?"

"Yeah. They're performing *Titus Andronicus* all week. One of my favorites. It was first performed in 1594, did you know that? You know the twentieth century poet, T. S. Eliot? He said it was one of the stupidest plays ever written." Katie laughed. "But I like it. It's about a guy who really gets pissed at some dirty bastards who screw him over, so he plots his revenge. Hoo boy, does he ever! You'll love it!"

"What if I don't?"

Katie shrugged. "Then screw you, Rock. We do it my way until we get back to my place. Then *you* can screw *me*." She laughed. "After the play I know a place where we can have drinks, talk a bit before we go back to my pad. Come on, let's get a move on."

During the meal Katie never shut up. She maintained a steady monologue on a variety of subjects that did not interest Claypoole in the slightest. But she was a good talker, obviously very intelligent and well-read. Idly, he wondered how she could eat so much and still maintain her figure. "I get plenty of 'exercise,' during the tourist season!" She laughed, almost as if she could read his mind.

"What happens when you get old, Katie?" Claypoole asked suddenly.

She shrugged. Around a mouthful of food she said, "Then I go out with older men. We have a retirement program here, you know? Everyone who works on Havanagas does. I figured when my tits get down to my belly button, I'm out." She laid down her fork and laughed so hard other patrons turned to look in their direction.

Claypoole couldn't help himself. He started to laugh too. They laughed until tears streamed down their cheeks.

After the play they stood on a corner waiting for a cab. "Whadja think of the play?" Katie asked.

"Well, I'm not much on plays, Katie. Sure kept my attention, though. I can still see those heads in that meat pie! God's hairy balls, I need a drink after all that cutting and slashing." Everyone in the 34th FIST knew the story of what had happened to Ensign vanden Hoyt and Professor Benjamin on Diamunde, and the grisly fate of Tamora's sons in the play came as an uncomfortable reminder of that real-life horror.

"Oooh, don't talk like that!" Katie chided him. "Bad luck to take God's name in vain. And you know, when you swear by God's parts, those parts actually hurt him?" Claypoole thought she was joking, but when he looked at her the expression on her face was serious. "Okay, I know just the place," she rattled on. "The library."

"What?" Claypoole asked sharply.

"The Free Library. It's a bordello on the other side of town. I know the girls there. The manager's been trying to recruit me for years. If we buy drinks, they'll let us sit in the parlor. They have real books they'll let us look at."

A taxi pulled up. Claypoole felt a twinge of nervousness. The library! They weren't due there until day after tomorrow. Would going early screw things up? No, he realized suddenly, just the opposite! What a break! Now, at the appointed time, he could go back there with the others and it'd look very natural. Hell, he'd just retain Katie's services for the rest of the week and she would go with them on Thursday. It was perfect.

Two huge stone mythological beasts, half animal, half human, stood beside the long flight of steps that led up to the Free Library of Placetas. Enormous brass doors with huge, highly polished handles swung wide to let them in. The foyer was all polished marble, ceilings twenty meters high. An enormous marble staircase led to the upper floors. To the right and left of the foyer were huge alcoves with shelves of books reaching from floor to ceiling. The carrels were comfortable nooks just big enough for two people, where customers met the girls and made their arrangements. Drinks—and books, the Free Library was a real library!— could be ordered from there.

"Gerry!" Katie shouted. Her voice echoed loudly in the enormous foyer.

An elderly man, beard neatly trimmed, somewhat stooped, and balding on the top of his head, smiled up at them from a reception desk. "Katie, my dear!" He stood up and they embraced warmly. "Have you changed your mind? Are you here to join my staff?"

Katie smiled warmly and tweaked Gerry's ear playfully. "Not tonight, love, just visiting. Gerry, this is Rachman. He's a retired Marine."

Gerry bowed slightly and extended his hand. "Good evening, kind sir! I am Gerry Prost, head librarian and manager of this establishment. I trust you will enjoy your evening with us. Come right this way."

Mr. Prost guided them to an empty carrel. "This is a real library, Mr. Claypoole," Prost said as he seated them. "We have some very rare volumes available. We have books that go way back to the dawn of printing, incunabula, they're called. We also have some original etchings by William Blake, the English poet. They are extremely rare. If you order anything from our rare books department you will be issued special gloves. Please wear them when handling those volumes. Otherwise, Katie knows how things work around here. Enjoy."

"Gerry's a real librarian, Rock," Katie said after Prost had left them. "He retired years and years ago and took this job here. The girls love him. He's a shrewd manager and he does not participate in what goes on upstairs. And he has single-handedly built up this wonderful collection. Do you read much?"

Claypoole shrugged. "Yes, novels and training manuals, mostly." Ooops! He was out of the Corps now! "Well, when I was in the Corps, that's what I read mostly," he added.

"What'll we have to drink?" Katie asked. She activated the computer. "We're ready to order," she said.

"I'd like a big glass of Reindeer Ale and let's smoke some thule."

"Sour mash bourbon for me, on the rocks," Katie told the computer. "And let me see the card catalog. There's a book I always love to look at whenever I come here," she said to Claypoole. "Give us the Speght *Chaucer*, please," she said after scrolling through the catalog and picking the call number.

"No drinking or smoking allowed while handling the books," the computer announced. The automated voice was that of Mr. Prost. "Please wear the gloves when you handle this volume." Obediently, they put their drinks onto sideboards.

A panel in a sidewall popped open and a metal box slid out. Katie slipped on the thin cotton gloves that came with the box and opened it. Carefully, she took out a large leather-bound volume and opened it up. On the flyleaf someone had written a long message by hand in ink. It was to "Jack" from "Dad" and dated April 12, 1931. Claypoole whistled; that was 522 years ago! His eyes fell on one line that stood out. It was in archaic English and the penmanship was difficult to decipher at first, but he puzzled it out. ". . . Chaucer 'ever ready to cheer the languor of your soul, and gild the bareness of life with treasures of bygone times'—"

"Now look at this," Katie whispered as she turned to the

title page. On the obverse of the first leaf was a full-page woodcut entitled "The Progenie of Geffrey Chaucer," and on the recto of the title page, "The Workes of Our Ancient and learned English Poet, Geffrey Chaucer, newly Printed. London, Printed by Adam Islip. An. Dom. 1602."

"This book was printed in 1602?" Claypoole asked, astonished. "Katie, this book is—is, good shit, 850 years old! I've never held any man-made thing that was this old! What do you think it's worth?" he almost whispered.

"Millions, I should think. The people who sponsor this place have money to burn. When they first hired Gerry, he went wild on acquisitions. People come from all over Human Space just to see the books he's collected, did you know that? Yes! Here, let me show you something." She turned to the prologue. "See this?" She pointed to a passage.

"What language is that written in?" Claypoole asked, peering at the strange black letters on the leaf.

Katie laughed. "It's archaic English, but what might make it difficult for you to read is that it's printed in 'black letter' type. But rendered into modern typology, you could learn to read Chaucer's English pretty easily. Here, let me read it for you:

"There was an Oxford student . . .
And he was too unworldly for employment
In some lay office. At his couch's head
His twenty volumes bound in black and red
Of Aristotle's philosophy pleased him more
Than a rich wardrobe or a gay guitar."

"Do you love books, Lance Corporal Rachman Claypoole, late of the Confederation Marine Corps?"

"Well, I—"

"I do. Oh, it sounds insincere, don't it, when a whore like me talks about love? But I think if I ever was to fall in love with any man, it'd be a man who shares my love of books. A man like Gerry Prost." She nodded toward the reception desk as she carefully put the ancient book back into its case and commanded the computer to return it to the stacks.

"Where'd you ever learn so damned much about books and plays and poets and stuff?" Claypoole asked, a tinge of wonder in his voice. He smiled. He was beginning to like the Havanagas scene. And although he would never tell Katie this—it really would sound insincere—he thought that old book a thing of surpassing beauty, even if he couldn't read it.

Katie shrugged as she peeled off the gloves; inwardly she was delighted. She'd seen how Claypoole reacted to the ancient book, and that pleased her no end. *I'm gonna give this guy a night he'll always remember.* "How'd I learn all that stuff? Well, I've got plenty of time to read in my business. Now," she settled back and stretched her legs, "let's finish our drinks and have a smoke. And then let's fuck."

CHAPTER
THIRTEEN

The Fighters grumbled among themselves, though they were careful to do their grumbling away from the hearing of the Leaders. The Masters and Leaders saw complaints as a challenge to their authority and power, and challenges were punishable by death. Normally, the Fighters kept unspoken any displeasure they felt, but this planet—

The Fighters had not been told the name of the world; they were told it was a secret. As though knowing the name of the pesthole could possibly threaten the True People, much less the Emperor. They called it the "Bog" because soldiers had to call the place where they were by some name. They did not tell the Workers they called the planet the Bog. The Workers might have grumbled among themselves, but they never did it within hearing of the Fighters. The Fighters saw grumbling by the Workers as a challenge to their superiority.

The Fighters who thought about it, few of them because Fighters were not bred to think, wondered why the Bog was so miserable. It was not that different from Home. The air was quite similar, damp and redolent with fish and vegetation. There were many swamps and much marshland. A plentitude of sluggish rivers threaded the land. There was frequent rain.

Maybe it was the rain; at Home it rained more often than not, a refreshing, cleansing rain that left one feeling rejuvenated when the sun came out so the True People could bask in its light. On the Bog, it rained all the time. They had been on the Bog for a few weeks, and there had not been a break in the rain. Sometimes the rain was little more than a mist, sometimes it was a monsoon. And it rained every way in between. Not once in the weeks they'd been on the planet had the sun broken through the solid cloud cover.

Or maybe it was the mud. There were many lush forests at Home, as there were on the Bog. But the forests at Home glittered with all the eight billion greens; they were speckled with flowers in all hues, birds sang in their branches, saplings and bushes carpeted the ground under the trees. The Bog's forests were muted in color, a few dull browns and greens, there were no flowers or birds, and only scraggly treeling-things poked up through the mud. Home had savannas with luscious green growth for browsing animals. The Bog had only small, weedy clearings in its forests and swamps.

Or it could be the animal life. The Bog was home to hideous creatures, like things out of some evildoer's nightmares. They walked on six legs, or climbed with them. They had no heads; instead their eyes were on stalks that poked out of their backs, the tops of their shoulders, and their chests. Their mouths were snouts—some long, some short, some in between—that protruded at a forward angle from their shoulders below the eyestalks. They breathed through tubed openings as far behind the shoulder eyestalks as their snouts were before them. They were brown or black or gray, the colors of the mud on which they lived. Only the fish looked natural, and they had too many eyes and fins.

One kind of animal, larger than a True Person, but not nearly as big as a Large One, walked and climbed with four of its legs and used the front pair as the True People used hands and arms. This kind of animal also used primitive tools and weapons, though it went about naked and did not build houses.

For all those reasons, perhaps, the Fighters, a hundred and more of them, were grumbling among themselves that day as they slogged through the mud. Mud spattered their legs with each step, caked their boots, seeped through the drain holes and squelched in their boots. Heavier than a drizzle, the rain pattered on them incessantly, soaked the uniforms that clung to their skin, runneled down their arms, trunks, legs, added its weight to the mud that built on their legs and feet and inside their boots. The dull colors in the forest further deflated their spirits. And they knew what awaited them at the end of the fatiguing march: a camp of the repulsive creatures that walked and climbed on four legs and had two arms. Creatures had come close to the base in the past several days since their arrival. The Masters had decided they were a nuisance that must be dealt with.

The leader and elders and other advisers stood in a circle under the spreading branches of a forest giant whose leaves diffused the heaviest rain so it fell on them delightfully. None of them bothered to step out from under the cascades of water that fell from the leaves, leaf-trapped rain that was channeled into funnels. Hunters not admitted to the circle gathered in clumps around it so they could listen. Females who were not tending young also edged close.

"Three hunters have gone out and not come back," the chief hunter said angrily, his primary eyestalks aimed rigidly at the leader. "It is past time we organized a search for them."

The leader wagged his primary eyestalks at the chief hunter, acknowledging the topic of the council he had called for, then pointed them at the eldest.

"When hunters go out alone, sometimes they do not return," the eldest said in a creaking voice. "If we search we will probably find no trace. If we do find anything, it will likely be a few scattered, broken bones."

"We must find out why they didn't return," the youngest elder interjected sharply.

The leader reached out and smacked the youngest elder between the eyestalks for speaking out of turn. The youngest elder bowed his torso low but did not point his primary eyestalks at the ground. He kept them defiantly on the leader.

"If we do not find out why they did not return, more hunters will go out and not return." One of the missing hunters was the youngest elder's younger brother, and the youngest elder was still an active hunter himself.

The leader pointed his primaries at the second oldest elder. *That* was the custom in council. The one who called it spoke first, to say why council was called, then the elders spoke in order of seniority. The leader said nothing more until all the elders had spoken.

The second oldest extended his pectoral eyestalks to look at the semiprostrate youngest. "Get up!" he snapped. He retracted his pectorals and aimed his primaries at the leader. "Both the oldest and the youngest are right. Hunters sometimes go out and do not return and cannot be found and we never know what happened. But when *three* hunters disappear in a short period of time, there is usually a reason for it, and we must deal with that reason or hunters will keep disappearing until we move to another hunting ground."

The leader wagged his primaries and looked at the third eldest. Her oldest daughter's oldest son was one of the missing hunters.

"My grandson is careful," she said in a voice so controlled it gave no indication of the anguish she felt at the loss. "He has never been injured on a hunt. He is also a careful hunter and always brings back food." She glanced at the chief hunter, who wagged his primaries in agreement. "There is a new danger out there. We must identify it before we lose more mothers' sons."

The leader acknowledged her, then turned to the next oldest, the only elder who hadn't yet spoken.

That elder retracted his primaries in reflection. When he finally spoke, he did so slowly, as though he wasn't certain his words should be said.

"During the night before the day the first missing hunter went out, I had to get up in the middle of the night." This elder was notorious for his lack of control over his excretory functions. "While I was up I heard thunder. It was not normal thunder. It did not crack or boom, it did not roll in a succession of booms. Instead it began almost too soft to hear, then slowly grew to the volume of middle-distance thunder. It stopped suddenly. I listened, but there was no more. I decided a storm did not threaten, so I returned to my nest and went back to sleep." He paused for so long the leader thought he was finished and began to speak. But the fourth eldest flicked up a limb to indicate he wasn't through and resumed speaking. "There was something strange about that thunder. It wasn't all in one place. It sounded," his primaries darted down in embarrassment, everyone knew his hearing was failing, "like it began very high in the sky and came closer to the ground as it got louder." He paused again, but resumed before the leader opened his mouth. "It was in the same direction the first hunter went in."

When it was obvious he was through, the leader looked at the youngest elder.

"I have said what I have to say."

Before the leader could speak, the chief hunter broke in, a breach of custom; the petitioner was not supposed to speak again until after the leader.

"All three hunters who are missing left in the same direction."

The leader didn't strike the chief hunter for speaking out of turn. Instead, he withdrew his primaries in thought. The circle waited patiently. The surrounding centauroids also waited quietly.

After a moment the leader extended his primaries and spoke solemnly. "We must go out as scouts to find why three hunters went in the same direction and did not return. We must be especially careful. If fourth-eldest's ears did not play tricks on him, the monsters may have returned."

Eyestalks, primary, dorsal, and pectoral, popped everywhere. Everyone was startled. The direction in which the hunters disappeared, and in which the fourth eldest heard the strange thunder, was not where the monsters had been before. But the leader was right, there was no reason the monsters should return to the same place.

"The monsters did not kill any people when they were here before," the second eldest said. "Why should they kill hunters this time, if they have returned?"

"Who knows what monsters will do, or why?" the third oldest snapped. Her primaries quivered at him.

No one had an answer.

"Prepare," the leader said to the chief hunter.

"Will you scout as well?"

"I will."

On orders from the Leaders, the Fighters bellied themselves on the mud and slithered in two lines that curved away from each other, then back again until they formed a circle. The slither through the mud was disgusting, but the lack of undergrowth in the unhealthy forest allowed the movement to be made in almost total silence. The biggest problem the Fighters had was keeping the nozzles of their weapons clear of the mud. None of the few who thought of such things wanted to think of the consequences of firing with clogged nozzles. Fortunately, there was little growth to snag the ammunition tanks they carried on their backs.

On further signal the Fighters slithered forward until they could see into the encampment of the headless monstrosities. Those few among the Fighters who thought of such matters saw the camp as a nesting ground, such as the migratory birds of Home might use—except for one disquieting detail. The nesting grounds of birds were raucous places, filled from dawn to dark with cries and caws, strobing with incessant movement. These creatures moved seldom, and were almost sedate about it when they did. Their vocalisms were restrained, and only one in a group spoke at a time. Most of them were gathered in one place under the dripping trees; they seemed to be listening to a smaller group in their midst, and those in that group spoke one at a time.

The six Leaders in the group observed; they ignored the social structure displayed by the creatures. They looked at the implements that might be used as weapons, where they were scattered in the camp, which creatures held them, which creatures that were not armed were in position to take up weapons. The Leaders needed to know those things so when the order to attack came, they could command their Fighters to kill the most dangerous of the creatures first.

There was a Master with the group. A very junior Master on a minor vermin-removal mission, but a Master nonetheless. Decisions and changes in orders were his responsibility. He observed the social structure displayed by the centauroids. He saw the tools and understood which were weapons and which were not. He thought deeply about such things. The way the centauroids attended each other, their evident communication, their use of tools—at least some of which were made rather than found—indicated to him that they had some form of intelligence. They were beasts, of course, but intelligent beasts. Intelligent beasts could be trained to labor. The Master thought about the amount of work to be accomplished to establish the staging base on that unpleasant world, the number of workers available, and the time constraints under which they worked. He came to a decision. He immediately dismissed the thought of checking with the Senior Master; the Senior Master couldn't see the things he saw. If the Senior Master disliked his idea afterward, the Junior Master would die. If the Senior Master did like it, honors would be heaped on the Junior Master. He believed his idea was one that would gain him honors. He spoke into his communicator and instructed the Leaders to have the Fighters take prisoners. Eradicate the nesting ground, he instructed. Kill all armed centauroids, kill all who are bigger than people, and kill the smallest ones. But take as many of the others prisoner as possible. Kill all who resist or attempt to escape.

The Leaders acknowledged the new command and awaited the order to attack. When the Master saw the central group of centauroids begin to break up, he ordered the attack.

All around the centauroid camp the Leaders jumped to their feet and screamed for their Fighters to attack. The Fighters rose, aimed their weapons, and sprayed killing juices into the masses of monsters. As the Leaders called out the changed orders, the Fighters adjusted their aim accordingly.

The centauroids panicked.

The leader and the council of elders were among the first to die horribly as thick, greenish fluid ate deep holes in their flesh.

Only the chief hunter survived the initial volley as he had broken from the council group to organize scouts an instant before the firing began. When the attack began, the chief hunter ran in unpredictable jigs and jags, changing direction and speed every step or two, as though dodging the spikes of a dangerous prey animal. As he ran he called out to the hunters, his full-volume honking carried easily over the panicked hooting of the females and young. A few hunters honked replies to his orders, too few. As he paused in his irregular movement to look for those who didn't call back, streams from three weapons struck him.

The chief hunter's honking turned shrill . . .

CHAPTER
FOURTEEN

Partly concealed by the other females who stood nervously around her, she huddled miserably in a corner of the barn. Spatters of rain splashed through the slit they'd made in the wall behind the huddling one. She needed the rain—they all needed rain; their skins were dry and cracked from being kept many hours each day under a roof that blocked the rain. The huddling female needed the rain more than the others; her birthing time had come.

With a sudden gasp, she struggled to a crouch. Three females helped her up. Gingerly, she moved her posterior over the pile of leaf fragments the females had sneaked into the barn despite the watchful guards. One female folded her mid- and hindlimbs to lower her torso until her primary eyestalks were level with the birther's channel.

The birther squeezed and grunted. Fluid gushed from her channel and two tiny balls plopped onto the pile of wet leaf fragments. She staggered from the effort and release, but the others held her up and the one by her posterior kept her from sitting or stepping on her newborns. They aided her in moving around until she could fold her mid- and hindlimbs under herself next to the two balls that were opening up on the pile of leaf fragments into miniature, incompletely formed centauroids. Each stood on all six wobbly limbs. The miniatures turned about uncertainly, their eyebuds poking out, searching for their dam. Shuffling, she slid a midlimb from under herself and nudged the leaves. Uttering feeble squeaks, the newborns scrabbled toward the disturbance. They found her midlimb and climbed onto it. Grasping with all their limbs, they struggled along its length, up the front of her torso to the sac slit beneath her mouth, and slipped inside.

The new mother sighed deeply, lowered her torso, and rolled onto her side. The small movements of the newborns inside the sac soothed her. She crooned softly and the irregular movements slowly matched the rhythm of her crooning.

"You should have left them," said a female who hadn't aided in the birthing.

The new mother paid no attention; it was her first birthing, and the feel of her babes in her sac obliterated everything from without.

"She should not have," said the one who had protected the newborns when they first fell from the birth channel.

"The monsters will see and they will kill us all."

The helper looked at the mother. She could easily spot the slight bulge on her chest where the sac held the newborns, but she doubted the monsters would notice. *She* certainly had trouble telling one monster from another, though they instantly recognized each other.

"They won't see," she said with certainty born of hope.

The monsters worked them hard, thought them ideal pack-animals, loaded them with burdens that weighed more than the centauroids did. Kicked them and beat them with clubs when they fell beneath the unbearable weight. The labor weakened them. The first of them to die had been beaten to death on their first full day of labor. That death taught them to struggle back to their feet as fast as they could when they fell instead of trying to release their burdens.

Each day as the sky lightened into dawn, they were fed. The food wasn't the diet of fish, leaves, and tubers to which they were accustomed. Instead they were given a gruel with bits of fish, fragments of leaf, and strange, pulpy, white seeds of a kind they'd never seen before. The pulpy seeds, not in a gruel, seemed to be the major diet of the monsters, though they ate many fish and strange leaves as well. In the evening, as the sky was darkening to night, they were fed again. The inadequate diet weakened them even more.

Then one day more creatures were brought in; frightened, bruised, and wailing. All were females of breeding age; no elders, no immature young. No males.

When the new group arrived, the monsters stopped the six surviving females and herded the newcomers, about thirty of them, to them. Gabbling unintelligibly, the monsters got across what they wanted—the six were to teach the newcomers how to be slaves.

How could they do that? They didn't know how to put the burdens on themselves; the monsters always loaded them and fastened the straps that kept the burdens on their backs. And they never knew when they were loaded from the flying nest which of the other nests they were to bear their loads to until a monster lashed them in the right direction.

"Follow us," the oldest of the six called out. She staggered as she turned, but she didn't fall. She led the way to the huge, strange nest to which they were carrying their burdens.

The newcomers were frightened, confused, but seeing that others of their kind were there and seemed to know what to do, they stopped wailing and fell in line behind the six. Soon, they were sure, their questions would be answered. Then the burdens were lifted from the six and the newcomers were filled with horror at sight of their oozing backs. They shrilled and cried and some of them tried to run.

The monsters beat one of them to death as an example to the others. Then the heavily laden females followed the six to the flying nest, almost collapsing under their burdens. In line they moved along to another nest, each stumbling at least once. Each received blows, but struggled back to their feet. No more were killed that first day. Most adapted and became too dulled by exhaustion and weakness to care.

The new mother was one of the third batch to be brought in. She gave birth little more than a week after her arrival. Her strength hadn't yet ebbed too low, and she thought she could manage. At each meal she allowed some of her gruel to dribble down from her mouth to the sac slit where her newborns lapped it up. She did her best to retain food in her mouth for her babes between her own meals, but often all she could give them was saliva she was barely able to work up. One of the two died several days after its birth, and, for a while it seemed that the other would survive. But it lasted only six days. Deprived of her babies, the young mother refused to rise for work the next morning. The monsters beat her to death. But the monsters didn't find the newborns; the other females had hidden the tiny corpses away.

The Senior Master growled, "You were right. They make very good slaves. It is too bad they are so much weaker than their broad backs would suggest."

The Junior Master bowed low to the Senior, uncertain whether to be pleased that the Senior Master thought his idea was good, or dishonored because the creatures were weaker than they looked. "Thank you, Master," he growled back. "You are right, Master."

The two Masters stood in the lee of a porch roof, watching the centauroids struggle under their burdens.

"If we had enough of them they would do nearly as much work as our tractors and we could unload the mothership in half the time."

"Yes, Master." The Junior bowed again.

The senior considered the slaves for a moment longer, then asked, "These are all females?"

"Yes, Master."

"The males are larger and stronger?"

"They are larger, Master. I believe they are stronger."

"Go out again. Bring back males this time."

"The males are all armed, Master."

"Kill any you must. Any you can disarm, bring back."

"Yes, Master." The Junior Master bowed a third time and backed away.

He lost two Fighters in the raid, but they brought back fifty male centauroids. The Senior Master had to laugh—the males were easier to break to the yoke than the females. And they *were* stronger. After additional raids, on which they lost only one more Fighter, they had more than two hundred male slaves. Construction and supplying of the staging base speeded up. The work was finished well ahead of schedule. The surviving beasts, all thirty-eight, were released.

Thoroughly disoriented as well as weakened, the freed centauroids swam across the river and wandered into the forest. Most of them survived the swim.

Two Junior Leaders watched the centauroids leaving, growled at each other, then went to the Senior Master with a proposal. The Senior Master barked out a laugh at their proposal and gave his permission for them to proceed. The two Junior Leaders stripped down to loincloths and took up swords. They followed the centauroids across the river and began hunting them. One hour later they returned and deposited the eyestalks they'd collected. One brought back twenty-one pair, the other seventeen.

The Senior Master peered at the eyestalks. "Did you kill them all?" he asked.

The Junior Leaders bowed.

"I think so, Master," said one.

"It is difficult to cut the heads off beasts that have no heads," the other replied.

The Senior Master laughed.

So did everyone else within hearing.

Within the scheduled time, more Masters arrived, some senior even to the Senior Master in charge of the staging base.

These Masters brought Leaders and Fighters with them. First they came in the thousands and then in the tens of thousands. When more than a hundred thousand had arrived, the operation was ready to begin. The most Senior Master ordered a ship to ferry the first wave to the target planet, a mere three light-years away.

CHAPTER
FIFTEEN

It was raining—again—on Thursday as the three Marines sat in the dining room at the Royal Frogmore, pecking away disconsolately at their breakfast. While none would admit to it, they were all very nervous as the hour of contact neared.

"Goddamn rain," Claypoole muttered, "I don't see why anybody'd want to waste his money on this waterlogged hole. The skinks would love it."

Pasquin cringed at the mention of skinks and looked hard at Claypoole.

"I just don't give a damn," Claypoole responded, twirling a piece of beefsteak on the end of his fork. "And they can have this damned chow too." He threw his fork down. "Reindeer steaks are better than this cowshit stuff anyway."

"Well, all this rain *is* depressing," Dean offered. "But Rock, don't forget, you met Katie here. The place can't be all bad then, can it?"

Claypoole brightened at the mention of Katie. "Yeah! Hey! I wanna take you guys someplace this afternoon."

"That library you been talking about?" Pasquin asked.

"Yeah. Let's go over after lunch. Hey, Raoul, maybe you can pick up a girl there!"

"Afternoon's a long way off. What do we do until then?" Dean asked.

"Get drunk?" Pasquin offered.

"I'll drink to that!" Claypoole responded. Then suddenly

he shot straight up in his chair and the color drained completely out of his face.

"Hey, buddy, what's up?" Pasquin asked, genuinely concerned. He turned around to follow Claypoole's gaze but could see nothing amiss in the dining room.

"Rock, what is it? Are you sick?" Dean asked.

Claypoole swallowed, "N-No. Turn around to your left, very slowly. Three tables over. She's sitting by herself. See her?" As he spoke, Claypoole concentrated on the food still left on his plate.

Casually, as if stretching, Dean looked in the direction Claypoole indicated. He saw nothing out of the ordinary at first, two or three tables with early morning diners enjoying their food. Then he too stiffened. "My God," he sighed, "it's a small universe, ain't it?"

"What? What? Whadaya see?" Pasquin followed Dean's gaze and then looked back at him anxiously and shrugged his shoulders. "Whadaya looking at?"

"That middle-aged woman sitting by herself over by the waterfall. See her?"

"Yeah. So what?"

"That's Juanita from Wanderjahr, Raoul," Dean answered.

Pasquin regarded the two quizzically and then it hit him. "You mean the woman who ran that bar where . . . ?" Everyone in 34th FIST knew that someone had tried to assassinate Dean and Claypoole as they sat out back of Juanita's, drinking with some girls. A woman named Maggie, apparently someone Claypoole had fallen for, was killed in his arms. He'd never quite gotten over it. "Jeez, what a coincidence," Pasquin muttered. "Do you think she still holds it against you?"

Claypoole nodded.

"Ah," Pasquin made a dismissive gesture, "who gives a shit? We're here, we got money, we're havin' a good time. No old bitch is gonna screw that up on us, right?"

"I wonder what she's doing here?" Dean speculated aloud.

"I don't know," Claypoole said, "but let's split. I've lost my appetite."

As the three stood and gathered their rain gear, Juanita looked up at Claypoole. Their eyes locked.

"Oh, shit," Claypoole sighed, "she's made us. Damn, what a way to start out an otherwise perfectly awful day."

Juanita stared silently at the three. To Dean and Pasquin, it seemed she fixed Claypoole with a particularly icy stare. She only looked at them for an instant but to Claypoole it seemed an hour. Then she got up, spun on her heel and stalked out.

"Whew!" Pasquin breathed again. "Someone just walked over my grave!"

"Aw, jeez, Raoul, I could have gone all day without hearing a remark like that!" Claypoole muttered as he shrugged into his rain gear.

By the time they got outside, Juanita had disappeared. "Now what?" Pasquin asked as he stood under the awning trying to avoid the pouring rain. Placetas boasted all the conveniences of modern life except the climate-controlled environment most twenty-fifth-century city planners preferred. It was thought natural weather enhanced the "atmosphere" of life on Havanagas, and for most visitors it did. But not for Marines. They got enough "natural" weather in the Corps.

"Let's go to The Suicide King," Dean suggested.

"And let's get drunk," Claypoole added, "but not too sautéed to pick up Tara and Katie and make it to the library this afternoon. Man, they got this book in there I want you guys to see—"

Dean smiled to himself and winked at Pasquin. Claypoole was getting back to normal.

It was a little past three P.M. when the cab let them out in front of the Free Library. None of them was feeling any pain by then. Laughing and shouting, they stumbled up the steps toward the giant doors. Impulsively, Katie tried to climb onto one of the mythical beasts standing guard, and on unsteady legs Claypoole tried to give her a boost, with the result that she slipped and they both rolled screaming with laughter down the stairs into the street. They lay there, gasping and laughing, as the rain streamed down from the skies and traffic swerved to avoid them.

Wearily, Pasquin came to their aid, and as he helped Katie to her feet he couldn't resist laughing at the sight of them, soaked through and bedraggled as a pair of alley cats.

The five of them stood, sopping, in the middle of the high-ceilinged foyer, tiny puddles of rainwater collecting on the floor about their feet. Tara giggled uncontrollably. Gerry Prost walked from behind his desk and, rubbing his hands together warmly, greeted Katie. "We'll have to get you out of those wet clothes," he said with a smile. "Can't have you handling our priceless books with all that water around."

Several of the unoccupied girls inside had come out to see what the commotion was all about. "Any of you unattached?" an attractive brunette asked.

"Yeah, him." Claypoole pointed at Pasquin and laughed.

"See you later, then," she said, winking broadly at Pasquin.

Prost gestured to one side of the foyer at doors marked with the ancient alchemical symbols for copper and iron. "In this season we have to be prepared for things like this. Put your clothes into the hampers provided and they'll be returned quickly, dried, cleaned, and pressed. Please come to my desk inside when you're ready."

Twenty minutes later, with their dried clothes returned and themselves considerably sobered up, the five stood before Prost's desk. Surreptitiously, Pasquin glanced at the time. Good. They had a few minutes before Culloden was due to show up. Despite himself, Pasquin's pulse had quickened the closer they got to the meeting time. Nervously, he fingered the reader attached to his belt as Prost droned on about the old book he had spread out before him. He glanced about the room. The brunette, sitting in a carrel off to one side, nodded at him. A man and a woman, arms wrapped around each other, slowly mounted the grand staircase to the upper floors. He found himself wishing he had come to the library first off instead of that dive he'd wandered into that first night.

". . . by Anton Koberger of Nuremberg, Germany, in 1493," Prost was saying. "Imagine! That was only nine months after Columbus discovered America! Koberger probably wasn't even aware of that momentous event when he printed this copy of the *Liber Chronicarum*, commonly referred to as the *Nuremberg Chronicle*! And here you have before you, my dears, an original leaf from that very same edition. Just this one leaf, children, but it's a beaut, ain't it? Cost us a pure fortune!"

"Gerry, is this a new acquisition? I've never seen it before," Katie exclaimed as she bent over Prost's desk, peering intently at the folio leaf in its slipcover.

"Ah, my dear, it just arrived this afternoon! I was able to purchase it from an estate sale on Gymnestra!" What Prost didn't know is that the mob's capo on Gymnestra had put the word out that he wanted the item, so as soon as the reserve had been met, bidding, strangely, ceased. But it was obvious Prost was in his element. "Now," he rattled on, "the very interesting thing about the *Chronicle* is these woodcuts, hundreds of them. See on this leaf for instance, we have all the kings of Persia. In 1493 Darius and those boys were still mighty big names. Now look down here, under Artaxerxes, these two guys are Democritus and Heraclitus, the Greek philosophers. It says, *'Heraclitus philosophus asianus cognomento,'*—that's Latin—*'Scotinus hoc tempe in—'* " Prost suddenly stiffened. He shifted his gaze to someone who'd just come in from the foyer. "Good afternoon, Lovat," he said, his voice carefully neutral. Katie and Tara did not greet the newcomer but it was evident they knew who he was and were afraid of him, because they looked nervously down at the floor as he approached.

Lovat! The three Marines almost whirled as one to shout

"Whores, fours, and one-eyed jacks!" but by now they'd learned to stifle such impulses.

Lovat Culloden stood over six feet tall with a chest as broad as a horse's and flaming red hair to match, so red it looked orange, and Dean's own red hair looked positively dull by comparison. He stood there silently for a moment, regarding the three Marines.

"Lovat is in charge of security in Placetas," Prost offered. "He often comes here to check on things," he added dryly.

"W-Well," Pasquin stuttered. This was not starting out as they had expected. Not at all! "Uh, have we done something, sir? I mean—"

"Button your goddamned lip, mister. You and your friends get your goddamned asses outside and into my car, pronto." He gestured toward the door. "You." He turned to Katie and Tara. "Don't wait up for these boys." He turned to Prost. "I'll see you later, Mr. Bookworm." The threat in his voice was obvious.

Outside, they climbed into Culloden's car. He was driving and there was no one else inside. He fiddled with a small handheld device. "That'll screen us from surveillance," he said, "but we've only got a few seconds, otherwise someone'll wonder why I turned it on." He put the device away. "Now, just what in the ever-living hell does Nast think he's doing? Does he want to get us all killed?"

"W-What do you mean?"

Culloden snorted. "You been fingered, that's what! And look at it this way: two thousand people a day arrive here. Any one of 'em could be an agent, understand? Who do you look for first? Mom and Pop Blitzflick with their kids, or three bozos who stand out like sore thumbs? You know the last time any discharged Marines visited Havanagas?"

The three shook their heads.

"Never. Never! I checked the records all the way back. Never. When does any Marine save enough of his pay to visit a place like this, huh? Any GI or any sailor for that matter? What was Nast thinking?" he pounded his knee in frustration.

"Well, I mean—" Dean began.

Culloden silenced him with a shake of his head. "I should have known it was you three. My office checks all the flight manifests. Now it looks as if I'm not doing my job and so I'm under suspicion too. Talk about dumb!" He smacked his palm into the side of his head.

"Who fingered us?" Pasquin asked.

Culloden shook his head. "Some old bitch, I don't know how the hell she knew who you were. Works as an independent agent for the mob and is very respected down here." Claypoole groaned out loud. "What? You know her?" Briefly, Dean explained, a sinking sensation growing in his stomach as he spoke. Culloden shook his head again. "Well, you guys better talk fast or we're all dead. Try to relax and get your stories straight. Act normal, or what passes for normal for Marines."

"Uh, sir, who is it we're going to see?" Claypoole asked.

"Johnny Sticks, counselor to the Ferris Family. He's your worst nightmare."

One look at his emaciated body and it was easy to understand why Gozo Paoli was called Johnny Sticks. He sat comfortably in his office—more like a fortress than a place of business—in the hills some thirty kilometers north of Placetas. As they drove up the mountain into Paoli's compound the Marines instinctively noted checkpoints, the number of guards, their weapons, fields of fire. Third platoon could take the place easily, they concluded individually, and all three wished fervently the rest of third platoon was with them.

The points of Johnny Sticks's bony knees showed clearly through the dressing gown he was wearing. "Enjoying your stay here?" he asked the three visitors. His voice rasped, dry as the wind across the Martac Waste. His eyes were too big for his narrow, hatchetlike face and, aside from his thinness, they were the most remarkable thing about him.

"We were, until this guy kidnapped us. Why the hell is this place so heavily guarded, if you run everything so well on Havanagas?" Claypoole asked bluntly.

Sticks smiled grimly and nodded at Culloden. "You're very observant, Mister, uh, Claypoole, isn't it? Well, tell me what else you know, Mister Claypoole, lately of the Confederation Marine Corps."

"My friends here and me, we saved up our money and paid a hell of a lot of it to enjoy ourselves here! This is a once-in-a-lifetime vacation for us. Goddamnit, we been through hell in the Corps, you goofy-looking sonofa—"

"Sir, we're all under some stress right now. But do you pull this sort of thing often on paying tourists?" Pasquin said, interrupting Claypoole quickly and rushing on. "I think not, otherwise nobody in his right mind would come here. What do you want with us?"

"Mister, or should I say 'Corporal' Pasquin, yes? Frankly, we think you might be spies." Sticks smiled again; it was thin and utterly humorless, like a reptile's grimace. But the word "might" was not lost on the three Marines.

"Oh, bullshit!" Claypoole said indignantly.

"We've been watching you very closely since you arrived," Sticks continued, unfazed by the outburst. "For instance, Mister Pasquin, you didn't enjoy your evening with Miss Giselda, the transvestite, did you?" At the look of embarrassment on Pasquin's face, Sticks gave a quick laugh. "We've been following you every moment of your stay here, gentlemen," he told them. "We even know who snores the loudest."

"Transvestite, huh?" Claypoole turned to Pasquin. "Raoul, we didn't know!" He laughed and patted Pasquin delicately on the shoulder.

"You asshole!" Pasquin shouted at Sticks. "Why the hell did you bring that up! You know I ain't no—"

"Gotta be Claypoole," Dean said. "He snores like a whole

battery of heavy artillery." The three looked at each other and laughed. Johnny Sticks watched them closely.

"Hey, do you spy on all the people who come here?" Pasquin shouted. "Word gets out, and your business is gonna nosedive, buddy." He nudged Claypoole in the ribs.

"Oh, Raoul! I didn't know you cared so very much!" Claypoole simpered.

Smart as he was, Johnny Sticks had never dealt with Marines before. By demonstrating to them how complete his knowledge of their activities was, especially revealing the embarrassing details of Pasquin's misencounter, he'd given them the perfect opening for the I-don't-give-a-damn, kiss-my-buttplate act designed to convince him they really were only discharged Marines on a spree. Sticks almost believed it.

He shrugged. "No, only on a select few, and you few were selected. I must confess, you haven't given any indication you are here for any other purpose than to enjoy yourselves, but someone recognized you this morning, and that someone does not like you very much. We are naturally curious. As Mister Culloden may have already informed you, not many—not any, in fact—Marines ever come here." He gave them a death's head grin.

"Yeah?" Claypoole interjected. "Well, maybe someday they'll land a fire team and they'll proceed to clean your clocks for you."

"I believe you could do that, Mr. Claypoole. But unfortunately, for the moment there are only the three of you, and alas, you are, shall we say, naked to your enemies?"

"Well, Mister, uh, Paoli, don't you think if anyone wanted to spy on you they'd send someone who didn't stand out so much?"

"Yes, Mister, er, Dean. Yes indeed. You've hit the mark. We look at them too, the ordinary people, of course. Everything here is subject to surveillance. It has to be. We don't allow cheating or any sort of criminal activity; that'd be bad for business. But with so much money around, the temptations are very great. But you three stood out, so naturally we are suspicious. Now, I want you to talk to someone." He turned to a very large man who'd been standing quietly in a corner of the room. "Bring her in, Hugo."

Juanita walked into the room. She regarded the three balefully for a moment. "Kill them," she told Sticks coolly. "I don't know the stupid-looking one," she nodded at Pasquin, "but these other two, kill them. Kill him too." She nodded back at Pasquin.

"Why, my dear? Oh," Sticks turned to the Marines, "Juanita is a very important member of our business community here on Havanagas—and elsewhere. She recruits young ladies to work in our various enterprises. I believe, Mr. Claypoole, your consort, Miss Wells, was specially recruited by Juanita. Why should we kill them, my dear?"

Claypoole bristled at the reference to Katie, but he bit his tongue.

"I told you what they did on Wanderjahr, Johnny." Her voice dripped hatred. "They ruin everything wherever they go. They destroyed my business on Wanderjahr. I don't believe they're here as tourists. Kill them now and avoid trouble later."

"Mister Paoli, sir," Claypoole said, "that girl was killed by rebels on Wanderjahr. We had nothing to do with it. Oh, they were after us, I'm sure of that. But they hit her instead. In that sense maybe we were responsible. But we didn't know they were laying for us. Now that's way in the past, we're out of the Corps, and we just want to enjoy ourselves for the rest of our stay here."

Juanita smirked at Claypoole's words. "You are incredibly stupid," she said. "I don't give a shit about that little whore. You Marines ruined my business on Wanderjahr, you destroyed Kurt Arschmann's Stadt, and Kurt was my benefactor in so many ways."

"Thank you, Juanita," Sticks said. Juanita turned to leave.

"Hey, lady," Claypoole called after her, "you can just go

fuck yourself! I wish to God it'd been you they killed that day and not Maggie!" he shouted. His face had turned deep red and the veins in his neck stood out.

Juanita turned back to Paoli. "Johnny, kill them. I've warned you." She turned back to Claypoole and pointed her finger at him. "I will see you again, Marine," she said, turned and walked out.

The room was silent for a few moments. Then Johnny Sticks sighed and handed each of the three men a plastic card. "I'm sorry for any inconvenience, gentlemen. Here are free passes to the library for as many visits as you wish to make while you're here. Lovat, please return these good gentlemen to the city?"

Just before he let them out in front of the library, Culloden put his lips very close to Pasquin's ear and whispered, "Here. Tomorrow night. Eighteen hours."

"Come on, Raoul," Claypoole shouted from the steps. He was elated. They all were. They'd carried off their impersonations. "Let's take these passes and make some passes!"

CHAPTER
SIXTEEN

As he strode into Brigadier Sturgeon's anteroom, Colonel Ramadan glanced at the corporal, who snapped to attention and acknowledged him with a slight nod that betrayed none of the surprise or curiosity he felt. He recognized the corporal, though he hadn't seen him in more than half a year Standard. It was Corporal Doyle, the Company L chief clerk who had been transferred to avoid having to face a court-martial for the same action for which he would have been awarded a medal had he remained with 34th FIST. He stopped in the open doorway to Sturgeon's office.

"Good morning, sir," Ramadan said.

"Morning, Colonel," Sturgeon replied. "Come on in." He signaled for his executive officer to close the door. His reds were slightly rumpled; he'd made planetfall just a half hour earlier, at the break of dawn, and come directly to headquarters. He'd called Ramadan on the way in and told the Chief of Staff to meet him in his office.

The door closed and Ramadan dropped all pretense of formality. He grinned broadly and stepped to the desk with his hand outstretched. "Damn good to have you back, sir." He noticed without comment an addition to the small display of photos of the chain of command—a portrait of Lieutenant General Aguinaldo, the Assistant Commandant. Aguinaldo's portrait, like the one of the Commandant, was a holo; the others were 2-D.

"It's good to be back," Sturgeon said, rising to take

Ramadan's hand. He grinned wryly. "But I'm surprised you're glad. With me back, you're no longer acting FIST commander. I've never known a Marine officer to willingly give that up."

Ramadan laughed. "It's a tougher job than I realized," he said. "Good thing we don't have 'up-or-out' anymore. I love the job I've got, but now that I've done it, I don't really think I'm cut out to be a FIST commander."

Sturgeon chuckled. "Sometimes I don't think I am either."

"You're a fine one, sir. One of the best."

"I'm not sure you'll be so glad to have me back when you hear what I found out."

"That's all right; I've got a thing or two that might make you wish you'd stayed away." Ramadan moved a visitor's chair to the side of Sturgeon's desk and sat down. He couldn't restrain himself any longer and asked, "What's he doing back?" with a nod toward the door and Corporal Doyle beyond it.

"What he's doing back here is part of what I learned on Earth." Sturgeon looked down at his desk and thought for a moment. When he looked up, there was no smile on his face; he looked as serious as Ramadan had ever seen him. "What I'm about to tell you," he said briskly, "is so far beyond ultra-secret that not even the Commandant is authorized to know it. It's something that no one in 34th FIST, including you and me, is authorized to know. Yet we need to know it, and so does everybody else in the FIST." He paused a beat, then continued, "We have to find a way to make sure all of our people know this, and that nobody else finds out about it."

Ramadan's mouth thinned to a line, but he didn't say anything.

"As you know, I went to Earth to straighten out whatever needed fixing because my Marines weren't getting their normal rotation orders. Colonel, they aren't going to get orders. All transfers out of 34th FIST have been canceled. So have retirements. Moreover, everyone in the FIST has been involuntarily extended for 'the duration.' "

"What!" Ramadan said, loudly enough to be heard in the anteroom. He caught himself and lowered his voice. "What war is going on that requires involuntary extensions for the duration?" he asked.

Sturgeon slowly shook his head. "There is no declared war. The Confederation is doing nothing out of the ordinary of a military nature. He"—he nodded toward the door and Corporal Doyle—"is back with us because he knows something nobody is supposed to know."

Ramadan looked at him blankly.

"You know about the Avionians that Company L encountered late last year. And about the skinks Company L's third platoon encountered on Society 437 nearly a year earlier."

Understanding washed across Ramadan's face. "It's because the Confederation is keeping the existence of the alien sentiences secret, isn't it?" He shook his head. "That's not a good enough reason to mess up everybody's life."

Sturgeon nodded agreement. "You're right, it's not. But there's more."

Ramadan's eyebrows went up.

"For reasons known only to the politicians and bureaucrats who make the decisions, knowledge of alien sentients is to be kept a state secret for the foreseeable future. There are at least *six* known sapient species." He held up a hand to hold off the question Ramadan obviously was about to ask. "I know what you're wondering. Why haven't astronomers heard their radio broadcasts? Because five of those species are relatively primitive. They haven't developed use of any part of the electromagnetic spectrum for communications beyond signal fires and ground-to-ground mirror flashing. The skinks are the only species we've met who are even close to being our technological equals. And some skink technology seems to be advanced beyond ours."

"What does that have to do with our rotations and involuntary extensions?"

"Since elements of 34th FIST are the only military units that have made contact with the aliens, we have been designated the official alien-contact military force. In order to keep the secret, we are, in effect, quarantined. There is even high-level talk of quarantining Thorsfinni's World altogether in case civilians learn about the aliens."

"They can't do that!" Ramadan snapped. Then, more calmly, he said, "I guess they can. And there are bastards in the government who would gladly stoop that low."

"And that's why Corporal Doyle is back. He was intercepted on his way to his next duty station and taken to Earth, where he was held in solitary confinement while they figured out what to do with him. When I showed up on Earth, someone pulled strings and he was handed over to me to bring back."

"What are we going to do with him? I'm sure First Sergeant Myer will want to court-martial him as soon as he finds out he's back."

"There will be no court-martial." Sturgeon drummed his fingers on his desktop, then decided to put the Doyle Question—he was beginning to think of it in capitals—aside for the moment. "The first thing we have to do is brief my senior staff and major subordinate commanders. Would you arrange that, please?"

"Certainly, sir." Ramadan rose. "How soon do you want it?"

"Right now." Sturgeon chuckled, knowing it wasn't possible. "Pull them from whatever they're doing and get them here as soon as they can. Then come back and tell me what's happened that should make me wish I hadn't returned.

"Incidentally . . ." He stopped Ramadan before the colonel opened the door. "I saw you look at the chain." He indicated the portrait display. "General Aguinaldo is up there now because he called in favors to find all the information I have. He's working on our behalf."

Ramadan nodded. He knew Aguinaldo and knew he was just about the best Marine to ever attain that high a position in the Corps. With Assistant Commandant Aguinaldo looking into their situation, Sturgeon was certain the problem would be resolved as well as possible.

The meeting with the senior staff and major subordinate commanders took only half an hour. They agreed with Assistant Commandant Aguinaldo that the men should be told that a problem in the Hexagon was preventing change of station rotations and that the ACMC was working on fixing it. That would be the official word for the time being; if the situation seemed likely to continue indefinitely, or if 34th FIST made another alien contact, the men would have to be told the truth. None of the subordinate commanders was comfortable with the idea of telling his men they were involuntarily extended—that could possibly create even worse morale problems than they were already experiencing—but it was the only fair thing to do. Both the infantry battalion and air squadron commanders wanted to brief their top people. Sturgeon agreed. He was relieved when Commander Van Winkle, the infantry commander, offered to handle the Doyle Question.

"If there are no questions, gentlemen?" Van Winkle said at the end of his briefing. His senior staff, company commanders, and first sergeants looked somber and reflective, but none had anything to ask. "Captain Conorado, First Sergeant Myer, please stay for a moment. The rest of you are dismissed."

The assembled officers and first sergeants stood and filed out of the battalion briefing room, leaving the commander and first sergeant of Company L in their seats. Battalion Sergeant Major Parant also remained; he knew what Van

Winkle wanted to see Conorado and Myer about and understood that he might be needed.

When the others were gone and the briefing room door was closed again, Van Winkle walked to where the Company L leaders were sitting and turned a chair around so he sat almost knee to knee with them. Parant took up station to his immediate left rear.

"There's something else I have to deal with, and I wanted to talk it over with the two of you before I decide what to do," Van Winkle said without preamble.

"Yessir," Conorado said.

Myer looked attentive.

"Corporal Doyle's back."

Neither reacted for a few seconds, then cords bulged on Myer's neck and his face turned red. "I want his ass court-martialed!" he almost shouted. "Nobody blackmails me and gets away with it."

"Brigadier Sturgeon was very clear that there will be no court-martial," Van Winkle said calmly.

To his left rear Parant patted the air in signal for Myer to calm down.

"Obviously," Van Winkle went on, as though Myer's outburst hadn't happened, "he can't return to Company L as chief clerk. If nothing else, you've already got a new chief clerk, and don't need a third clerk."

Conorado nodded. He promoted PFC Palmer to lance corporal and gave the job to him when Doyle left. Palmer was one of the men far overdue for rotation. There was a new PFC in the clerk's billet.

"Unless," Van Winkle went on, "the whole matter of Doyle's insubordination gets cleared up, I can't really assign him to one of the other companies either—and Headquarters has a full complement of clerks. So, gentlemen, what do you suggest we do?"

Parant fixed Myer with his eyes, leaned back on his chair

and crossed his arms. Myer glared back and tightened his lips over his clenched teeth so he wouldn't say anything.

"He's a clerk, sir," Conorado said slowly, his mind racing to come up with a solution.

Van Winkle waited. He knew, as the best superiors do, that usually the best solutions come from the people who have to deal with the problems, not from those who hand solutions down from on high.

Conorado looked at Myer, who kept his eyes locked with Parant's. He stifled a sigh and said slowly, "Doyle's a career clerk, but he has experience as a combat infantryman. Maybe Charlie Bass will take him."

Myer's head jerked toward his company commander when he heard that.

"Doyle's a dipshit fuckup! You can't put him in a blaster platoon."

Conorado calmly looked at him. "Charlie Bass didn't think Doyle was a 'dipshit fuckup' when he got that Bronze Star. Charlie was there when Doyle earned it. He's the one who recommended him for it."

Myer clenched his teeth but didn't respond.

Van Winkle nodded. "Sounds like an excellent solution. Will you put it to him?" To his left rear Sergeant Major Parant was grinning.

"Yessir. Regardless of what he did one time, he *is* a clerk, and there will be problems with putting him in a blaster platoon. As long as I have any say in the matter, I won't tell a platoon commander he has to take on a problem like that."

"Understood. That's it, then. Let me know if Gunny Bass doesn't accept the challenge." The battalion commander stood; the others stood with him and turned to leave.

Parant caught up with Myer just outside the door.

"I understand how you feel. Let Charlie deal with it. I don't believe Doyle will ever pull a stunt like that again."

"But—"

"No buts. Remember, what Doyle did worked wonderfully. Even if he had to defy you on how."

Myer glared at the battalion sergeant major, then spun about and marched after his company commander. The muscles of his neck and shoulders visibly bunched under his uniform shirt.

Parant shook his head. "That man needs to calm down before he tears a muscle," he murmured, then looked around for his commander.

Gunnery Sergeant Charlie Bass sat at his tiny desk in third platoon's minuscule office. Staff Sergeant Wang Hyakowa, the platoon sergeant, lounged with arms crossed over his chest against the wall next to Bass's chair. Sergeant "Rabbit" Ratliff, the first squad leader, mimicked Hyakowa's posture against one sidewall; Sergeant Tam Bladon, second squad leader, leaned against the other sidewall; arms akimbo and ankles crossed. Sergeant "Hound" Kelly, the gun-squad leader, stood against the door—there wasn't space for him to lean back or to place his arms anywhere, other than to let them hang straight down.

Between Kelly and the desk, Corporal Doyle stood at rigid attention. Doyle had a choice; he could stand with his thighs pressed tightly against the desk, or with his back against Kelly's front. He didn't want to think about what Kelly might do to him later for such intimacy, so he got as close to the desk as he could without tripping over it. Even with his feet together, the office was so small Bladon's toe brushed his ankle. He'd tried to will sweat not to pop out of his forehead, but sweat beaded and dripped from his brow and dribbled down his sides from his armpits.

Bass, the very image of relaxation save for the drumming of his fingers on the desktop, looked at Doyle with an expression that could only be described as mild curiosity. None of the other NCOs in the room displayed any more emotion than their platoon commander did.

"Corporal Doyle . . ." Bass's mild voice broke what had become an extended silence. "You present me with quite a quandary. All of us, for that matter." He stopped drumming and lifted a hand to indicate the other NCOs. That wasn't true, there was no quandary. He'd discussed the situation with these men immediately after Captain Conorado's briefing with the platoon commanders and sergeants. Everyone involved agreed with his plan, though Corporal Kerr had agreed with less enthusiasm than the others.

"You've been assigned to third platoon," Bass continued. "Everybody in the company—hell, probably the whole FIST—knows the Top wants to court-martial you. And with good reason. Having you in my platoon puts me at odds with the first sergeant—a most undesirable position for anyone to be in, let me assure you." He chuckled softly. "But you know all about that, don't you?" He paused as Doyle swallowed.

"Moreover, this is a blaster platoon, and you're a clerk. On the other hand, I've seen you in combat and you acquitted yourself quite well under the circumstances. I even seem to remember saying at some point that if you ever decided to change MOS to real Marine, you were welcome in my command. My word is good, so you're welcome here. I'll deal with the Top. Under that gruff exterior he's really a sweetheart."

He ignored Kelly's snort, but Hyakowa shot the gun squad leader a look that said *I'll deal with you later*.

"But, Corporal Doyle, you're a corporal, and that's a problem. You see, corporal is a fire team leader's rank. There is simply no way I am going to entrust you with the lives of two of my Marines. You have neither the training nor the experience to be a fire team leader. That seems to mean I have to reduce you in rank. Which brings us back to the court-martial the Top wants to give you."

"But—" Doyle's knees wanted to break and his bowels threatened to let loose.

Bass held up a hand. "No buts from you. I'm the only one

who gets to say 'but' just now. But, if the Top court-martials you, you'll be facing a long, hard time in a very serious brig. Which in turn would negate the welcome I just extended to you. So, do you understand my quandary?" When Doyle merely swallowed again, he added, "It's all right for you to speak now."

"Gunny Bass . . ." Doyle's voice squeaked. He swallowed and tried again. "Gunny Bass, I'll do anything you say. And I won't insist on having the job my rank calls for. But please, don't let the Top court-martial me." His voice cracked on "court."

Bass decided to ease some of the pressure. "Be easy, Doyle. There won't be a court-martial. That's on direct order of Brigadier Sturgeon."

Corporal Doyle sagged with relief. Sergeant Bladon flexed his knee muscles and rapped Doyle's ankle with his toe. Doyle stiffened again.

"You're a corporal, but the only thing I can do that doesn't unreasonably jeopardize anybody else is give you a PFC's job. Are you sure you're not going to be upset about that?"

"Yessir, Gunny Bass, that's all right. I know I can't do a fire team leader's job." He would have agreed to giving away his testicles; at that moment all he could think of clearly was he wasn't going to be court-martialed.

"Good. The platoon's short a couple of men, so we—" A hand wave included the other NCOs "—came up with a reorganization of the platoon. I'm putting you in Corporal Kerr's fire team. That's Sergeant Bladon's second fire team."

Bladon smiled a shark's grin, which Doyle caught out of the corner of his eye, and tapped his ankle once more.

"I know Corporal Kerr. He's a good Marine."

"One of the best," Staff Sergeant Hyakowa growled.

"Any questions?" Bass asked.

Why not? "Who else is in the fire team?"

Bass smiled beatifically. "Lance Corporal Schultz."

Doyle blanched and groaned. He knew Lance Corporal

Schultz too. Schultz was reputed to be the toughest man in the Marine Corps. Doyle believed it. Schultz scared him.

The room wasn't big. None of the fire team rooms in the barracks were. It held three single beds—one alone, two stacked one above the other. The single bed and the lower of the bunk pair had a bank of drawers under them. A narrow set of drawers climbed the foot of the bunk pair. There were three small desks against available wall space. A low table centered on the floor completed the room's furnishings. Personal items stood on the desks, and a few hanging 2-D images kept the walls from being blank. A door on one sidewall led to a not very large closet that was divided into three sections. On the other sidewall a door led into the head the occupants of the room shared with the occupants of the room on the other side of the head.

Sergeant Bladon rapped on the doorjamb.

"Come," said a voice from inside the room.

Bladon poked his head inside. "Corporal Kerr. Schultz." He nodded at the two men in the room.

Corporal Kerr looked up from the Marine Corps Institute course he was studying. "Sergeant Bladon," he replied.

Schultz glanced up from his desk and nodded, then returned to the book he was reading.

"I brought your new man," Bladon said.

Kerr stood and faced the room's entrance. "Bring him in."

Schultz gave no indication that he heard what his squad leader said. He knew who was coming, he didn't have to show any curiosity. Even if he didn't already know the identity of the new man, a new man would be another Marine. That and the man's name were really all he needed to know.

Bladon stepped in and gestured toward the corridor. Corporal Doyle stepped in and gave Kerr an apologetic smile. His eyes darted nervously at Schultz, then quickly back to Kerr.

"You already know Doyle," Bladon said.

Kerr leaned against his desk and folded his arms across his chest. "I know more about Doyle than he realizes."

"Well, he's yours now. Get him settled in."

"Oh, we'll do that all right. Won't we, Hammer?"

Schultz grunted and kept reading.

Corporal Doyle let his eyes wander. He swallowed. The room was the same size as the one he used to share with then-PFC Palmer. That room had felt crowded with two men. This one was home to three. He swallowed again.

"Well, he's yours now. Going on liberty tonight?"

Kerr shook his head. "Nah. I've got too much studying to do." He nodded at his course material.

"Good idea. That'll help you get these." Bladon self-consciously tapped the rank insignia on his collar. Before Kerr had gotten almost killed, he'd been senior to Bladon. During Kerr's extended absence, Bladon had been promoted and was now Kerr's squad leader. There was no particular tension, but both men were aware that except for the wound their positions would most likely be reversed. "See you at chow?"

"Sounds good. Seventeen hours?"

"I'll stop for you on my way." Bladon left, headed for the end of the corridor where the squad leaders' room was.

Doyle stood nervously, waiting for his new fire team leader to say something.

Kerr let the silence stretch long enough for Doyle's nervousness to make itself visible with a twitching of one leg before he broke it.

"Got your gear?"

Doyle jerked at the sudden words. "Ah, yes." He scrambled out of the door and came right back in, clumsily carrying his issue seabag, a civilian suitcase, and a few smaller parcels.

"There's closet space," Kerr said, "and the drawers under the bottom bunk are yours."

"Top bunk's mine," Schultz growled without looking up

from his reading. Schultz held the high ground and nobody ever argued the point with him.

Scrabbling, almost tripping over himself in his desire to do things right, Doyle hung his reds and some civilian clothes in the closet and put other items in the drawers. When his clothes and most other items were put away, he looked longingly at the desks.

"The one by the head's yours," Kerr said.

Doyle's head bobbed several times. He loaded his personal comm unit, vid, library, medals—Kerr shook his head in wonder at the Bronze Star—and a few other items into the desk.

Before he was finished, Kerr came over, picked up his library crystal, and popped it into his own vid to read the titles.

"I'm not surprised at all the novels you have in here," Kerr said as he popped the crystal out and handed it back, "but that's more military history than most of the Marines in the platoon have. I might want to borrow it sometime. You've got several books I haven't read."

"Well, Corporal Kerr, I may only be a clerk—"

"Belay that, Corporal Doyle," Kerr snapped. "You *were* a pogue. You are now in the *real* Marine Corps. Let me remind you your primary MOS was changed."

Doyle fish-mouthed for a few seconds. "Right," he got out.

"You were saying," Kerr said encouragingly.

"Well, I've always had an interest in military history and tactics."

Suddenly Schultz was there. He had his personal vid in one hand and the other extended. When Doyle simply looked at him dumbly, Kerr picked up the library crystal and handed it over. Schultz popped the library into his vid and scanned the titles.

"You don't have Oberholtz's *Sun Tzu: Twenty-fifth Century Relevance*," he said. "Lend you mine when I finish. Too scholarly for its own good, but some good shit in it." Having spoken nearly an entire evening's worth of casual conversation in one burst, Schultz returned to his desk and his copy of

Oberholtz. Doyle stared after him—the thought of "Hammer" Schultz reading scholarly analyses of classical literature was a shock.

"Sit down," Kerr said when Doyle was finished unpacking.

Doyle pulled out his desk chair and sat on its edge. Kerr pulled his own chair over and sat down nearly knee-to-knee with him.

"Here's the way it's going to work. This is my fire team, I'm in command, what I say goes. When I say jump, you wait until you're up in the air before you ask how high."

Doyle's head began bobbing as though it was on a spring.

"Technically, you outrank Lance Corporal Schultz, but he's got more experience and knowledge than you'll ever have. He's second." He ignored Schultz's snort. "That means you're on the bottom of this particular totem pole. For that matter, everybody—" His eyes flicked to the Bronze Star ribbon on Doyle's chest and he nearly shook his head again. "—nearly everybody in this platoon has more knowledge and experience than you do. You need to get a couple deployments under your belt before you can begin thinking about becoming an acting fire team leader."

Doyle's head was still bobbing. He stopped it with visible effort.

"Corporal Kerr, I know that. Once upon a time I thought maybe I was good enough to be a salty lance corporal in a blaster squad." That was when he won the Bronze Star. "I know more now. I don't know nearly enough to be a salty lance corporal." He made a face. "I think you're right about me not knowing as much as anybody else in the platoon. I was only in a real firefight one time, and that was more than two years ago."

Kerr burst out laughing. "Great Buddha's balls! One firefight, and you got a Bronze Star out of it." Kerr hadn't seen it; it happened when he'd almost gotten killed, but he'd heard about it more than once.

"He earned it," Schultz snarled. He'd been with Doyle on that particular action.

"I know he did, Hammer," Kerr said, still chuckling. "That doesn't mean it's not bizarre." He reached out and clapped Doyle on the shoulder. "Keep alert and I think you'll do all right."

Then it was 1700 hours and Sergeant Bladon was back, rapping on the doorjamb. "Chow call!" the squad leader shouted.

"Chow call!" Kerr shouted back. The two NCOs left.

Doyle still sat on the edge of his chair, not sure of what to do.

Schultz turned his vid off and stood over Doyle. "Remember," he intoned. "This is the best FIST in the Corps. We have the best company commander. The best platoon commander. The best fire team leader. You be the best."

Doyle swallowed. He'd heard an emphatic "or else" in that.

Schultz stepped back and said, "Chow call." When Doyle didn't get up he jerked a thumb in the direction of the mess hall. Junior men in the same fire team usually took their meals together. Schultz wasn't going to leave Doyle out of that tradition, even if he was a corporal and was really a pogue.

CHAPTER
SEVENTEEN

Olwyn O'Mol stood back in the shadows of a doorway across the street from the Free Library. He was why Sticks's headquarters was so heavily guarded. Sticks had refused to answer Claypoole because neither he nor any other member of the mob wanted to admit that a man like O'Mol existed in the well-ordered world the crime families had created on Havanagas.

A gust of icy wind blew cold rainwater into the doorway. O'Mol stepped farther back into the recess, tightening his cloak more securely about him. Absently, he fingered one of the several weapons he carried. Arms were necessary to O'Mol's survival. He was one of the most hunted men on Havanagas. Only his wits and his caution had kept him alive—and his guns.

O'Mol and his confederates had been keeping a close watch on the three Marines since they'd come through customs at Intourist, but not for the same reasons the mob had been watching them. O'Mol needed help.

Olwyn O'Mol was descended from one of the families that had originally settled the world now known as Havanagas. For generations his ancestors had farmed successfully, cultivating crops imported from Earth which thrived in the Hanavagas soil. In time his people had become one of the major landowning families on Havanagas. Now the family holdings had shrunk to a few miserable farms. Most of their land had been expropriated by the mob, once it got control of the local governments. Ironically, most people on the other worlds in the Confederation would have still considered O'Mol a rich man, judging just by the property that still remained in his hands, but he smarted constantly over the forced reduction of his family's wealth and prestige. He dreamed of getting it back.

The first colonists on Havanagas, organized by a company based in northern Italy on Earth, had named the place Neo Milano. They had gone there for the simple reason that they wanted a chance to run their own lives on their own terms, the age-old motivation for moving to a new place. The population on Neo Milano had remained small over the years, and when the crime families—calling themselves the "Havanagas Conglomerate"—started investing in the place, the natives had welcomed them with open arms. Havanagas had brought jobs, security, and tourism. Everyone benefited. But as Havanagas's operations expanded, droves of new settlers were required to run them, and many were rootless people recruited from all over Human Space. They owed everything to their employers. The original inhabitants found themselves being absorbed into this system, and most of them did not object to that. But Olwyn O'Mol did.

Life on Havanagas was good for those who did not ask questions, stayed in line, and let the crime bosses make all the major decisions for them. But ask for a raise or a promotion? Ask where all the money the Havanagas operations were making was going? Ask why your neighbor had suddenly disappeared without a trace? Any of those questions—or a dozen more anybody would normally ask of his government—got you "replaced." The mob on Havanagas was utterly ruthless in its enforcement of discipline.

Worst of all, the mob deliberately stifled its employees. For instance, Katie knew she would always be a whore. The mob had brought her to Havanagas to be a whore, and she would whore until she was too old to whore anymore, and then and only then would she be allowed to do something else, like help in the management of a whorehouse. She could live a long and comfortable life if she were careful, but she would never marry or have a family, get into another line of work, or capitalize on her intelligence and the first-class education she'd managed to pick up on her own. She could never share her interests with anyone, except maybe the john she was with for the night, and always the only thing he wanted from her was what he had paid for.

People like Gerry Prost were a little better off because they had careers elsewhere before being recruited for employment on Havanagas. But now that the mob paid his salary and bought his precious books for him, he was their man too, for the rest of his life. No library in the universe except the Free Library on Havanagas had the money to build a collection like the one Prost had put together, but the mob's pockets were bottomless and their methods effectively ruthless. Prost did not know this because he did not care to know. For him the end—exquisitely rare books available to those who worshiped them—justified the means. So do decent people accommodate themselves to evil.

Olwyn O'Mol vowed he would die before he'd live like that. So far, though, the mob had not been able to pin him down. He was rigorously careful about his movements, never staying in one place for very long, constantly on the move and never establishing a pattern to his moves. His confederates provided safe houses and hideouts for him. He became used to living outside what passed for law on Havanagas. The few times he had been cornered, he'd shot his way out. Superstition had grown up around him, and there were many in the Havanagas underworld who were convinced Olwyn O'Mol lived a charmed life. Huge amounts had been placed on his head, but no one had collected. O'Mol had discovered a great secret: when criminals settle down, when they become so powerful they run things, when they are no longer fugitives, relying on their wits and initiative to survive, then they become as vulnerable as the society upon which they once preyed.

O'Mol had been standing in this doorway for two hours now, since the agent assigned to follow the Marines had signaled that the trio had been picked up by Culloden. He had come to the scene personally and relieved the agent, whom he'd sent to watch the Frogmore instead. He knew where Culloden had taken the Marines and why. He had to know if they were allowed to return. His guess was that since the men had come in with women, Culloden would return them to the Free Library instead of their hotel—if they returned at all. Well, he'd know soon enough.

The "Havanagas Liberation Front," as O'Mol and his associates grandly called their tiny movement, posed no real threat to the mob—yet. But O'Mol had plans.

Havanagas had no army, navy, or even a police force. The mob kept control of things through a vast network of informants and agents, overseers and minor bosses, who ran and supervised every business enterprise and government operation on the planet. When force was needed to keep someone in line, goons were available. If a tourist was found cheating or creating disorder, the casino or park security personnel handled the matter—usually by putting the miscreant on the first ship off-world. If an employee went bad, he or she was quietly disposed of by professionals.

The inflexible rule on Havanagas was that tourists were never cheated or molested in any way, and while they were guests in the casinos and theme worlds on the planet, they should never be troubled by internal disciplinary problems. Thus, to billions of people Havanagas was the most peaceful and delightful spot in Human Space, and whole families pooled their life savings for a week or two in its pleasure palaces.

But the venery behind every aspect of Havanagas had not gone entirely unnoticed by the Confederation of Worlds. Politicians and social critics regularly inveighed against the

Barkspiel show as appealing to the basest form of cupidity, enticing its millions of viewers to risk bankruptcy just to sample the transient pleasures of a fantasy world created by gangsters. But since there was absolutely no admissible evidence of crime or corruption on Havanagas itself—and since Havanagas and *Barkspiel* had become cultural icons—the families could only be attacked in their off-world enterprises, which would never reach the capos themselves, safely ensconced on Havanagas.

O'Mol knew he had to take out the mob leadership if he was to break their hold on his home. But he was shrewd and he was patient. He had initiated several low-key and very clandestine programs to weaken confidence in the families. Among them was a clever propaganda scheme designed to play on the natural discontents of a population under the total control of the mob, and a sophisticated campaign of cyber sabotage. His most recent coup had been wiping out all the records of a casino in Placetas, forcing the place to close down for a week. He had also engineered several successful burglaries. If you can't hit the mobster himself, he realized, then rob his bank.

But now he had begun to hit the mobsters, with a terror campaign against the lower-level family members—the assassination of an underboss here, a soldier there. Those first-level employees of the families were beginning to go around looking over their shoulders. That is why Johnny Sticks's headquarters was surrounded by armed men. O'Mol was beginning to make the mobsters understand what it was like to be under the gun.

And now these three Marines. Marines were fighters. No matter what their jobs—clerks, supply men, drivers—they were infantrymen and knew weapons and tactics. Olwyn O'Mol had a job for them.

Another gust of wind howled into the doorway. The street outside was deserted. Everything might hinge on whether these three, or even one of the three, would accept his offer. O'Mol had money; the robberies had been very successful.

O'Mol began to consider, as he did constantly, what he would do once he had broken the families' hold on Havanagas. The rudimentary forms of civil government that existed on Havanagas would have to be expanded beyond mere caretaker status. There was a vast infrastructure to handle logistics, run the casinos and theme worlds, process the millions of tourists who visited Havanagas every year. What Havanagas lacked was a political structure to make fair and honest decisions about how the world would be run. O'Mol had no intention of closing down the parks and casinos. They could continue to run virtually by themselves. But Havanagas had no real laws or regulations, and there was no mechanism for a new government to obtain feedback from its citizens. Before the mob, the planet had been run by a loose confederation of landholders who remained essentially autonomous in their own geographical areas. That would not work in a postmob environment.

O'Mol was thinking he would have to call on the Confederation of Human Worlds for assistance and that he would be the chief spokesman in that process, when Culloden's landcar pulled up in front of the Free Library.

Ah! O'Mol realized he had guessed right. He smiled as the three Marines got out of the car and mounted the steps, laughing and slapping each other on the back. Culloden drove off. Now to make contact.

"You know me, Johnny," Juanita was saying. "You know I have good intuition. You also know I don't give a damn about that girl who was killed, the one that fool, Claypoole, is mooning over. Yes, Johnny, that one's an incurable romantic, in love with the ghost of that girl."

"And your valued intuition tells you?"

"There's a rat in the woodpile, Johnny. Nothing happens in

this life by chance. There's big trouble in store for your family if you don't take action right now."

"We're in danger from three Marines, Juanita?" Sticks laughed. "Now if they were four—"

"No laughing matter, Johnny."

"I know, I know. I do trust your insights, Juanita. We all do. I could've killed them, but I didn't because I want to know who their contact is. It was very fortunate that you came to me. Oh, we were suspicious from the time they came through customs, and what you told me is very valuable. I owe you for that. Oh, sure, they were sent here, as you suspect. Only an idiot would fail to catch on to that. Jesus, Nast must be slipping in his old age."

"Yes? He's pretty damned quick on the draw, Johnny," Juanita said, tacitly reminding him of the failed assassination attempt in Fargo.

Johnny nodded and pursed his lips thoughtfully. "Well, he was lucky, Juanita, but still, he's got fast reflexes, I hear. But our sources at the Ministry of Justice haven't all dried up, you know. We know he's up to something. He hasn't been seen in months, did you know that? What I can't figure is why he would send in these three clowns to make contact with his agent here."

"Maybe it's a diversion," Juanita suggested. "You look at the left hand and the right hand is free to move."

"Hmm." Sticks was silent for a time. "No. He knows we're too sophisticated and alert to fall for a substitution play."

"Well, get rid of them and there'll be no contact."

"I'm keeping my eye on them, Juanita, and when the time comes . . ." He drew a finger across his throat and smiled evilly. "They won't get out of here alive."

"Let me know, Johnny, before you kill them. I want to be there. I want to see their blood and hear their screams."

"Ooh," Sticks pretended to be frightened, "and we don't hold anything against the Marines, do we?"

Juanita's expression hardened. "Johnny, they blundered

into my world and upset it. I cannot tolerate interference. What will you do to them?" She leaned forward eagerly.

"Oh, the usual. First we'll find out what they came here for. Nobody can resist spilling his guts after Hugo's been at them for a while."

Juanita smiled. "I want to be there for that. Will you promise to let me watch, let me participate a little, even?"

Johnny nodded.

"And then what?"

"Ah, and then, my dear Juanita, 'all roads lead to Rome,' as they say."

Juanita Cruz, known as the "Old Woman" on Havanagas, was a procuress for the mob. From her headquarters on Wanderjahr she scoured all of Human Space, recruiting young women and boys for employment in brothels, the ones she owned and the ones on Havanagas and other worlds that the mob ran. She was a key figure in the prostitution rings the mobs ran on a dozen other worlds too. The obscure bar near Brosigville's spaceport on Wanderjahr where Dean and Claypoole had spent a boozy afternoon two years before was merely a front.

Juanita was not really that "old"; middle-aged, really. Nor was she that bad looking. Her stern, businesslike demeanor—hair pulled back into a severe bun, no-nonsense clothes, and lack of makeup—just made her *look* dumpy and grandmotherly. Johnny Sticks found himself more than a little attracted to Juanita, and she knew it. While she did not encourage his advances, she never rebuffed them either. Johnny, who had the pick of the most beautiful women on the planet, was used to getting any woman he wanted. He knew he couldn't do that with Juanita, however, because she was more than his equal in the mob hierarchy, so instead he settled for the verbal cat-and-mouse game they played. Business, after all, is business.

* * *

"Ah, gentlemen." Prost greeted them as they approached his desk. "Good to see you've come back." He smiled wanly, as if saying, *Good to see anybody come back after an interview with Paoli.* It was obvious he was surprised he'd ever seen them again. "I'm sorry, your consorts departed long ago. They, uh, thought you'd be retained, er, beyond a reasonable time." He gave another sickly smile. "Well, would you care to spend the night with us?" Dramatically, like the three musketeers drawing their swords, they presented the cards Paoli had given them. "Well," Prost exclaimed, "I am impressed, very impressed. Johnny doesn't give these out to everyone. Take your pick." He waved his arm at the carrels.

"I don't know if I can get it up anymore, Mr. Prost, with someone listening to every little fart we make," Claypoole said.

"Yeah," Dean said, speaking loud enough to be sure whoever was monitoring them heard the remark. "Some people get their jollies listening to other people's farts." The other two laughed. That'd give Mr. Paoli's goons something to think about.

Now that it was out that they were under surveillance—something they'd known all along anyway—it was all right to talk openly about being spied on.

Since Katie had gone home and it was too late to go after her, Claypoole had decided to spend the night. Besides, he did not want to find her in the company of another man, which was probably just where she would be at that hour.

Pasquin looked around for the girl who had winked at him before. Suddenly, almost as if called, she appeared from around the other side of the room, a bright smile on her face. He waved at her and smiled back.

"Please sign our guest register, gentlemen," Prost said. He shoved an old-fashioned ledger at them. Boldly, Pasquin picked up the antique pen, dipped it into the inkwell and signed "John Hancock" in huge black letters. "That's striking a blow for liberty!" Prost exclaimed with a flourish.

The girl gave her name as Marilyn, and despite the fact that

Pasquin knew the room was bugged, as soon as she started to undress he forgot all about it. Quickly, he began to shed his own clothes. He watched her in the mirror. Suddenly, she had a strange little device in her hand, like that thing Culloden switched on to shield their conversation in the car. In the other hand she had— Then everything went black.

CHAPTER
EIGHTEEN

"The Kingdom of Yahweh and His Saints and Their Apostles." That was the charter name of the human world commonly called "Kingdom." The formal name was used only by the theocracy in its formal pronouncements and publications. Everyone else, including the government of the Confederation of Human Worlds in its official pronouncements and publications, simply called it "Kingdom."

Sometime during the twenty-third century, when Human Space hadn't spread far enough to include the planetary system around a particular nondescript Class G star, the leaders of a number of small or disregarded religious sects— and splinter groups of well-established religions—thoroughly dissatisfied with what they saw as the rampant materialism and humanism of the day, and further convinced the day of reckoning wasn't as near to hand as they would have it, pooled their churches' not inconsiderable resources to purchase a starship. The starship shuttled back and forth a number of times and eventually brought some two million like-minded colonists to an Earthlike planet orbiting the nondescript, off-the-beaten-path, star.

Thus was founded the Kingdom of Yahweh and His Saints and Their Apostles. It was hard going at first. The colonists didn't have the full panoply of occupations that were normal for settlement on new worlds. While one may find farmers, husbandmen, woodsmen, teachers, machinists, and truck drivers among the ranks of religious fundamentalists—metallurgists, biologists, and medical technologists tend to be in short supply in those ranks.

The leaders of those half-dozen sects weren't willing to surrender their dream of a shining city on a hill to an impoverished agrarian landscape, nor were they willing to give up the benefits of modern medicine in favor of a short, brutish life. So they had their followers build a walled compound outside Haven, the capital city of Kingdom. They hired contract workers from off-world to live in Interstellar City, as they called the walled compound, to provide the talents and skills they didn't have in their own populace and, meanwhile, to prevent contact between the off-worlders and the Chosen People.

The attempted isolation didn't work.

The off-world metallurgists and geologists had to cooperate and coordinate with the miners, smelters, and machinists of Kingdom. The biologists, botanists and zoologists both, had to work with the farmers, husbandmen, woodsmen, and hunters. The medical technologists had to teach the doctors, nurses, and midwives. Etcetera.

Quickly, a religious overseer was assigned to accompany each off-worlder every time one left the walled compound in order to assure that there would be no contamination. The citizens of Kingdom weren't allowed into Interstellar City, not even as cooks, maids, or janitors.

At first the attendant overseers were able to prevent contamination, but that lasted only for the first generation. The ruling theocrats attempted to bring up later generations to believe theirs was the only righteous way of life and only heretics lived off-world.

Yet some in each generation saw for themselves that the off-world scientists and technicians with whom they came into contact bore neither horns nor barbed tails. Even when the off-worlders said nothing that was not absolutely necessary to their work, they showed there was good in other places—and how they moved, dressed, and spoke suggested that life elsewhere could be better than it was on Kingdom. Some of those among the common people who didn't have access to the modern medical technologies the theocrats kept to themselves, or to the other modern conveniences and comforts, reasoned that anything had to be better than the short, brutish lives they led.

Beginning with the third generation, there was at least one rebellion in each generation, some large enough that the theocrats were forced to request Confederation assistance in putting them down. The first intervention convinced many in the Confederation government that Kingdom's theocracy deserved the rebellions it faced. After that, the Confederation intervened only when the lives of the contract workers, most of them citizens of member worlds, were threatened.

It became a game. When the theocracy wanted help badly enough, it manufactured an incident to blame on the rebels. The Confederation then had to intervene, however unwillingly. The Confederation never, ever intervened before such an incident.

The shuttle blinked out of Beamspace just long enough to send out a radar pulse and get the blips back, then popped back into Beamspace. That deep in a gravity well and its attendant atmosphere, any longer than a blink at the speed the shuttle traveled would overheat the hull. The onboard computers analyzed the returned blips in nanoseconds and set a course change. The shuttle blinked out of Beamspace, fired vernier jets to make the course correction, blinked back into Beamspace. The shuttle repeated the process. Any active radar that picked it up when it was in Space-3 would probably see the widely separated blinks as unconnected anomalies.

The shuttle's braking jets were already on full when it blinked out of Beamspace for the last time. It shuddered violently before its wings extended and bit into the atmosphere, then almost lazed onto the ground in a near perfect landing a few kilometers from the village of Eighth Shrine. Its maw clanked open and four vehicles of a design not previously seen on Kingdom roared out. The vehicles were mud-colored, bore strange symbols, and were obviously armored and armed. As soon as the vehicles were a hundred meters away from it, the shuttle lifted off and rapidly gained speed until it was able to blink back into Beamspace, not to be seen again until it blinked back into Space-3 on its next relay to the surface of the planet.

Flanked by a brace of Large Ones, the Over Master in command of that phase of the planetside operations stomped off his command vehicle and glared around the village his Fighters had just ravaged. The bodies of Earthmen lay on the ground, many still bubbling where the acid of his Fighters' weapons hadn't yet finished eating the flesh. The houses and other buildings of Eighth Shrine were scattered debris, struck by kinetic energy weapons designed to destroy steel and stone constructions instead of the flimsy woodframe used by these primitives.

The Master who led the raid scampered to the Over Master and bowed deeply. The Over Master inclined his head in response.

"Did you allow any to escape?" the Over Master growled.

"Yes, Master. Three of them fled, sufficiently uninjured to live long enough to carry word of the raid."

"Good!" the Over Master barked. "How are preparations proceeding?"

The Master in command of the raid nodded toward a hillside half a kilometer away. "Construction of the tunnel complex has begun." In the distance, clots of mud could be seen as they were flung from a hole in the side of the hill. Thanks to his workers and a nearby forest, when the digging was finished there would be little trace other than the opening in the hillside, and that would be camouflaged into invisibility.

When the Over Master grunted provisional approval of the tunnel works, the Master said, "I have placed squads in observation posts at these locations." He turned on his mapper and

a true-color topo map of the area materialized in front of the
Over Master. Seven squad-size observation posts were indicated. "Reaction platoons are stationed here." Three spots on
the projection lit up with the symbols that indicated platoons.

The Over Master studied the map and compared it with
what he recalled from his own maps. Then, satisfied that the
observation posts and reaction platoons were stationed where
he would have put them, he grunted "Good," turned to one of
the Large Ones flanking him and issued the order to set up his
command post.

"Now we wait," the Over Master said.

They waited for three days before a remote radar station reported rapidly approaching aircraft.

"Lock on and prepare to kill them on my command," the
Over Master ordered.

Two Avenging Angels of the 357th Attack Squadron of
Kingdom's Aerial Defense Corps approached the destroyed
village at Mach 3. Avenging Angel was the name the King-
domites used for the Strike Eagle, the ground attack aircraft
used by the Confederation Navy and Marine Corps before
they upgraded to the Raptor. It might be obsolete on a
modern battlefield, but the Avenging Angel was quite deadly
against ill-trained ground troops who lacked modern antiair-
craft weapons.

"Lead to Wing," the pilot of the lead Angel said into his
radio as soon as their destination became visible on the
horizon. "Give me cover at angels ten, I'm going down to angels one for a closer look."

"Roger, Lead." The wingman pointed his plane's nose up
and hit the afterburners. The Avenging Angel gouted flame
and shot upward.

The leader throttled back sharply and hit his braking jets.
The sudden deceleration slammed him forward in his har-
ness. The Avenging Angel bucked and, almost out of control,
shed altitude. It was a crude maneuver, but effective for

making an abrupt change in velocity and altitude. He was at altitude and four hundred knots when he overflew the village.

"What the . . . ?" What he saw on the ground didn't look like the aerial or satellite photos he'd studied during the briefing. None of the buildings were there, though the roadways seemed to be intact. The few structures that were standing didn't at all resemble anything he expected to see in a subtropical agricultural area of Kingdom. He saw no people or farming equipment in the fields, but people were evident in the village itself. Most of them seemed to be carrying tanks of some kind on their backs; none of them waved at him when he waggled his wings.

"Bogie! Bogie!" the wingman suddenly screamed.

"Where?" None of the alarms in the lead's cockpit had gone off. He looked around wildly but didn't see anything approaching. Then he looked up.

"Sacred Yahweh," he breathed. Far above, where he should have seen his wingman's Avenging Angel, he saw only tumbling specks. The pilot hit the afterburner and yanked hard on the stick in case something undetected was coming toward him. The maneuver was in vain. An invisible force slammed into his aircraft and disintegrated it.

Both aircraft went down without getting off a message to their headquarters. Three hours after the air reconnaissance failed to report in, a battalion of armored infantry mounted up and headed toward the village of Eighth Shrine.

Colonel Deacon Truthly Godsservant stood tall in the commander's hatch of his Gabriel armored fighting vehicle. He relished the growling, clanking, and rattling of the Gabriel. He shook with the rattling of the vehicle and imagined that shaking was the trembling of God's will filling his body. It gave him a feeling of power, imbued him with certainty that his force would easily smite the heretics who had usurped the devine authority of the priests in the village of

Eighth Shrine and somehow managed to knock out two Avenging Angels.

He scanned the landscape. To one side of the roadway the ground sloped upward toward the mountains. That side was terraced for rice paddies. Golden wheat for the sacred wafers grew on the level ground to the road's other side. Well ahead, dust rose from the churning treads of the six Gabriels that scouted ahead of the main column of twenty-one. Far to the flanks four more churned the rice paddies, grinding the golden wheat in their protective screenings. The loss of the rice and wheat would teach the local peasants not to harbor heretics. Ahead, the road wound through a small range of low, wooded hills that were too rocky to farm.

Godsservant's own AFV was fifth in the main column of twenty-one vehicles. Twenty-one plus the scouts and flankers. Thirty-five Gabriels, righteous avengers of the Lord! And four hundred Soldiers of the Lord rode in those blessed chariots. They were a fearsome sight to the sinners on whom they brought down the Lord's righteous wrath. A thin smile creased Godsservant's harsh face. He glanced at his map. Ten more kilometers. His scouts should break through the wooded hills into view of Eighth Shrine in a few more minutes.

"First platoon, hold up," ordered First Acolyte Loveoflord. Around him the six Gabriels of the scouting screen clanked to a halt just inside the trees. Loveoflord, the platoon commander, raised his telescope to his eye and surveyed the open land ahead. "Check our position," he ordered the gunner, who doubled as navigator.

"Sir," the gunner-navigator said sharply, "we are 1.4 kilometers from the heretic village, azimuth 327."

"Double-check that," Loveoflord said.

"Right away, sir." The speed with which the navigator said, "Reading is the same: 1.4 kilometers, azimuth 327," told Loveoflord either the navigator had already rechecked their position or was confident enough of his navigation he didn't bother to.

"Then Eighth Shrine is in sight?"

"If we're through the trees, yessir."

"Come up here." The gunner-navigator couldn't see outside from his navigation position, instead he had to rely totally on his instruments.

There were scrabbling noises from below, then the navigator squeezed up into the commander's hatch next to Loveoflord. The officer wordlessly handed him the telescope. The navigator took it and looked ahead.

"That's odd," he murmured. He lowered the telescope from his eye and checked his wrist compass. Then he looked again, this time in a sweep that let him view the entire landscape beyond the woods. He handed the telescope back and said, "I've been here before, sir. I recognize the land." He looked at his platoon commander but fear was visible in his eyes. "Where did the village go? And what are those buildings?"

Loveoflord shook his head. "Take your gun station." Then he got on the radio and reported to Colonel Deacon Godsservant.

At a range of two kilometers, closer where the trees obstructed their vision, thirty-five Gabriels, each armed with two 12.7mm projectile machine guns and a 75mm cannon, ringed the place where Eighth Shrine should have been. The four hundred infantrymen had dismounted and split into two groups before the vehicles moved into position; two companies remained with Colonel Deacon Goddservant at the approach to the village, while the third swung around in a wide arc to form an anvil on the other side of the village for the main force's hammer.

Godsservant finished his visual inspection of Eighth Shrine. The village's buildings—the temple, the silos, the barns, and houses—seemed all to be gone, though he could still see the roads and pathways. In place of the buildings there were seven squat constructions; flimsy looking, ugly, mud-colored things in no architectural style familiar to him. No people were in evidence.

"Commence," he ordered.

Fifty meters to his left a platoon, thirty-four men, rose from cover and trotted for the village. The platoon moved in good order; spread out, each man with his flechette rifle held at the ready. A hundred meters from the nearest of the strange structures the soldiers dropped to prone positions.

"Report," Godsservant ordered into his radio.

"Sir," the second acolyte commanding the advance platoon replied instantly, "I detect no movement among the structures. I hear nothing other than the wind and distant animal calls."

"Hail them."

"Yessir." The junior officer rose to his feet and spoke into the boomer he carried. "In the village of Eighth Shrine, show yourselves! We are Soldiers of the Lord and wish no harm to any other than sinners!" His voice echoed off the low hillside behind the village. There was no other reply. He repeated his message. Still no reply.

"Advance," Godsservant ordered.

The platoon rose again and continued its advance. The strange structures proved to be as flimsy as they looked at a distance; they opened easily and fell apart at a blow. In moments all seven were knocked down.

"Sir, the place seems to be totally abandoned."

Colonel Deacon Godsservant gave a signal to his driver, and his Gabriel rumbled out of the trees and sped into the village site.

"Sir, I found some odd things," the second acolyte said when Godsservant dismounted and joined him. "Look." He pointed at the surface of one of the village's roads.

A swath about three meters wide was swept at an angle across the road—no debris, not even a pebble, was in the swath. Pebbles and twigs were scattered out from its sides, as though tossed or blown from it.

"And over here, sir." A rectangular patch of ground cover on the edge of the village site was crushed, as though something heavy had rested on it.

Godsservant stood at one end of the crushed area and looked into the village. "It looks," he said after a moment, "like an off-worlder shuttle landed here and debarked hovercraft." He pointed. There were several swept swaths across roads. Many of them were in line with the crushed area.

"Unbelievers landed here, sir?" The young officer's voice cracked.

Godsservant grunted. "We will find them. We will take them. The Collegium will find out what they did to the village."

The second acolyte swallowed. The Collegium was the very core of Kingdom's disciplinary arm. When people were called before it, they might go in whole, but they always came out broken if not dead.

Godsservant ordered the battalion's officers to join him for a meeting. In a few minutes all the officers in the battalion were gathered near the crushed area.

Suddenly, plugs of turf popped up all around the officers, and creatures stood up in the holes that had been concealed under the plugs. The creatures were manlike, but smaller. They held nozzled hoses in their hands, pointed toward the officers. One of the creatures shrilled a command, and they sprayed the officers with a thick, greenish fluid. The officers screamed in agony as the fluid hit them and ate into their flesh and bubbled it away.

In seconds the lead sword of the advance platoon was the senior man left functional. He started shouting orders to the infantrymen, but a stream of greenish fluid took him in the face. He couldn't scream because the breath he drew in sucked the acid into his lungs. More turf plugs popped open and creatures stood up in the holes. Only four soldiers managed to get off shots before they were all down, writhing in agony. All the shots missed.

Inside the treeline a company first sword realized that all the battalion's officers were dead or dying, as were all of the soldiers in the village. Even though he was but an enlisted man, he was the senior remaining man in the battalion. He took command and ordered the Gabriels to open fire with their cannons and obliterate the site.

Lost to the men in the armored vehicles in the blasting of their own guns was a rapid-fire cracking along the length of the hillside behind the village. They saw nothing coming and their threat alarms sounded no warning. Every one of the Gabriels was hit by a force equal to two tons of dynamite before they could get off their second salvo. The force was concentrated to punch a hole through the armor. The secondary explosions when their magazines went off tore them apart and violently flung their parts great distances.

The riflemen in the two companies that formed Godsservant's planned hammer saw their officers killed most hideously and came close to panic. When the Gabriels blew up and many of them were wounded or killed by shrapnel, they closed the short distance to panic and ran. In their flight many of them passed near the still hidden observation posts and died as horribly as their officers had.

The soldiers in the one company of the planned anvil didn't see the officers die, but they heard and saw the deaths of the Gabriels near them. No one rose up to take command immediately, so they dithered fearfully, waiting for someone to tell them what to do. Suddenly, doors opened in the hillside in front of them, the back side of the hill behind the village, and combat vehicles smaller than their Gabriels sped out. The soldiers didn't have any antiarmor weapons; they broke and ran. The small vehicles that pursued them were nimble and chased them wherever they went, spraying a greenish fluid from their cannon nozzles whenever they came close to a fleeing soldier. All of the soldiers in the anvil died.

Before nightfall, the invaders were gone along with all their equipment and supplies. They left behind only the tunnels they dug under the hill and the holes in the village area, all still well-concealed, all booby-trapped.

The next day a specially trained reconnaissance team came to investigate. Not knowing it was unnecessary, they remained fully concealed. They retrieved fragments of one of the shattered Gabriels to take back for forensic examination. One of the reconnaissance soldiers, braver or more foolish than the others, crept into the village site during the night and picked up partial remains of one of the dead to take back for the same reason. When the technicians of the Kingdom's Army of the Lord were unable to determine what had killed the soldier or destroyed the Gabriel, the pieces, organic and metallic, were handed over to off-worlders for analysis. The scientists in Interstellar City were fascinated by the remains and wanted to know where they came from so they could visit the place and gather more pieces for analysis. Such a visit, the scientists were told, was impossible, and there the matter lay. For a while.

CHAPTER
NINETEEN

Gradually, Claypoole became aware of rushing water, far away at first and then louder as he slowly regained consciousness. He opened his eyes. In the dim light shining through a dirty window high above his head, he could see that he lay on the floor of a warehouse of some kind. Boxes stood stacked in neat rows along one wall. He could just make out a door at the far end of the building. The place was enormous. He coughed and the sound echoed loudly in the damp gloom.

The last thing Claypoole remembered was some girl named . . . ? He couldn't remember. What the hell had she hit him with? Someone nearby groaned. His eyes now adjusted to the dim light, he could make out two other figures stretched on the floor nearby.

"Oof! I feel like I been shot at and missed and shit at and hit," one of the figures groaned. It was Raoul!

"Raoul! How are you?" Claypoole asked. Pasquin only grunted. The other figure had to be Dean. Claypoole nudged him. Dean groaned. "Deano, we been zapped! How you feeling?"

"You telling me?" Dean muttered. Damn, this kind of roll job wasn't supposed to happen on Havanagas!

Pasquin sat up slowly. "Oh. Last thing I remember was Marilyn's big jugs, and then the lights went out. Do you think that bastard Paoli did this?"

"Not at all, gentlemen!" a voice boomed from behind them. A dark figure approached, its heels smacking loudly on the concrete floor. A man in a dripping cloak stood before them, his face obscured by a floppy-brimmed hat pulled down low. "I apologize for this," the figure gestured vaguely, "but since you are under constant surveillance, I couldn't risk exposing myself to invite you to be my guests here like a gentleman." He laughed.

"And just who in the hell are you?" Pasquin asked, real anger in his voice.

"Never mind for now, Corporal Pasquin. Oh, yes, I know who you are, or who you want to be known as. We've been watching you too."

"Who's this 'we'?" Dean asked.

"Well, let's say I represent a group opposed to the criminals who run this world. How's that, Lance Corporal Dean?"

"You are with the Havanagas Liberation Front?" Claypoole asked.

The figure regarded Claypoole for a long moment before it answered. "Yes. Strange, three recently discharged Marine grunts know about the existence of the Front?"

"Culloden told us about you," Pasquin said quickly. That goddamned Claypoole, he thought, should engage brain before mouth.

"Oh?" The figure was silent again for a moment. "What else do you know about the Front?"

Pasquin got shakily to his feet and pulled up an empty crate, which he sat on. It was marked FERTILIZER. "We know the mob doesn't really consider you a threat." Pasquin's mind rushed. Nast had briefed them on the Front. This was a warehouse. It contained fertilizer. There was running water nearby. Yes! O'Mol. This guy had to be him. Somebody-or-other O'Mol, the gentleman farmer who owned property along a river. He couldn't remember the full name or the name of the river, but this had to be the guy.

"That's going to change, and very soon," the figure replied. "You know Johnny Sticks doesn't believe you're really three discharged Marines on a spree. Neither do I, come to that.

Just what are you three doing here? Discharged servicemen never come here."

Silence. The water continued to flow outside, and far above them the rain thrummed steadily on the tin roof. Dean and Claypoole had now gotten up and were squatting on their haunches.

"Okay," the figure said at last, "I really don't care what you're doing here. I have a request of you, that's all. Will you listen to me? If you won't help, that's all right too. You'll be free to return to Placetas and I won't bother you again. Deal?"

"Do we have a choice?" Dean asked.

"Just hear me out and then I'll take you back to the city." Pasquin nodded. Quickly, the figure stepped over to the row of boxes and pulled one out. It was heavy and he dragged it with difficulty over to where the Marines sat. He ripped the lid off and threw it onto the floor, where it clattered noisily. With a knife he took out of a pocket, he sliced open the foil wrapping of a package inside and peeled it back.

The three leaned forward to see what was inside. Dean emitted a low whistle of surprise. "Am I dreaming or are those M-1A semiautomatic miniaturized oxyhydrogen plasma shooters?"

"Blasters!" Claypoole exclaimed. He reached inside and pulled out a disassembled stock and receiver.

"Where in the name of Mohammed's dirty fingernails did you ever get these?" Pasquin asked. "It's against every law on the books for anyone but legitimate military and police forces to have these!"

O'Mol snorted derisively. "Corporal, you are on Havanagas. If you have money, you can get anything you want here. I have money. There are six of these in there, each with four power packs, sixteen hundred rounds per weapon. I need someone to teach us how to use them."

The three began pulling out the disassembled weapons. "Oh, jeez, I am beginning to feel like a Marine again!" Pasquin sighed as he pulled the wrapping off a blaster and fished around in the crate for the barrel and sighting mechanism.

"Gentlemen, I will pay you well to teach us how to use and maintain these weapons. I'll give you more than enough to pay for your stay here on Havanagas, plus set you up when you get back home. With these six weapons I'll have enough firepower to make myself heard on this planet. I'll have a fighting chance to clean this mess up."

"So you're going to go after the mob?"

"Yes."

"I'll drink to that," Dean said. "You know, there are instruction manuals in here. You don't need us to learn how to use these weapons."

"Yes, I do. The manuals will tell us how to assemble and disassemble them, how to maintain them and how to clean and store them, but they won't tell us how to shoot. That's what Marines do."

"You sure got that right," Claypoole muttered.

"Look," O'Mol said, "it'll only take a couple of days to get us off to a good start, and after that you're free to go."

"Oh, yeah, and the mob finds out we're working for you and I know where we'll 'go'—to hell in a hand basket," Claypoole responded.

"I'll put you up here and I'll get you off-world. I can do that."

"If we do this for you, I want Katie Wells to go with us, mister," Claypoole announced, standing up.

"What the—" Pasquin shouted.

"Rock!" Dean exclaimed.

Claypoole shook his head stubbornly. "If we work for this guy, I want Katie to go with us when we leave. I'll work for you for free if you'll do that for me, sir," he said.

"I'll pay you and I'll get the girl out for you too, Mister Claypoole. What do you others say?"

Pasquin moved close to Claypoole and put his nose right into his face. "Lance Corporal, we have a job to do and we are going to do it! You hear me? We are gonna do that job and I don't want to hear any more of this shit from you, understand?" He turned to O'Mol. "No, we can't help you. Now we want to go back to Placetas, if you please."

Dean flexed his fingers nervously, looking from Claypoole to Pasquin. "He's right, Rock," he whispered. "I wish you success fighting the families, sir, but Marines follow orders and we have our orders." He started to put the weapons back into their crate.

"Hold on!" Claypoole shouted. "It won't take three of us to do what we came here for! I'm staying! You guys can carry on without me."

"Claypoole, you are deserting in the face of the enemy. Do you know what the Corps will do to you when you get back to 'Finni's World? Do you?" Pasquin had stepped back a pace and stood facing Claypoole with his fists on his hips.

"This not a military mission!" Claypoole shouted. "We get every shit detail in the universe and we're supposed to lap it up and grin, right? Orders, orders, orders; cover down, dress right, dress, hup, toop, threep, fo? Well, this time Lance Corporal Claypoole, R, CMC 2130242L, is gonna do what he wants! I don't care! I'm staying." He paused and stood there breathing heavily. "Fellas, listen to me, okay? I'm not giving this girl up to these fucks. You know what they told us, once you work for the mob you're theirs forever. Here's a woman who could go places but she'll just be a whore forever unless I do this for her. Look," he was pleading now, "ever since Maggie—"

"Okay, okay, Rock, we get the picture," Pasquin said sarcastically, "you get a little pussy and you flip your buddies the bird. You get a little screw and you bring it back to the barracks and give the rest of us a screwing, is that it? You worthless goddamned civilian!" Pasquin spit the word out, and it echoed around the warehouse.

"Now listen here, you goddamned candy-assed pogue!" Claypoole shouted back.

Quickly Dean stepped between them. He remembered all
too well the fight he'd had with Claypoole back on Wanderjahr over Hway Keutgens, and he could see another one
coming on now.

"Stop! Stop! Wait a second!" O'Mol held up his hand.
"Listen! Listen!" From far away came a metallic whooshing
sound.

The door at the far end of the building slammed open with
a crash and a man came running in. "They're coming! We've
been made, Olwyn! Get to the boat!"

"Wait! Wait! How many, how far away are they?" O'Mol
asked. He didn't have to ask who was coming.

The man ran up to the little group, panting, his hair plas-
tered to his head with rainwater. In one hand he clutched a big
pistol of some kind. "They're at the house! Lots of the Ferris
men! They came in three ships at least." From outside they
could hear the sound of gunfire and explosions. "They don't
know you're in here, Olwyn, but they'll be on us any minute!
They had to have seen me running this way!"

"Oh, that's just fucking peachy," Pasquin said as he began assembling one of the blasters. "Marines, you know what
to do."

"Hoooheee!" Claypoole sang. "We're Marines again!"

"We can assemble these weapons in thirty seconds—in the
dark," Dean informed O'Mol, "but in here, well . . ." He
stood up, a fully assembled blaster at port arms, a power pack
inserted securely in the magazine well.

The rain had let up for now and they could clearly hear
men shouting from somewhere outside.

"I have a hydrofoil at the river," O'Mol said. "We'll make
a break through the backdoor, it opens onto the riverbank.
If you Marines'll hold these goons off for a few minutes,
I'll get her started and we can make it to the open sea, we'll
be safe."

"You damned sure better be waiting there for us, mister,"
Pasquin muttered as he jammed power packs into his pockets.

"Dean, you cover the inside here. If anyone comes in through that door, you know what to do. Rock, come with me. We'll cover the approaches from either side of the building." He grinned fiercely. "We got a big surprise for these bastards!"

"Not so fast!" the messenger said, stepping back a few paces, his pistol leveled at O'Mol.

Pasquin shot him from the hip. A plasma bolt punched a hole through his chest. The stench of burnt flesh filled the air as the man toppled. Pasquin coughed. "You never know who to trust, do you?" he said to O'Mol. "Okay, Marines, let's get a move on."

O'Mol picked up the carton with the remaining three blasters in it and ran for the door.

Dean lay on his stomach just inside the rear door, the muzzle of his blaster trained on the entrance at the opposite end of the building. From outside came the *hiss-crack!* of Pasquin's and Claypoole's weapons. Dean smiled. Goddamn, we're a team! he thought. The door he was covering burst open suddenly. Dean fired three rapid shots through the open door. Instead of the thuds of falling bodies, he heard the excited shouts of men who found themselves up against an unexpected weapon. He fired several shots as fast as he could at the wall to the side of the door and slagged a hole through the metal. Outside, it was raining again. A small group of men was milling around, shouting and beating at their clothing where molten metal had set it afire. Dean shot into them, one, two, three quick shots. Three of the men spun and dropped, with charred holes where they'd been hit. The others ran, screaming. The only emotion Dean felt as he watched them burn to death was satisfaction. This undercover shit was for the birds, but combat—he could handle that!

"Dean! Come on, we're leaving!" It was Claypoole.

Dean got up and dodged out the backdoor. About a kilometer away stood what looked like a farmhouse. Three huge jet-powered aircraft sat around the structure, their engines running. A large number of little black figures were dashing up to them and climbing on board. Off to the left in a field of grass he saw the unmoving bodies of men that Claypoole had killed.

"Come on!" O'Mol shouted from the hydrofoil docked at a small wharf on the riverbank fifty meters below the warehouse.

"Not yet! Raoul!" Dean shouted. Pasquin ran up to him from his firing position, a fierce grin on his face. He gave them high fives all around. "No, Raoul, we can't leave until we've taken out those aircraft!" As Dean spoke the first one lifted off.

"Oh, shit, Marines, taking on enemy aircraft in the open! That's great tactics!" Claypoole shouted, but he went to one knee and took steady aim at the cockpit of the lead jet. It skimmed slowly over the grass, coming on steady and level. It was a great shot and Claypoole took it. His bolt flashed on the bubble of the cockpit and the machine skittered crazily to one side, out of control, and nosed into a field of crops, where it exploded into an enormous fireball. They could feel the concussion of the explosion and the heat of the burning fuel where they stood.

The other two pilots, seeing the fate of their partner, veered sharply left and right and came on quickly from the flanks. Suddenly, the air around the Marines cracked and hissed with the deadly noise of supersonic projectiles; bullets smacked and whacked into the metal roof and walls of the warehouse.

"Do something and do it quick!" O'Mol shouted from the riverbank.

Pasquin fired from the offhand position, using the corner of the building to brace himself. He snapped off three quick shots at the aircraft approaching from his side. They all missed. He cursed, went to one knee and fired again. The jet exploded in a massive flash of fuel, parts, and bodies. Dean's first round at the remaining jet hit it in the tail section, and smoke began to pour out of it. The pilot climbed rapidly to gain altitude and get out of range. At about three hundred meters the jet suddenly went totally vertical, its nose pointing straight up in the air, engines screaming, and just hung there for a full ten seconds as the pilot tried desperately to level off. The Marines held their fire, watching, fascinated. Little black figures leaped out its open passenger doors and plummeted to earth, making great splashes as they plunged into the wet fields. Slowly, gracefully, the machine rolled over on its back and fell screaming into the earth, ending its flight in another huge fireball.

The whole scene went deathly quiet, except for the hissing rain. "Jeez," Claypoole said, "you know the worst thing about all this? We won't even get credit for shooting those bastards down."

CHAPTER
TWENTY

With O'Mol at the controls, the hydrofoil zoomed along at sixty kph, sending up a huge roostertail of spray behind it.

"Shouldn't we take it a bit easy?" Pasquin asked. "I mean, aren't you worried about rocks, shallows, floating logs?"

"This part of the river is dredged frequently," O'Mol shouted back, "so tourists can take leisurely trips. But we can't worry about that now; we've got to put some distance between the farm and us. Some of those men must've survived, somebody had to have sent a message!"

"How far to Placetas?" Dean shouted.

"Seventy-five klicks!" O'Mol answered.

"And to the ocean?"

"Maybe another twenty-five klicks. Piece of cake!"

O'Mol sounded the klaxon. Its harsh *arooo! arooo!* made the Marines jump. Directly ahead of them was another boat.

"Goddamn, we're gonna hit!" Dean screamed. O'Mol only laughed and increased his speed. At the last instant the boat swerved into the bank and the hydrofoil roared on past, thoroughly soaking the passengers on its open lower deck.

"Goddamned tourists!" O'Mol shouted. "I always wanted to do that to those goggle-eyed freaks! What the hell are those fools doing out in this weather anyway?" He sounded the klaxon several more times. "Toooot, toooot!" he screamed. "Make way for Steamboat Willie!" O'Mol laughed delightedly, thoroughly enjoying his role as captain of the tiny vessel

219

as the three Marines crouched in the cabin, weapons covering the riverbank as it sped by.

As soon as the light began to fade, O'Mol slowed the hydrofoil. After a few more minutes he pulled it up into some reeds. "We'll wait here until dark," he said. "I have equipment to mask our signatures in case they have more aircraft out looking for us. We'll be reasonably secure once it gets full dark. This river runs right by Placetas. We'll cruise by quietly in the dark. I've got a boat at the mouth of the delta. We can take it to some islands out in the Ligurian Sea where nobody'll find us. We can hole up there and make plans."

Slowly, carefully, O'Mol guided the hydrofoil into a thick patch of reeds growing in the shallows. He cut the engines and the craft settled silently down to its gunwales. "It's an hour to dark. The overcast and the rain'll hide us from the air." O'Mol laughed. "Besides, there's nothing on Havanagas that can compete with those blasters of yours anyway. But the mob'll be out looking for us; you can count on it. What *I'm* counting on is they'll be extra cautious because of what you did to them back there." He went into the tiny galley and came back with four bottles of beer.

"How come we can't stop at Placetas?" Claypoole asked.

"Too dangerous. The city's the mob's territory. It'll be crawling with agents and security goons anxious to make a big bonus for being the first to spot us. I figure we can coast by in the dark, open her up on the other side of the city, and make the ocean by dawn."

"We're supposed to meet our contact at the Free Library at six hours tonight," Pasquin protested. "Once our contact hands over the evidence the Ministry of Justice needs, we can call in plenty of firepower. Put these families out of business and you'll be in business, Mister O'Mol."

O'Mol shook his head. "No can do. Too dangerous, I said. They'll get you for sure if you go into the city."

"Not if we have these." Dean patted his blaster.

"Mister Dean, if you go into the city, you will have to use it there. Do you really want to take a chance on burning up innocent bystanders with that thing?"

"Hell, they all work for the mob," Claypoole protested.

"No, they don't, Mister Claypoole," O'Mol answered forcefully. "I could have launched a terrorist campaign all over this planet, blown up hotels and casinos, all that. The reason I didn't was because Mom and Pop Citizen who come here for a vacation may be fools to spend their life's savings like this, but they don't deserve to get roasted in a crossfire between the good guys and the bad guys. You understand what I'm saying?"

Claypoole looked at his feet. "I have to go back in," he said quietly. He looked up at O'Mol. "I said I'd work for you, but you promised to get Katie out of there. I won't help you unless you let me get her and bring her to the islands with us."

"But the whole situation has changed! We're on the run now! Sticks'll be looking for us! Claypoole, he'll round up everyone who even smiled at us and interrogate them to find out if they know our plans. It's standard mob procedure. They probably have already snatched the girl. And if they don't keep her, they'll put a watch on her in case you show up." He looked to Dean and Pasquin for support, but they said nothing.

"I will not go unless you let me get Katie and bring her out to the islands with us. That's final."

"We haven't agreed to work with you, Mister O'Mol," Pasquin said.

"You have to now! I'm your only chance to get out of here alive!"

"We have to make contact with our agent in Placetas," Dean said.

O'Mol drained his beer and threw the bottle over the side. "I normally hate litterbugs," he said, apropos of nothing, "but screw it." He belched into the palm of his hand and regarded the three in the semidarkness. "Boy, you guys are sure stubborn." He shook his head. "Okay, Claypoole, I'll drop you off at the docks. How long will it take you to find the girl and get back to the river?"

"Jesus H. Mohammed, how the hell do I know?" he protested. "I know where she lives. I'll move as quickly as I can. I suppose I can get a cab at the docks?"

"Get a cab!" O'Mol exploded. "I can't believe any of this," he moaned.

"Can't you call someone in the city and have them pick Rachman up at the docks?" Pasquin asked.

"Yes, I can. But I can't do that until we're there. They'll be monitoring all telecommunications systems now. For all I know, whoever told them I was at that safe house also compromised my people back in Placetas. I have people in other cities too, but the Placetas cell was the strongest and most active. That man you killed back there was one of my most trusted assistants. I have to assume now that my whole organization's been infiltrated, or the reward they have out on me is so great even my best friend would be tempted to turn me in. We may have to fight our way out. You'll just have to forget about contacting your controller. There's no way you can do that without getting caught. He'll just have to wait for another time. How do you contact him, by the way?"

"All we can do is send a signal we're ready, and he'll home in on us, but we can't give him the sign without the evidence he sent us here to get. Can you infiltrate us back into the city once things have had a chance to quiet down?"

"Yes. Who's your contact?"

Pasquin hesitated only briefly. "Lovat Culloden." They were in too deeply with O'Mol now to play games with each other or hold things back.

"Culloden!" O'Mol whispered in amazement. "Okay, here's the deal. I'll get someone to pick Claypoole up at the docks. We'll wait for him there. If we're discovered, we have the firepower to hold the attackers off. But it might get very, very hot. If we make it to the islands, I'll get you back into the city somehow—I don't know how right now—so you can get in touch with Culloden. I mean, damn, if I can help make your mission a success, I win, because you'll remove the family heads for me. You Marines are a godsend, if you don't somehow screw this up on me. You agree?"

"I agree," Claypoole said at once.

"Okay, I guess we don't have any choice," Pasquin put in. "Dean, what do you say?"

"Well, the man on the spot has the tactical initiative. Good plans allow for that and Marines have to be flexible. We change the plan. We have to change it. I'm with Mister O'Mol."

O'Mol blew out his breath and smiled. "Now that that's settled, let's drink up the rest of this beer."

O'Mol quietly nosed the hydrofoil into a slip at the marina at the Franklin River Docks. Pasquin gave him a quick orientation on how to use a blaster and they took up a 360-degree defensive position.

"You will need something," O'Mol told Claypoole. He handed him a small pistol. "This is a Sig-Walther semiauto. You load it by pulling back the slide and—"

Claypoole pressed the magazine catch and dropped the magazine into his hand. Quickly he thumbed ten rounds into the palm of the other hand and pulled back the slide several times to be sure there wasn't a round in the chamber. "You ought to carry this thing with one up the spout, ready for immediate fire," he advised O'Mol. Then he reloaded the magazine, rammed it into the butt, and racked a round into the chamber. "Double action?" he asked. O'Mol nodded. "Good. I'm off." He climbed up onto the dock and began walking toward the street.

"Where did he ever learn to handle a projectile weapon like that?" O'Mol asked, impressed.

"Place called Wanderjahr. It's a long story," Dean said.

A car in the street flashed its lights once. O'Mol's agent was ready.

Nobody had said anything about how long they would

wait for Claypoole, but Pasquin and Dean didn't intend to leave without him. If he wasn't back by dawn, they would go into the city and get him. O'Mol knew enough not to argue about it.

A woman was driving. "Take me to 134A Bilko Strand," Claypoole announced as he climbed into the passenger's seat. Claypoole glanced at her as she put the car into drive. She had a hard face, and the dim light did not improve it much. He realized suddenly her tight-lipped expression was one of fear, not anger at being called out on a night like this. "Piece of cake," he said easily, hoping to break the tension. She did not respond. They turned into a major thoroughfare leading into Center City. Claypoole realized with a sudden twinge of fear that Katie's apartment was in the suburbs on the far side of the city. They'd have to go all the way through town and then back again. Nervously, he fingered the pistol in his pocket.

"You armed?" he asked the driver.

"Yes." She stared ahead at traffic, which was quite heavy at this hour, even in the rainy season.

"What do you do for a living?" Claypoole asked the question in the hopes of getting her to relax by talking about something familiar.

"I drive this taxi." She shifted her position to get more comfortable. "I know where you're going, I live in the same neighborhood, a place on Cramden Square. Who are we picking up? The message just said I was to drive you somewhere."

"A girl I know. Then we go back to the docks on the riverfront."

The woman looked at Claypoole anxiously. "That'll work if they don't make us, but if they do, we'll never get back through the city."

"Yes, we will," Claypoole replied with a confidence he didn't feel. "My name's Lance Corporal Rachman Claypoole, Confederation Marine Corps. What's yours?"

"Grace."

"Okay, Grace, we're gonna pull this off. Relax. But be prepared. I don't know if Katie'll be home. If she isn't, we're gonna have to go down to where she works and get her there. Just take it easy and act naturally. I presume you can use whatever weapon you're carrying? Good. If we do have a fight, aim at the center of mass and squeeze off your shot. You know this town, do you?"

"Like the back of my hand."

"Well, be thinking about alternate routes and all that, just in case we gotta get a move on. Otherwise, you're a taxi driver and I'm your fare." He settled back in his seat and Grace grinned over at him. "Grace, we get back to the docks in one piece, can you come with us? We need every hand we can get. Can you jump out of here without any advance notice?"

"Damn right," she replied. Claypoole smiled in the dark.

Katie's apartment was on the ground floor of a two-story complex on a pleasant suburban street. Claypoole had Grace park a block from Katie's door, so he could approach on foot. "If you hear any shooting, I'm gonna need your help real quick, Grace. I can rely on you, can't I?"

"I'll pull up in front of the apartment and you get your ass in here real quick, Marine." Now that they were well into the mission, her initial anxiety had disappeared, replaced by a cool professionalism.

It was raining as Claypoole sauntered down the street, trying to look like he belonged. He stepped under the overhang and tapped the Query button on the entry keypad. Nothing. He tapped again. Still nothing. Uncertain what to do next, he stood there. Maybe Katie was working. He tapped the keypad a third time, leaving his finger on the bell icon for a full ten seconds. Nothing. He turned to go just as the heavens opened up and dumped water on the city.

"Yeah?" a man's voice said from behind him. Through the privacy screen in the doorway he could see only a dim outline of someone on the other side.

"Is Miss Wells in?" Claypoole shouted over the downpour.

"Yeah, but she's busy. Go 'way."

"Excuse me, but I just gotta see her! I'm her brother and we've got a family emergency going. Just ask her to step outside for a second, will you?"

The privacy screen turned transparent. A very big man stood there. "She ain't got no brother, you stupid—"

"Hey hey! One question, man, okay?"

"Be quick, asshole." From inside came a muffled scream.

"Can you run 350 meters in one second?"

"You wiseass—" The man reached over to reactivate the privacy screen as Claypoole shot him between the eyes. The shot was muffled in the roar of the downpour. The big man spun around and then slowly fell over backward through the doorway. Claypoole stepped over him into the apartment. Another very large man had Katie pinned to the floor. As soon as he saw Claypoole, he slammed Katie's face into the floor to stun her, then stood up, reaching inside his coat as he rose.

Claypoole shot the man in the center of his chest.

"Goddamn!" he exclaimed, looking down at the fist-sized dent in the vest he wore beneath his coat. "You bastard! I'm *really* gonna kick your ass now!" He staggered toward Claypoole, who backpedaled until he almost fell over the corpse in the doorway. He raised the barrel and fired again, hitting the man in the mouth, taking out his lower front teeth before exiting through his upper jaw, just in front of his left ear. The man clapped a hand to his face and grunted. He stood there, blood streaming through his fingers. Carefully, Claypoole aimed his gun at the center of his forehead.

Katie slammed a heavy chair onto the top of the man's head and he collapsed to the floor. "Sonofabitch!" she swore. Her face was bloody and one eye was almost swollen shut. She was breathing hard. "He didn't hit me hard enough," she gasped.

Claypoole decocked the pistol and put it away. He had seven shots left. He grabbed Katie by the shoulders. "We gotta leave, now, Katie! These guys were after me, weren't they?"

Katie nodded. "They said they're rounding up everyone who's had anything to do with you since you've been here. What's going on? They wouldn't tell me."

"I'll tell you later. Come on, don't bother to grab anything." He propelled her toward the open doorway. The rain was coming down in sheets outside now and it hit them like a huge hand as they stumbled out onto the sidewalk. At that moment two cars roared up and slammed to a stop almost in front of them.

Claypoole pulled Katie away from where Grace was parked, because the cars blocked his way in that direction, and they ran as fast as the fear of death could carry them. Something went *crack!* beside his head, and Claypoole felt a very uncomfortable sensation in the small of his back. Anticipating the hammer blow of a bullet at almost any second, he looked back. They were coming on fast, stopping only to snap off a few shots, which fortunately were going wild. Suddenly the rain stopped.

"I can't run any faster!" Katie gasped. Claypoole grabbed her by an arm and pulled her along with him. They reached the end of the building and, without hesitating, Claypoole ran around it, putting the edge between them and their pursuers. Three of them doubled back to go around the opposite end of the building and cut them off. Claypoole dragged Katie behind the building with him.

A man leaned around the edge of the building and fired three quick shots. They sounded loud, now that the rain had stopped. Could Grace have heard them? Katie crouched beside Claypoole, panting to get her breath. Behind them was a chain-link fence about two meters high. "What's on the other side of that fence?"

"Another complex," Katie gasped.

"Let's go!" They ran for the fence. Claypoole boosted Katie up and gave her a massive shove that sent her sailing over the top. She plunged to the ground on the other side, splashing into an enormous puddle. Claypoole scrambled up after her. Shouts and the thud of feet sounded behind him. *Crack! Spang! Crack!* Bullets whistled all about him. He felt an impact through the links in the fence but none came near him. Then, abruptly, it began to rain again. He was over now and on the ground on the other side. Crouching as low as he could get, he pulled Katie into some nearby shrubs. They plowed through and out the other side into a quiet cul-de-sac.

Behind them someone was climbing the fence. Then all sound was drowned out in the torrential downpour. "Let's go!" Claypoole shouted into Katie's ear. They ran between two buildings and into the street. Water poured through the gutters like a fast mountain stream, and their feet made big splashes in the puddles. The rain was coming down so hard now the air was full of spray, which limited visibility almost as much as a thick fog. Breathing was difficult. Gasping heavily, they stumbled up the street.

A car roared down on them out of the roaring mist, its headlights flowing only dimly through the curtain of water. "Oh, hell," Claypoole muttered, and pulled out his pistol. The car almost ran the two down before the driver saw them and hit the brakes. The machine fishtailed and slid down the street sideways, its tires throwing up a bow wave as it came on, slewing to a complete stop only centimeters from where the fugitives stood frozen in their tracks.

"Get in here!" Grace screamed.

With the last of his strength, Claypoole shoved Katie in through the passenger's door and dived in behind her. Grace spun the wheel and gunned the engine as she turned the car around. They roared back up the street. She stopped before entering the main street to check traffic, and when she pressed the accelerator, the wheels spun helplessly on the rain-slick pavement. Something went *Thwank!* in the back of the car, and Grace put the car into four-wheel-drive. They shot out into traffic, narrowly missing an oncoming truck.

"They're everywhere!" Grace screamed. "I don't know how you made it!" A heavy object bounced off the right fender, slammed into the windshield and thudded over the roof. In the instant it was visible, Claypoole was horrified to see they'd hit someone. "Serves the dumb shit right!" Grace shouted. They were thrown left, then right, then left, as Grace took corners on two wheels. She reached a major road and mashed the accelerator to the floor, throwing her passengers back into their seats.

"You gotta slow down!" Claypoole screamed. "How can you see anything in this rain!"

"I know where I am!" Grace shouted over the roaring of the engine.

The rain stopped again. They were back on the main road leading into Center City. Grace braked suddenly and swerved down a side street. "We can't go through Center City, not at this hour! Besides, they'll have roadblocks up. Hang on!" Skillfully, Grace guided the cab down narrow streets, more like alleys. Waves of standing rainwater flew up from under their tires as they roared through the night. She pumped the brakes at last. "Get ready!" she shouted. "This is Franklin Boulevard coming up. It's two kilometers from here to the river. I'm gonna make it as fast as this crate'll fly! If they've set up roadblocks, we'll have to run 'em!" She stopped just off the main road, revving her engine. Claypoole looked out the back window. Way behind them he could see the bouncing lights of another vehicle, coming on fast.

"Okay, Grace, go for it! We're being followed! How ya doing?" Katie nodded that she was all right. Claypoole took her hand and kissed her. "Katie, I gotta ask you something. Will you—" His question broke off as Grace stepped hard on the accelerator and they shot out into the early evening traffic on Franklin Boulevard. One hundred, 110, 115, 120 kilometers per hour; the speedometer needle crept up and to the right.

"Pray the rain holds off!" Grace shouted, maneuvering

around the slower vehicles in front of them. "Here!" She handed Claypoole a large pistol she'd been carrying under her left armpit. "I'll drive, you shoot!" The gun was a much larger version of the one O'Mol had given him. Carefully, he eased back the slide just far enough to see if there was a round in the chamber. He was rewarded by the bright gleam of a brass cartridge. He checked for a safety. There was none, just a decocking lever. He made sure it was in the up position.

Behind them, but not that far away, another vehicle weaved in and out of the traffic. Behind that one, two more bobbed along at top speed.

Grace's cab boasted a sunroof over the passenger compartment. Claypoole opened it and stood up, bracing himself with his legs. He held the big pistol in both hands and used the roof to steady his aim. As soon as the lead vehicle appeared to be within range, he squeezed the trigger. The gun went off with such a flash, Claypoole was almost blinded, and the recoil flung both his arms upward. He held on to the pistol only because he was too surprised to release his grip. But that first bullet had a devastating effect as it smashed through the driver's side of the pursuer's windshield. The car abruptly swerved into the back of a slower vehicle, throwing it out of control too. As both spun around, other vehicles got involved, until several sat smoking and blocking the thoroughfare. By the time the other two following cars were through the mess, Grace was already several blocks ahead of them and pulling away rapidly.

"I think we'll make it!" she screamed. Claypoole, his torso sticking out through the sunroof, couldn't hear her, but it didn't make any difference. With that monster pistol in his hands, he wasn't afraid of anyone.

Another car roared out from a side street not more than fifteen meters behind them! Bullets smacked into Grace's cab and whizzed by Claypoole's head. Instinctively, he ducked back inside. The rear window had been shot out in the fusillade. Katie, crouched down on the floor, screamed, "Get down! They're shooting!"

The new car managed to pull up alongside them, and a hail of bullets smashed through the right side of the cab. Claypoole covered Katie with his own body. Then the rain came down in sheets again, and the other car slammed at full speed into the back of a tour bus that had slowed down because of the sudden reduction in visibility.

"Anybody hit?" Claypoole asked. Nobody said anything.

Grace sped ahead of the wreck and flew into a wall of water as thick as smoke. They could feel a concussion behind them although they couldn't see the wreck through the rain. "Fuel cells must've ignited!" Grace shouted. So much for keeping the tourists untroubled by "internal disciplinary matters" on Havanagas, Claypoole thought. He pressed a button and the sunroof closed. The floor of the passenger compartment was ankle deep in rainwater.

Suddenly, they stopped. "We're here!" Grace shouted. "Get out and down to the river! Quick, gimme my gun back!" She took the pistol and slid out of the driver's door. Claypoole dragged Katie out the passenger's side. Grace leaned over the hood of her cab and leveled the pistol in the direction they had just come. "Run to the boat! I'll cover you!"

The rain stopped again. In the silence, his voice sounded loud. "You don't have to," Claypoole shouted. "We have plenty of firepower! Come on, Grace, don't stay here!" She half turned and pointed at her side. Claypoole was horrified to see a large stain spreading there. She'd been hit.

Claypoole dragged Katie down a flight of stairs to the water's edge and they ran along the dock. Behind them they could hear the deep-throated roar of Grace's pistol. Other shots answered it.

"Come on! Come on!" Pasquin shouted. Already O'Mol was at the helm, revving the hydrofoil's engines. Dean rushed to help Katie aboard as little flashes of light winked at them from the street. Pasquin opened up with his blaster. The shooting ceased abruptly. Pasquin fired several more bursts. Something exploded above them. In the orange glow of the fire, Pasquin could make out figures clambering down the stairs from the street level. He flamed them with two quick shots.

O'Mol guided the hydrofoil out into midstream and then opened up the engines to full throttle. Pasquin and Dean, joined now by Claypoole with his blaster, sent bolts into the docks as they receded behind them. Things began exploding back there.

"Hey, lighten up!" O'Mol shouted. "I may own that property someday!"

"We are 'lightening up'!" Dean screamed, and fired another burst back at the docks. A boat in its slip began to burn.

"Hoohaa! If you, absolutely, positively must have it destroyed overnight," Pasquin shouted.

Claypoole was silent, thinking about Grace. It started raining again, and it rained all the way to the islands.

CHAPTER
TWENTY-ONE

The maps of the priests and bureaucrats called it Sacred Spring Five. The farmers, husbandmen, and tradesmen who lived there called it Hole in the Mud. The spring after which the village was named burbled out of the rock near the base of a cliff at the foot of the mountains. The water was sweet where it left the rock, but the land it flowed into was a shallow, flat-bottomed bowl, the remnant of an ancient impact crater, and it had poor drainage. The spring that gave the village its name, and several other springs, poured more water into the bowl than could conveniently drain away. The ground was sodden. The central area of the bowl, a broad ring around the badly eroded central peak, was covered with sluggish water ideal for growing rice without dikes or terraces. The rest of the ten-kilometer-wide bowl was too wet for growing other crops.

The village itself, forty-odd structures not counting fowl houses, was built on pilings along the northeastern edge of the rice waters. Its "streets" were simple walkways of board that rested on top of the mud. It was important that the streets be easy to move. The ground was soft and soggy to such a great depth that the pilings on which the houses and commercial buildings were erected regularly sank and new pilings had to be placed for the houses and shops to be moved onto. No matter what the maps of the priests and bureaucrats said, Sacred Spring Five did not have a stable layout.

The people wore simple garb cut from cloth woven in mills

in other parts of Kingdom. Their shoes were from the hides of
kine raised in yet other regions. They kept their shoes in
closets or chests where the constantly wet ground would not
bring mildew and rot to them, and they wore the shoes only
on those rare occasions when they left the village.

Early in its history, on orders from the priestly hierarchy,
the farmers had valiantly attempted to raise sheep, but the wet
ground rotted the sheeps' feet. Swine might have thrived in
the bog of Sacred Spring Five, but too many of Kingdom's
founders saw swine as unclean, so there were no swine to
raise. Instead, the husbandmen of Hole in the Mud raised
ducks and geese. The ducks and geese required constant vigilance to keep them from eating the growing rice, which made
it important to have a gaggle of goose-boys. The goose-boys,
despite all strictures to the contrary, found ways to turn their
herding into play rather than allow it to be the drudgery it
would have been. The ducks and geese of Sacred Spring Five
were known for their high-strung natures and the piquant
flavor of their meat.

So it happened that it was a ten-year-old goose-boy named
Heronymous Blessed, delightedly engaged in stalking a duck
that was stealing rice on the western side of the central peak,
who was the first resident of Hole in the Mud to see the unexpected visitors.

Young Heronymous Blessed jumped when he heard a
noise, a crack as if the sword of the Archangel Raphael had
rent the air. Terrified, he looked toward the sound, expecting
to see the Archangel himself coming to discipline a goose-
boy for not obeying the strictures. Even the determined duck
broke off its stalking of the rice to fly from this danger, but its
clipped wings prevented it from rising into the air, and all it
could do was plash along the water, crying *waack* and futilely
beating its useless wings.

Heronymous saw the Archangel's chariot speeding through
the air and quailed. He wanted to duck down, to hide behind
something, but the grouse was too low to the ground and the

ferns too thin to offer concealment. Wide-eyed, he watched the chariot as it slowed to touch land. The chariot was huge. If it hadn't been that of an Archangel, he would have thought it could not possibly land without sinking without a trace below the surface of the fen. It was only when it was close enough for him to see the chariot's immense size that Heronymous realized the chariot wasn't coming directly toward him; it was coming down more than half a kilometer to his south.

He dared to release the breath he hadn't realized he was holding and sucked in another. Perhaps one of the other goose-boys had drawn the Archangel's wrath. He offered up a quick prayer and vowed, should he be spared, to follow the strictures in the future.

The chariot did not sink into the fen. Instead it opened its front and four smaller chariots sped out of it and raced toward Hole in the Mud. The chariot immediately levitated and flew off from whence it came.

"No!" Heronymous shrilled. He sobbed as he ran toward his home, convinced that vengeful Yahweh was sending Archangels or even Dominions to punish his family for his transgressions.

Fortunately for him, he ran around the rice paddy rather than through it. By the time he came in sight of the village of Sacred Spring Five, its buildings were just charred and shattered fragments floating on top of the mud. All that remained of its people were pitted bones that steamed where bits of flesh exposed to the air still bubbled. The chariots were gone. Much later Heronymous learned that once the destruction of the village was complete, the chariots had zigzagged back across the rice paddies seeking out and killing what farmers and goose-boys they could find before their shuttle returned to whisk them away.

It took the rest of that day for Heronymous Blessed and the three other goose-boys who were the only survivors of the attack to come out of hiding and find each other. It was another day before the frightened boys could accept that they truly *were* the only survivors. They settled down to wait for an adult to come to their succor.

Nearly a hundred bishops, ayatollahs, chief rabbis, and metropolitans gathered in the sanctuary of Mount Temple in the heart of Haven. It was the only holy place on all of Kingdom revered by all the denominations that had settled the world—its site marked the landing place of the first star-ship's colonists. When there was a problem that affected all, the spiritual leaders had to meet in a place none considered a Palace of Shaitan.

Chairmanship of the Convocation of Ecumenical Leaders rotated annually. That year it fell upon Bishop Ralphy Bruce Preachintent, the head of the Apostolic Congregation of the Lord's Love and Devotion. As soon as the last member of the board took his place in the rear pew, Bishop Ralphy Bruce stepped out of the vestry and strode to the center of the chancel rail. He raised his eyes to the abstract sunburst on the wall behind the altar, the only symbol of divinity that all of the founding leaders could agree was not blasphemous, and prayed silently for a moment.

His prayers finished, he turned to face his fellow leaders. His hands were clasped over the butter-yellow necktie that bisected his starched white shirt. His silver-gray sharkskin suit shimmered with his every movement, and patent leather shoes flashed reflected light. A wig of office with its high-coiffed pompadour completed his traditional vestments.

Bishop Ralphy Bruce unclasped his hands and spread them wide at shoulder height. His eyes rolled up in their sockets until only their whites showed.

"MY FRIENDS!" he suddenly called out in the rhythms of the holy cadence. "We are faced with a TRIAL sent by THE LORD to TEST us! TROUBLES abound in the hinterlands and the FAITHFUL are being MARTYRED by SINNERS most foul!" As he spoke he began the sacred choreography, briskly striding from one end of the chancel rail to the other, bent forward at the hips, half turned toward the nave. His hands clenched and he stabbed his index fingers at the assembly in emphasis to his words.

"Strutting popinjay," muttered a scarlet-gowned prelate to his pewmate, a rigid, dour-faced man in a severe black suit of an ancient cut and a flat crowned black hat.

The black-garbed man clenched his jaws in agreement and kept his attention on Bishop Ralphy Bruce.

"Our GODLY soldiers," Bishop Ralphy Bruce continued, "have gone forth to SMITE the unbelievers who MARTYR the FAITHFUL and been MET with Satan's FIRE!" He paused in his striding, faced his audience, looked up and flung his hands heavenward. "LORD! WHY have You visited this TRIAL on us? HOW have we SINNED that we bring down YOUR displeasure?"

An old man in a white cassock and squared turban in the front pew slowly rose to his feet and cleared his throat.

"BROTHER!" Bishop Ralphy Bruce threw an aggressively inviting arm toward him. "Do you wish to give TESTIMONY?"

"Bishop Ralphy Bruce," the old man said in a quavery voice, "we all know how devout you are, and how you revere the Almighty. But now is not the time to beg answers from Him. Our followers are being killed by rebels even as we listen to you. We must decide, and decide quickly, how to learn the identity of the heretics perpetrating these crimes so we can send them to the perdition they deserve." He gathered his cassock around his legs and gingerly sat back down.

A very tall man, whose vestments were of the same cut and material as Bishop Ralphy Bruce's, though their colors were less gladly praiseful of the Lord, stood. "Reverend Ayatollah Fatamid is right, Ralphy Bruce," he said in a voice that sounded like it came from the depths of a crypt. "We all need prayers all the time, but right now we need decisions and action more than we need invocations."

"We never need decisions and actions more than we need

prayers and meditation!" shouted an abbot swathed in a saffron sheet.

Abruptly, half of the assembled leaders were on their feet taking sides while the other half attempted to silence them and pull them back into their seats.

"MY FRIENDS!" Bishop Ralphy Bruce shouted into the pandemonium. "BRETHREN! I BESEECH you!" But his voice wasn't loud enough to cut through. He looked about in consternation, then stepped to the pulpit and turned on the amplifier that Mount Temple's acoustics needed only for the feeblest speakers.

"MY FRIENDS!" His amplified shout boomed through the sanctuary, rattled windows, staggered a few who stood off balance. "We must not quarrel among ourselves!" The sheer volume of his words stopped the arguments and turned faces toward him.

"PLEASE, my friends, JOIN with me in a MOMENT of silent PRAYER." He clasped his hands and bowed his head. There were a few muted grumbles, but the others faced front and stood or sat or kneeled as their particular beliefs required, and prayed along with him.

"LORD!" Bishop Ralphy Bruce cried after a moment, "I beseech YOU to guide us in our DELIBERATIONS!"

Then they made some decisions. The decisions didn't come easily or quickly, but theological discussion was put aside for a few hours and they *were* able to reach them. Even though they continued to disagree on some particulars:

The rebels had some weapon, they had no idea what it was, that defeated aircraft and armored vehicles. Therefore they would instruct the Army of the Lord to send only foot soldiers after the rebels. The identity of the rebels was another matter. Beyond the fact that they were unbelievers and heretics, there was no agreement.

The rebels had destroyed a dozen villages in an area sixteen hundred kilometers long by three hundred wide, so there must be large numbers of them and several legions needed to be sent to put them down. There was time between attacks, plenty of time for soldiers to walk from one widely spaced village to another between attacks, therefore it must be a relatively small band and not more than one regiment would be needed to destroy them once they were found.

The rebels were led by a messianic leader who wished to wrest control of the Kingdom of Yahweh and His Saints and Their Apostles from God's anointed representatives for his own devil-worshiping purposes. Clearly they were simple peasants weary of tithing and frequent worship services—which services obviously weren't frequent enough.

The rebels wanted to disrupt the farming or mining or fishing or manufacturing segments of the economy to sow discontent and bring about a wider rebellion. The rebels were vandals who didn't care what they damaged as they destroyed villages that contributed to all segments of the economy.

In the end, still in total ignorance of who the rebels were, they decided to ring the area of destruction with brigades and wait for the next depredation, then speed the nearest three brigades to the scene and have them fan out in search of the rebels.

CHAPTER
TWENTY-TWO

The Egadi Island group, so named by the early settlers after islands off the west coast of Sicily, consisted of hundreds of points of rock in the Ligurian Sea, stretching a thousand kilometers to the south of the continent on which Placetas was situated. Some were literally just points of rock that jutted out of the ocean floor, but many of the islands were big enough to support the plant and animal life native to Havanagas, mostly lichens and arthropodlike amphibious creatures. The seas, however, swarmed with both vertebrate and invertebrate creatures reminiscent of the early Silurian Period of Earth's Paleozoic Era.

Over the three centuries humans had inhabited the planet, the seeds of terran flora had drifted to the islands on the currents and established themselves. So the larger members of the island group actually sported forests and other plant life that would have looked familiar to anyone sailing in the Mediterranean Sea back on Earth.

The Egadis had never been settled. They were too remote for settlement and they boasted no mineral or animal life worth exploiting. As a result, they had never been adequately charted, and most of the islands did not even have names. Several of the larger chunks of rock served as vacation sites or getaways for rich Havanagasans, but essentially the tiny oases of civilization were deserted most of the year. If there had been pirates on Havanagas, the Egadis would have been their favorite hangout.

* * *

Nast had picked a forested but rocky, medium-sized islet about four kilometers square in the center of the chain, about thirty minutes' Mach 2 flight time from Placetas. The landing had been successful using the stealth suite and under cover of a meteor shower and a tremendous rainstorm that blanketed the landing area and most of the hemisphere in which Placetas itself lay.

"I ain't never seen rain like this!" Chief Riggs exclaimed as he guided the second Essay to a faultless touchdown in a grove of trees on the leeward side of the island.

"Good navigation, Chief." Nast clapped Riggs on the shoulder.

"Ah, I just followed the guy in front of me, sir. Mister Nast, someone's gonna have to go out in that and set up your camp. We can't remain in here for two whole days."

"We can and we will. I can't take a chance on compromising our presence here. I know, I know, Chief, who's gonna be conducting flyovers in this weather, right? Nobody. I'm sure of it too. But I've worked a long time setting up this operation and I'm not leaving anything to chance. We stay buttoned up until we get the signal from Placetas. When the rain lets up a little, we can go out in shifts to stretch and so on."

Chief Riggs looked glum. "I just follow orders, sir."

"Well, Chief, when the time comes you'll get your blood pressure up, I guarantee you. And when that time does come to make the snatch, I want all of you to be so mad you'll be looking forward to it. Okay, let's look sharp. I need 360-degree surveillance out to the horizon and up to 25,000 meters. Maintain the stealth system to mask our signature."

"Aye aye, sir! Three hundred and sixty degree surveillance, horizon-to-horizon and up to 25,000 meters!" That had been agreed upon before they launched from the *Wanganui*. Chief Riggs had volunteered to pilot the Essay because he smelled an adventure coming up. He was not too sure he'd done the right thing. "Ah, Mr. Nast," he protested, "it's really gonna get funky in these Essays with all these guys cooped up in here for two full days!"

Nast found it highly ironic that Chief Riggs would complain about anything "funky" after all the time he'd spent on the *Wanganui*. He smiled. "Put me in touch with the other Essay. Okay, Chief, I see your point. I'll issue an order nobody's to fart for the next forty-eight hours."

By the time they reached his hideout, a rocky pinnacle three kilometers square in the middle of a small group of islets, they were all seasick, except Olwyn O'Mol. Huge seas were breaking against its cliffs. O'Mol, an accomplished seaman, was in his element. "I used to race my yacht in the annual Havanagas Cup," he shouted over the roar of the wind. He had been standing at the helm of his small boat for hours but seemed just as fresh as the first time they lay eyes on him. Huge gray-green waves surged all around the tiny vessel, rising so high at times that their view of the island was cut off. Still, O'Mol kept the bow steady.

His four passengers slumped wearily about the cabin, their stomachs empty. O'Mol laughed. "I thought you were Marines!"

"Spacegoing Marines, not seagoing," Pasquin answered weakly.

"Oh." O'Mol laughed again. He was really enjoying all this.

"Have you—have you—urk—" Katie couldn't finish the question.

"Have I ever done this before, you ask?" O'Mol shouted. "Yes, once. In calmer weather, though. We almost didn't make it that time either!" He laughed riotously.

"Ohhhh," Dean groaned, "do we need this shit?"

"Hold on, children!" O'Mol shouted. "We're going in!"

Timing his entry to match the surge of the waves, O'Mol expertly guided his boat between two huge cliffs and into a small cove encircled by sheer rock precipices. Immediately the wild pitching ceased. The cove was about half a kilometer wide and no more than a thousand meters deep, but it offered perfect protection from the sea and aerial surveillance. At the far end was a stretch of sandy beach on which someone had built a wharf. Two ramshackle buildings stood there, nestled against the base of the cliffs. The muted grumble of the boat's engine echoed loudly off the cliffs. The cove was also protected from the rain, which instead of pouring down in sheets from above, hung suspended over it in a heavy mist, a vast relief from the constant pounding they'd been receiving in the open seas.

"Who lives here?" Katie asked, somewhat revived.

"Nobody, now. This place was only used during the summer. Too difficult getting in here in any other season. You might have noticed."

"Well, who put up the buildings, then?"

"Cousin of mine. He's been dead two years. He used to come here to get away from his wife. I don't think she even knows this place exists."

"How did he die?" Katie asked.

"Wife killed him. She found out he was messing around. One of you lads jump up there and secure the boat and we'll go ashore."

Claypoole clambered up on the wharf. "Oops!" he said. "Lost my balance there."

"It'll take you a few minutes to get your land legs back," O'Mol said. "Don't be alarmed. Hey, look at it this way: you get to make the trip again in a couple of days!"

"Are we going to be safe here, Mister O'Mol?" Katie asked.

O'Mol snorted. "Miss, no aircraft can get at us down here in this weather, and for damned sure not even Homs Ferris himself or Johnny Sticks could find anybody crazy enough to take a boat out in this season. We're safe here for as long as we want to stay safe. Now let's get under cover."

Katie looked out over the cove. The water was perfectly calm. The rain descended from above in a thick mist that gleamed wetly on the rocks all about. "It's really quite beautiful in here," Katie said.

The larger of the two buildings proved to be a comfortable bungalow, more than big enough to accommodate the five of them. The water cisterns were full of fresh water from the rains, and the pantries were stocked with gourmet food and drink.

"Old cuz liked his creature comforts," O'Mol said as they made a brief survey of the pantries. "He liked his 'creatures' too." He nodded at Pasquin, who did not ask O'Mol what he'd been doing out here the one time he'd made the trip. "There's a generator in that other shed. If one of you boys can get it going, we can have power in here." Because the cove was so sheltered by the cliffs all about, the place was always in deep twilight, even on the brightest days. Pasquin went outside and in a few minutes the lights and other utilities sprang to life.

O'Mol rummaged about in the closets, pulling out towels and dressing gowns. "Whew! These are a bit fusty after sitting in here for a couple of years, but they're dry and they'll fit us until we can dry out our own clothes."

"Im not going to complain about 'fusty' after that ride we just had on the open sea," Dean remarked.

Katie produced a bottle of fine brandy and some glasses. O'Mol raised his glass for a toast. "Here's real poo to my sham friends and shampoo to my real friends, which all of you could use after that long trip we just made!"

"You don't smell very much like a rose garden yourself," Katie replied.

"Touché!" O'Mol exclaimed. They sat around the tiny living room wrapped in the gowns, sipping on the brandy, waiting for their clothes to dry.

"Everything depends on you now," O'Mol announced. "My organization, what there is left of it, is powerless to operate without me. I think now it was a mistake to exercise such tight control, but there it is."

"Everything depends on you, Mr. O'Mol," Pasquin corrected. "You don't get us back to Placetas to contact Culloden, and Nast can't send in the cavalry to clean this shithole out."

O'Mol nodded. "Call me Olwyn, will you?"

"How long do you think we can hold out here?" Claypoole asked.

"We can 'hold out' as long as the food and water lasts. Weeks, maybe months. But how long do you want to stay here? That's the question."

"We were supposed to contact Culloden Thursday, but that was delayed until yesterday, and now we've missed that meeting. So we're two days late sending the message that it's ready for Nast to come in. We don't know where he is or how to get in touch with him to tell him what's happened. We must get back to Placetas and get hold of Culloden."

"Hard to do right now, with what you and Grace—" O'Mol paused for a moment. "Grace," he said quietly, "she was one of the best. Do you think they got her?"

"Yeah," Claypoole answered. He took Katie's hand in his.

O'Mol shook his head as if to clear it. "How are you going to call Nast in? And where is he?"

Pasquin smiled. "We can't tell you how we're going to contact him. As to where he is, somewhere here on Havanagas. He didn't tell us where. Just rest assured—if you can get us back to Placetas in one piece, we can get through to him."

"Hooboy," Claypoole exclaimed, "Mister O'Mol—Olwyn— you think we raised hell back at that farm? You just wait'll Nast and his boys get here. The damned mob'll think an army landed on top of their heads! We'll see how tough Johnny Sticks is then!"

"I'll get you back to Placetas. Today's Saturday. We'll head back Monday, soon as it gets dark. In this weather it'll take us ten, twelve hours, put us back into the Franklin River just before dawn. I know where Culloden lives. We'll figure out how to get there once we're back in the city. You up to another voyage in this storm?"

"No!" they all answered at once, and laughed. They lifted their glasses and toasted O'Mol.

They talked about themselves for a while. O'Mol admitted he'd never been married. "And what about you?" he asked the Marines.

"We aren't allowed to marry until we reach the grade of staff sergeant," Dean said.

"How do you two feel about that rule?" he asked Katie and Claypoole.

At first neither answered. Frankly, beyond getting Katie out of the clutches of the mob, Claypoole had no idea what would become of her. "Guess we'll get married," he said at last. Katie let out a gasp of surprise. Dean and Pasquin just looked at him in wordless surprise.

This conversation was déjà vu for Dean. "I remember something like this on Wanderjahr, old buddy," he said, "that time you told me—well, you explained how 'unrealistic' my chances were of marrying Hway. Need I go on?"

"I'll wait for you, Rock!" Katie said. "You get me out of here and I'll marry you, goddamned straight I will!"

"You'll wait a long time before this idiot ever makes staff sergeant," Dean said, slapping Claypoole lightly on the top of his head.

"I got three more years on this enlistment, Deano, and if I can't get the Commandant to give me an exception to the regulation, I'm going back to PFC—'poor fucking civilian.' Count on it. I can write a letter to the Commandant and send it through channels, can't I? Regulations can be excepted, can't they? It isn't that I'm a bad Marine. I bet the brigadier'd approve it in a minute."

Dean and Pasquin just looked at each other. "Well," O'Mol said at last, "this calls for a celebration." He uncorked the brandy bottle and poured everyone's glass full with what remained. "Here's to you, Rock, Katie! I'll do my best to get you out of here and I'll dance at your wedding!"

Then they opened tins of imported Carthusian oysters and

caviar harvested on Melbourne—one tin cost a lance corporal's annual salary—and ate them on salted crackers. Rummaging through the cupboards, they found a supply of fine Davidoff Anniversario No. 1 cigars and lighted them up, Katie too. O'Mol opened another bottle of the exquisite brandy and poured liberally all around.

Outside, nature raged and the seas pounded the cliffs. Homs Ferris, Noto Draya, their counselors and minions raged in their fortresses, casinos, and parks all across Havanagas. But down in the cove on an uncharted islet in the vast Ligurian Sea, the five fugitives ate and drank and laughed and told stories far into the night. When at last they sought refuge in slumber, it was the peaceful sleep of the good and the brave.

Thom Nast raged inwardly. "What the hell has gone wrong now?" he asked Brock. "They should have sent the signal Thursday. Jesus, it's Saturday, and not a peep from them. I think the families got them, Welbourne."

"Maybe they got Culloden, and your boys are stranded in some casino somewhere, drinking and playing blackjack with the ladies. I told you we should have had some way for them to contact us if anything went wrong. Don't we have any doughnuts around here?" Brock was a good beat cop and a good special weapons and tactics man, but he was very short on tact. And doughnuts.

Nast did not reply. Culloden was not important to Nast's plan, so long as his deep-cover agent was still operating. His Marines didn't need any way to check in with him. All he really needed was someone to mash the button. If his deep-cover agent hadn't been compromised, he still had that someone. "Okay. Wednesday there's a big gladiatorial contest in the Coliseum. Noto Draya and Homs Ferris will be there. They love to bet on these events. What's the flight time to that hemisphere?"

"Four hours," Chief Riggs answered.

"The seasons down there are the reverse of up here, so the

weather will be excellent. The contests start at noon. We'll leave here at eight hours. We'll 'drop in' on the bastards before the first match is over, when they'll be most vulnerable. We'll snatch them right out of the Coliseum, right in front of everybody."

"What good will that do, boss, if we don't have the goods to put them away?" Brock asked, always the honest street cop. Back home he'd never stop a citizen on the street without probable cause. Now, of course, he was under the orders of the Ministry of Justice.

"I'll have it," Nast said with confidence. Well, then again, he thought, maybe I won't. He really didn't care.

In the Bavarian city of Würzburg under the reign of Bishop von Ehrenberg (1623–1631), nine hundred people, including persons of high standing, were burned at the stake for the crime of witchcraft. Those who admitted their guilt and repented were strangled first and then burned; the others were burned alive.

The Renaissance theme park on Havanagas featured a burning every day, Monday through Sunday, at noon, weather permitting. In that hemisphere in that season the weather usually permitted, but if it turned inclement, the trials, which were held indoors, emphasized torture so the tourists would feel they'd gotten some of their money's worth. The crowd that morning was small, about two hundred people. They sat around a huge gallery, in the center of which was a dais for the judges, witness boxes, the usual appointments of a courtroom. Off to one side stood the executioner and his assistants, masked and stripped to the waist, their instruments ready. In the real historical setting the tortures were administered elsewhere, but the Renaissance theme park colocated them so the tourists would not have to move to another location. Once the trial was over the victim went right to the stake, which was just outside.

The program for that morning's trial announced the woman

would not admit her guilt or repent, so the spectators sat in anticipation of witnessing a live burning before lunch.

A young woman in chains stood before the court. As the trial unfolded a well-modulated voice, supplied through individual headsets the tourists could rent, commented quietly on the action, like a sportscaster at a golf tournament. The spectators in their gallery boxes could clearly see what was going on below.

Witnesses were brought in who swore they saw the woman flying through the air. One said she had been present at a sabbat in the forest and saw the accused having intercourse with a demon. The accused hysterically denied her guilt and called upon the audience to intervene and help her. "I'm not a witch!" she screamed. "This is real! Murder! Murder! They're murdering me!"

She was then bound tightly into an iron chair studded all over with sharp points. "This is called the witch chair," the commentator intoned softly. The accused witch screamed piteously as the guards tightened her bonds, pressing her flesh onto the points. At a nod from the presiding judge, the executioner stepped up and with pincers ripped off a fingernail and into the bleeding flesh he drove a red-hot pin. The victim's shrieks reverberated throughout the gallery, and some of the tourists shifted uncomfortably in their seats. Questioned again, she babbled about how someone was trying to punish her. Several more fingernails were removed.

Released at last from the chair, the accused was hauled, literally supported between two guards, before the judges and questioned by several men dressed in clerical robes. More witnesses were called. One testified to how the accused had killed her cattle by pronouncing strange words as she passed by their fields. Another accused her of poisoning her husband with a spell because of an argument they'd had in the market about the price of vegetables he was selling.

"She shall now be given the ladder," the commentator announced. The ladder had rungs studded with sharp wooden points. Arms twisted over her head, the accused was hoisted up on this device and suddenly dropped, hoisted up again and dropped, and so on for several repetitions.

"Gosh," a twelve-year-old from Sisyphus visiting with his parents exclaimed, "this is so real! Dad, do you think they're really going to burn that lady?"

"Well, that's why people come here, son, because on Havanagas they know how to re-create the past. Just watch carefully. This is a valuable lesson for you. Back a thousand years ago they really did torture and burn people at the stake for being witches. This'll give you a real appreciation for the civilization we live in today."

"Now the court has ordered application of the Bamberg torture," the commentator intoned. "This consists of a series of varied and prolonged scourgings. It is so called because it was invented by a bishop of the German city of Bamberg over a thousand years ago." During the Bamberg torture several tourists got up and left. The accused fainted several times during her ordeal and had to be revived with the application of cold water. At a quarter to twelve the presiding judge announced their decision: death by burning.

Everyone filed out into the courtyard where the stake and faggots had already been set up. The accused, barely conscious after her ordeal, was stripped and chained to the stake. While priests invoked God's blessing and solace, burning brands were applied to the faggots. The flames rose quickly and the victim began to scream. Although the onlookers stood back fifty paces or more from the pyre, they could feel the heat of the flames on their faces. The girl's skin began to burn and her hair flared up like a torch.

"This is so realistic you can actually smell the burning flesh," the mother of the boy from Sisyphus exclaimed. "I read in the brochure where sometimes people get sick at these shows."

"It sure is," the son agreed, shifting uncomfortably. Burning flesh! Wow! He'd have something to tell the kids back home after this was over! "Phew, is that stink her burning?"

"I think it's her hair," his father answered. "She had a lot of it. But you can smell burned meat too, can't you?"

"Goddamn you! Goddamn you all to hell!" the girl screamed as the flames rose and increased in intensity. Her head slumped forward and then the flames completely surrounded her and the screaming ceased.

"Ohh," the boy's mother exclaimed, shivering, "I think a cat just walked over my grave!"

"Careful, Mother," her husband chided playfully, "around here they might consider that evidence of witchcraft!" The three laughed nervously.

The crowd lingered until the fire died down. All that was left of the girl by then was a blackened, doubled-up skeleton secured to the stake by the iron manacles about its wrists and feet.

"Wow, Dad, that was really something!" the boy said as the crowd gradually dispersed into the cafés about the square. "How'd they do that?"

"Special effects," his mother said.

"Well, you think that was good, Darryl? The best is yet to come, son. Wednesday we're going to Rome to watch gladiators fight! Anybody want a latte?"

Out in the square workmen cut Tara's blackened corpse from the stake.

CHAPTER
TWENTY-THREE

Sword Simon Cherub was a squad leader in Heaven's Vision. His job was neither to fight nor to lead fighters in holy battle, though both he and the men he led were highly trained fighters who had fought fiercely in their previous units. The regiment named Heaven's Vision was the eyes of the Army of the Lord. The regiment supplied a platoon to each of the twelve brigades assigned to Operation Cleansing Flame—Sword Cherub's platoon was attached to Thaddeus Brigade. The squad, one of four in its platoon, was divided into two teams for the opening phase of the operation, as was each of the Heaven's Vision squads assigned to the operation. Each of the ninety-six teams prowled a grid approximately ninety kilometers on a side, an extremely difficult area for five men on foot to cover, especially since they had to move about unseen. Nobody seriously expected the Heaven's Vision reconnaissance teams to locate the rebel base before the rebels struck again. Archdeacon General Lambsblood, who was in overall command of Operation Cleansing Flame, did however expect them to spot the rebels when they made their next raid and then track them to where they went, so the Army of the Lord could follow and smite.

Sword Cherub's squad was assigned to ranchland. He chose to lead the team with the most difficult terrain: scrub fit only for grazing by widely scattered kine. The scrubland gave the great advantage of longer sight lines than were usually possible in orchard farms or through the rows of windbreak trees found on grain farms, but there was the disadvantage of poor concealment. The herdsmen roaming about on the lookout for dangers to their charges could easily spot the team if its members weren't vigilant. Nobody had any way of knowing whether those herdsmen were with the rebels, so it was imperative that the soldiers of Heaven's Vision not be seen by them. That was why Sword Cherub, the most experienced and skilled member of his squad, chose to lead the team himself.

They had been out for a week and a half, and Sword Cherub was beginning to feel unclean. Not dirty. As a soldier he was often dirty and was used to it. Unclean. The need for unobtrusiveness and constant vigilance had kept him and the team away from Sunday's church service. In two more days they would miss a second church service. Cherub was not particularly devout; a soldier could not afford to be so devout that he could not bear to miss Sunday service. But he was devout enough that missing two services in a row gave him serious pause.

Because of the chance of being seen, the team did most of its moving at night. At dawn that day they'd settled into a shallow, boulder-bordered hollow near the top of a rock-strewn low hill. When the sun came up, Cherub had found the location to be even better than he'd originally thought—it gave clear view of a village and the herdsmen between it and the village. His map told him they were twelve kilometers from the village called Twelfth Station of Jerusalem. Two twelves, most auspicious, he thought, and felt slightly less unclean. Perhaps today the rebels would launch their next attack. The operation, or at least his team's part of it, might well be over before the coming Sunday, and he and his men would be able to go to service.

The boulders that bordered the hollow were sufficiently jumbled that men lying or sitting still could peer between them without being seen unless someone came very close.

They were large enough to cast shade sufficient to keep the soldiers from baking in the harsh sun. The gaps between the boulders allowed slight breezes to waft through the hollow, enough to keep the flying gnats that were the bane of men in the scrubland from congregating too densely on them. Sword Cherub assigned his men to watch and sleep by twos in three-hour shifts. He himself would watch and sleep at irregular intervals to ensure that each of the men had the advantage of his experience for at least part of his watch.

The morning passed without incident. On the land stretched out below, herdsmen wandered about checking on the small bands into which the kine gathered for grazing. The forage was too thin for the herd to graze together, but the kine were too strongly herd animals for many of them to wander about alone in search of fodder. Those few who did wander alone were more likely to be brought down by predators, removing them from the gene pool, decreasing over generations the willingness for solitary pursuits among the kine. Once, the soldiers were entertained by watching three herdsmen chase away a wolf, a predatory lizardlike animal somewhat smaller than its Earthly namesake.

"That wolf is fortunate," one of the watching soldiers said. "Had it been me down there, we would dine on fresh meat." He patted his flechette rifle.

The other watching soldier snorted. "Had it been you down there, the wolf would have been in a pack and *they* would dine on fresh meat." He watched the wolf as it slunk away, and shivered at the thought of the pack the wolves normally hunted in. His entire team could be in danger if there were a wolf pack nearby. He increased his vigilance and vowed to tell the other soldiers about the wolf when they were awakened for their turn at watch.

High above, flying scavengers glided away on thermals, their attention already diverted from the wolf, which was not going to bring down a meal for them.

The sun was near its zenith and the herdsmen were finding shady spots near their kine when a sonic boom shattered the peace.

Sword Cherub bolted awake and dove for a gap in the rocks in the direction he thought the sound came from. Without conscious thought he grabbed his flechette rifle as he moved. The other sleeping soldiers moved almost as sharply into defensive positions as he did.

"Do you see anything?" he asked.

"No, Sword," replied one of the soldiers who was on watch.

The other watching soldier grunted that neither did he.

The boom continued for several seconds, rattling into a higher register. Then it abruptly broke.

"There!" a soldier shouted, and pointed.

Cherub saw it at the same instant, a fast-flying aircraft in what looked like a landing approach, except it was flying entirely too fast for a landing. Was it possible that the rebels had aircraft, and that this one had been damaged in an aerial fight and gone supersonic to make its escape? It was too far away for Cherub to identify. He groped for his telescope and put it to his eye. The blocky thing with stubby wings that he saw speeding like a flung brick wasn't an aircraft, it was a shuttle! He'd seen a shuttle once when he was briefly assigned to duty in Haven. It had descended from its several degenerating orbits to spiral gently down onto the landing pad inside Interstellar City. It did not come down on a straight, fast glidepath like this one. If his memory was right, it had also looked different than this one as well.

Sword Cherub braced his arms and the barrel of the telescope itself against rocks to keep the field of view as steady as possible as he swiveled the telescope to track the shuttle. Still the shuttle stuttered and jittered in his view as the air it slammed through buffeted it. He saw flame shoot from its front and the shuttle stagger more violently, and then, suddenly, it wasn't where he was looking. He swung the telescope back and found it again, moving much slower now. The stubby wings appeared to grow, and the shuttle seemed to stagger again as the wings bit into the air. Within seconds the shuttle was clearly in controlled flight.

Cherub removed the telescope from his eye to get a view of the shuttle's path. He estimated that unless it altered its course, it would touch down three kilometers from Twelfth Station of Jerusalem. He picked up his radio.

"Heaven's Vision Seventeen to Host. Heaven's Vision Seventeen to Host. Over," he said into it. "A shuttle is about to land at . . ." He gave the map coordinates when Host acknowledged his call. "That is right," he said when the incredulous radioman at Host questioned him. "An orbit-to-surface shuttle. Yes, I'm looking at it right now. Yes, I've seen a shuttle before, I know what I'm looking at." He waited while the Host radioman called for the watch officer, then repeated his information to the officer and added, "It just touched down." He propped his telescope on a boulder and looked at the shuttle through it. "It's disgorging something that looks like armored personnel carriers, looks like four. They're headed into Twelfth Station of Jerusalem. Yes, four of them, headed toward the village."

He flinched at the crack of another sonic boom and turned his telescope toward it.

"Sir, that boom was another shuttle. Sir, I have no idea where they came from. We didn't see anything before the sonic booms told us where to look. Yessir, I'm sorry, sir. This one looks to be in the same landing pattern as the previous one. If so, it will be maybe thirty seconds before it lands. Yessir, wait one." He shifted his telescope back toward the landed shuttle and scanned the scrub for the APCs. "Sir, the first shuttle is sitting there. The APCs it dismounted are about to enter Twelfth Shrine of Jerusalem. Yessir, that's right, it's just sitting there." He turned to one of his men. "Use your GPS and get a fix on that shuttle's position."

The soldier looked through the scope of the GPS spotter he carried. "I can't get a precise reading," he reported. "The GPS doesn't have a size match for that shuttle."

"Give it to me as near as you can." The soldier did, and Cherub relayed it to the officer. "Understood, sir. We will stand by to guide the Avenging Angels."

The watch officer at Host signed off.

"Avenging Angels are being scrambled to strike the shuttle while it's still on the ground," he told his men.

They grinned. Watching an air strike from a safe distance was exciting.

The second shuttle didn't follow the path of the first all the way down, it altered its course and landed midway between the Heaven's Vision soldiers and the village. Three of the vehicles it debarked followed the first wave to the village. The fourth turned about and sped for the low hill.

"They can't know we're here," Cherub assured his men. "It's scouting, and it's mere chance that it began scouting in our direction."

But the armored and armed vehicle wasn't scouting and it wasn't chance that sent it toward the low hill any more than it was chance that had its shuttle alter its path and land closer to the hill. Sword Cherub's radio transmissions had been picked up and his position pinpointed, and now he and his men had held their positions too long to have any chance of getting away.

They didn't live long enough to see the carnage in the village, or to see the four Avenging Angels disintegrate before they could get off their first missiles. They barely had time to hear the sonic boom of the third shuttle. They completely missed the way the twelve nimble land vehicles chased down and slaughtered the herdsmen and all the kine they could not carry off. Sword Cherub's last thought was a sincere prayer that he'd be forgiven his uncleanliness.

* * *

Bishop Ralphy Bruce Preachintent again stood before the Convocation of Ecumenical Leaders. His eyes were downcast on his hands, clasped in front of the pale rose necktie that bisected his starched white shirt. His main vestment was a suit of silver-gray sharkskin picked with a delicate gold pinstripe. When the herald finished reading the report, Bishop Ralphy Bruce raised his head and spoke in the holy cadences.

"BRETHREN! You have all HEARD the herald's REPORT." Today he didn't strut back and forth along the chancel rail in the sacred choreography, nor did he stab fingers at his listeners. His mood was entirely too somber for such joyousness. But nothing could remove the sacred cadences from his speech. "It is quite CLEAR that the HERETICS who PLAGUE our hinterlands and MARTYR our blessed PEOPLE are not APOSTATES from among us! Rather, they are GODLESS ones come from AFAR to launch a CRUSADE against the PEOPLE of THE LORD!"

Yes, the assembled leaders had heard the herald's report. At least, those of them who hadn't dozed through it, or hadn't been otherwise occupied in conversation with their neighbors or engrossed in their own thoughts. They had all read the report before assembling, and discussed it with their highest staffs and advisers. Many of them had other reports as well, made by their own agents within the Army of the Lord. The report of the attack on Twelfth Station of Jerusalem was far the most appalling they'd heard, even without considering the off-world implications of the shuttles.

"MY FRIENDS! Archbishop General Lambsblood has CONFESSED to me that the ARMY of the LORD does not know what weapon this FOE has that can so SMITE our aircraft from the SKY! YEA, the archbishop general TREMBLED when he made this CONFESSION! I do not know whether his FEAR was from his lack of KNOWLEDGE or if it was righteous FEAR of the LORD'S WRATH for his FAILURE!

"Archbishop General Lambsblood was so CONTRITE

over his FAILURE that he offered his RESIGNATION." He dropped his voice. "Of course, I refused it.

"BRETHREN!" He flung his head and hands heavenward. "What are we to DO with HERETICS descending UPON us from AFAR!"

The same aged cleric in white cassock and squared turban who spoke first the last time the convocation met rose slowly from his position in the front pew.

"BROTHER!" Bishop Ralphy Bruce threw a hand toward him. "Do you WISH to give TESTIMONY?"

"Bishop Ralphy Bruce," the old man said in his quavery voice, "I have been a member of this convocation longer than anybody else. I have stood where you stand more often than anybody else. I have seen more heretical movements come and be put down than anyone else here."

"Do you have a point to make, Ayatollah Fatamid?" Bishop Ralphy Bruce asked impatiently.

The old man cocked a rheumy eye at him. "If you will be patient for a moment, young man."

Bishop Ralphy Bruce took a half step back. For all the grandiosity of his speech and gestures, he fully understood the delicate balance he was responsible for maintaining among the powers of Kingdom. "Forgive me, Ayatollah Fatamid, I beg you."

Ayatollah Fatamid stared at him a moment longer, then spoke again. "I have seen more heretical movements come and be put down—I think I already said that. It does not matter who the heretics are or whence they come. The righteous people of the Lord will always prevail, even if we must contract with off-world mercenaries to take jihad to the home world of these heretics. *Allah akbar.*"

Someone gasped at the old man's use of an invocation specific to one religion, but was quickly hushed by those nearest him. Ayatollah Fatamid might have breached protocol with his last words, but he was widely respected among his peers.

Besides, most of them knew he was somewhat senile and shouldn't be held responsible for everything he said. But his mention of hiring mercenaries to take jihad to the homeworld of the unbelievers who were raiding the Kingdom of Yahweh and His Saints and Their Apostles, *that* bore discussion.

The only outcome of the meeting was the appointment of a delegation to Interstellar City for the purpose of enlisting the aid of the off-world unbelievers in learning whence came the heretics. Maybe the Confederation would send its military there to teach them a lesson. After all, Kingdom was a full member of the Confederation of Human Worlds, and it was a violation of the Confederation's constitution for one member world to attack another without approval of the central government on Earth. Even then, the attacked world had to be served notice of the coming invasion. Violation of that section of the Constitution merited swift punitive action.

Dr. Friendly Creadence, a career diplomat, was the ambassador to Kingdom from the Confederation of Human Worlds. Before his arrival on Kingdom, he'd thought the reports he'd read and heard about the local government were somewhat exaggerated, if not downright hyperbolic. During the year and a half since he'd arrived to take over as the Confederation's primary representative to the theocracy, he'd come to the conclusion that those reports were understated almost to the point of criminal irresponsibility. The theocrats, in his view, were as vile as the worst despot on any other human world. In his entire thirty years as a Confederation diplomat, he had never seen so much repression in the name of religious freedom. So he wasn't in the least pleased when a delegation arrived to request Confederation assistance with what sounded to him like a rebellion that raged out in the countryside.

"But we are not asking for assistance in putting down a 'rebellion,' " insisted Metropolitan Eleison.

"Oh . . . ?" Creadence asked slowly. "Then—" He held out a hand palm up.

"We believe we are being invaded by off-worlders. What we ask is assistance in discovering the identity of those off-worlders and where they come from."

Creadence looked to his chief-of-station, an engineer by the name of Harly Thorogood.

Thorogood looked surprised. "But Metropolitan, the only starships that have entered Kingdom's space in the past— well, since Kingdom joined the Confederation of Human Worlds more than a century ago—have been scheduled trade ships or Confederation Navy vessels on routine patrol."

"Their base must be hidden on the far side of our moon, and they are coming down when you aren't looking. That would account for the irregularity of their raids."

Thorogood shook his head. "Not possible. We have a station of our own on the moon's far side; it would have noticed. And we have constant satellite surveillance all around Kingdom."

Metropolitan Eleison bit off a grimace. The string-of-pearls satellites the Confederation Navy had put in place a generation earlier was a sore point with the theocracy—they believed the ring of satellites spied on them despite the Confederation's assurances that the satellites were restricted to weather forecasting, geological surveys, and watching the approaches to Kingdom.

"Besides," Thorogood continued, "ships leaving Beam-space are quite distinct. Believe me, we'd spot anyone coming here."

Metropolitan Eleison looked thunder and lightening at the two Confederation representatives. "Then you are saying you need proof that orbit-to-surface shuttles are bringing in men and weapons before you will give us the aid we request, as is our right as a Confederation member?"

"That would help," Creadence said.

"Will you help us get that evidence?"

Creadence almost salivated at the opportunity to put more people—and observation equipment—in Kingdom's rural areas. There was no telling what they might learn about how the theocracy operated where it couldn't be seen from Interstellar City. He appeared to consider the request, then said:

"I think some form of assistance can be arranged."

CHAPTER
TWENTY-FOUR

"Okay, candyass, I'll see your damned pair of fives and raise," Klink said. He shoved a handful of coins into the pot. Klink was a burly man with powerful, hairy forearms and a closely cropped bullet-shaped head. He had not bothered to shave in several days. In his younger days he had spent a lot of time in prison, hence "Klink." He sat at the table in his undershirt, a huge pistol tucked into a holster under his left arm.

Bug, who was sitting to Klink's left, hesitated. Five stud, one more card and he couldn't beat the fives. "Playing three-handed is for the tourists," he said disgustedly, throwing in his hand. Bug was short and thin with a narrow face and a prominent hooked nose. It was difficult for him to sit still very long. He was always crossing and uncrossing his legs, moving his hands, twitching. Hence "Bug."

"You trying to bluff me outta my pot, Klinker?" the man with the fives showing, whom everyone called Fader, accused Klink. "Okay, buddy, I call and—" He pretended to be counting his money. "—raise you back. How's that for balls?" Fader was squat, unshaven, his hair thin and graying; an unlit cigar stub stuck out of one corner of his mouth. Every now and then he'd spit masticated cigar fragments onto the floor. He was very fast with his hands and a dangerous opponent on his feet, thus the nickname Fader. Like Klink, he carried a pistol in a shoulder holster.

"If you got any, you won't have them for long," Klink replied, but he only called. "Whatcha got besides them fives?"

"Two pair," Fader replied, flipping over a jack in the hole to match the one faceup.

Klink swore mightily and threw his hole card down. He'd been betting on a pair of kings. Fader whistled merrily as he took in the pot.

"Hey, fellas," Bug said, "don't you think we should be out looking around?"

"Shaddup, Buggy! You want to check, go check, but it's raining like hell out there. Besides, they ain't coming to this hole, so relax," Klink said.

Johnny Sticks had dispersed many of his men along the coast. Klink, Fader, and Bug had been assigned to keep an eye on the coast from Royale, in case O'Mol and the Marines tried a landing. They were heavily armed and ruthless, but Klink and Fader saw no reason to get wet on what they considered the very remote possibility that the fugitives might come back through the village of Royale.

"These people don't like us," Bug sniffed. "Bastards. I bet they're all rebels. The place stinks too, like goddamned fish."

"Fish smell, like something else I could mention, ain't bad, once you get used to it." Fader laughed, winking broadly at Klink.

A powerful gust of wind rattled the inn's windows. Bug got up nervously and looked out into the main—and only—street. Nothing moved out there. Windblown gusts of rain swirled over the stones. It was nearly noon but already lights showed in the windows of some of the homes along the street. In such bad weather, the fishermen could not go out. Normally in that season they spent their days at the inn, drinking and socializing, but the three men from Placetas had taken over the inn as their "headquarters" and made it clear no one was welcome until their business was done.

"Hey, Buggy, go out back and tell that bitch to make us up some sandwiches and bring in some beer," Klink said. "God-damn woman must think she's on vacation or sumptin'. I hate these freaking hicks almost as much as the freaking tourists. Come on, come on, Fader, deal."

"Move your ass, Buggy, I'm thirsty!" Fader yelled. Reluctantly, Bug turned from the window and walked slowly into the kitchen.

Klink swore. "The guy's useless, Fader. Okay, just two of us? How 'bout some blackjack? Cut to see who deals."

Someone knocked at the door.

Fighting strong headwinds and very high seas, O'Mol and his passengers reached the mainland coast just before dawn on Tuesday. There was no sun that day, just rain and dense fog. He guided the boat into the mouth of a little bay fed by several streams. He anchored in the middle of the bay.

"We'll hold up here until full dark," he told Pasquin. "Royale is about five kilometers from here. It's a fishing village but we should be able to commandeer ground transport once we get there. Then we'll pay Lovat Culloden a call and wrap this adventure up. How's that sit with you?"

"How many people live in this village—Royale, did you call it?" Dean asked.

O'Mol shrugged. "Maybe a hundred or so. The mob never used to keep an eye on the place, so we should be able to pass through there undetected."

"Wait a minute, Olwyn," Claypoole interjected. "You said 'never used to keep an eye on the place.' Does that mean now they will be keeping an eye on it?"

O'Mol paused before replying. "Maybe," he admitted. "Look. They know we fled Placetas on the river. They know the river opens into the sea. It's a good possibility they've put a watch along the Franklin as well as along the coast. I think we have the element of surprise on our side. We disappeared for two days. They won't be looking for us to come back so soon, if at all. If there are watchers in Royale . . ." he drew a finger across his throat.

"You mean we kill them?" Katie exclaimed.

"Yes, Katie, that's just what I mean, and that's what we'll do."

She looked imploringly at Claypoole, who just nodded. "Katie, it's kill or be killed," Pasquin said. "We're on the very thin edge of a disaster here. We've got to act quickly and decisively or we'll all die. It's that simple."

"Olwyn, why wait until dark?" Dean asked. The boat rocked gently in the water as the wind drove sheets of rain against the cabin windows.

"Better cover traveling at night."

"I don't think we'd better wait, Olwyn," Pasquin said.

"Well . . ." O'Mol thought. "Okay, Raoul, this is your mission. I'll guide you. The weather's bad enough so we can travel overland on foot to Royale without being seen."

"What's the countryside surrounding Royale like?" Dean asked.

"Open grassy fields, some forestation. It's been a while since I was up there, I don't quite remember how the land lies."

"Got maps, a compass?"

O'Mol consulted his onboard computer and called up a 1:25,000 scale map of the area. The three Marines crowded around the screen and studied it. Pasquin looked out the cabin window at the steep bank on the north side of the bay. At the top was an opening through the trees. In the shifting mist and fog he could see that it had been used frequently; evidently this spot was used for recreational purposes in good weather.

Pasquin took a compass reading. "That's the path that leads to the village," he said.

"We can't use the path," Dean remarked.

"Why not?" Katie asked, a pained look of disbelief on her face.

"Because it could be under surveillance," O'Mol replied. He'd spent enough of his life in hiding to know that much about basic infantry tactics in enemy territory.

"This big patch of forest along the south side will screen us for about two klicks," Calypoole pointed out.

"And then we cross this open space." Pasquin put his finger on the screen. "You know how that'll work. Then more trees up to about two hundred meters from the first house in the village." He smiled. "I think that'll be a pretty easy cross-country march—for Marines." He looked at O'Mol and Katie. "We'll have to do some low crawling. Are you up to it?"

"If my life depends on it, I can do anything," Katie replied. O'Mol just nodded.

"Okay," Pasquin said, "load up. Katie, here's a blaster and some extra power packs. Before we get off the boat I'll show you how to load and fire the thing. We may need all the fire-power we can get before this day is over. Olwyn, you and Joe take point. Rock, you're rear point. Katie and I'll stay in the middle. Keep five-meter intervals on the march. I think that's all we can afford in this fog. No talking, use standard hand signals. Olwyn, run this thing to shore. Oh, yeah, deep six the last blaster in that crate. We don't want some citizen stumbling onto your boat and falling in love with the thing."

They had not penetrated more than two hundred meters into the woods when Dean signaled a halt. Before them was a wide firebreak. "This goddamned thing wasn't on the map!" he whispered into O'Mol's ear.

"It gets hot and very dry out here in the summer and fall, so forest fires are a real threat. This must've been cut recently, that's why it's not on the maps yet. By the way, why are you whispering?" O'Mol whispered back. "Nobody can hear us in here."

"Because I've got laryngitis," Dean whispered back as he signaled Pasquin to come forward. Dean shook his head. O'Mol was a rare breed for a civilian, but he'd never make a good infantryman.

Pasquin took in the situation with one glance. He motioned

for Katie and Claypoole to come forward and join them just inside the fringe of undergrowth bordering the firebreak. "Line up," he whispered. "When I give the sign, we all walk across together as fast as we can. Everybody, check the safeties on your blasters." It was the third time he'd had them do that since they left the boat.

Katie's blaster went off with a loud *hiss-crack!* The bolt arced into the trees across the firebreak and flashed briefly but brightly. The foliage was so wet it did not catch fire, but the flash and the sound of the explosion caused fliers to take wing in all directions despite the driving rain.

"Well, that did it," Pasquin said in his normal voice.

"I just forgot!" Katie protested, near tears.

Pasquin sighed. "Don't worry about it, Katie. Rock, show her again," he said patiently. He sighed again. "Okay, everybody, move out, same formation, and make it quick. We'll know soon enough if that gave us away. Be prepared to deliver immediate fire if we're challenged."

It took them another hour to get to the other side of the woods. They crouched inside the treeline, scanning the wide open space between them and the next concealing patch of woodland. The open field was deep in swaying grass about a meter high. It took them another hour to get across. By then each was thoroughly soaked and Katie had begun to shiver from the exposure. "We have to get under cover soon," Claypoole said, his teeth chattering, "or we'll all drop from hypothermia."

Pasquin remained silent, staring at something in the woods. Claypoole nervously followed his gaze but there was nothing to be seen. "Raoul," Claypoole said, "did you hear me?" Pasquin did not acknowledge.

Dean stepped forward and laid his hand gently on the corporal's shoulder. When Pasquin was with Force Recon in the 25th FIST on Adak Tanaga he'd lost men in his patrol because he got careless. That was the reason he'd been assigned to 34th FIST in the first place, to get rid of him. But everyone in the 34th knew Pasquin was neither a screw-up nor a coward. "Raoul," Dean said quietly, "we're all counting on you." Pasquin did not respond. "Raoul, come on, we need you, buddy. Snap out of it."

Pasquin shook himself. "Uh, I was just thinkin', this has happened to me before, you know, Joe?" he said quietly. The others watched them with concern on their faces as the two talked in low voices. Pasquin smiled weakly and shook his head. "Thanks, Joe. Okay," he turned to the others, "as I re-member from the map, this woods extends about two klicks to the village. Is there anyone who doesn't think he can make it th-that far? Oooh." He shook himself. "It's getting to me too, Rock." He was shivering. "Let's get moving, if we move we can k-keep w-warm."

It was nearing 11 hours when the village at last came in sight. Pasquin made them stop just inside the treeline again. They had to get inside one of the houses and get warm, but Pasquin knew it would be suicide if watchers were in the village.

"Come on, Raoul," O'Mol urged, "let's run to the nearest house and get under—" He shook his head. His teeth were chattering so violently he couldn't get the words out.

"No," Pasquin answered. "We do this by the numbers. Olwyn and I will go to the nearest house with a light on and check it out." He paused briefly as a bout of shivering took hold. The others stamped their feet and flexed their arms, their faces white and eyes staring. Pasquin wasn't sure he could keep them from bolting, despite the possibility of danger. "The rest of you stay under cover. Huddle close to-gether to preserve your body heat. We won't be long." They took off at a lope across the narrow strip of grass and through the winter-dead gardens that separated the woods from the nearest house.

Dean, Claypoole, and Katie huddled shivering inside the tree-line. It was raining so hard they could barely make out the house with the light on in the window. Dean and Claypoole put their arms around Katie and drew their own bodies as close to her as they could get.

"This is real togetherness, isn't it?" Claypoole said. "I hate this rain!"

"Do that again," Katie said. She was shivering so badly now it was hard to understand her.

"What, whisper in your ear?" Claypoole asked.

"No, breathe on me! At least my ear won't freeze!" The three of them began to laugh despite their desperate condition.

It seemed an hour had passed but it was only minutes before O'Mol returned carrying three fisherman's slickers. "Put these on! Be careful, there are watchers at the inn, but the people in that house are very glad to see us, I can assure you," he smiled. "We are going to kick somebody's ass real good before this day is out!"

"Go 'way!" Klink shouted at the knocking. "Nobody's in!" He laughed and dealt another hand of blackjack. The knocking persisted, louder and more insistent.

"Better see who it is," Fader said.

"You see, then. I'm busy."

Fader got up and went to the door, drew his pistol and, standing to one side, called out, "Who is it?"

"I've seen strangers!" a muffled voice called from the other side. Fader glanced back at Klink, who nodded and drew his own pistol.

Fader fumbled with the unfamiliar brass key and pulled the door open after several tries. O'Mol stepped in, his blaster held underneath his slicker. "Good afternoon, gents." He smiled and shot Fader, with the barrel less than one meter from his belly button. The bolt seared a hole straight through Fader's midsection. Klink was fast. O'Mol swung the muzzle toward him, firing several bolts in quick succession. Klink leaped away from two bolts and had leveled his gun at O'Mol when the third bolt struck his gun arm, searing through flesh and bone, and the arm below the hit flopped down limply. A fourth bolt burned through his torso. He screeched and stumbled away from the table, then crumpled to the floor.

Dean and Claypoole rushed in, seized the two bodies by their feet and dragged them swiftly outside. Pasquin, covered by O'Mol, ran back toward the kitchen. The residents in the first house had described the layout of the inn and the three watchers there, besides the widow woman who ran the place.

Bug stood in the center of the large, old-fashioned kitchen, a gun to the head of the hostess, who he held tightly with a stranglehold around her neck. "Don't come any closer!" he shouted.

"Hey, okay, okay! We won't shoot," Pasquin said soothingly, but the muzzle of his blaster never wavered.

O'Mol crept to the side along a wall. Seeing him, Bug didn't know which way to turn, so he ground the pistol into the woman's head all the harder. "Back off or I'll kill this bitch!" he screamed.

The kitchen was full of the smell of scorched flesh from the bar, where Dean and Claypoole, assisted by the villagers, were busy putting out the fires.

"You hurt that woman and you die," Pasquin said. "Drop the gun, let her go, and you live. It's that simple."

"I—I called for help!" Bug screamed. "The boys'll be here any minute now! You ain't got a fucking chance."

Pasquin had no doubt the rat-faced little man had sent a distress signal. But how far away were his reinforcements? The fight in the bar had been over in about six seconds; give him another five to get to the kitchen, and they'd been talking maybe ten seconds already. Less than a minute. They'd have to defuse the guy and get moving pronto.

"I'll count to three," Pasquin said, holding up a free finger.

"Okay! Okay!" Bug dropped the pistol to the floor and shoved the hostage toward Pasquin. As soon as she was clear, O'Mol flamed the little man. He screamed and O'Mol hit him two more times.

O'Mol looked at Pasquin and shrugged. "We can't take prisoners. If we'd left him here, he'd have implicated the villagers. Besides, I owe these bastards a killing or two."

Pasquin nodded. That's the way it would have to be. "Ma'am," he said to the landlady, "we will pay for the damage to your place."

"Pay, hell!" she shouted. "Goddamn, it's I who should pay you boys! You cleaned these bastards up for me!"

Outside, the entire village had gathered in the street despite the rain. When Pasquin and O'Mol emerged, a rousing cheer went up.

"Listen, people!" Pasquin shouted. "We don't have much time. How far is it to Placetas from here by road?"

"Fifty kilometers!" someone answered. Several men volunteered to drive them but Pasquin shook his head.

"Is there any other road to Placetas except the main highway?" Pasquin turned to O'Mol, who shook his head. "Any side roads, back roads where somebody could get here without using the main highway?"

"No, sir," a grizzled fisherman answered. "We seldom use the road. It's only one lane. We take our fish to market up the Franklin instead."

"One lane?" Pasquin grinned at O'Mol, who saw immediately what the corporal had in mind and grinned back. "Listen, people. One of those men got a message off to Placetas before he was killed. More men are on their way here. Go back to your homes! Stay indoors! There will be more fighting today, and soon! But with any luck, these guys will all be out of business by this time tomorrow."

"Let us help!" several of the men cried out.

"You can help by lending us a lorry. But let me tell you up front, you may not get it back. When we leave, everybody get under cover."

A man raised his hand. "I have just the thing. Follow me." Behind one of the houses he pulled a large tarpaulin off a ground-effect car. "Had a very good catch a couple of years ago—and some luck at the casinos—and bought this thing. Wife thought I was crazy, but always wanted one. Haven't used it much. It's no good for hauling fish to market. Take it."

O'Mol let out a gasp. "You'd let us take this?" The man nodded. "Sir, if I come through this I promise to make everything up to you!"

The man shook his head. "Take the damned thing and go. You've done enough for this village by getting rid of those three bastards."

"Okay, people," Pasquin shouted, "let's mount up and move out!"

CHAPTER
TWENTY-FIVE

O'Mol drove. About a kilometer outside Royale, where stone walls closed in on the highway from both sides, Pasquin had him stop in the middle of the road. "El-shaped ambush, one hundred meters from here. Katie and I will form the base of the el, on the left side of the road where I can deliver enfilade fire and stop the front vehicle dead. You three take the flanking ambush, down the right side of the road. Claypoole, you take out the rear vehicle, if there're more than one. Nobody fire until I do, and then pour everything you've got into them. I'm betting these guys'll be coming on like the wind, no security. If we can stop 'em here, we can kill them all before they can even get out of their vehicles.

"If they're smart and come down both sides of the road through the fields, we've got a problem and we'll just have to fight it out. We've got the firepower advantage. If that happens, use what cover you can get and fight your way back to our car. We'll make a run for it. But I don't think they're that smart. Set yourselves up at about ten-meter intervals."

O'Mol, Dean, and Claypoole took up the flanking ambush along the long side of the el.

Katie and Pasquin jogged along the stone wall to a point about one hundred meters from their parked car. Pasquin picked it because hedges grew up there and would give them cover. Across the road the three crouched behind the wall, their weapons ready.

"I'll tell you when to take the safety off your weapon,

274

Katie," Pasquin told her as he checked her weapon's safety visually and by feel. He smiled. "Don't worry, this time you can shoot all you want to. But remember, finger off the safety until I start shooting, okay? All you have to do is point the muzzle in the direction of the oncoming vehicles and squeeze the firing lever. Don't worry about hitting anything, just start shooting when I do. If you forget at first to remove the safety and your weapon doesn't fire, don't panic, just flip 'er down and shoot." He checked the power magazine to be sure it was properly seated and then patted Katie reassuringly on the shoulder.

"Raoul, I wanted to go with Claypoole," she said suddenly.

"No. I brought you with me for a very good reason, Katie. Rock loves you. His mind has got to be on his weapon, not on you. That's why you're here with me instead. Hey, once you get to know me, you'll like me!"

Katie laughed. Very careful to make sure the safety was still on, she pointed the muzzle of her blaster over the wall and aimed it experimentally down the road.

They waited twenty minutes before the sound of speeding vehicles reached them at last. Everyone tensed. Pasquin smiled grimly. "Get ready." From around a bend in the road about a thousand meters away the first vehicle came into sight, barreling along at about a hundred kilometers per hour. Water flew in a spray from beneath it. There were four of them.

The column slowed when the lead driver spotted the landcar standing in the middle of the road. He came on slowly. None of the vehicles stopped to dismount troops. The men were professional criminals, not infantrymen, and Pasquin was counting on that. He was right. When the lead vehicle was well into the kill zone, he stood up suddenly and fired a quick succession of bolts into the cab. The windshield exploded and fire broke out in the interior. Then Pasquin raked the left side of the column with a quick volley. Katie started shooting at the same time. Some of her bolts hit the wall, others bounced harmlessly into the nearby fields, but enough hit the vehicles to add to the devastating effect that Pasquin's aimed fire was having.

The three in the flanking ambush, firing at point-blank range, poured a withering fire into the stalled vehicles. Claypoole's first bolt killed the driver of the last car, then he methodically pumped bolts into it until its interior was set ablaze. The other two vehicles were unable to maneuver, trapped between the stone walls on either side and the burning vehicles in front and behind. It was a perfect ambush. Screaming men burning like torches stumbled out of the vehicles and ran about crazily until they collapsed in the road. In seconds all four vehicles were fiercely blazing wrecks. The fire was so intense the three along the long side of the el had to retreat into the fields to escape the heat. Then fuel cells began to cook off, turning the road into a deadly inferno.

A man, weaponless, his hair and clothing burned away, plunged over the wall and ran stumbling toward Dean. Without thinking about it, Dean killed him with one bolt. No one else emerged from the conflagration.

Pasquin whistled loudly from the road and waved the three back to their car. O'Mol was breathing heavily. His face was flushed and his eyes glittered with excitement. He was also laughing. "We did some damage, by God, we hurt them!"

"That's for sure," Claypoole muttered. While the shooting had been going on he'd fired his weapon in the full rage of combat, but now that it was over and men were frying in the road, criminals or not, they were men, and he felt sick. "It—It was like slaughtering animals," he said, "not a single shot was fired back at us."

"How many do you think we got?" Dean asked. Personally, he wished all the fights he'd ever been in had been so one-sided.

"All of them!" O'Mol exclaimed happily.

"Between these here and the ones at the farm, we sure

made a dent in their numbers," Pasquin said. "I won't forget this piece of work anytime soon."

"I'll never forget those screams!" Katie said.

The one-lane highway from Royale eventually led into a beltway complex on the outskirts of Placetas. This modern highway network was necessary for such a small city because tourists used it to get to resorts situated in the nearby mountains. During the tourist season the road network was heavily used, but that day not another vehicle was to be seen.

Taking advantage of the city's side streets, O'Mol guided them into the suburbs. He explained that Culloden's home was in an exclusive neighborhood with its own elaborate security system. "We'll never make it in unless Culloden gives us the clearance or agrees to meet us somewhere else."

"How do we make contact, then?" Pasquin asked. "Originally he was to meet us last Thursday at the Free Library. He has to know what happened at the farm and now at Royale. What if he goes to ground? Maybe he considers it too dangerous to have any contact with us now."

"You may be right. The only way to find out is to contact him. But I think this is the ideal time to make contact. Frankly, the mob's never been dealt a blow like we've given them these past few days, and I'm betting they're confused as hell right now. And we'll make contact by calling him on your comm unit. You wouldn't have his number, would you?"

Culloden's telephone number? The three Marines looked at one another. It was the last thing they ever thought they'd need on this mission.

"Often in life survival boils down to something very insignificant like a nail, a bullet, a telephone number," O'Mol said. "I'll get him through the central computer." O'Mol pulled the telephone from its dashboard recess, picked up the handset and pressed 0. "Lovat Culloden, Chief of Security," he said.

Almost immediately a male voice answered, "Please identify yourself and state your business."

"I must talk to Lovat Culloden."

"That is impossible, sir. He is out. May I help you?"

"Tell him that his whore and his four jacks are in town," Pasquin whispered.

O'Mol winked broadly and said, "No. I must talk to him personally. This is a matter of the most urgent nature. Kindly inform him that his whore and four jacks are in town."

The line went silent for a moment. "Culloden here." Pasquin nodded. That was Culloden's voice.

"We need to see you," O'Mol said.

"Who the hell are you?" Culloden said, but he knew who they were and was just saying that to cover himself.

"We have the information you hired us to get for you."

"My place, fifteen minutes." The line went dead.

"Katie, Katie, Katie," Claypoole murmured, "in a little while this'll all be over."

"Look sharp, Rock, we aren't out of the woods yet," Pasquin warned.

"Well, we're getting there, we're getting there," O'Mol said. "I can see the 'light at the end of the tunnel.' " It was full dark when he pulled up to a huge iron gate set in a high stone wall. "Tell Mr. Culloden the whore and four jacks are here," he told the hard-faced men in a shack behind the gate. One of them nodded and the gate slid open slowly. They drove up a winding drive bordered on both sides by large trees. At the top of the drive, straddling a steep ridge, sat Culloden's villa.

"All right, stick together," Pasquin said. "Got your readers?"

O'Mol snapped his fingers. "Now I see why you guys were always fiddling with those things! There is a code in there that activates a transmitter, right? Christ on a handcar, I should have known."

"All we've been through, we gotta be sure the innards haven't been screwed up," Dean said. There it was, *Knives in the Night,* a novel that'd been on the Commandant's reading list forever. Even now, on the cusp of the most dangerous dilemma he'd ever faced, the opening lines stirred him: "The sun rising over the South China Sea cast long shadows . . ." He smiled. Like those Marines in the ancient story of a war nobody even remembered anymore, they were a team on Havanagas, just like they always were, Pasquin, Claypoole, and himself, and no goddamned civilians could touch them! He clipped the reader back on his belt, checked his blaster. He was ready.

They dismounted and walked into the foyer in a tight group, weapons held casually but ready. Their footsteps echoed loudly on the flagstone floor. Culloden stood in the center of the living room, off to one side.

They marched in and stood facing him. "Well?" O'Mol demanded. He exchanged glances with Pasquin.

"Well, what?" Culloden smiled. Suddenly the room was swarming with armed men. They burst in from every direction. Before any of the fugitives could get off a shot they went down in a tangle of wildly flailing arms and legs. "Thank you! Thank you for being so naive!" Culloden shouted above the uproar. In seconds the five were hoisted to their feet, bound and manacled.

Johnny Sticks walked in. "Thank you, Lovat, thank you very much."

"You are welcome, sir."

"Wh-What the hell's going on, Culloden?" Pasquin raged, struggling against the manacles. Dean and Claypoole screamed defiance and rage at Culloden, who just smiled calmly.

"Survival, Mister Pasquin," Culloden answered. "Who do you think betrayed the pitiful Mister Woods? I've been working for Johnny all along. We didn't kill you at once because we thought you'd lead us to the real undercover agent. We know all about your readers." He motioned to one of the men standing by, who stepped forward and plucked them from the Marines' belts. Culloden hefted them. "You'll never send any messages on these things now." He threw one to the floor and crushed it under his foot. The second one followed. He tossed the third one to Sticks.

Sticks approached the small group of prisoners. "I must admit, gentlemen, you certainly have caused us a lot of trouble, a hundred of my men killed, three aircraft destroyed, four—or is it five?—expensive landcars up in smoke. Good thing Nast didn't send a full squad of Marines or your lives might have turned out differently. As it is, Mister Ferris is not happy, not happy at all. He's prepared special treats for all of you."

"And what might they be, you ugly little shit?" O'Mol asked.

"Ah, yes, O'Mol! Freedom fighter O'Mol! You are an unexpected prize. You'll make a noise in the world when you die."

"Look, Mister Sticks," Claypoole said, "let Katie go. She had nothing to do with any of this. I got her into this mess! For Christ's sake, please don't hurt her!"

"Ah-ha! A love affair here, eh? I'll tell you what, Mr. Claypoole. You tell me where Nast is and who his deep undercover agent is and I'll not only let her go, I'll let you and your friends go. You are nothing to us. You are entertainment to us. What do you say, Marine?"

"Aw, go fuck yourself! I wouldn't tell you if I knew!"

"Tut tut, Mister Claypoole. Make your good-byes." He nodded to the men holding Katie and they dragged her out of the room. "She is going to light up the world a bit, Mister Claypoole. She's going to Würzburg."

"No!" O'Mol shouted. "Not the girl, Johnny! For the love of God, not her!"

Sticks only laughed. "My, my, gentlemen, have we gotten religion? All this calling upon the deity?"

"What? What?" Claypoole shouted. He saw the look on O'Mol's face at the mention of Würzburg. "What is he going to do to Katie?"

"You don't want to know, Rock," O'Mol muttered.

"Oh, yes he does!" Sticks gloated. "He shall know the truth because if you know the truth, well, you shall be—dead." He laughed. "Würzburg was an ancient city in the country of Germany, and a thousand years ago they tortured, tried, and burned people at the stake as witches there. Your girl is going to be burned at the stake as a witch." He chortled. "She'll be one truly hot piece of pussy when they get done with her." Claypoole cursed Sticks. "Oh," he pouted, "such a vile temper! Ah, Mister Dean! I am truly sorry I've ignored you! Your girl? Miss Tara? She's already been there, and I must say, she made a complete ash of herself!" He laughed so hard he began to cough. Dean just glared.

"I'll kill you! I'll kill you!" Claypoole raged impotently.

"Oh, yes, you, freedom fighter." He turned to O'Mol. "You're going with the girl. Take him away."

The guards dragged O'Mol out.

"Oh, one more thing." Sticks held up his hand. "An old friend wants to say something to you. Juanita?" he called.

Juanita came in from an anteroom. "What an artful display, Johnny. Get anything out of them yet?"

"Not yet, my dear. The interrogations come later. You wish to address these gentlemen?"

Juanita stepped close to the three Marines and slapped Dean and Claypoole hard. The sound of her hand echoed like a shot in the room. Pasquin saw what was coming for him so he lifted his leg and blocked the kick to his groin. Unbalanced, Juanita staggered. "You'll regret that, you bastard!" she hissed. "I'll see you three again," she warned, "and when I do, you'll wish you'd never been born."

"I'm scared shitless, lady," Pasquin told her. He turned his attention to Sticks. "Well, needle-dick, what's the treat in store for us?"

"Ah, for you, Corporal Pasquin, and your two friends here, why, all roads lead to Rome."

CHAPTER
TWENTY-SIX

The surveillance techs had probably less to do than anybody else in Interstellar City. The treaty that had admitted Kingdom to the Confederation of Human Worlds expressly prohibited Confederation representatives and agents from performing any and all manner of covert surveillance on the local population. Weather, geological, and geographic surveys were allowed so long as they were required for programs designed to aid the population. The theocracy made final determination of what programs aided the population and banned any that would allow the Confederation to peek into their operations or view the lives of their people. For its part, the Confederation did not reveal to the theocracy the capabilities it had on hand out of fear the theocracy would demand to use them for its own purposes. The theocracy's purposes, the residents of Interstellar City were convinced, were largely geared toward spying on the population so it could be more completely repressed.

The only variation in belief the theocrats allowed was between their various sects, not within them. Attempts at proselytizing across sects had caused great problems during Kingdom's first couple of generations. The only solution, the theocrats decided, was to ban proselytizing all together. Not everybody found that solution acceptable. Prominent among those who found it unacceptable were Mormons, Seventh Day Adventists, and the followers of Sun Myung Moon. Which was why there were no longer any Mormons, Seventh

Day Adventists, or followers of Sun Myung Moon on Kingdom. Conversion from one religious belief to another was a capital offense. Proselytizing was punishable by burning at the stake. It took a lot of burnings-at-stake to convince the surviving Mormons and Seventh Day Adventists to leave. The followers of Sun Myung Moon were more tractable and had left after only a few of their members were immolated.

Naturally, the theocracy didn't tell the Confederation about the penalties for conversion; there was too great a chance that the unbelievers in the Confederation would try to make them stop. Public executions for religious transgressions were too important a form of education to allow off-worlders, no matter who they were, to put an end to them.

When the theocracy asked for assistance in locating and identifying purported off-world raiders, it was too rich an opportunity for the surveillance technicians to pass up. They were like children on Midwinter's Day morning. Except they weren't opening gifts, they were planting them.

The first thing they did was turn on an unused geosync satellite that included in its broad range of view the area of the purported off-world raids. It wasn't their fault, they reasoned, that the satellite had sat idle for so long that the mechanism that would normally focus it strictly on one specific area had died and it would take, oh, six months to a year Standard to get a replacement part.

The ground surveillance techs just about cackled with glee as they went through—and beyond, if the truth be known—the area the theocracy said would provide the needed proof of the off-worlders the next time they launched one of their murderous raids. They installed cameras that did such a good job of mimicking birds' nests that birds sometimes added to them and claimed them as their own. Motion detectors were planted in such overlapping profusion that a large, dung-eating beetlelike creature endemic to the scrub could be tracked to within millimeters throughout its range. Listening devices sprang up all about, except "sprang" was not quite the word. Some of them were disguised as burls on tree trunks, others as pebbles that almost miraculously didn't wash away in a heavy rain.

And they didn't stop there. Finally released to play with their toys, they installed infrared detectors, UV viewers, and myriad other devices that covered most of the range of the electromagnetic spectrum. Nothing would appear, move, or make a noise without the surveillance techs knowing about it.

They'd worry about how to sift through all that data after they started getting it. In the meanwhile, Oh joy! What fun simply installing all those devices!

They installed so many things that nobody could blame them if some were inadvertently left behind when they picked them up again at the end of the authorized surveillance, could they?

Surveillance Tech (15th grade) Morley Christopher scratched his neck as he peered at the bank of monitors he was supposed to watch over.

"Think we overdid it a bit?" he asked. There was no way he was going to stay on top of the data being analyzed and laid out for him by the thirty computers feeding data from six hundred surveillance devices into the fifty monitors in front of him.

"Not a chance," replied his partner, Surveillance Tech (14th grade) Elizabeth Rice.

Christopher screwed up his face and tried to count how many monitors he could clearly see without moving his head. Not enough. "Are you sure, Betty?"

Rice laughed. "Mor, we only have a few months, maybe only one or two, before we have to bring it all back in. We're getting enough data to keep us busy analyzing for years."

"But we're being inundated with so much we probably won't be able to spot the raiders when they hit again."

She smiled at him. "Mor, you've been stuck here in Insanity too long. You sound like you believe the theocrats' nonsense about off-world raiders."

"Well—"

"Come on, Mor. You know better than that." She went happily back to the Olympia Mons of data building up in front of her. The next raid would come, the theocracy would demand the identity and location of the off-worlders who made it, the techs would check the data for that time and location, and Ambassador Creadence would duly report that they'd found no sign of off-worlders and their shuttles. Even if they had to break down all their surveillance devices immediately afterward, they'd still have mountains of data to plow through.

The mullahs had told them about the infidel crusaders who came from a demon world to rapine and burn the faithful, so when the people of Almedina heard the distant thunder on a day when the sun shone and the sky was clear, they fled to predetermined hiding places.

Hetman Mohammet paused before he fled to turn on the village's radio, its sole communication with the district capital, to inform his superior, Pasha Alaziz, of the matter. The radios given to the villages were of an ancient design, necessary to restrict villages' communications to their own district capitals. Open communication between villages or, far worse, with the infidels of Interstellar City, was deliberately made so difficult as to be nearly impossible. Hetman Mohammet had to wait a moment before the radio was ready to transmit. Then he had to fiddle with the dials to bring the district radioman's voice in clearly enough that he could understand the man's responses to what he said. Finally, his communication complete, he turned the radio off and went outside to where his donkey waited. He mounted the beast, kicked and geed it into motion, and began the briskly clopping journey to his hiding place some three kilometers to the northwest. But it had taken too long to establish communications with the district capital, and the makers of the distant thunder traveled *very* fast.

Hetman Mohammet hadn't even reached the last house in the village when the first infidel fighting machine roared in and began blasting the houses to cinders. He cried out a prayer and heeled his donkey. The frightened beast didn't need the urging, it had broken into a gallop even before Mohammet's heels touched its flanks. They ran into another fighting machine that was entering from the northwest, its snout already firing at the first house it encountered.

When the mullahs said the infidels came from a demon world, Hetman Mohammet had thought they spoke in a religious sense; he hadn't realized they meant the infidels were truly demons. But that was most assuredly the ugliest djinn he'd ever heard of standing in the cupola of the fighting machine. Its skin, where he could see it, was a jaundice yellow. Its eyes were slanted and its teeth pointed in its sharply convex face. When it saw him, the demon's eyes grew wide and its mouth curved in a scimitar smile.

Hetman Mohammet wailed out prayers to Allah, and bent over his donkey's neck to make a smaller target when he saw the demon point what must be a weapon at him. He pointlessly kicked his beast to induce greater speed; the donkey was already at its fastest gallop.

Far too slow. A greenish fluid shot out of the nozzle of the demon's weapon and splashed on both rider and steed . . .

It took mere moments for the eight fighting vehicles that converged on Almedina to reduce all of its structures to cinders and charred briquettes.

Then they set out in pursuit of the fleeing villagers and their hiding places.

"I beg your pardon?" Ambassador Friendly Creadence said.

"YOU FAILED!"

Creadence thought Metropolitan Eleison looked and sounded like a prophet from the Old Testament, one condemning his followers for worshiping a golden calf or something.

"How—"

"The off-worlders came again and you have not yet told us who they are!"

Creadence had been a diplomat for entirely too long to let any reaction show on his face at the stunning news. In his peripheral vision he saw Harley Thorogood murmuring into his personal comm unit.

"Tell me when they came and where."

"Had you done as you agreed, instead of planting things to spy on our faithful, you would be telling *me* not only when and where, but who they were and whence they came!"

"Sirs, if I may speak?" Thorogood said as he slipped his comm unit into his pocket.

"Yessir, I can do that," Surveillance Tech Morley Christopher said into his headset as his fingers tapped a rapid staccato of commands on his keyboard. "I'll have it for you in a moment—if there's anything to have."

At the next workstation Elizabeth Rice was entering the same string of commands. Locate: sonic boom. Locate: unscheduled aircraft. Locate: explosions. Locate: fires larger than cooking. Locate: screams other than children at play.

"Blessed Mothers," Rice whispered as the flick-flick-flick on her main monitor resolved into an unidentified orbit-to-surface shuttle on what looked like a crash landing glide path.

Christopher was silent save for the heavy breathing coming from his gaping mouth. He hit the rapid forward to speed the action on his main monitor.

The shuttle didn't crash land. It fired braking rockets and made a safe touchdown. Four armored vehicles rushed out of it and sped toward what a scrolling legend identified as the village of Almedina. A second shuttle landed near the first and spewed out four more vehicles which sped after the first quartet. A third let out four that went elsewhere.

The picture jerked as Christopher gave the command to follow the groups of vehicles. The monitor focus changed to the outskirts of the village and showed eight vehicles burning everything to the ground. Then it jerked to a different view, this time of wilds the legend identified as within a kilometer and a half of the village. The vehicles started killing people in a manner neither Christopher nor Rice had ever heard of.

Christopher found his voice again. "Sir," he said, his voice strained, "it's a place called Almedina. Some kind of fighting vehicles came off shuttles and attacked . . . Yessir, that's right, orbit-to-surface shuttles." His fingers worked the keyboard again. "I've got the computer doing a search now to identify the shuttles and vehicles." A new window opened on his monitor. Automatically, he expanded the window to take up the entire screen; he'd already seen enough of the carnage to give him nightmares.

The window gave its search results. Shuttle: unidentified. Armored vehicles: unidentified.

"Sir, the computer doesn't recognize them. . . . Right. As soon as we have more I'll notify you."

He glanced at Rice. She was still watching the visuals on her monitor. Then she jumped. He heard her exclaim:

"That's impossible!" Her fingers hit Playback so she could see it again.

"Metropolitan," Thorogood said soothingly, "our technicians are working at this very moment to identify those who attacked Almedina. I am fully confident we will have their identity shortly. When we do, we will notify you."

It took a few more minutes, but Metropolitan Eleison finally left with his entourage, only slightly less angry than he had been when he arrived.

Thorogood swiveled his chair to face Creadence. "Shuttles, unidentified manufacture or place of origin, three of them," he said soberly. "Each carried four unidentified armored fighting vehicles. The AFVs went into the village of Almedina and destroyed it. Then they went hunting for the people who fled before they arrived. It seems they found most of the people and killed them. Maybe all of them."

"My God," Creadence murmured.

"I doubt any god," Thorogood looked at the door through which the religious delegation had just departed, "had anything to do with it." He stood. "I think we need to look at the pictures."

Creadence agreed. They went to look at the pictures.

"Can't you show them before the sonic boom?" Creadence asked.

"I'm sorry, sir," Rice said. "When we planted our devices, we really didn't think anything would come from above, so we didn't set anything to watch the sky."

"The only reason we have the visuals of the shuttles on approach," Christopher added, "is some cameras were set to turn to and focus on the sources of loud, unexpected noises."

"At that," Rice picked up, "there's a good fifteen or twenty second gap between when the shuttles broke the sound barrier and when our cameras picked them up."

"Mostly because of the length of time it took for the sound to reach the receptors," Christopher added. He had to try to salvage *something* from what might well turn into a debacle. Who'd have thought they actually needed to watch the sky? Nobody except the nuts who ran that asylum had believed they were being hit by someone from off-world.

"All right, let it run. Show me what happened when they touched down." Creadence let the visuals run while the shuttles off-loaded their AFVs, all still unidentified, even though he had them run through the computers on whatever navy starship that was in orbit on some routine patrol, or whatever it was navy starships occasionally did that brought them into

Kingdom's planetary space. He didn't have the visuals pause until one showed a good image of an AFV commander.

"Stop there. Focus on the vehicle commander and enlarge, then let me see some movement."

Creadence did, and swallowed at the image on his monitor. He stared at it for a long moment. He'd seen a few genetically engineered modifications to the basic human, made to suit the needs of a few worlds, but he'd never seen—or heard of—modifications that extreme. If he hadn't known humanity was alone, he'd have sworn the AFV commander was an alien. Why, that man even seemed to have nictating membranes on his eyes!

"Continue," he said.

He didn't speak again until the visuals showed vehicle commanders spraying people with some kind of greenish fluid from a hose attached to tanks mounted on their backs. Then it was again focus, enlarge, show movement. He turned to Thorogood.

"Have you ever heard of a weapon like that?"

Thorogood, looking somewhat greenish himself, simply shook his head.

Then it was forward again until the point where Rice had exclaimed, "That's impossible!"

"What happened?" Creadence demanded. "Why'd the visual cut off then?"

"It didn't," Rice said. She pointed with a shaky finger at a dot on the screen. She focused on it and enlarged. It was a flying scavenger gliding on thermals, clearly in motion. The picture hadn't stopped.

"Where'd the shuttle go?"

"Sir, I've run that sequence several times. I have no idea."

"Run it through again," Thorogood said. "Stop it at the instant the shuttle vanishes."

She did.

Thorogood studied the frozen frame for a long moment.

The sky seemed to ripple a bit into different shades of blue, violet, and green, some of them not quite possible.

"I've never seen—" He stopped and snorted. "Hell, nobody's ever seen anything shift into Beamspace in an atmosphere. But I read a blue-sky paper on it once. The author hypothesized it would look something like that."

"But you can't shift into Beamspace in an atmosphere. Or deep in a gravity well."

"And a shuttle can't vanish into thin air either. But we just saw one do exactly that. Do you have a better explanation for what we just watched?"

Creadence didn't have a better idea, but he did have a disquieting thought.

"Do we have infrared images of any of the raiders?" he asked.

Christopher and Rice both tapped commands. An infrared view of two of the AFVs pursuing villagers popped up on their main monitors. The four studied the images, then read the scrolling legend. There was nothing unusual in the infrared about the AFVs. The pursued villagers had slightly elevated temperatures, as was to be expected under the circumstances. The two AFV commanders had body temperatures not far above the ambient air temperature.

Thorogood and his boss exchanged haunted glances. Christopher and Rice looked at them and shivered.

"I don't give a damn about the treaty," Creadence croaked. "Full planetary surveillance as of now. I want to know where those shuttles are coming from."

CHAPTER
TWENTY-SEVEN

"Well, well, well, well," Noto Draya rumbled, his voice echoing hollowly off the dripping walls of the dungeon. It was very early in the morning, so the Coliseum was empty except for the prisoners and their guards.

On the flight from Placetas the three Marines had been thrown together with Mr. Prost, who, like everyone else who'd had more than just casual contact with them, had been arrested on suspicion and tortured. Now they all lay chained to the walls, awaiting more torture and then death. During the flight, guards had taken turns beating them with their fists and clubs, not enough to injure them permanently, just to pass the time. Ferris had ordered his men to go easy on the captives because he had special plans for them.

Homs Ferris, his bulk rolling along behind Draya's, put a hand to his mouth and yawned. "Too damned early for me, Noto. Big day today, so let's have our fun and get some rest before the games." It was three A.M. Wednesday.

It was Wednesday, and a huge gladiatorial contest was scheduled to begin at noon. It would be kicked off by the slaughter of the four men in chains.

"I rather like the effect of these torches," Ferris said.

"We only use them when the tourists are let in here before the games," Sal Richter, counselor to the Ferris Family, responded. The actors who played the roles of gladiators and prisoners scheduled for sacrifice in the arena were mustered in that cavernous prison before the start of the games so the tourists could gape at them. "You ought to visit us more often."

"He's right, Homs," Draya wheezed, "you ain't made it down here in a while. You ought to take a week off, especially this time of the year, when the weather's so bad up there, and spend it with us."

"We've had business to take care of recently," Johnny Sticks replied for his boss. Avoiding the puddles, he walked carefully through the dirty straw covering the stone floor. Juanita clung to his arm, her eyes glittering with anticipation.

A guard clanked open the iron gate to the cells and the party stepped through.

"Well, if it ain't the goddamn Tons of Fun!" Claypoole croaked. His face was swollen and a tooth had been pried loose in the front of his mouth as punishment for just such wisecracks. One of Sticks's goons had done it with a knife. The gap was still bleeding.

In a corner two huge men, stripped to the waist, stood next to an array of torture instruments.

"I see what you mean about this one, Johnny," Ferris said. "He does have a smart mouth. Noto, which one shall we start on?"

Draya put his hand on his chin and thought for a moment. "The librarian. I hate books. Put that scrawny old fart into the boot for a while." The "boot" was an iron shoe that could be filled with boiling water or hot coals while it was fastened to a person's foot. "Uh-uh, just one foot, boys," Draya cautioned the guards. "He's got to be able to do some maneuvering later this morning, when we put him in the arena." Draya's body rumbled with laughter.

Two guards unchained Prost and dragged him to the torturers.

"Mr. Ferris," he shouted, "this is unfair! I had nothing to do with these spies! Please, sir, please!"

Ferris laughed. "You eat with the crows, you get eaten with the crows!"

Prost was strapped into a chair and then the iron boot was fixed to his right foot. He still did not believe any of this was really happening to him. One of the men took a pot of boiling water off the fire and inserted its spout into a hole near the top of the boot. Prost screamed and pulled against his bonds. He kicked his right foot against the inside of the boot—it could be heard thumping hollowly against the metal, but his struggles were useless. The torturer paused and looked up at Draya. Prost groaned and thrashed about in the chair.

"More?" Draya asked his companions.

"My dear Noto, of course more." He nodded. The executioner began pouring more scalding water into the boot. Prost's screams echoed off the stone walls. As the executioner looked up for instructions, Ferris continued nodding, until the pot was empty. Tendrils of steam seeped out the top of the device and the room filled with the stench of parboiled flesh.

"How much longer to breakfast?" Johnny Sticks asked, and everyone shook with laughter, even the torturers. Prost had passed out from the agony and sat limply in the chair.

"You didn't ask him any questions," Draya said with a pout. "I was hoping we could get information out of the old bastard."

"He don't know nothing," Ferris answered. "He's useless. Time we got a real manager to run that place. He overspent his budget like crazy! He was supposed to get more girls through Juanita, but instead he went out and bought all these expensive goddamned books! Books! Who the hell needs that shit in a fucking cathouse?" He shrugged. What was done was done. "We'll use the books for decoration. I just brought him along to get things started. Let him loose." He gestured at the guards, who unstrapped Prost's bonds and unfastened the boot. Hot water spilled out onto the floor. "Oh," Ferris exclaimed when they could see Prost's foot, "cook spoiled the roast again, I guess." His companions smiled heartily. The guards dragged Prost's unconscious body back to the wall and chained him there.

"Make you hot?" Johnny Sticks whispered into Juanita's ear.

She nibbled playfully at Johnny's earlobe. "I'll get hot when we start on them." She gestured at the Marines. "Especially that one." She pointed at Claypoole.

"Hey, boss," Sticks turned to Ferris, "take that one," he pointed at Claypoole, "and ask him how this thing works." He held up the last of the readers his men had taken from the Marines. "Also, maybe he knows who the deep-cover agent is. Be useful to know that."

Ferris shrugged. "Whadaya think, Noto? I don't think Nast told these guys. He didn't tell Culloden, and we know Nast trusted him. I think he sent us these three dummies to distract us. If we had the time we could drag 'em over to Doc's and get the truth out of them."

"Hah," Draya answered. "We don't have the time. I think you're right." He turned to the Marines. "How does it feel to be Nast's patsies?" And back to the others, said, "And who cares where Nast is hiding out? We got our security up, and without the proof he needs, he can raid us until Sunday and it won't do him any good. Besides, torturing these guys is more fun. I like to see my victims squirm. Let's take these Marines in turn, by IQ. Take the corporal first."

"They don't promote by IQ in the Marines! We're smarter than he ever will be!" Claypoole and Dean shouted at once.

"You made the right decision," Pasquin said through his split lip. "These two are too stupid to feel pain."

Sticks was disappointed. He knew how much Juanita hated Claypoole, and he was hoping that torturing Claypoole would excite her to the point where he might be able to coax her into a more intimate relationship in the time left before the contest.

"Give him a nail job," Draya rumbled. "Only one hand, though, and not his fighting hand either. He'll need that later, to make it look good."

Guards unchained Pasquin and dragged him over to the torturers, where he was strapped into the chair just vacated by Prost. "You left- or right-handed, boy?" one of the torturers asked.

"Fuck you, asshole! I've killed better men than you!"

The executioner looked at Draya. "Take a chance. Left hand. If he's left-handed, too bad." The capo chuckled. In one swift motion the man ripped the nail off Pasquin's left forefinger. His assistant immediately plunged a red-hot pin into the flesh.

Pasquin heaved against the straps holding him and groaned. Perspiration broke out on his forehead. He grunted and sucked breath through his clenched teeth but he did not scream.

Dean and Claypoole screamed curses at the gangsters.

"Another?" the torturer asked. Draya nodded, and he plucked the nail on Pasquin's middle finger. The corporal gasped this time and grunted. When another needle was plunged in, he let out a short bark of a shout. Blood trickled out the side of his mouth where he'd bitten himself to keep from screaming. He breathed heavily and his eyes flashed hatred at the gangsters but still he did not scream.

"Give him the boot," Ferris said.

"Don't look, fellas! Don't look!" Pasquin gasped at Dean and Claypoole as his right foot was placed into the boot. When the first trickle of scalding water dribbled down the outside of his lower foot he gave a shout of pain and anger. As the boot slowly filled, his agony increased until he could hold it in no longer and screamed until he was hoarse. Finally he slumped forward, exhausted and overcome with pain.

"It's almost four in the morning," Draya said as he yawned. "I gotta have at least eight hours of sleep a night or I'm worthless in the morning. Let's leave these birds. They'll get theirs at the show later. Come on, let's head back to our rooms," Draya told the others.

"Noto, Noto . . ." There was a note of desperation in Juanita's voice. "Let me stay for a while? I have a score to settle with these two." She indicated Dean and Claypoole.

Draya shrugged. "Never deny a lady her pleasures. Okay, I'm outta here," he said.

"Juanita, come on along with us," Johnny Sticks urged.

She pecked him on the cheek. "You run along, Johnny. I'll join you in a little while." She patted him in an intimate spot.

Johnny's eyebrows rose and he smiled. He turned quickly and joined the bosses as they plodded down the torchlit passageway.

The guards and torturers stood waiting for the woman's instructions. "Stand aside and let me work on them for a while," she commanded. Obediently, the guards retreated into the passageway, where they lit up smokes and the torturers settled down among their instruments with cold drinks.

She pulled down Claypoole's trousers and grabbed him by the crotch. "Scream," she whispered, "this has got to look real."

"Fuck you," Claypoole muttered.

"Goddamnit, holler, you idiot!" she whispered. "I want them to think I'm really hurting you."

"Eat shit, you old bitch," Claypoole shouted.

Juanita yanked on his jewels and Claypoole grunted. "Is that all you can do?" he asked through clenched teeth.

She leaned close and bit his earlobe so hard her lips came away stained with blood. One of the guards watching from the passageway laughed. "I work for Nast, you idiot," she whispered, wiping the blood from her mouth. "Give me the code and I'll call for help."

Claypoole snickered. "Get on with it," he said.

"No, no, you goddamned fool, I am Nast's secret agent, Claypoole! Give me the goddamned code! I'll get your reader and call him in!"

Claypoole stared at Juanita. She yanked his jewels again, harder this time.

"You . . . ?"

The other prisoners were chained far enough away from where Claypoole was lying they could not hear with Juanita had been saying. "Rock, what the hell's going on?" Dean whispered.

"Shut up!" Juanita screamed. She jumped up and kicked Dean in the head. He cursed foully but she turned back to Claypoole. She leaned over him, bracing herself on both arms. "Now Claypoole, listen to me," she whispered, her voice intense. "I don't blame you for not believing me." She brought her knee up between his legs to make the guards think she was whispering her hatred to the chained Marine. "But you have got to believe me! I am your only chance! I know Nast is somewhere on Havanagas, waiting for your signal. Tell me how to send it! I've got what he needs to put these bastards away forever." She leaned forward as she spoke, punctuating her whispered words with forceful slaps to Claypoole's face.

Claypoole thought fast. It made sense. But if Juanita was the deep-cover agent . . . ? A nasty thought began to form in his mind. What was it that fat bastard had said? Sending the Marines here was a diversion of some kind? Anger surged through Rachman Claypoole. If this was a setup—

"*Knives in the Night, chieu hoi*—"

"What?"

"C-h-i-e-u-h-o-i, *chieu hoi*," Claypoole whispered.

Juanita stood up and signaled the guards. "I'm going to see Johnny," she said. "Get these fools ready for the show." She turned and walked out.

"What was that all about?" Dean asked.

Claypoole was not ready to tell anyone what had passed between him and Juanita. If he were wrong . . . "She likes me," was all Claypoole would say. Dean grunted and lay back against the stones.

"I'm all fucked up," Pasquin groaned from his corner of the cell. "Oh, God, I'm no good with only one foot, guys. You'll have to carry me out in the morning." He lay back and groaned again.

"We're going to stand together and go down together,"

Dean said. "Us and Mr. Prost there, if he can get up on his good leg. We're going down fighting, like Marines."

"Guess this might be it for us, eh, Joe? What a way to go!" Claypoole whispered. He lay back against the cold stone. Was Juanita telling the truth? If she were—a quick surge of hope flared up in his breast, but he suppressed it immediately. No, there'd be no last minute rescue on this mission. Why did Nast pick us? he asked himself angrily. Why did he put us into this shit? Marines would never do this to anyone. He shook his head. I gotta stop feeling sorry for myself, he thought.

"I may only have one leg to stand on," Pasquin said with effort through the red cloud of pain enveloping him, "but we're a team, we're going out standing up and—oh, Jesus, Mary, and Joseph, it fucking hurts, guys!" His voice shook and he was breathing heavily and soaked in perspiration. The others did not even dare look at his leg.

One of the guards approached them. No, it was Hugo, Johnny Sticks's man. He carried a small case and a pitcher of water. "Mr. Ferris wants you guys to look good tomorrow," he announced without preamble. "I'm gonna give your buddy and the bookman there a shot to knock them out and then apply these compresses to their feet. At least they'll be able to stand up tomorrow." He gave them all a drink from the pitcher and then plunged a syringe into Pasquin's good leg.

"I don't need no goddamn—oh, Jesus, oh—" He slumped unconscious to the stones. Hugo did the same thing for Prost, who had not regained consciousness. Then he applied what looked like a shoe to the foot that had been broiled.

"These compresses will harden so they can stand on their feet, and they're impregnated with a powerful analgesic that'll help deaden the pain," Hugo explained.

"What's the plan?" Dean asked.

Hugo hesitated and looked around. "You're going up against jackels, you know, dinosaurlike raptors? You know what happened to Nast's last agent? Prost is going first, on his own, to get the crowd stirred up. Then you three go. If by some miracle you should win, then professional gladiators will be sent in to kill you."

"When?" Claypoole asked.

Again Hugo hesitated. "Half past eleven, five hours from now."

"Should we thank you?" Claypoole asked cynically.

"No. I've made my bed. I follow orders, whatever they might be. But you guys don't deserve to go out like this, no man does. Go for their snouts. Good luck tomorrow," he whispered, and he was gone.

Johnny Sticks was naked under his robe, throbbing with anticipation as Juanita stepped into his suite. "Did you enjoy your little session with the boys downstairs?" he asked.

She walked over to where he was standing. "Of course, Johnny. I feel much better now." Sticks grabbed her and pressed himself up against her. She could feel him underneath his robe. "Johnny," she whispered into his ear, "I know how to send the signal to Nast."

"What? They told you? How?"

"Give me the reader and I'll show you," she whispered.

Her hand touched him ever so lightly under his robe. Johnny was so wild he would have given Juanita his pistol. "It's over on the dresser," he croaked.

She stepped to the dresser, and there among Johnny's personal items sat the reader. She picked it up and turned it on. Johnny came up behind her and pressed himself into her back. She whirled around and drove the blade of a tiny stiletto between his ribs. Johnny grunted in surprise and staggered backward. Juanita followed and stabbed him twice more. "Urk! You—" Johnny doubled over and grasped his stomach. The blood flowed between his fingers. He went to his knees, gasping and choking. "You—You goddamned—" He pitched forward on the floor.

Absently, Juanita wiped her hand on her skirt. She scrolled

through the table of contents. Ah, there it was, *Knives in the Night*. She smiled. Just what you'd expect a Marine to be reading. She activated the search function and punched in c-h-i-e-u-h-o-i. She wondered what the words *chieu hoi* meant. She never felt the bullet that crashed into the back of her skull. Poor Johnny Sticks was not as naked under that robe as she had thought.

CHAPTER
TWENTY-EIGHT

The iron gate to their prison cell slammed open with a tremendous crash, snapping Dean out of the semicomatose state he had been in, not fully awake but not quite asleep either. He thought he had been dreaming, talking to his mother. She had been alive, in perfect health, and he was a boy again, looking up at her as she spoke. "Joseph," she had told him, "your Honor is in Fidelity."

"All right, boys, your time has come," one of the guards grunted as he kicked the four men into upright positions from where they lay on the cold stone floor. "Look lively, look lively. In less than three hours now you won't be anymore." He and his several companions laughed harshly. They hauled each man to his feet, taking off the manacles and chains as they did.

"I ain't worth a damn in the mornings without a cup of coffee," Claypoole said, stretching. Several of the guards laughed. They admired his pluck. Dean looked at him in admiration too. They were in desperate trouble and Claypoole was cracking jokes! A sudden wave of affection for his friend brought moisture to his eyes. Claypoole thought to himself, Where the hell is Nast!

"Damn!" Pasquin said, "I can actually walk on this thing!" He tested his weight on his injured foot and it held, with little pain. "Remember," he told the others as the guards unchained him, "we're in this together."

"Not him," a guard gestured to Prost. "He's going in first all by himself."

Already people were gathering in the Coliseum stands above, taking their seats in the early morning freshness, relaxing, buying their breakfasts from the vendors who plied the aisles. Out in the arena itself, clowns initiated mock battles for the amusement of the early crowd. Even in their subterranean prison the Marines could hear the muted laughter, like the audio from a vid being played two rooms over.

"Gate receipts are gonna top the record today," one of the guards remarked. "All right, into the showers with you birds."

Held by three guards each, the four men were hustled into a modern shower facility adjoining the mock dungeon. The warm water revived them somewhat after their ordeal. "We can't jump them," Claypoole observed, standing under the cascading water. "Too many of 'em."

"Listen," Claypoole told Prost, "the raptors' hamstrings have been cut, so they can't jump. We've encountered these things before. You do have a chance! Attack! Catch them off balance! They're only animals!"

"Go for the snouts," Dean advised.

"No talking, damnit!" one of the guards shouted.

"I'm very afraid, gentlemen," Prost whispered.

"So are we," Pasquin admitted, "but we're Marines, we've been shot at and shit at and this is the worst scrape any of us have ever been in, but we are not giving up! We are not going out quietly. Don't you give them that satisfaction, Mister Prost."

"Actually," Claypoole said, "the worst scrape I ever been in was on Elneal, when we were lost in the Martac. Remember, Joe? We were—" He shut up when the other two looked at him very strangely. Well, they didn't know what he knew. "I got a score to settle with these bastards," he went on, "and no Wanderjahrian jackals and no gladiators are going to stop me. They got a fight on their hands today, by God, and we are gonna win it!" His voice rang off the walls, causing the guards to look at the four men suspiciously.

"I told you guys to shut up!" a guard hollered.

Claypoole's companions regarded him as if thinking, What the hell's gotten into him? Then they broke into cheers. "Kill! Kill! Kill!" they shouted and gave high fives all around. Dean, Pasquin, and even Prost felt a sudden surge of hope, so infectious was Claypoole's defiance. Claypoole thought, If Juanita's sent the message— But still he dared not tell his companions, in case the hope of their rescue proved false. He still didn't know if he could trust Juanita, if he'd done the right thing by giving her the code. Who can you trust? Claypoole asked himself. He looked at the other three and he knew.

Nast had finally agreed to set up a shelter between the two Essays, so he could get all his men together for a preflight briefing. An aerial blowup of the coliseum had been projected onto a screen so all of them could see it. They had been studying smaller versions for three days and knew the place by heart. But Nast insisted on one more rehearsal.

"They won't be expecting us," Nast said. "I'm going to be in the lead Essay. We'll land right here." He pointed to a spot in the arena just in front of the emperor's box. "The bosses will be seated there, with their whole menagerie. Those walls are about four meters high. From the roof of an Essay that'll be an easy climb. We'll assault the mob bosses directly from the Essays. Number two will follow us in and provide security for the snatch. Do not fire unless you have to. We don't want to harm any of the spectators. But if you're fired on or if anyone tries to interfere with this operation, shoot to kill." They'd all heard that before too.

"Any word from our Marines?" Chief Riggs asked.

"No," Nast answered quickly. "Nothing. We have to assume they've been compromised. So have my agents."

"Then how're you going to get the evidence you need to put these rats away?" Brock asked.

Nast paused for only an instant before he said, "I have

enough evidence from their operations on a dozen worlds to extradite them from Havanagas."

If he already had what he needed, then why— Chief Riggs asked himself. A sudden thought occurred to the old navy chief that made him start but he dared not give voice to it. "We'll snatch Draya, Ferris, and their henchmen and transport them to the *Wanganui*. She should be in orbit by now. I know, I know, customs will have queried Perizittes why he's here, and he'll tell them it's to effect emergency repairs to their Beam drive. I anticipated something like this might happen. We're off schedule, I know. But we have the element of surprise and we'll get them by the balls."

Brock and several other policemen looked dubious.

"Brock, you and your team'll be on the lead Essay with me. Soon as we're down, up you go and into the box. You all know what our targets look like; any doubt, secure or disable everyone. Don't let anyone get out of the boxes. Is that clear? If you have to shoot anyone to stop him from getting away, shoot him. We'll sort out who's who when we get back to the *Wanganui*."

Brock looked at the officer sitting next to him and they exchanged glances. Was this a license to kill?

"Chief," Nast turned to Riggs, "we go in as if this were a wartime combat assault. You know how to do that. When the prisoners are secure, you take off for the *Wanganui* immediately. The rest of us will remain on the ground until you can get back for us. Gentlemen, it might be a very hot hour down there for those of us who stay behind. Make sure you have plenty of ammunition. Chief," again he turned back to Riggs, who then briefed the men on how an assault landing would go, despite the fact they'd practiced dry runs many times over the previous days.

Riggs explained again that they would go in at wave-top level at supersonic speed. When they approached the coast of the continent where Rome was situated, they would rise to

treetop level. That way they should be able to avoid any surveillance radars the mob might have in operation. Nast was
not worried about armed interference while they were air-
borne, just that their quarry might get advance warning and
get away.

"Okay, men, thirty minutes to 8 hours," Nast announced
when Riggs was done. "Team leaders, review your assignments with your men. Once we're away you can catch some
sleep.

Nast turned to go but Brock stopped him. "How're we
gonna make an arrest that'll hold up in court if you don't have
that evidence your agent was supposed to get for you?"

Nast regarded Brock for a moment. Still the dumb street
cop from back in—where was it, someplace called Fairfax
County? "Welbourne, look at it this way. I'm the number two
man in the Ministry of Justice. I have a phalanx of lawyers
just waiting to go into action, and besides, the President of
the Confederation bought into this operation months ago. But
if that's not enough for you, there won't be any trial for these
swine. They're going straight to Darkside, those who survive
the raid. It's not the first time and it won't be the last. Now get
with your men and get them ready. And Welbourne, the fewer
of those rats that survive the assault, the better it'll be for the
taxpayers."

The four prisoners sat chained to a wall just inside the
staging area. From outside came the hubbub of the crowd
waiting impatiently for the games to begin. There was a
sudden burst of laughter.

"What time is it?" Claypoole asked one of the guards.

"Eleven twenty-two. Eight minutes to show time." He
laughed and came over to where the four sat. "Look. We're
only following orders. We're not responsible for this. There'll
be at least two jackals out there. You've got a chance if you
stick together and cooperate." He glanced sideways at Prost.
"But he doesn't," the man whispered.

"Where the hell are the cops when you need them most?" Claypoole muttered. The others laughed briefly, thinking it was Claypoole's dogged sense of humor, but he really meant what he said. Where the hell was Nast, anyway? On the other side of the planet? What could be taking him so long? Now he had serious doubts Juanita had ever sent the message. He could see her now, schmoozing with Johnny Sticks, laughing at how easy it was to get the code. More laughter from the crowd. "Jesus," he muttered, "don't any of those fools realize what's really going on down here?"

"No, they think it's all done by special effects," Dean answered. "When Tara and I—" he stopped short. Tara. Burned at the stake. Anger bordering on madness swept through him. He got control of himself after a moment. "They don't think these fights are any more real than the vids all of us watch," he said in a tired voice.

A very big man in gladiatorial armor came up to them. "If you survive the raptors, and you just might, you'll have to deal with us," he said. "We'll kill you quickly, if you cooperate. That's all I can promise. Quick and clean."

"I'm sorry to disappoint you, sir," Pasquin replied, "but you kill us and you'll know you've had a goddamned fight on your hands."

The gladiator stared silently at the Marines, shrugged and touched a hand to his helmet's visor. "We who are about to die salute you," he whispered.

"These guys take this stuff awful serious," Dean whispered. He thought the remark sounded extremely nonchalant and he was proud of himself for saying it. Claypoole wasn't the only one with a sense of humor.

Pasquin had to laugh. "I'll miss you fools," he whispered to his two teammates. There were tears in his eyes as he spoke.

"No! No!" Prost protested as two guards unchained him and hauled him to his feet.

"These things never start on time," one guard said, grinning. "Your life has been extended by approximately two minutes. Hope you used the time to good advantage."

It was precisely 11:32.

Dressed in a loosely fitting toga that came to just below his knees, and armed with only a short sword, Gerry Prost was thrust unceremoniously into the arena. The door slammed shut behind him. The sun was blinding! As his eyes adjusted, he saw thousands of people looking down at him from their seats in the galleries. The arena was empty. He staggered forward and then stopped. From the opposite wall another door opened and out hopped two of the most horrible creatures he'd ever seen. His heart pounded wildly in his chest as the animals stood blinded by the strong sunlight, seeking their bearings. The crowd erupted in an enormous shout of delight.

Bent low to the ground, sniffing the sand as they came on, the jackals advanced cautiously to the center of the arena. Prost stood rooted to the spot, unable to move, his sword dangling uselessly from his hand. They saw their prey at last and scuttled forward rapidly in short hops.

The faster of the two jackals skidded to a halt inches from where Prost stood. Suddenly, a survival instinct took over and the old man swung his sword and brought it straight down onto the creature's snout. It gave a piercing *skree!* and reared back on its haunches. Prost dashed around to one side as the second monster lunged at him, its fangs bared and dripping. Dodging nimbly under its neck, he whacked it on the side with his sword. To his horror the weapon bounced harmlessly off the thing's hide and out of his hand into the sand.

The crowd was on its feet, screaming and cheering, but Prost could've been alone in the world for all the notice he took of the noise. The first jackal fastened its jaws upon his injured leg and lifted him bodily off the ground as it got back on its hind legs. Prost screamed in agony as the beast began shaking him like a rag doll. His leg separated just below the knee and he fell heavily into the sand, rich red blood spurting from the arteries in his severed limb. The jackal tossed back its head and swallowed the leg. The second creature leaped upon him. Prost had just enough time to turn facedown on the ground. The thing gripped him firmly with its short upper arms and raked him viciously with its hind claws. Prost screamed in agony as the razor-sharp talons shredded his back and buttocks. Attracted by the source of the screams, it dipped its head quickly and decapitated Prost with one bite. The two then went to work on what was left of their victim.

It was 11:34.

"Jeez, Dad, that was great!" the young lad from Sisyphus enthused, sitting in the gallery between his parents. "First that witch thing and now this! Boy, I can't wait until the gladiators come on!"

The crowd shrieked as one of the jackals ripped the intestines out of its victim and gulped them down like slimy red sausages. "Oh, that's disgusting!" The boy's mother said, and laughed.

"Animal entrails," her husband said knowingly. "But wonderful special effects. I've read where they use several hundred pounds of raw meat here each day, to simulate human body parts."

"Look! Look!" their son shouted, getting to his feet in his excitement, "Three guys! Now there's gonna be a real fight!"

"Siddown up front! Siddown!" a fat man sitting behind the family from Sisyphus shouted around a mouthful of hamburger.

It was 11:39.

The jackals looked up from their meal as the three men entered the arena. They were dressed like Prost and also armed with the short gladius swords.

Something red and stringy dangled from one of the jackal's jaws. "Oh, Christ," Dean groaned when he realized what it was. The sand around where the two creatures crouched was stained dark red; chunks of meat lay scattered about.

"Ah, goddamn, they're gonna pay for this!" Claypoole shouted, and started toward the jackals.

"Hold it, Rock! We stick together." Pasquin grabbed Claypoole's shoulder and restrained him. "We stand here and let them come to us. Save our energy."

The jackals seemed in no hurry. The crowd began to jeer and throw things into the arena. "Fuck you!" Dean shouted as a half-eaten piece of fruit bounced off his shoulder.

"Steady, steady," Pasquin muttered. More fruit, half-eaten sandwiches, even a shoe or two, pelted them from the galleries. The corporal laughed. "We can take this for another six months."

A third jackal suddenly skittered into the arena.

It was 11:44.

"Uh-oh, that one hasn't been fed this morning," Claypoole said.

The beast hobbled forward, snarling. The crowd cheered wildly. The three Marines arranged themselves in a tight triangle and faced it. As soon as it lunged, Pasquin stepped backward quickly while Claypoole and Dean attacked it from the flanks, banging their swords on its snout. A look almost of surprise came over the thing's face as it reared back to get away from the pounding. At that moment Pasquin lunged forward and plunged the tip of his sword into one of its eyes. The jackal *skreeked* shrilly and shook its head. Dean and Claypoole closed in on it from the flanks and, holding their swords in both hands, rained fierce blows on its head. The blades were too dull to cut but the heavy blows opened its hide and blood spurted out. Dean managed to close the thing's other eye.

Blinded, the jackal whirled about and staggered off toward the other two, which jumped on it and began tearing it apart. The three Marines withdrew and reformed their little group, panting and catching their breath. The spectators went wild.

It was 11:48.

* * *

"What the hell's going on?" Noto Draya rumbled. He and Ferris, their aides and guards, sat in the emperor's box. The two capos were decked out in purple togas fringed in gold; golden coronets graced their heads. They drank wine from silver goblets and puffed on Davidoff Anniversarios No. 1.

"They won't last a lot longer, Noto," Ferris said. He held out his goblet and a nubile serving girl poured more wine. He laughed. "Man, they disposed of my librarian in no time at all!"

Draya laughed. "Hey, sorry to hear about Johnny and that bitch, Juanita. Goddamned women are more trouble than most men can handle."

Ferris made a dismissive gesture with his cigar. "I'll miss Johnny but he should have known better than to mess with that bitch. He went down shooting, though. One bullet right in the back of her head, and him lying dying on the floor when he did it. Pretty cool, Johnny, right up to the end."

"Shoulda sent the whole crowd to Würzburg," Draya rumbled.

"Ah, yes, but then we wouldn't have a chance to see them tortured—and this spectacle!" Ferris laughed. "On with the show! On with the show!" he shouted. Those nearby took up the chant, and soon the entire Coliseum rocked with the roar of thousands of voices.

"Did you see how they fought him off?" the lad from Sisyphus hollered in his father's ear. "Boy, was that some fight, eh, Dad? Just three guys with those little swords! Wow, this is great, Dad! The greatest vacation ever!"

"Keep your eye on the one in the middle, son. I think he's in charge."

The screaming of the crowd, the stomping of thousands of pairs of feet, was so powerful it seemed a physical force, like the concussion of an artillery barrage.

The three Marines stood together, watching the jackals. The sweat streaming off their bodies mixed with the dust from the arena floor to cake them in brown mud. They wiped the sweat from their palms on their togas and they turned brown too.

"Maybe they'll take a nap when they're done," Claypoole said.

"Nah, you remember Wanderjahr. Those things don't kill just to eat, they kill because they like it," Dean responded. "They'll be at us soon enough."

Pasquin's foot was beginning to hurt again. "I can't last much longer," he confessed, "and I'll be on one leg. If I fall, leave me there. We'll close in on the first one to come within range of our swords. You two hack away at its head, I'll try to keep the second one at bay. If he gets me, I'll try to distract him until you can finish his partner. Then you'll have a fighting chance."

"Then we only have to worry about armored gladiators," Claypoole said.

"We'll cross that bridge when we get to it," Pasquin answered. "Uh-oh, here they come!"

It was 11:50.

"All hands secure for landing!" Chief Riggs announced.

Nast flicked his comm unit to the command channel. "Heads up, just so you haven't forgotten, here's the drill one more time: soon as we're down, get out and into the stands. Secure your weapons until we're completely stopped and Chief gives us the green light to dismount. You guys carrying the scaling ladders, get them in place fast. Covering team, give them a volley of grenades as soon as you're topside and be prepared to suppress any fire from the boxes. The grenades won't have the same effect as in a room, but they'll stun them long enough for you to get up there and among them. Brock, I'll lead and you follow with your men. Shoot anyone who—"

"Mr. Nast," Chief Riggs interrupted, "the second Essay bosun reports he's losing power fast. Shall we abort?"

"Negative! Negative!" Nast yelled without hesitation. "We will proceed as planned! Men," he turned back to the command net, "be prepared for a hard landing. Anyone gets sick, he wears it." He didn't bother to tell them they were on their own now. He had no idea what he would do. Once on the ground he'd figure things out. "Chief, take us on in."

It was 11:52.

Before it could even get its mouth open to let out a roar, Dean and Claypoole were hacking away at the first jackal's head. It ducked and weaved, trying to avoid the blows. The second creature warily stalked around the small group and tried coming at them from the rear, but Pasquin was on guard. He shouted, waved his word and stomped his good foot in the dust. His bad foot was an agonizing ball of pain but he could not afford to ease up.

The first jackal let out a shriek of agony as Claypoole put out its right eye. Dean stepped in from the other side and plunged the point of his sword into the monster's other eye. Blood spurted out and coursed down his arm. The jackal backed away and squatted back, emitting long shrieks.

Pasquin's leg gave out at last and he went down hard. The second jackal was on him instantly. It grabbed the corporal's head between its short arms, but Pasquin brought his legs up to his chest, so its deadly hind claws were not able to reach his vital parts. He pounded the side of its head with the edge of his sword in his right hand and managed to keep its jaws up with his left arm. Claypoole, in a frenzy of blood lust, straddled the thing's back and began hammering powerful blows down upon the top of its head. The spectators in the stands could clearly hear the hollow thunk of the blade striking through the skin and hitting the bone of the animal's skull. Each blow elicited a shout of approval from the crowd. The blinded jackal stumbled and staggered about the arena. Eventually it crouched on the far side of the field, breathing heavily, refusing to move.

Pandemonium reigned in the Coliseum. The crowd was on its feet screaming for the men. The sound washed over them like a wave. Claypoole's jackal managed to fling him off its back. It staggered to its feet and hobbled away from the trio as quickly as it could. When it reached its companion it began eating him. The *skreeks* and shrieks of the dying animal penetrated even the victorious howling of the crowd.

Dean helped Pasquin to his feet; he could not stand unassisted because both legs had been so severely lacerated by the jackal's hind claws. Pasquin sank to a sitting position. Claypoole joined them. The roar of the crowd enfolded them. Thousands of people were standing in the galleries now, screaming and holding their thumbs up. Claypoole raised his arms over his head, his sword gripped firmly in his right hand. He turned around slowly, so everyone could see him. Dean did the same. Pasquin clenched his fists and raised them over his head.

"We beat them! We beat them!" Claypoole screamed triumphantly. "We beat them, goddamn you all, we beat them!" He had never in his life felt such power. It seemed now that he was leading the crowd in its wild enthusiasm. There was nothing he couldn't do! He looked to the emperor's box. Ferris and Draya were clearly visible from where he stood, standing out in their purple robes. He shook his bloody sword in their direction. "You're next, you fucking pigs!" he screamed. "Come on," he shouted at Dean, "we can scale that wall and get into their box! Let's get them!" Dragging Pasquin between them, they started running toward the box.

It was 11:57.

They stopped abruptly. Blocking their way was a line of gladiators rapidly trotting out of the staging area. Claypoole counted a dozen of them, heavily armored and bristling with nasty looking weapons.

"Drop me!" Pasquin shouted, "You can't fight and hold on to me! Drop me, I said!" The line began to advance on them. The crowd went wild again. Without a word, the two released

Pasquin and took up a defensive stance over the corporal's prostrate form.

Suddenly, the advancing line of gladiators stopped. The men stood silently. The crowd also went silent. After all the screaming and shouting an eerie calm descended over the arena. The three Marines could clearly hear themselves panting. A big, heavily armored man stepped out from the center of the line. He carried a long sword. He stood facing the Marines. Slowly, the sword held vertical in one hand, he raised the hilt to his chin, the blade standing straight up in the air, flashing brightly in the sunlight.

"Get on with it!" a reedy, angry voice shouted from the emperor's box. Otherwise the Coliseum was plunged into total silence, all eyes fastened on the lone gladiator.

"We salute you!" the gladiator shouted in a voice that carried to the far reaches of the Coliseum. The other gladiators raised their weapons and shouted, "We salute you!"

"Well, I'll be goddamned!" Claypoole exclaimed.

It was noon.

CHAPTER
TWENTY-NINE

Homs Ferris waddled to the front of the emperor's box, his vast bulk jiggling obscenely. "Get on with it! Get on! You are all dead men if you don't!" he shouted, his face as purple as his robe. The big man standing in front of the line of gladiators did not even bother to look up at the box. "Get that man's name!" Ferris screamed at an aide. Obediently, the man scurried off to find out who the gladiator was. Ferris turned to Draya, who lolled in his enormous chair, a huge goblet of wine in one hand. The sunlight sparkled brightly off the diamonds in the rings on his sausagelike fingers.

"Sumbitches gettin' beyond themselves," Draya rumbled. He shifted his cigar from the right to the left side of his mouth. An expression of annoyance came over his face. He removed the cigar and probed in his mouth with a finger, extracting a masticated wad of tobacco. He flipped it away. It landed on Johnny Sticks's former aide, Hugo. The men sitting around him laughed. Embarrassed, Hugo surreptitiously removed the mess with a napkin.

"Noto, I'll tell you what—" Ferris began.

Draya sat forward in his chair and held up a hand. "Listen." From far off to the northwest of the Coliseum there was a rumble. Draya sat back in his chair. "Goddamn storm coming! Are we gonna have to sit here in the rain?" he asked an aide.

The aide shrugged. "Weather report says clear and hot through the end of the week."

"We ought to build one of them domes, you know," Draya said, "so we could have climate control in here. This first-century Roman shit's fine once in a while, but goddamn, this is the twenty-fifth century and we oughta be able to sit in here without sweatin' our jewels off."

"We could build a special box, boss, just for the emperor," the aide offered.

"Nah." He waved a huge hand dismissively. "Then they'll want them too." He gestured at the thousands of spectators. "Buddha's prick on a stick, that thing's moving fast!" He gestured off to the northwest, where the distant rumbling had now risen in volume and intensity. "It's gettin' closer!" There was a small tinge of alarm in Draya's voice. "If I wasn't so damned comfortable I'd get under cover." A woman sitting beside him put her hand between his legs and smiled. "What's a little rain?" Draya laughed.

But now others had taken note of the approaching storm. People began looking up apprehensively at the sky, but it was cloudless. The rumble turned to a splitting roar, and suddenly, over the roof of the stadium, a massive black object appeared, spitting fire. Panic seized the spectators.

"Mom! Dad! It's a Confederation Navy Mark IV Essay!" the lad from Sisyphus shouted. "See, the forward stabilizer is mounted at a forty-five-degree angle instead of fifty-five, like on the Mark VI's! Goddamn, Dad, this is the greatest fucking vacation since the beginning of the world!"

"Sonny!" his mother exclaimed. "Where did you learn to talk like that?"

"He's right, Mother!" the father shouted, also on his feet. "Holy jumping shit, they're raiding the emperor's box! Goddamn, this is so real, goddamn, how do they do this stuff? Goddamn, lookit that, lookit that! What a goddamned surprise this is! Are we getting our money's worth or are we?"

The mother shook her head. Then she laughed. "Am I

going to have a talk with you two when we get back to our hotel!"

Chief Riggs guided the Essay to a perfect landing directly behind the gladiators and only a meter from the wall. While the dust was still in the air, its rear ramp dropped and armed men raced out of it. The gladiators threw down their weapons.

"You take care of Raoul!" Claypoole shouted. "I've got work to do!" He ran unopposed through the gladiators, hopped nimbly onto the skirts of the Essay and hoisted himself topside. Two men in protective armor where putting up a short ladder to the emperor's box. Several others crouched nearby, firing stun grenades. To the utter amazement of the assault team, Claypoole dashed between them and flung himself up the ladder.

"Claypoole!" someone shouted behind him, but he paid no attention.

Two men wielding hand-blasters were trying to shepherd Homs Ferris to safety. Noto Draya sat dazed and confused in his seat, temporarily stunned by the grenades. Claypoole screamed and brought his sword down on Ferris's head with all his strength. Bone crunched and blood spurted from the wound. Claypoole dodged under one man's arm and his gun went off with a harmless *crack!* He drove his knee into the other's groin, and as the man doubled over, he rammed the hilt of his sword down onto the top of his head. Executing a perfect pirouette, he smashed the blade of his sword into the first man's face, sending him backward in an explosion of blood.

Homs Ferris lay unprotected, groaning, blood flowing from his head wound. Claypoole descended on him like St. George on the dragon, raining a quick succession of terrible blows onto the fat man's skull. He stopped only when he saw pieces of brain on the blade of his sword. Behind him big men in black body armor were climbing into the box, firing weapons. It was pandemonium. Claypoole leaped over the seats and fell on Draya. A woman with a gun, blood running from her nose, stood in front of him. He broke her gun arm with a blow from his sword and body-blocked her into the next row of seats, but his sword flew out of his grip on impact and skittered under the seats, where he couldn't reach it. He dived on Draya, a savage scream welling up from somewhere deep inside his soul. Lance Corporal Rachman Claypoole, Confederation Marine Corps, was not a man at that instant but an avenging devil. At least that is what Noto Draya thought he saw thundering down on him.

Draya screamed in primal fear as Claypoole grabbed his throat, threw him bodily between the seats and began smashing his head on the floor . . . He smashed Draya's head again and again.

The next thing Rachman Claypoole knew, several men were holding him. Someone was talking to him. Gradually the red haze obscuring his senses cleared.

"Rock! Rock! For God's sake, are you all right?" It was Dean. Over Dean's shoulder he recognized Chief Riggs, and beside him that big cop, Brock. And there was Nast!

"They burned Katie!" Claypoole gasped. "They burned her." It was the only explanation he could give for what he'd just done. It was the only one he needed. He looked into the faces surrounding him. "Good old Juanita got the word off, didn't she? I was right to give her the password, then."

"Let him go," Nast signed to the policemen. "Clean this mess up here." He laid a hand on Claypoole's shoulder. "Rock, Juanita never sent me a message. I came today because I knew the bosses would be here."

"Then—Then—" Claypoole stuttered.

"Yes, she was my ace in the hole, Claypoole. You say you gave her the code? You were supposed to, but I couldn't tell you that. This thing had to go down a certain way or it would never have worked. But—" He hesitated. "I knew Ferris and Draya attended these games every Wednesday, so my fall-back was to raid them here if anything went wrong."

"Where is that Sticks bastard anyway?" Dean asked.

"Dead," Nast replied. "That's what the survivors here told us anyway. We haven't had a chance yet to recover the bodies. Juanita killed him, but apparently before he died he was able to put a bullet into her."

"But—" Claypoole was not sure he understood, or that he wanted to understand. "Patsies" is what they'd been called down in the dungeons. Patsies?

Nast saw the confusion on his face. "I had to have a way to get the evidence Juanita had accumulated. She sat in on many of the mob's most secret meetings and recorded them. But she had no way to get them off-world. The mob doesn't trust anyone that much to let them get out of here without a full scan. So I had to get the recordings from her here, on Havanagas. I couldn't take a chance on giving her a device when we met on Wanderjahr two years ago either. I knew what happened in her bar when you were deployed there. That's why I picked you two, and I told her to watch out for you. I wanted someone she could recognize easily, and someone it would be convincing for her to pretend to hate."

"But you don't have the recordings!" Brock interjected.

"Maybe we can find them. But I really don't need them. There never was to be any trial for these guys. You, Claypoole, you too, Dean, know what I mean." He was referring to the men Nast had sent to Darkside for poaching on Avionia.

"We were bait! We were your bagmen!" Dean exclaimed.

"Yes, you could put it that way. I knew Culloden had been turned. But I couldn't take a chance on compromising Juanita. She was my last hope to get these guys. I needed the authority first to mount this operation, and by promising to get the evidence to put these guys away, I got it. Oh, Juanita hid the recordings somewhere, and we'll find them. You know how evil these men were. You know all this was worth it."

"Worth our lives?" Claypoole shouted. "Worth the lives of O'Mol and Grace and Tara? Worth Katie's life? They killed Prost too, the librarian! He never did anything to anybody.

You got all those people killed! And all you had to do was just come here yourself and get Juanita! They burned Katie, you bastard!" Claypoole shouted. "They burned her at this Worstburg, Würstberg place! Burned her so you could get your worthless 'evidence'!"

"We don't need the evidence now, Claypoole! You killed the capos! You killed them with your bare hands. That evens up the score, doesn't it?"

Claypoole's mouth fell open. He was not proud of what he had just done, even though those men deserved death; he was not proud to have been turned into an animal by this officious, arrogant police bureaucrat. Trading Katie's life for those two fat slobs didn't even up the score, he thought.

Claypoole swung his arm in a 180-degree arc then, and brought his fist sharply onto the bridge of Nast's nose. The snap of the cartilage breaking echoed loudly in the emperor's box. Blood spurted from Nast's nose and he staggered backward. As Claypoole stepped forward to deliver another blow, Brock stopped him.

Nast stood with one hand over his broken nose. "Dad's okay! Dad's okay!" he muttered. "Led imb go, Brock. Led imb go. I deserbed dad. I'mb sorry, Caypoole, I'mb sorry."

Claypoole hit him again, this time over the right eye. Brock made no effort to restrain him. "I oughta smack you for everyone you got killed on this operation, you worthless, manipulating bastard!" he shouted. Claypoole was almost in tears he was so mad. He couldn't believe they'd been used like that, and worse, that innocent people's lives had been sacrificed by Nast. This man was not the Special Agent Nast he remembered from the operation on Avionia.

Nast raised his hands. "Okay, dad's id, Caypoole! You god yur shot. No more shit oudda you, Marine!"

Claypoole clenched his fists, trying to get control of himself. All around them the members of the assault team were securing prisoners. One of them was Hugo, Johnny Sticks's aide. "I need to tell you something," he hollered at the Marines.

Brock signalled that the officer securing him should bring him over.

"That's Hugo," Dean said. "He tried to help us last night. Go easy on him, will you?"

"Look," Hugo said, but before he could finish, the second Essay roared over the Coliseum and gracefully landed amid a cloud of dust and flame. "Look," he tried again, "they took your girl to Würzburg. That's about three hours from here by suborbital aircraft."

"I know that." Chief Riggs had just joined the group. "Wanna go to Würzburg, boss?" he asked Nast, then did a double take when he noticed his broken nose.

"Yeah? Why do we need to know dad?" Nast asked, speaking carefully now, to be better understood.

"Well, the burnings only take place when weather permits, because they're held outside. It's been raining heavily in Würzburg these last three days. I know 'cause Sticks was concerned about losing money on the event."

"Thank God for the rain!" Claypoole shouted at the top of his voice. "Nast?"

"Brock, take ten men and these two Marines. Chief, you drive. Take our Essay to Würzburg. You should make it before dark. I've got to stay here and tie up loose ends. We'll have Pasquin on board the *Wanganui* and in stasis in just a few minutes, so don't worry about him. Come on, get a move on!"

Claypoole seized Nast's hand and shook it. "Thank you! Thank you! And thank God for the rain! I'll never complain about rain again as long as I live!"

Olwyn O'Mol, flanked in the prisoners' dock by Grace and Katie, both of whom were still weak from the scourging that had just been administered—to the indifferent response of the tourists in the gallery—stood as straight as the burden of his chains would permit. Grace was in particularly bad condition since the bullet wounds she'd sustained in the fight at the docks had never been attended to.

Outside, the rain poured down in sheets. O'Mol was aware that if it hadn't been for the rain, they'd all be dead. But then again, now they were facing further ordeals at the hands of the torturers instead.

"Olwyn O'Mol, how do you answer to the charge of witchcraft?" the presiding judge bellowed.

O'Mol hesitated. If he pled guilty and repented, the sentence of strangulation would have to be carried out immediately, rain or not. In that regard, the rules of the Renaissance park would prevail. If he denied his guilt, he'd live until the rain stopped and things dried out a bit, but that would mean more torture. He had no more fingernails to lose, but there was always the boot, the witch's chair, the ladder, red-hot scourging, and castration. Was continued life worth it at that price?

"Olwyn O'Mol, we have sworn testimony that you are a warlock and these detestable whores are your accomplices. Confess, divulge the names of the others in your coven and repent your sins, and your death will be merciful."

O'Mol remained silent. The rain pounded on the roof above. He wondered idly what the weather report said about the storm. How long would it last? And what of the three Marines? He thought back to that night on the island. God, they should've stayed there! Claypoole announced he would marry Katie, beside him now, barely able to stand, her body wracked by steaming iron pincers. How victorious they'd been that night! But now look at us, he thought mournfully. And those three good men were no doubt dead by now, probably a lot quicker and cleaner than the way he was going to die. No! They would've gone down fighting!

"Fuck you!" O'Mol shouted. He turned to the spectators in the gallery, no more than a hundred bored tourists, going through the motions because they'd paid to see a show. "You fools! This is real! We're being murdered by the men who run this world because we dared to oppose them!" The judge motioned for the torturers to silence O'Mol. They were big men, masked, bare-chested. O'Mol swung his manacled hands into the face of the first man, bringing them down on his nose, which broke with a sickening crunch. He staggered back into the second man, who shoved him aside and advanced. Grace, swiftly recovering from a feigned coma, drove her knee into his crotch, and as he doubled over, O'Mol brought both hands down on the back of his head.

"Guards! Guards!" the judges screamed.

Three men in jumpsuits, carrying modern weapons, ran out of the wings. That was a big mistake. "Hey!" one of the tourists shouted. "They aren't wearing the right costumes! What the hell's going on here?" The other spectators murmured excitedly among themselves, and a woman shouted, "They must really be hurting those people!"

The three guards kept O'Mol at bay with their weapons. Realizing they'd broken the harmless Renaissance illusion by coming out in modern dress, they looked at the judges for instructions. But Johnny Sticks himself had told them to make sure those people were burned. That's what the guards were there for.

The judges looked at each other in bewilderment. People in the gallery were beginning to shout at them. Then, from the top of the gallery, an old-fashioned glass bottle, something a tourist had picked up in a gift shop on the town square, hurtled out into the courtroom and shattered in front of the judges' bench. That was all it took. The tourists, on edge because of the bad weather and the delay in the executions they'd come hundreds of light-years and spent a fortune to see, began ripping up the wooden benches in the gallery and tossing them down into the courtroom. A large chunk of wood struck one of the judges on the head. A look of surprise on his face, he stood frozen for an instant, then his eyes rolled back into his head and slowly, gracefully, he rotated halfway around and slid flu-

idly to the floor, ending with an audible thud as his head struck
the cobbles. The people in the gallery laughed, and continued
ripping up benches and throwing chunks of wood, all dignity,
caution, and pure common sense evaporating.

A panicked guard fired his weapon into the air and a large
section of the roof disintegrated. A torrent of rainwater poured
down on guards, judges, torturers, and prisoners. Fragments
of wooden benches, brass fittings, miscellaneous personal
items, rained down on them from the gallery. Dragging the
two women with him, O'Mol surged out of the dock and
threw himself onto the guards. They all went down in a tangle
of arms and legs. People began climbing down out of the
gallery and rushing into the fray.

The remaining "judges" fled through a back door. Over the
sound of the rioting tourists and the rain, there was a roaring
noise.

"I don't dare set this baby down in the town," Chief Riggs
said as he circled Würzburg in his Essay. "The town square's
too small with that goddamned fountain in the center, and the
buildings are too close together. There's an open field on the
north side. I'll set down there, but you'll have to find your
friends on your own." Chief Riggs clutched a cigar butt between his teeth. He wore a dirty bandanna around his head,
hadn't shaved in days, and around his neck dangled a gaudy
necklace made of animal teeth he'd picked up somewhere on
a cruise. To anyone else he would have looked like a pirate,
but to the two Marines, no man had ever looked more professional and reliable that he did just then.

"Okay, there's twelve of us, counting the two Marines,"
Brock said. "Split up into six two-man teams and spread out.
Keep in touch on the squad net. Uh, Claypoole? You come
with me."

As soon as they ran down the ramp they were engulfed in
the rain. The town was just an indistinct blur about three hundred meters from the soggy field Riggs had used as a landing

zone. Claypoole, still wearing the toga he'd been dressed in at
the Coliseum, took off down the road toward the center of
town, running as fast as he could. When the sandals he was
wearing began to slip on his feet, he ripped them off and ran
barefoot. Brock, his weapon at port arms, ran behind, trying
to keep up with Claypoole, shouting for him to slow down,
but nothing could stop Lance Corporal Rachman Claypoole
at that point!

He ran into the town square and stopped. There were lights
on in the shops around the square, but not a soul was in evidence. The rain hissed down steadily. From behind him, up
one of the narrow side streets, he heard the pounding of feet.

Where . . . ? He looked around in despair. Then from
straight ahead, across the square, he heard a tumult of voices
coming down a street that led to a large building with a bell
tower. The voices coalesced into a crowd of people. They
were shouting something. The crowd poured into the square,
about a hundred people, soaked to the skin, some drinking
from bottles, all of them singing and shouting and dancing in
the rain. They were carrying people on their shoulders.

Brock ran up behind Claypoole, breathing heavily. "What
the—" Seconds later the rest of the assault party joined them.
The twelve men stood in a tight formation, weapons ready,
facing the crowd. Abruptly, the rain stopped. There, in the
front of the crowd, hoisted on the shoulders of several men,
was—

"Olwyn!" Dean shouted. "Olwyn! It's Dean! It's Claypoole! We're here to rescue you!"

"Rescue *him*, hell! Where's Katie?" Claypoole yelled.

Utterly bedraggled from the rain, weak from torture and
confinement but standing erect, Katie stepped out from the
crowd. "Rock!" she shouted. The crowd broke into loud
applause.

Claypoole started forward but Dean restrained him with a
hand on his shoulder. "Better get rid of that," he said, gesturing at Claypoole's right side.

Claypoole looked down in surprise. He was still carrying the sword from the Coliseum! He grinned at Dean and threw the weapon onto the cobblestones.

Dean reached down and retrieved it. "Make a good souvenir." He looked up at Brock and grinned. "I guess we will dance at that dumb shit's wedding after all," he said.

CHAPTER
THIRTY

The Convocation of Ecumenical Leaders assembled in Mount Temple for its third consecutive day since the off-worlders of Interstellar City had analyzed their data and confessed they couldn't identify who the raiders were or where they came from. Bishop Ralphy Bruce Preachintent's hands were folded in front of his tie and shirt in the same manner he always folded them when he first faced the assembly. The tie was askew and a stain showed on the shirtfront. His iridescent lavender vestment, though fresh, was rumpled, as though he'd slept in it. His eyes, which normally glowed with the fervor of his calling, were sunken and distant.

The heretics who sporadically rebelled in outlying areas had never been more than a minor nuisance to Bishop Ralphy Bruce. He'd never even thought of the more serious heretical rebellions, which occurred about once a generation, to be any true threat to the theocratic rulers of the Kingdom of Yahweh and His Saints and Their Apostles. Not even on those few occasions when the aid of the Confederation had been called upon to put down a rebellion had the theocracy been truly in jeopardy of overthrow.

As the current chairman of the convocation, he'd just been to Interstellar City for a more detailed briefing on what the off-worlders had found than the one they'd given to Metropolitan Eleison and his delegation. What he'd seen on the monitors had horrified him. That the off-worlders couldn't identify the shuttles or ground vehicles terrified him. The possibility that the strange-looking creatures in the vehicles might not be of this flesh nearly traumatized him. He'd raised no objections when the ambassador told him he'd ordered a violation of the treaty, that he had the entire planet under close surveillance to find where the shuttles came from; instead, he'd agreed to it.

In a different time and place Bishop Ralphy Bruce would have been solidly in control. But right here and now, he was in way over his head—and he knew it.

"My friends . . ." he said, his voice strained to keep it from cracking. Today he was unable to speak in the sacred cadences of the saver-of-souls, much less dance the holy choreography. "I have just come from Interstellar City. They told me everything they know, showed me all the evidence they have. It is most . . ." What word should he use to describe his reaction? Terrifying? Horrifying? Neither felt as soul-wrenching as the blow he had felt when he realized what he most probably was looking at. ". . . most disquieting." The word was thoroughly inadequate, but the somber expression on the faces of the leaders who watched him so closely assured him he touched them in a soul-felt place.

"It was with great pain that I authorized—" He couldn't keep his voice from cracking on the word. "—planetwide surveillance in order for them to locate the, uh, unholy raiders." How unholy, he didn't say. He'd promised Creadence he wouldn't divulge what they all suspected about the nature of the raiders. Surprisingly, his revelation of the unprecedented surveillance raised no more than a few muted murmurs of protest. Encouraged by that, he continued with somewhat more strength in his voice, "It is my exceedingly strong belief that this extraordinary step was necessary in order to protect the faithful from these—these visitors from somewhere else. The off-world unbelievers also feel threatened by them. They will give us the information we need for the Army of the Lord to root them out, or they will call for assistance from the Confederation of Human Worlds if we cannot do it ourselves. Ambassador Creadence gave me his most solemn word on this. Unbeliever though he is, I trust his word on this matter.

"Yes, brother," he said as Ayatollah Fatamid slowly rose to his feet. "Do you wish to give testimony?"

The aged cleric stared silently at Bishop Ralphy Bruce for so long, only the harshness of his look showed he was aware of where he was.

"Ralphy Bruce," he finally said in his quavery, old man's voice, "I have sometimes suspected your heart might harbor thoughts and ideas that run counter to the precepts upon which the Kingdom of Yahweh and His Saints and Their Apostles was founded. If you are wrong in this deep belief about the truth of the off-worlders, you will regret the day you chose to betray us in favor of the infidel!" The silence as he resumed his seat was palpable. Never in the memory of any member of the convocation had one of them made so thinly veiled an accusation against another, nor so serious a threat.

"You are righteous in what you say, brother," Bishop Ralphy Bruce said so softly his voice barely carried to the far end of the sanctuary. "But I am equally righteous in my belief in the depth of the threat we face and the earnestness of the off-world unbelievers when they say they will give us all the aid possible in defense against it."

Someone in the room applauded. A few cheered.

"BRETHREN!" The reaction of the few to his response to Ayatollah Fatamid so encouraged him that Bishop Ralphy Bruce suddenly felt the strength to sing the sacred cadences. "When they toil for the sake of HIM and his faithful, THE LORD will give strength even unto UNBELIEVERS!" His shoulders pulled back and he stood straight, his arms flung toward heaven. "Even as OUR LORD," he dropped his eyes to Ayatollah Fatamid, "or Prophet, as some call him, washed the FEET of the sinners, so may we TREAT with the unbelievers when it is in HIS cause! Let us pray!"

* * *

Four divisions quietly moved into place to encircle the swamp lands below the Mountains of Abraham. Twenty-four squadrons of Avenging Angels assembled at three widely spaced and hastily built airfields a hundred kilometers from the swamps. The raiders had obliterated another remote village—and laid waste to a small Army of the Lord patrol base since Bishop Ralphy Bruce Preachintent gave his after-the-fact approval of the planetwide surveillance. The surveillance paid off. Following each of the raids, the vanished shuttles had reappeared low in the air above the swampland below the Mountains of Abraham and disappeared into them.

Nobody had any idea how large the off-world unbeliever force was, but except for the first raid—the one on Eighth Shrine, where no one could know how many there had been—there were no reports of more than three shuttles and twelve of the small, nimble AFVs in any one raid. The markings on the shuttles seen in the surveillance images were identical in each raid, which strongly suggested they might represent most or, with the Lord's blessing, all of the force the enemy had. If that intelligence was correct, the Army of the Lord was sending one regiment of infantry or light armor plus one squadron of attack aircraft against each of the twelve AFVs.

It was a ratio Archdeacon General Lambsblood found comforting. He'd seen the devastation wrought by the off-world raiders and wasn't in the least sanguine about their destructive power. Only a fool, he believed, would go up against them with anything less than absolutely overwhelming numbers and strength. Even with the odds so greatly in favor of the Army of the Lord forces under his command, he expected heavy casualties.

Every hovercraft and water-skimmer on the planet was commandeered for the operation. There weren't enough, so the Army of the Lord borrowed more from Interstellar City. There still were too few. Chief Administrator Creadence used his authority to have the CNSS *Douglas County*, then in orbit around Kingdom, lend its six Essays and twelve Dragons to the operation. He was so wrapped up with watching the coming operation unfold it didn't occur to him to wonder why an old troop ship was plying the spaceways without a load of combat-ready Marines.

As well-equipped as they could get with vehicles capable of negotiating the swamp, the four divisions split into their regiments, the infantry regiments into battalions, and slithered into the miasmatic morass. The light armor regiments sent their vehicles as deep into the swamp as they could find ground solid enough to support their weight. A hundred kilometers away, twenty squadrons of Avenging Angels rose into the air and halved the distance from their bases to the swamp, where they orbited in holding patterns. If needed—the pilots kept hoping "when" they were needed—they were mere minutes away from striking.

Hours went by, then half a day, with neither contact nor sign of any life not indigenous to the swamp. Then one of the regiments lost contact with one of its battalions. Scouts sent frantically to its location found a surprising and horrible sight: swamp scavengers and opportunists writhing in agony as acid ate away their bodies from the inside out. Of the missing five hundred soldiers, all they found were a few weapons and acid-scarred scraps of uniform cloth.

Archdeacon General Lambsblood knew what must have happened. The unbelievers had weapons that acted silently, and they had attacked so quickly the Soldiers of the Lord hadn't had time to fire their own weapons before they were killed or captured. The swamp scavengers and opportunists devoured the remains of some before the acid of the enemy weapons dissipated. The remains of others sunk into the murky waters or were sucked into the mud and quicksand. Many, perhaps most, of their weapons went the same way.

Archdeacon General Lambsblood was glad his battalions were converging. The closer they were to each other, the less chance another could be attacked without the next one knowing in time to counterattack.

Fifty kilometers away the Avenging Angel pilots chaffed. They had been orbiting for hours and had grown impatient for targets to attack.

By then the four divisions, less one battalion, had penetrated three-quarters of the way to the heart of the swamp.

"What's that?" Soldier Augustian asked in a panicky voice.

"Where?" Sword Lutherson demanded. His eyes scanned the foliage, his hands keeping his flechette rifle pointed where he scanned. His squad occupied the rear half of the skimmer.

"In the water. I saw something, maybe a man swimming under the surface.

Sword Lutherson looked at the water, his hands automatically shifting his rifle's aim. The water was murky, as though tainted with the devil's own urine. It certainly smelled thus to Lutherson.

"Nothing's there. Your fear is making you see things. Nothing but the vile beasts of the swamp can be in that water."

"But, Sword, I swear I saw a man under there."

Sword Lutherson snorted and returned his attention to the foliage that edged and overlapped the waterway their skimmer floated along, foliage that appeared to rot even as it grew. He did his best to ignore the insects that buzzed about his ears and crawled on his flesh. The rank vegetation grew dense in that part of the swamp and sight lines were short. Twenty meters ahead of the skimmer he saw a hovercraft following a bend in the channel. Another skimmer was barely visible through the foliage an equal distance to the rear.

Something thunked the skimmer's bottom. It jolted.

"Watch where you're going!" Lutherson shouted at the boatman operating the skimmer. "You'll run us aground."

The boatman didn't bother to reply. His wide eyes probed the waters to the front and sides of the skimmer. He didn't know what it was that hit his skimmer, but he hadn't run it aground or hit a sunken log, of that he was positive.

There was another thunk against the bottom of the skimmer's hull.

Seconds later a soldier fired off a burst from his rifle into the water abeam of the skimmer.

Lutherson open-handed him across the back of his head, hard.

"Stop that! Don't fire unless you have a real target. You'll give us away if anyone is close enough to hear. And don't waste your ammunition on the water, the flechettes lose their energy within inches. Even if there was something to shoot at, you wouldn't hit it underwa—"

A dual explosion tore the skimmer in two.

The nearest soldiers were shredded by shards of shattered hull. Those near them screamed as splinters tore into their flesh. Uninjured soldiers yelled at each other as they fell into the vile water and grappled for something that would keep them afloat. Some of them retained enough of their senses to reach for wounded comrades to pull them to safety, but hardly any thought to look for an enemy to fight. And none of them looked far enough into the distance to see that the hovercraft before them was also broken, as was the skimmer to their rear.

So hardly any of the soldiers saw the things that looked like deformed men rise, dripping, from the water and aim hoses in their direction. Those few who got off quick bursts riddled two or three of the horrid apparitions before the viscous green fluid coated their flesh and sent them into the agonies of the damned.

The scene was repeated throughout the area of operation, eighty of the five hundred skimmers and hovercraft in the operation shattered by explosives attached to their hulls; 160 of the thousand infantry squads were killed, 10 percent of the force was wiped out. The initial loosing of the minions of hell lasted less than two minutes.

Before all the reports of death and destruction of his soldiers even reached Archdeacon Lambsblood's headquarters, skillfully hidden doors, set into the more solid portions of ground less deep into the swamp than the infantry had gone, opened. Weapons of unfamiliar design rose on platforms from the holes. The weapons crackled when they fired, and each crackle sent an invisible crushing force into the Gabriels that couldn't penetrate the swamp as deeply as the infantry had. Their work done in seconds, the weapons were lowered and the doors closed over them, once more hiding them from any but the most carefully searching eyes. Behind them they left one-third of the operation's armored force shattered, fragments of exploded Gabriels sizzling where they landed in the mud and water.

Less than a minute after the first Gabriel exploded, orders were issued to six of the orbiting Avenging Angel squadrons to obliterate the areas around the killed vehicles. Filled with righteous joy, ninety pilots banked out of their holding patterns and sped toward the swamp, dropping as they went so they would be at attack altitude when they arrived on target. The pilots of the other eighteen squadrons enviously watched them leave.

As the Avenging Angels neared the swamp, skillfully hidden doors in the ground just inside the wetland opened and weapons similar to those that had killed the Gabriels rose on platforms, already aimed heavenward. They crackled.

Every Avenging Angel of two squadrons disintegrated.

The three Avenging Angels of one squadron that weren't destroyed in the opening volley spun about and sped away; one didn't get out of range fast enough.

Five Avenging Angels of another squadron managed to escape, and the commander of a trailing squadron spontaneously ordered his pilots to fire all their missiles where he spotted the strange weapons. The commander's instinct was good; his squadron destroyed two of the weapons. Nine of that squadron's fifteen pilots paid for the victory with their lives.

Eight Avenging Angels of the final squadron made it through the protective fire to their designated target. They totally obliterated the ground in the vicinity of one of the killed Gabriels and destroyed one of the enemy's weapons. Then they sped on and were lucky enough to exit the swamp through an area not covered by the invader's remaining anti-aircraft defenses.

"Everybody, into the water!" Second Acolyte Talas screamed when the skimmer to his hovercraft's rear exploded; he realized boats had suddenly become unsafe places to be. He was the first soldier to leave the illusory safety of the hovercraft and drop into the scummy, waist-deep water. His soldiers, having seen or heard the skimmer explode, scrambled into the water behind him. Even the boatman jumped ship.

The turgid water was almost as difficult to wade through as it had looked from the deck of the boat. It felt thicker than water had any business being. Sodden clumps of rotting leaves drifted in it, as did fragile waterlogged twigs. Things the men didn't want to think about bumped or wriggled against them as they followed their officer to the edge of the watercourse. The slurry of muck on the bottom of the water sucked at their feet and more than one boot was left behind. Intent on their officer, the men didn't see anything rise up behind them.

Second Acolyte Talas, still crying out "Follow me," reached the vegetation along the bank of the watercourse and broke his way into it. When he felt the mud under his boots begin to rise, he grasped a buttress root and stepped upward. His foot found precarious purchase on a slick root and he pulled himself out of the water. There, less than a meter away, was land. It was just a more-solid mud and didn't look very inviting, but it did appear capable of supporting a man. Watchful of his balance on the root, Talas stepped across the narrow gap and soon had both feet on the ground. Only then did he turn about to see how his men were doing.

Behind them the hovercraft was still making its way against the current; unguided, it was angling toward the opposite bank of the watercourse. But of his men, he saw none.

"Lead Sword," he shouted, "report."

The indignant scream of a swamp creature a few meters away was the only response.

"Squad Swords, report!"

Not even the swamp creature replied.

"Anybody in first platoon, sound off!" Second Acolyte Talas's voice climbed the register toward panic.

Somewhere, a swamp flier cawed, an amphibian croaked, another creature cried. Flying insectoids buzzed about, water drip-dripped, clumps of rotted leaves heavy with moisture plopped into the water. But not one soldier from first platoon sounded off.

Second Acolyte Talas's breath came in shallow, rapid pants. He slowly lowered himself to a crouch. His officer's sidearm shook in his sweaty grip.

He slowly became aware of a different sound, one that was neither made by the swamp creatures nor rotted matter falling into the water. It was a low-pitched, slow huffing, as though something was breathing nearby. Slowly, he turned his head to look behind him.

A creature stood a few meters away. Manlike in its overall appearance, its face was sharply convex and it had fluttering slits on its sides. A nictating membrane swept across the creature's eyes from the inner side to the outer. The teeth exposed by its evil grin were pointed. It had tanks mounted on its back. A hose led from the tanks to a nozzle in the creature's hands. Then a greenish fluid shot out from the nozzle.

Second Acolyte Talas screamed briefly.

*   *   *

Ambassador Friendly Creadence listened to the report of the battle with mounting horror. When Archdeacon General Lambsblood finished, the ambassador got control of himself and thought briefly.

"Archdeacon General, I thank you," he finally said. "Let me be sure of what you are asking. You lost nearly a third of your force in a battle that lasted less than ten minutes. You then withdrew from the swamp without opposition."

Lambsblood didn't reply; that was what he'd told the off-world ambassador.

"It is your studied professional opinion that the armed forces of Kingdom are not powerful enough to defeat these intruders."

Lambsblood nodded. The disgrace of his failure had him so tense that his neck audibly creaked when he bent it.

"You believe that the only way to defeat the intruders is with the aid of the Confederation military."

"Yes." The word was almost unintelligible.

Creadence turned to Bishop Ralphy Bruce Preachintent.

"Bishop, do you concur with the Archdeacon General?"

Bishop Ralphy Bruce nodded weakly. "Yes, Mister Ambassador. As much as it pains me, I formally request military assistance from the Confederation of Human Worlds in rooting out whoever it is that has invaded." He took a deep breath. "May I remind the ambassador, as a member world of the Confederation of Human Worlds, the Kingdom of Yahweh and His Saints and Their Apostles has every right to make this request. And as the foe we face is obviously from off-world, the Confederation of Human Worlds is obligated to come to our assistance."

Creadence nodded. "That is true, Bishop. It is my opinion that, in accordance with law and treaty, you have the right to request military assistance, and in this instance we have the obligation to provide it. I will dispatch an urgent request today."

"Thank you, Mr. Ambassador."

They rose and shook hands all around. Bishop Ralphy Bruce led his delegation out of the ambassador's meeting room.

When they were gone, Creadence said to Thorogood, "This is definitely serious enough to send for the Marines."

Thorogood simply nodded.

Despite his years in the diplomatic service, Ambassador Creadence had never had to send for military assistance and didn't know what details he should put in his report. Since they only had a suspicion of the nonhuman nature of the invaders, the urgent request for Marines was vague on that point; it was necessarily vague on the size and strength of the force the Marines would face.

CHAPTER
THIRTY-ONE

Navy doctors determined that Pasquin's leg would have to come off below the knee. "No problem," the orthopedic surgeon at the Bethesdan Naval Medical Center's Dahlgren Surgical Clinic told him the first day he was out of stasis. "We'll have you back on active service in no time at all."

"Ma'am," he grinned up at the lieutenant commander surgeon, "I've got nowhere else to go right now." He'd been in stasis for two months before arriving at Bethesdan. Dean and Claypoole were already back on Thorsfinni's World spreading lies. He wondered what 34th FIST had been doing while they were away. Training, as usual. The three of them had been gone long enough that there might well have been a deployment. He vowed never again to complain about Marine Corps field problems.

The doctor studied his chart for a moment. "You have an infantry MOS," she said, "but you were on a survey ship, the *Wanganui*? That's an odd assignment for a grunt."

"Something new, ma'am," Pasquin answered. "They were going into a sector where pirates have been operating, and we went along as Marine security for the crew and the scientists."

The doctor raised her eyebrows. "Never heard of such a thing. I wouldn't think a survey ship would have room for all your Marines."

"There were only three of us, ma'am."

"Only three, to deal with pirates?"

"Well, ma'am, if there were a lot of pirates, they'd have sent four of us to deal with them."

The doctor laughed and patted Pasquin's good leg. "Corporal, Marines make the best orthopedic patients. You don't let the bad stuff get you down. You and I are going to be seeing quite a bit of each other these next few days."

Pasquin grinned. He wouldn't mind that at all. She was not bad looking for a Squid pill pusher.

Katie had decided to remain on Havanagas. "I'm used to life here," she explained to Claypoole, "and now that the mob's no longer in control, I think I can make something of myself. They'll need someone to run the Free Library now that Mister Prost is gone. Who's better qualified than me? I'm a whore and I know books." She shrugged. "But Rock, you know where I am when you're ready. All you have to do is let me know and I'm on my way."

"It may be a while," he warned her.

"I don't care, take your time. But you know, I sort of wish you'd wait until you're promoted to staff sergeant. If I have to leave here, I wouldn't mind being a Marine's wife."

"When we get married, whether I'm still in the Corps or out, you'll still be a Marine's wife, Katie."

Nast had many details to take care of on Havanagas, shutting down the families' control of operations, so he'd agreed to let Dean and Claypoole spend the time in port rather than on the *Wanganui*. They were to leave the next day. Claypoole was of two minds. He wanted to stay with Katie, but he knew his place was back with 34th FIST. Already, he was looking forward to drinking beer in Big Barb's and swapping sea stories with his fellow Marines.

Nast had given them their cover story about providing security for the *Wanganui* and warned them they must stick to it. Pasquin had been injured in a shipboard accident. Lieutenant Perizittes had filed the official accident report, and Pasquin's records would reflect injury in the line of duty.

There could be no mention that they had ever been on Havanagas. "You know what happens to people who talk too much," Nast reminded them ominously.

Claypoole had taken that seriously—for a while. Then he went over the details of the fight at the farm, his rescue of Katie in Placetas, the fight in the Coliseum. Well, fuck you, Mr. Nast! he told himself. After what Nast had pulled on them, Claypoole resolved that as soon as he was back on Thorsfinni's World, the Marines of third platoon were going to hear about their adventures. He was tired of people telling him to shut up; he was good at performing the impossible missions nobody else would dream of taking on.

"Hey," he said, holding up a reader, "look at what I've got here!" he handed Katie the reader. A look of surprise and then deep pleasure came over her face. She leaned over and planted a very long kiss on Claypoole's lips. He was reading *Canterbury Tales*.

"Well, if it isn't the prodigal sons!" Top Myer exclaimed as Dean and Claypoole reported back into the Company L office at Camp Ellis. "Where the hell have you been, and where's Corporal Pasquin?"

"Security duty on a survey ship, First Sergeant!" Dean responded.

"Corporal Pasquin's in the hospital, First Sergeant! Shipboard accident. He'll be back soon, though," Claypoole said.

"Security duty on a survey ship?" The First Sergeant looked askance at the two Marines standing before his desk. "I never heard such crap in my life! The Commandant of the Confederation Marine Corps is going to reach all the way down to 34th FIST and pick two birds like you for goddamned 'security duty' on a goddamned survey ship?" He held out his hand, and they handed over the crystals that contained their reassignment orders. He popped Dean's into a reader. Sure enough, there it was, along with a strong letter of commendation from the captain of the *Wanganui*.

"It was crap, Top. Dullest duty I ever pulled. Never fired a shot," Claypoole said.

Top Myer glared at the two lance corporals. He screwed up his right eyebrow. He took a cigar out of his pocket and lit it. He leaned back in his chair and blew out a cloud of smoke through which he regarded the two balefully. There was something mighty fishy there; he'd get to the bottom of it sooner or later. "Well," he said at last, studying the glowing end of his cigar, "next goddamned time they need someone for 'security duty' they damned well kin get 'em from M Company."

EPILOGUE

The Great Master sat cross-legged on a thick mat behind the low, lacquer table at the back of a large room. The rectangular gold plates that shimmered softly on his robe were worthless as armor, but that didn't matter, the ancient form of armor was ceremonial. A sword, sheathed in precious wood that curved with the blade, lay across his lap. Two Large Ones sat close to his rear, one to either side. A third Large One sat with his back to the Great Master's back. The armor the bodyguards wore was fully functional, as were the unsheathed swords they held. A diminutive female knelt at his knee and delicately poured a steaming liquid into the small, handleless cup that sat in easy reach of the Great Master. Finished pouring, she set the pot on a small mat on the table and bowed as low as she could in the small space between the table and her master's knee.

In front of the table, opposite the Great Master and his bodyguards, the Over Masters sat in open ranks on thinner mats. Their armor, like the armor of the bodyguards, was functional; their swords, like that of the Great Master, were sheathed. Ten more Large Ones sat around the sides of the room, unsheathed swords across their laps, facing in toward the Over Masters. No acid-guns were visible, but from the tops of the walls four were trained on the Over Masters.

For the moment, the Great Master ignored his subordinates. He lifted the small cup and brought it to his lips. He sipped the steaming liquid and his eyes closed in ecstasy.

He gently replaced the cup on the table and spoke briefly to the female. His voice was a growl that invoked the rumbling of water crashing at the foot of a mountain cliff. The female murmured a few words of reply, her voice the sound of a gently babbling brook, then rose gracefully and backed from the room, her eyes cast downward. A moment later several females entered the room. The tightness of the ankle-length skirts of their robes made them shuffle. Each carried a small, stub-legged table. Each table bore two small cups and a pot. Steam rose from the pot spouts.

The females gracefully knelt, each between two Over Masters, and set the tables down where the Over Master to either side could easily reach it. They poured from the pot into the cups, rose gracefully, and exited. The female who served the Great Master returned and knelt between his knee and the table, her head bowed low.

The Great Master picked up his cup and sipped again. A rolling bark of contentment came from somewhere deep in his chest. He put the cup back down. Only then did he look out at the assembled Over Masters. As though in response to a command only they could hear, they bowed so their foreheads nearly touched the mats in front of their folded legs.

"The Earthmen of this dirtball have sent a message to their so-called Confederation," the Great Master growled liquidly. "The Confederation will send their Marines, as they have done before.

"Rise!" he barked.

The Over Masters raised themselves from their bows and looked with grimly eager faces at the Great Master.

"The Grand Master's plan is for us to severely damage the Earth Marines when they come. Then, when they think they have defeated us and are beginning to relax and lick their wounds, he will send in the second wave to defeat them.

"I have a different plan." He chuckled with the sound of gravel washing down a sluice. "The last time we fought their Marines, we fought from well-prepared positions, but we were spread too thinly and they defeated us in detail. This time, we will make our preparations to spread *them* out. And we will then defeat their Marines in detail." He grinned. "When the second division arrives, they can help us celebrate our victory."

With a flourish, he lifted his cup and held it high in salute. The Over Masters picked up their cups and returned the salute.

"My staff will give you each copies of the plans when you leave here. Using the Earthman prisoners as slaves, some of you will see to the preparation of our positions. Others of you will continue to kill or enslave the pond-scum Earthmen who inhabit this world. If any of them remain alive and uncaptured when the Marines arrive, they will be too demoralized to give the Marines any aid." He grinned again. The nearing fulfillment of a holy mission shone in his eyes. He brought the cup to his mouth and tossed back its contents. The Over Masters did the same.

"Victory will be ours!"

The Over Masters roared out cheers.